Carry the Light

Stories, Poems and Essays from the
San Mateo County Fair

Volume III

SHRP

Sand Hill Review Press

Carry the Light
Stories, Poems and Essays from the San Mateo County Fair,
Vol. III
San Mateo, California
© 2014

Published by Sand Hill Review Press
www.sandhillreviewpress.com
P.O. Box 1275, San Mateo, CA 94401 (415) 297-3571

Front cover art, Through the Darkness, Rita Beach
Back cover art, Enchanted, Randy Marlow
Cover design by Joanne Shwed, Backspace Ink
(www.backspaceink.com)

Library of Congress Control Number: 2012940159

ISBN: 978-1-937818-25-8

SHRP
Sand Hill Review Press

Introduction

A reader lives a thousand lives before he dies.
The man who never reads lives only once.
—George R.R. Martin

Whether it is non-fiction or fantasy from poetry to short stories, reading transports you to a separate space. When you read, you get to see through the eyes of another. Yet, it is even more special – and you feel a different connection to the work – when you get to read from authors in your own community.

I have had the opportunity to read some of these works from our community during the compilation of the San Mateo County Fair's third anthology. I could not be more proud that the San Mateo Peninsula and the San Francisco Bay Area could be home to such creative minds.

With that said, the San Mateo County Fair is thrilled to continue offering our literary entries the opportunity to be published in this anthology. None of this could be possible without the Literary Department, driven by Bardi Rosman Koodrin and her group of dedicated volunteers. All of their efforts have played a major part in growing and producing a high-quality, literary event.

In addition to this dedicated team behind Bardi, special recognition needs to be given to the Board of Directors. It is with their guidance and direction that the San Mateo County Fair has been able to become an event that showcases our community in time-honored methods, but with new twists, following our slogan of 'Where Tradition Meets Innovation'. As the San Mateo County Fair evolves, we look forward to reading many more pieces of literary art and supporting the growth of our authors.

Let us live a thousand more lives.

Matt Cranford
Fair & Festival Manager
San Mateo County Fair

Foreword

We are pleased to launch our 2014 Carry the Light Anthology Vol III. It appears to be the only published collection of a county fair's literary stories, poems and essays in the country, especially during the fair's run. Considering we had over 200 entries and a dauntingly short production time, we are proud of our efforts. My appreciation goes to Matt Cranford, San Mateo County Fair and Festival Manager, for supporting my ideas despite how impossible they might seem, and to Tory Hartmann of Sand Hill Review Press for once again accomplishing this feat with aplomb.

Our front and back cover images of trees reflect the deep roots of our artistic community and how much it has grown since my husband Boris Koodrin and I took directorship of the Fine Arts Galleria in 2009. Perhaps these stately images also represent our personal family tree with the birth of our first grandchild, Gael Alexander Koodrin, the day before fair opened last year. Gael just might grow up thinking his grandparents own a Ferris wheel, a sweet belief we will not discourage.

Boris and I believe "The quality of one's dream will determine its power." The literary stage was designed to express creative collaboration. An example of creating something new and wonderful was the search for the first San Mateo County Poet Laureate, which we were honored to launch during the 2013 San Mateo County Fair. Seventeen of the county's brightest poets were considered for this prestigious position, and the process was brought to a delightful conclusion in Jan 2014 with the inauguration of Caroline Goodwin, MFA, a former Wallace Stegner Fellow in creative writing at Stanford. Local poets will perform two rousing Running of the Poets performances; our four classes of poetry received the highest number of submissions this year; the rap/jazz/fusion ensemble COPUS will again open our program; first-time presenter Michele Jessen will show how to integrate poetry into novel-writing; and we'll host words and music acts at night so three cheers for the spoken word.

This year our stage schedule boasts a whopping fifty-five "events within the event." The San Francisco/Peninsula branch of the

California Writers Club (CWC) is afforded the unique opportunity the San Mateo County Fair offers: a weeklong, 90-plus hour venue in which to offer mini conferences, workshops, book sales, author presentations and even music in the evenings that ordinarily would cost thousands of dollars to book. Other clubs and organizations must pass such costs on to their participants, resulting in high registration fees. For the nominal price of a fair ticket, people can attend every event on our literary stage for free. As far as we know, San Mateo is the only county fair to offer a full schedule of in depth, professional-level writing workshops and events in the United States!

This would not be possible without the dedicated efforts of the SF/Peninsula Writers* www.cwc-peninsula.org. Special thanks to stage managers David Hirzel and Laurel Anne Hill; Maurine Killough for booking musical talent; and Martin Shane Dowd for coordinating an army of volunteers. Boris relies on Kayte Van De Mark and I couldn't do my job without Sue Barizon, but there are countless others who give this project their time and energy.

We offer our sincere gratitude to everyone who has stepped up to Carry the Light!

Bardi Rosman Koodrin
Literary Director of the Fine Arts Galleria

San Mateo County Fair contests are open to entrants across the world https://sanmateocountyfair.com/contests/departments/literary-arts. Follow us at http://carrythelight2013.wordpress.com and www.facebook.com/pages/San-Mateo-County-Fair-Fine-Arts-Galleria.

* CWC members Teresa LeYung-Ryan (Immigrant Experience sponsor), Frank Kahren ("I'm Dying to Tell You" Mystery Novel Chapter sponsor), Karen Blake (Phillip's Wild Africa and Adventures in Science sponsor), Laurel Anne Hill ("Heroes Arise" Science Fiction/Fantasy Novel Chapter sponsor), David Hirzel, Martin Shane Dowd, Maurine Killough, Christopher Wachlin, James Hanna, Ann Foster, Lisa Meltzer Penn, Darlene Frank, Elise Frances Miller, Audrey Kalman, Wendy Walters, Sue Barizon, Tia Creighton, Lucy Ann Murray, Linda Oker, Marjorie Bicknell Johnson, Cheryl Levinson, Frank A. Saunders, Tina Gibson, Mary E. Knippel, Michele Jessen, and Beth and Ezra Barany, among many others too numerous to name.

The Winners

We think everyone is a winner, but here is the official list. There were 15 judges. Not all judges awarded first prizes or gave honorable mentions. A few of the entries were not published in this volume because of the author's wishes. They have been indicated by an asterisk.*

Div 326 Memoir
First Place: *69 Lengths*, Mary Ruth Coffey
Second Place: *To Hypnotize a Chicken*, Marjorie Johnson
Third Place: *Whispered Confession*, Gail Jenner
Honorable Mention: *The Principal of the Matter*, Evie Groch
Honorable Mention: *Gone*, Valerie Stoller

Div 327 Phillip's Wild Africa
Honorable Mension: *South African Tears*, Evie Groch

Div 328 Adventures in Science
First Place: *Heavenly Halos and Their Angelic Arcs*,
    Stanley Gedzelman
Second Place: *Granny Says Life Began Between Mica Sheets*,
    Helen Hansma
Third Place: *Condensation Day at Cloudopolis Academy*,
    Amberleigh Stipicevich *

Div 330 CWC Writer of the Year
Kevin Arnold, *Knock on the Door*

Div 331 "I'm Dying to Tell You" Mystery Novel Chapter
First Place: *Death on Route 66*, Carolyn Donnell
Second Place: *Catch and Release*, Madeline McEwen
Third Place: *Gun Smoke*, Linda Brown

Div 332 The Immigrant Experience: Novel, Memoir, Short Story, Or Monologue
Third Place: *From Munchenberg to the City of Angels*,
    Evie Groch

Div 333 *Parenting on the Peninsula* Children's Novel Chapter or Story
First Place: *Dragon's Baby Teeth*, Carolyn Donnell
Second Place: *Bag Girl*, Robert J. (Jamie) Miller
Third Place: *Cat with No Meow,* Kimberly Schultz

Div 334, Poetry, Class 1, Free Form
First Place: *Palimpsest*, Renae Keep
Second Place: *Oysterville Fame,* Renae Keep
Third Place: *I Dream,* Maurine Killough
Honorable Mention: *Monet's Garden*, Maurine Killough

Div 334, Poetry, Class 2, Senior Free Form
First Place: *Brotherhood of the Midnight Snack,* Ellaraine Lockie
Second Place: *Time... and Time Again,* Ellaraine Lockie *
Third Place: *The Buzz,* Evie Groch
Honorable Mention: *Closure,* Bernadine Fornesi
Honorable Mention: *Sounds of August*, Evie Groch
Honorable Mention: *The Children,* Margaret Vose

Div 334, Poetry, Class 3, Structured Poem, Exhibitor 54 years or younger
First Place: *Words,* Jeannine Gerkman
Second Place: *Nestle,* Jeannine Gerkman
Third Place: *Flossing,* Jeannine Gerkman
Honorable Mention: *Ode to a Canyon,* Hannah Giarrusso

Div 334, Poetry, Class 4, Senior Structured
First Place: *O Bind Not My Words in Paper*, Frank Saunders
Second Place: *Other Americans*, Ellaraine Lockie
Third Place: *Three Tankas,* Frank Saunders
Honorable Mention: *Clean-up in Rwanda*, Ellaraine Lockie
Honorable Mention: *Elegy to a Beloved Colleague,*
    Jo Carpignano
Honorable Mention: *Beyond Words,* Thomas Ekkens

Poetry Best of Show
***Palimpsest* by Renae Keep**

Div 335 Essay, Class 1, Exhibitor 54 years old or younger
First Place: *Half Foods, Whole Moments*, Katie Burke
Second Place: *Tommy's Story*, Michele Jessen

Div 335 Essay, Class 2, Senior Essay
First Place: *Creative Pursuits*, Teresa Harbin Lebeiko
Second Place: *Social Insecurity*, Rudie Tretten
Third Place: *Barefootin'*, Terry Toomey
Honorable Mention: *The Reset Button*, Sally Shunsky-Hernandez

Essay Best of Show
***Creative Pursuits* by Teresa Harbin Lebeiko**

Div 336 Short Story, Class 1, General Fiction
First Place: *Table for Two*, Kimberly Schultz
Second Place: *Premonition*, Amy Kelm

Div 336 Short Story, Class 2, Senior General Fiction
First Place: *Cassie's Valentine*, Valerie Stoller
Second Place: *The Call*, Kevin Arnold
Third Place: *Ghostly Messenger of Truth*, Cheryl Levison

Div 336, Short Story, Class 3, Science Fiction/Fantasy Exhibitor 55 years old or younger
First Place: *The Eyes Have It*, Lisa Meltzer Penn

Div 336, Short Story, Class 4, Senior Science Fiction/Fantasy
First Place: *Cliff Soaring*, Robert J. (Jamie) Miller
Second Place: *One Slightly Weird Sister*, Robert J.(Jamie) Miller
Third Place: *Open Road*, Doug Baird
Honorable Mention: *Bookwus*, Robert J. (Jamie) Miller

Div 336, Short Story, Class 6, Senior Mystery Thriller
First Place: *The Poisoner's Handbook*, Marjorie Johnson
Second Place: *Ditch-Rider*, Bernadine Forenesi
Third Place: *The Trolley*, Judy Jette-Hansen *
Honorable Mention: *Repo Man*, Linda Brown

Div 336, Short Story, Class 8, Senior Western
First Place: *The Last of the Oatmeal*, Carolyn Donnell
Second Place: *Link N' Milton,* Greg Erion

Div 336, Short Story, Class 10, Senior Historical
First Place: *The Great Fire*, Eugenia Budman *
Second Place: *The '90s, Golden Era...*, Camincha Benvenutto

Short Story Best of Show
***Cassie's Valentine* by Valerie Stoller**

Div 337 California State Parks 150th Anniversary
First Place: A California Summer with Marie, Jo Carpignano

Literary Exhibitor of the Year: Carolyn Donnell

Div 314 Fine Arts Book Cover Art Contest
"Carry the Light" for The San Mateo County Fair
Literary Anthology
First Place: Through the Darkness, Rita Beach
Second Place: Enchanted, Randy Marlow
These pieces have been used on our front and back cover.

Congratulations to all of the winners!

* Not published in this volume due to the wishes of the author.

Carry the Light

Stories, Poems and Essays from the San Mateo County Fair

Volume III

Vegan Speed Dating
By Valerie Stoller

I was tired of covering campus demonstrations for my college newspaper. So, when Bobby Marshall, my editor, sauntered over to my desk, I hoped he had something exciting for me to work on. Bobby's red bushy hair flamed especially bright that morning.

"Check this out, Lois."

One of Bobby's strange habits was calling reporters by names right out of Superman. I was Lois Lane, not Pamela Baker. Bobby, of course, with his thick black glasses was Clark Kent.

"Hey, Bobby. Don't tell me there's another protest."

"No. Even better." He pulled out a flier and waved it in my face. I grabbed the flier. Rows of dancing tomatoes and smiling zucchini. What?

VEGAN SPEED DATING: a round-robin style dating system to find your vegan soul mate.

"Isn't it great, Lois?" Bobby stood close to my desk, reading over my shoulder. "Isn't what great, Bobby?" I looked up at him. "Are you going to this?"

"No." He grinned, showing teeth stained from too much coffee and cigarettes. "You are."

"What?" I waved the flier back at him. "You want me to cover this?"

Bobby laughed, his wild red hair dancing a polka.

"Yeah, Lois. He winked at me. "You're gonna be an undercover vegan."

Oh, not me, a hardcore carnivore. Besides, speed dating was so lame. I wanted to find a guy on my own.

The event was scheduled for 7:30 pm at the Mars Café, a new vegetarian restaurant near campus. I wore a Hawaiian shirt over cotton drawstring pants. No dead animals on me.

"Welcome." The woman seated at a table near the entrance smiled up at me. "What's your name?"

"Uh, Lois. Lois Lane." I waited for her to burst out laughing.

"Okay. Hi, Lois." Not even a chuckle. "I'm Joanie."

She handed me my name tag with "Lois" in large print. A perky orange carrot dotted the "i".

Oh God, let me out of here now. This was all Bobby's stupid idea.

Joanie picked up a cordless mic.

"Welcome to what I'm sure will be a very fun night. Each of you lovely ladies will have a booth. The guys will rotate through every few minutes."

I grabbed an open table. My stomach gurgled, reminding me I was way out of my comfort zone. Why had I agreed to do this?

"Hi there." My first date plopped down in the booth. His face shone with sweat, a few bright red pimples lit up his cheeks.

"How old are you?" I couldn't resist asking.

Jacob, according to his name tag, wiped his forehead with an eco-friendly napkin.

"Everyone thinks I look young." He crushed the napkin in his fist. "I'm 22. Do you wanna see my license?"

Jeez, I'd already pissed off a guy without even trying.

"Sorry." I managed a smile. "Have you done this kind of thing before?"

Jacob told me all about his last speed date event. We were interrupted by Joanie's voice from the mic announcing time was up. On to my next dream date. I could almost taste the juicy hamburger I'd pick up later. Wiped a little drool off my lip as Bachelor #2 sat down.

Trevor. Thin, tall, pale, with a wispy goatee that made him look forlorn. He leaned across the table.

"Do you like quinoa? I make an amazing quinoa salad."

Kin-wah? What the heck was that? Fake it, Pam.

"Um, yeah, I love it." I nodded. "Especially smothered in ranch dressing."

"Wow." Trevor's eyes widened. He stroked his sad goatee.

"How long have you been vegan, Lois?"

"Gosh, it's been about three years since I let a dead animal pass these lips." I puffed out my mouth in what I hoped was a provocative come-on. "How about you?"

Trevor rambled on until Joanie's voice pierced our special moment. He scribbled something on his notes before he left.

Probably to try that ranch dressing.

Two down, eighteen to go. Too bad they weren't serving alcohol.

Bachelor #3 eased into my booth. Tall, slim, light brown hair, green eyes. He smelled like he'd showered recently. His name tag was partly covered by jacket. Name ending in r-y. Gary? Harry? Larry? I pushed my hair behind my ear and sat up.

"Hi. I'm Pam." Oh shit. "I mean Lois." Great job playing my part. A smile spread across his face. Dimples. Check. Nice teeth. Check. Damn, maybe I had hit the jackpot.

"Hi, I'm Jerry." He pulled his jacket open, flashing me his name tag. "At least for tonight."

Huh? I wasn't the only one using an alias. What was the deal with this guy?

"Nice to meet you, Jerry-for-Tonight." Damn, I sounded downright flirty.

"So, Lois." His face relaxed into another dimpled smile.

"Aren't you going to ask me why I'm here? Or if I've done this before?"

Oh, right. I was supposed to be checking him out. Instead, I was back in eighth grade, with adorable Eddy Newman talking to me in the school cafeteria. Tongue-tied.

"Okay." He smiled. "I'll go first. What do you like to do for fun?"

"Uh, let's see," I stammered. "You mean besides eating vegetables?"

Jerry laughed. "I hope that's not the highlight of your life."

"Well, uh, I do have a thing for old movies," I said.

"Really?" His dimples again. "Me too. I'm a sucker for Myrna Loy."

"Yeah, well, I heard she had a thing for steak tartare," I teased. What was I doing? I couldn't help myself.

Joanie's voice snapped me out of my trance. My impulse was to grab Jerry by the wrist and claim him as my prize.

Too late. He shrugged his shoulders and stood up. The one attractive guy in the room, walking out of my life. Forever.

Then he leaned in close to where I sat. Was he going to kiss me? "It really was nice to meet you, Lois." His breath smelled like mint toothpaste. Then he whispered into my ear. "Bobby was right."

What? I stared at the back of his head as he walked away, but he didn't turn around. He knew Bobby? My mind exploded with possible explanations. Had Bobby played a joke on me?

The rest of the evening passed in a blur. When the event was finally over, I grabbed my purse and looked for the one guy I needed to find.

He was already outside, talking to a pretty blonde.

Oh crap. Too late. He'd met the woman of his dreams, and they'd ride off into the night. I marched through the front door, staring straight ahead. Didn't want to see those green eyes ever again.

"Hey," he called out. "Wait up."

He walked over to me. Blondie was gone. Good riddance.

"So, Lois," he said, grinning as he emphasized my name.

"Would you like to get a drink?"

"I don't know," I lied. "Who are you?" My eyes met his.

"How do you know Bobby? Was this his idea of a joke?"

"Look, I'm sorry." He'd stopped smiling and extended his right hand. "My real name is Jesse."

Bobby, as it turned out, was his cousin. He'd wanted Jesse to meet me, but he knew I'd never go for a blind date. So he'd come up with this crazy plan to get us together. Bobby the matchmaker.

"Why did you call yourself Jerry?" It didn't really matter but I was curious. Jesse laughed, his green eyes shining.

"Bobby told me you'd signed up as Lois Lane. So I decided to register with the name he'd stuck me with as a kid." He gave a half bow with his left arm bent in front of him.

"Jerry, as in Jerry Garcia. You know, the Grateful Dead. Bobby's a huge fan." Jesse sighed. "Pretty stupid, huh?"

"Yeah." I nodded. "One more thing. Are you really a vegan, or was that part of Bobby's twisted sense of humor?"

"Yeah, I really am. For about three years now." He leaned in. I could smell his minty breath. "Does it really matter?"

Maybe. Maybe not. Maybe I'd be thanking Bobby later.

Three Tankas
By Frank Saunders

For Barbara
I sneeze. Spring's early this year.
Acacias spray their pollen in
the breeze.
Pistils and stamens rejoice:
Yellow love is in the air.

For Maryanne
Blue bird on a branch, whistling
to an azure sky, doesn't know or
care
that another spring has come or
another year has passed.

For Thom
A poet listens,
hearing what cannot be said.
Through what alchemy does he
evoke a feeling
through marking on a blank page?

The Poet Laureate
By Stanley Gedzelman

I have to tell you a gruesome story
About an envious girl named Laurie
And a sweeter girl you'd much rather meet
Lived in bigger house across the street.
All the neighborhood fell in love with Kate
She was pretty and her poems were great.
The difference between them was day and night,
Laurie was ugly and she couldn't write.
While Kate won all laurels on the town stage
Laurie swore revenge with a grisly rage.
But as good as Kate was in her town's eyes
She never did win a National Prize.
So when Laurie fricasseed tender Kate,
Kate was at last the Poet Laurie ate.

The Wood Shed
By Patricia Bradley

Behind the white farm house and slightly to the left, a weathered wooden shed sheltered the firewood that had been split and cut for the stove in the kitchen. In the field running up the hill behind the house, a stern committee of many uniform tree stumps stood, as if protesting the conversion of the trees for this purpose. It rained a lot here in Washington and the shed kept the wood fairly dry. On the right side, a door was somewhat ajar and he could be seen just inside, sitting on a pile of the firewood and staring at the floor. He was a good looking man, this thirty-year-old with the black hair and sparkling blue eyes now filled with pain. Bib overalls, shirt with the sleeves rolled to the elbows revealing a farmer's tan, a rumpled hat askew. A man who was used to solving problems, fixing things, with hands that had seen many days of hard work. Capable, in charge. This challenge, however, was more than he could handle and so he continued to stare at the floor, a white collie sprawled at his feet, on guard.

Inside the house, big pots of hot water boiled frantically on the stove. Nellie dropped wide strips of wool torn from blankets into the steaming pots. Her beautiful long auburn hair was wound in a bun and she brushed from her damp forehead a few of the strands that had escaped. Her apron was dotted with water spots.

"Where's your father?" she asked Annamae, the ten-year-old. "I'm going to need some more wood soon."

Annamae went out the back door and spotted her father sitting inside the wood shed. He held out his hand to her and drew her to him. She could feel his anguish but did not understand it. Why was he hiding out here? Maybe Harvey was really, really, really sick. He was only six. After all, she was the one they usually paid attention to with her coughs and wheezing. Her mother made her wear long, wool stockings even in the summer time as a possible help for her continual asthma. Sometimes she would cough into the towel to keep her mom from hearing her in hope that the stockings could come off and she could run around with bare legs.

"Mommy says she needs more wood. I'll take it. Daddy, am I going to get sick too?" He didn't answer her. Annamae gathered up firewood in her small arms and Daddy added one more large stick on top. She marched off toward the house with great responsibility for a ten-year-old, struggling to open the back screen door without dropping any of her load, her large hair ribbon bouncing like a butterfly on top of her head. She added the pieces to those in the wooden box next to the black, wood burning stove, and peeked into the bedroom.

Harvey was lying on the bed and Nellie was talking to him as she wrapped his legs with the hot wool strips, taking off the cool ones. No one knew much about this polio thing and no one could agree about the best thing to do. Doctor Tiffin said that he had read about a Catholic nurse named Sister Kenny who had tried this method and sometimes it helped.

Annamae wondered whose sister Kenny was. She didn't know those girls. As soon as Harvey's legs warmed up again, Nellie began to massage them from top to bottom and back again. Annamae went into the other room to see what her sister LaVerne was playing. She was only two and had golden curls. Annamae had black hair and a Dutch Bob and fixed you with her blue eyes in a very serious look sometimes. Pictures of her revealed that one of those eyes was slightly smaller than the other, a hereditary trait unnoticed in person. The baby of the family was playing with the blocks and her dolly with the china head and hands. Annamae sat down with her. She thought the baby was kind of little to play with but today no one was paying any attention to either of them.

Outside, he continued to maintain his vigil in the wood shed. The muscles in his arms tensed as he clenched his hands. Was his strength of any consequence now? This was the little boy he had taught to ride horses and had shown how to milk the dairy cows in the barn. This boy with the dimple in his chin who looked up at him. The dimple that was going to cause him trouble shaving. Oh God, please let him grow up to shave.

Again, he reviewed in his mind their move from Montana. Maybe if they hadn't come to Washington where it rained so much, maybe they should have stayed where the cold weather might have killed the bugs that caused this, maybe this was his fault. He was supposed to keep them safe.

Three days and three nights with almost no sleep, Nellie continued her march from the stove to the bed. Heat the legs and massage them, heat the legs and massage them. On the extreme periphery of this scene he moved, helping the girls with something to eat, bringing in a load of wood and filling the pots with water. But mostly he manned his post in the wood shed. Surely this would turn around. Surely his son wouldn't be crippled. Surely he wouldn't die. The doctor came and went, came and went. A neighbor arrived to help with the girls and looked out the kitchen window at him. Their eyes met, his filled with despair, hers questioning. And then she looked away.

The year was 1927 and this dairy farm in Enumclaw was an experiment he had entered into after much discussion with his father and mother. This Irish mother of his, very forceful and yet still possessing those Irish superstitions which caused him also to distrust new things, and then his quiet, reticent father, who had been a former scout with the Army chasing Chief Joseph through Yellowstone Park. He had hoped his family would have a better opportunity here than in the small town in Montana. But the price of feed and hay had been going up and the price of milk had not kept pace. None of that mattered now that there was the march between the stove and the bed. His hopes and dreams hovered in the air as if they would evaporate into nothing or blow away with the slightest breeze. He had never felt so helpless.

A week of this and the doctor got Harvey up on his feet and they walked together into the kitchen. A rest on the chair and back again. A rest on the bed and back again. It seemed the crisis had passed. The threat was over. The girls showed no symptoms. Exhausted, Nellie looked deeply into his eyes, this man who had huddled out in the wood shed in his fear and helplessness. Did she understand him or was there resentment or accusation in her gaze? Did he try to explain his feelings to her, his immobility, and could she understand? Had their relationship changed? Only those two knew the answers to these questions.

Harvey went on to ride many horses, including showing his horse at the auction when their farm went into foreclosure. The money gained from the sale of his horse, $25.00 in those hard times, was the family's bankroll to return to Montana. His saddle, however, was not for sale his father said. Harvey danced many dances, charmed and wooed many ladies, told many tales, and he learned to shave the cleft in his chin. There were no after effects of the dread polio. None that were visible.

Words
By Jeannine Gerkman

Words for me can be
Something ethereal
And fine. Like
Diamonds in the sunshine
And gold spun in my mind.
I can touch them in a moment.
Don't need a special place
Can feel the tingle in my fingertips
And the warmth upon my face.
They help me rise above my sorrow,
Throw off the fetters of my fear.
Make my life shimmer and sparkle
Like notes from a summer symphony,
They draw me ever near.

The Passenger
By Rita Beach

"Lilly, you have to stop this. It's not healthy mentally or emotionally." He saw the fire light up in her dark brown eyes as she whirled around to face him.

"What do you care? Why is this any of your business? I'm not hurting you or anyone else." She opened the car door and slid into the driver's seat. "Stay the hell out of the affairs of my heart."

"What good does it do, Lilly? You drive him around everyday. He's so out of it, he doesn't even know where he is." He paused, then said once more, "What good does it do?"

"You think anybody who isn't handling issues of grief by self-medicating the way you do must be off her rocker. Is that it?"

"Why, why do you always have to make my drinking a subject?" Then he spoke softly saying, "Yes, maybe sometimes that is my coping mechanism."

"Sometimes! Carl, you have a heap of issues the way you hit the sauce." She was in a rage by this time, springing from the car into his face like a tiger upon her prey. "You think you are capable of judging my state of mind. What gives you the right—thirty years together? Wrong! Do not assume you know me. You have never known me."

His face morphed into a submissive, wounded casualty, incapable of fighting back. His tone softened. "You two enjoy your drive. I'll see you when you get back." He paused beside the car door. "I worry about you, Lilly. That's all. I just worry."

Lilly did not look at him. She backed slowly out the driveway onto the neighborhood street and then turned right at the first light towards Crow Canyon Road.

"Boy, what a gorgeous day for a drive!" Her passenger let out a little moan. "You okay?" she asked. She drove for an hour. Her passenger never lifted his eyes or raised an eyebrow. He slumped further down in his seat, wilting to one side, unable to sit up straight, making no sound other than an occasional whimper. Lilly looked over at him. "There is a park right up here. We can take a nice walk. You always loved your walks."

She turned in and found a spot under a shady tree. Coming around the car, she opened the door, and literally had to grab her passenger to prevent him from falling to the ground. "It's okay, it's okay... I got you. A nice walk... that's what you need." She struggled trying to help him stand on his own, but it was no use. He was too weak.

"Goddammit, try harder! Don't you want to live?" she shouted at him in desperation. Lilly wrestled with the inert body until she managed to return him once again to the passenger seat. Suddenly, her passenger let out a loud, awful cry.

Lilly did not bother to wipe away the tears streaming down her face like an overflowing fountain as she drove home. As she turned into the driveway, Carl walked quickly out of the house to assist.

"That won't be necessary, Carl. He is suffering," Lilly said. "Will you go with me to have him put to sleep?"

"Are you sure you want to go, Lilly? I can take him if you want."

She did not seem to hear his words at first. "Do you realize, Carl, he has been with us for over half of the years we have been married."

"Yes, Lilly. He has been a remarkable companion."

"Yes, yes he has," she said with a quiet in her voice close to a whisper. "Maybe, if you don't mind, I'll wait here. That might be best."

"Of course, dear. I'll take care of this."

"Carl," she called as he closed the door.

"What Lilly?" he asked tenderly as he rolled down the window.

"I'll have a drink fixed for you when you return."

The Last of the Oatmeal
By Carolyn Donnell

Eleven-year-old Suzie sat in the rocking chair on the farmhouse porch and watched the pink and azure sunrise spread across the sky over the flat Oklahoma pasture. "Nothing for you today," she whispered to the doves congregating around the old oak. "There's barely enough for us. But it's still a beautiful morning, isn't it?" The doves cooed in agreement. Suzie smiled. This was the only time she had to herself, a few minutes after dawn, a small space for dreams. Her thin body cast an even thinner shadow as she walked back into the house.

Sunlight filtered hazily through a tiny window in the kitchen. Suzie had to stand on a stepstool to reach the pan on the old stove. She tapped on the bottom of the Quaker Oatmeal box to empty the last crumbs into the boiling water. She hoped it would be enough to feed them all this morning. Her stepfather, Frank, had left before dawn. Suzie hoped he would return soon with something from the nearby orchards.

Frank picked at the calluses on his right hand. He detested having to take the older children into the fields of others during the summer like common laborers. His own land, along with his house, the café, and even his blacksmith tools had gone back to the bank and tax collector. Proud of his ability to support his family, he had always assumed that the poor, if not ill or handicapped, were just lazy. But that was in regular times. These days there were no jobs. Even with his skills as farmer, blacksmith, carpenter, and merchant, not to mention a cook and even a bagpiper, he had been unable to find work. No one had any money to hire anyone to do anything. Landowners couldn't even hire hands to gather the ripening crops. They had to rely on "picking on the halves"—the pickers got to keep half of what they gathered.

This morning he went alone so the children, especially the boy, could go back to school. He found only enough peaches at a neighbor's orchard to fill half a burlap sack. Where was he going to look for food tomorrow? What were they going to do?

Pain shot through his right temple. He shifted the bag to his other and and opened the porch door. Stomping into the cabin, he dropped the sack of peaches on the table. The door slammed behind him with a shotgun-loud bang.

Startled by the noise, Suzie lost her footing. The pan clattered to the floor. Oatmeal flew everywhere.

"What's wrong with you?" Frank bellowed. "Clumsy girl! Look what you've done. Can't even stand on a stool!" Crimson crept up his neck. "That was the last of the oatmeal. We'll all starve because of you." Swiveling heavily, he swung at her with the back of his hand, forgetting his strength and her frailty.

Suzie flew into the far wall. The two babies in the makeshift playpen began to cry. Suzie lay very still. Finally she stirred.

Frank stared at the wall, absentmindedly rubbing his hand over the surface of the wooden table. The finely sanded and oiled surface and the softly curved legs seemed oddly out of place in the shack, like a Renoir in a tenement room.

Suzie recalled the hours he had spent carving and smoothing it to perfection. There wasn't a finer table in the town. It was all they had left from their old house—their old life.

"Shh. Don't cry." She crooned to the babies as she began cleaning the mess. Her back hurt, but she didn't let it show. This was not her stepfather, strong and wise—the one who had always been there for her. A stranger stood now in the dark shadows. She shivered. Without a word, Frank, with shoulders bent, shuffled out the door.

Suzie's older brother, Will, bounded into the room and landed heavily in one of the wooden chairs. "Where's breakfast?"

Suzie pointed to the peaches. "Put a couple in a sack."

"That's all?"

Eight-year-old Carrie followed Will. She grabbed the back of his chair. "Hey! That's my chair."

"Get off me, sister. Go away." He reached up and yanked her pigtail.

"Ow! He pulled my hair," Carrie cried out.

The two babies joined the cacophony.

Suzie stomped. "Stop it! Now look what you've done. I just got them quiet." Will crossed his arms and slumped in his chair. "Don't worry. I'll be gettin' out of here soon. Leave me alone, skinny girl! You're not my mother."

"Well, Mr. Smarty Pants, I may be skinny, but I'm the one who takes care of this family. And don't you forget it."

"Phhht," he exhaled. He grabbed his books and lunch sack and left the cabin, followed closely behind by Carrie.

"Skinny girl, skinny girl," the two taunted, now in as much harmony as they had been in discord a few minutes earlier.

Suzie watched them go. "I sure hope our momma gets home today," she said to the two babies. "I don't want to miss school." She wiped away a tear with her apron. "No. No time for that." She resumed cleaning.

Frank walked for what seemed like miles. Squeezing his aching head with his hands, he staggered over to a spreading oak in a nearby field and slid down into the shade.

How could I have done that! How did things get so bad? He thought back to the beginning of the hard years. I've been a good provider for my wife and her three children. Even when two more babies came along, I managed. But now... He pulled at the roots of his thinning hair. A wave of hopelessness washed over him. I can't go on any more.

No longer happy with merely sucking everyone's pocketbooks dry and emaciating their bodies, the Depression was demolishing their souls. He didn't know what they were going to do. Their only remaining food consisted of some turnips he had buried out back of the cabin and the peaches picked that morning.

He tugged on his worn leather belt. The newly punched holes kept up his sagging pants. Not much of a catch any more, am I? He sighed. His wife no longer seemed interested in him now that he couldn't provide a good living. It didn't matter to her that no one else was doing well either these days. She spent most of her time criticizing him or running errands. That's what she called it. He tried to eke out a living from what he could find, while Suzie did most of the household chores, fed everyone and cared for the two babies.

"Sweet Suzie," he murmured to himself. She had always been his favorite of his three stepchildren—the smartest one and the hardest working. Her younger sister was a winsome creature; her mother's favorite because of that, but not so bright. And the boy— Frank grimaced. He had been a problem from the beginning. The two babies were, well, they were babies. Suzie was the only one who always offered to help.

He remembered the night the sheriff had come to warn him of an impending raid. Suzie helped him hide the contraband whiskey he kept on the top shelf in the back of their café.

"We can get through this, Pop," she had told him. Her valiant spirit always encouraged him when he needed it and he had repaid her today by hitting her, maybe even injuring her.

His thoughts boiled. Hasn't she had enough from her mother? She lost her own father when she was four. She deserves better and I've failed her. I failed all of them. Oh, God.... A sob shook his lean frame. He collapsed against the tree.

He had lain in the tree's shadow for a long time when a movement in the distance caught his eye. A familiar figure was approaching. He screwed his eyes to focus on the blurry object. He groaned. Here it comes. Please, Lord, spare me today. A shuddering sigh escaped his lips.

The small, dark woman came closer. "Frank? What are you doing?"

He didn't respond.

"Frank! Are you listening to me?" She bent down and shook his shoulder. "Wake up, you lazy ..." Her push sent him sideways. His limp body crumpled like an old rag doll that had lost some of its stuffing. Only then did she see his slack mouth, a sliver of drool escaping from one side. She began to scream.

Strains of "Amazing Grace" floated up from the lawn behind the white-steepled church as Frank's funeral moved outside to the cemetery. Suzie sat to one side, away from the others.

"When I'm gone, I want this sung at my funeral," he had said. Suzie had had to remind her mother and the preacher of that wish.

The whine of a bagpipe joined in. Suzie jerked her head toward the creek. Frank was the only piper in this town and his bagpipe still hung on the wall at home.

Misty at first, then clearing, an image in full piper's regalia, kilt and all, came into view. His beard was no longer scraggly and his girth had regained its former prosperous dimensions.

The kilt and pipes looked fresh from the maker. Everything about Frank looked renewed, reborn. The bagpipe's accompanied the singers' voices, but its plaintive wail was for Suzie's ears alone.

Amazing grace! (how sweet the sound) That sav'd a wretch like me! I once was lost, but now am found, was blind, but now I see.

Suzie answered the chorus. "His strength failed him at last. But now he's in a better place."

'Twas grace that taught my heart to fear, And grace my fears reliev'd; How precious did that grace appear, The hour I first believ'd!

"He's found his peace and I know he asks me to forgive."

Thro' many dangers, toils and snares, I have already come;'Tis grace has brought me safe thus far, And grace will lead me home.

"I've seen two fathers buried now. Will I find grace to see me through?"

The Lord has promis'd good to me, His word my hope secures; He will my shield and portion be, as long as life endures.

"I hope he's right. Can I endure? My heart can't stand much more."

The apparition stopped playing, looked at Suzie intently, then nodded. Suzie took a deep breath. "Yes, you're right, Pops. I am strong." She watched him turn. The tassels on the pipes fluttered in the breeze as he dissolved back into the fog.

The funeral was short. The congregation small. No headstone would ever mark his passing. That would have cost money.

That evening Suzie took a copy of Little Women, a gift from Frank, and placed it in a box hidden under her bed. The book joined a faded rag doll and a rock collection, treasures given to her by her first father before they moved here from New Mexico.

"See those girls," Frank had said, pointing to the book. They had problems just like you, and they got through them. You're a smart girl. And strong. I want you to grow up to be a lady, just like them."

Suzie returned her treasure box to its hiding place. She straightened her spine and lifted her chin, trying to emulate the ladies from the book.

"I promise, Pops. I will stand. I will carry on."

The '90s, Golden Era of Open Mics
By Camincha Benvenutto

YACKETY YACK was another Open Mic that appeared at the same time as they were enjoying Above Paradise, Sacred Grounds, The Blue Monkey, Babar. Suddenly it was a must to go there. Regulars got published. Featured. Photographed.

The club was located on Sutter St. in the Theater District. Friday evenings 7:30 to 10. Alba, to avoid parking problems, took BART from Pacifica to Powell station, then walked five blocks to Sutter, turned left and walked three more to the café. She was a city person. Imagined herself walking among many, unleashing her desires that enjoyed the busy streets, night lights, stores, hotels. Restaurant fronts that suggested characters, life styles full of mystery that caused her imagination to entertain exotic thoughts. Unusual sounds, sirens, variety of smells of food, perfumes, people. Loved the tall buildings. And as she walked on Powell checked the latest fashions at Victoria's Secret, the new books in the windows of Barnes & Noble. This trajectory worked its magic got her adrenaline high. By the time she arrived at the Open Mic she was ready to tell it like it is. And on her way home it was The Golden Dust Lounge that seduced her with its murals on the ceiling, framed currency in the bar and music that called her in to dance before catching the last train home.

Yakety Yak, as many others, was a converted something or other. The bathroom, smelling strongly of Clorox, was a calamity, the one toilet didn't always flush, the faucets were reversed so you often burned yourself. How did it ever pass the sanitation inspection? Maybe it hadn't. The floors were uneven, walls needed painting, cleaning, anything would have helped. Some small rooms must have been torn down so there were two salons were people congregated, with standing space only. The few chairs, tables there looked like leftovers from some disaster area. The café's doors to Sutter St. were kept opened and that salon had a counter at the back that served coffee, tea, beer, wine, pastries. But it was the smell of freshly baked pastry right out of the microwaves that greeted you and made you forget all the shortcomings.

Vincent was a long time friend of one of the regulars, Bob. Single, heavy, short, balding, pleasant with a melancholic air. He was not talkative at home or the café but got things done. A local writer, poet with a day job, lived a few blocks away. Vincent liked to invite people to spaghetti dinners in his tiny studio-basement apartment. His company had to spill into the long hallway that lead to the front door. And because he owned only two chairs, all had to sit on the floor or the casing of windows that looked out to the building next door. Nobody minded. Many were thankful to have a free meal where no one paid any attention to how many helpings they had.

Vincent managed the readings with precision and a strict demeanor. He gave you seven minutes and didn't let anyone go a second over it. Had an alarm clock set each time. It was obnoxiously loud. He would let it run while dealing with whoever was going over time and if necessary the culprit would be physically escorted from the tiny stage located in the back of the inner salon. Therefore the readings ran like clockwork. Each time we turned a city corner, walked into a restaurant, library, bookstore, café, or bar we listened to poetry. And Alba believed it was the discipline exercised by Vincent that attracted such a mob. Everyone had a turn, no one went away disappointed and the variety of voices was exciting. Filled up the place and overflowed out of the locale into the sidewalk, making it very tight for the crowd inside. Seats were at a premium. But the readers could be heard, appreciated, because the stage was well built, high enough, though small. And she was glad for smokers; it masked the odors floating around. Alba loved that place, enjoyed the intense energy it generated. People shouted their approval. Laughter was sonorous. The crowds were mixed, in ages and lifestyles.

As time went by, the writers formed a tight group that could be found in all the venues. They called each other questions if got stuck on a line. If needed info on a date, name, address. Some stand out. Kelly, whose poems Alba remembers more like short stories that told of when he was a sailor, musician and what got him writing and made him a regular at Open Mics. Specially she remembers one piece in which he reminisces of an evening of music and as an aside tells of how teenagers were allowed in the clubs, but were separated from the adults by a screen of fence wire. And he described the young kids admiration, joy, to be able to listen to their favorites, to the Masters in a real club. And in the same piece he reads their names and ends with: ...and so many others whose names I can't remember anymore. When Kelly died his family eulogized him at Yakety Yak. His widow and grandchildren listened to our words and told us how much he had enjoyed being part of our group.

And there was Bob who worked very hard at not keeping a job and used his time to publish everyone as often as he could, organized readings in San Francisco at elegant, famous bars, public libraries where no one had ever heard of us. And Magda, who had her own way of promoting the group. Was in love with the then famous Mexican rebel Comandante Marcos. So she got us to contribute a poem, Dreams turned to nightmares/ and clipped wings laid to rest? a paragraph in his honor and got them published in a special magazine that she designed.

Vincent wanted to feature Alba. She said, Yes. I'll be happy to. He laughed, as if she had said something funny. Truly hilarious. She laughed harder. Would you like to choose your partner? Anyone you like? Alba had in mind the guy who liked her jokes. Talked to her in Spanish. Who thought everything she read was great. And himself read silly nonsense he made up about his parents. P. T. Paarty. At the time she thought it was a name he made up but found years later it was his real name. The night they were Featured she didn't feel well all day. Had a bad case of stage fright. Thought of not going, canceling. She called, seeking sympathy, Brennan and Onyx— his chosen nickname— they were taking Vincent's place. He was going to be away in his monthly visit to his mother. They cheered her up, cheered her on: You'll be fine. Come. You'll see. You'll be fine.

So. Yes. Alba picked herself up and got on her way. And it helped that when she got off BART her mood changed, she became energized with all the activity around her, the noise, lights, crowd so she entered the first pastry shop she found and bought herself a jelly donut oozing with . . . JELLY. Rich, sweet, pure sugar, calories. Pure fat for thighs, FAT belly, FAT FAT FAT. Half a block later she retraced her steps and bought another Jelly DONUT. She felt even better after she devoured it. Later standing on the stage she was full, of the DEVIL. Enthusiastic, exhuberant.

P. T. Paarty read. He was good. Specially his piece about the naked virgins. Alba had heard it before but now the whole piece fitted together. Or did it? Well, Alba thought maybe that's the plan, it's not suppose to make sense. Next Brennan was on stage introducing her, how wonderful she was and how, YOU ARE GOING TO LOVE HER.

She read her most picaresque, funny pieces poems, fiction:

The Pink Ladies winked at her. Smiled at a homeless man. Tried to trip a business suit going ......

Pausing over the clatter at McDonalds he shouts, Remember me when you take a shower......

Play me your saxophone./ Tell me your lies./ Looking at you I'll be/ enjoying your sexy, fun loving body...../

When she protested, the lipstick on her lips just pushed onward saying....

They did love them, being the Featured, she had ALL the time she wanted to use. She didn't take advantage of that. She didn't over do it. Had timed herself at home, so after 15-18 minutes was ready to wrap it up. . . Rather that her public said, I wish she had read more, than, I thought she would never shut UP!!!!! So she told the crowd: And now I leave you with my signature poem, PEOPLE, dedicated to all of you 'cause without you there would be NO readings, NO Open Mic.
Give me gridlocks,
grime and dirt,
noise and lights
out of control Muni buses
and BART trains.
But give me
PEOPLE.......

Once more thank you for coming. Thank you all for your company. And made her way to the table where her group awaited her to celebrate while the crowd was hopping, hooting, laughing. And they were still so, barely sobering up, like Jello rippling, before slowly settling down in their seats, red faces, eyes moist, lips parted holding on to the merriment, ready to break out in laughter again.

Some months later with no previous notice Yakety Yak was no more. The sign on the door said, CLOSED FOR RENOVATION. It had been sold to a Chinese realty company with agents in the USA.

Next, when it opened for business again it was as an elegant French Café, full of mirrors, at the door enormous bouquets of fragrant fresh flowers, waiters in impeccable uniforms waiting to take your orders with a smile.

Whenever Alba goes by now, is curious, do the toilets flush? She wonders. Never went in to find out. Didn't want to tarnish the great memories she has . . .

Flossing
By Jeannine Gerkman

I really don't like to floss my teeth,
My lame excuses are beyond belief.

Sometimes I'm simply not in the mood
To dig around for bits of food.

Or maybe, I'll express my fear
There'll be flocks of goop upon the mirror.

My fingers will smart with lines of red,
I'll taste iron, my gums will have bled...

I'd rather brush with a toothpaste taste,
Dragging lines through my teeth seems a waste.

But I promised my dentist and do what I'm told.
A healthy smile is worth a pot of gold.

So I faithfully floss my pearl-ies each day,
I'll keep my teeth and won't have to pay
A sum of thirty thousand or so
To my dentist, Dr. Rideau.

The Eyes Have It
Lisa Meltzer Penn

I don't know how to tell you this.

Your name is not your name.

Your skin is not your skin. The tiny, fine hairs—perhaps. The beauty marks—maybe. But never the skin.

Your eyes—brace yourself, my rosebud—the eyes through which you see everything around you are all that you possess.

After you protest, after you reject all that I am telling you, then you will search. You will try to trace yourself back. I know you will try. With those smoldering, angry eyes, you will search as far as you can for your real name, for your real skin. Away from here, away from us, who have been your family and supporters, away from even your brother who has loved you more than anyone. I hope you come back to him someday. I fear you will be gone a long time. I fear you will be gone for good.

But, that is your right and prerogative. Just remember: you will be walking on feet and legs that are not yours. Touching with hands you do not own. They were never yours to hold or keep.

You don't believe me, do you?

But you will.

Because I will bring you to your knees, my cloudlet, my little bee. I will bring you down on those knees that do not belong to you.

I will have your back. It is not yours.

I run the edge of my finger along your nose and your throat. If I must, I will silence the pink muscle of tongue in your mouth.

But your burning, watchful eyes, I cannot have. They are truly yours.

Let those eyes watch. Let them see. Let their sight fall upon every moment that is lit for their taking.

You should know, my milk thistle, my pussy willow: you own everything that comes through your eyes. All the light and images they absorb are sent to the brain and changed into you. What you see overrides even smell and touch—the deepest, most primordial senses—from as far back as can be traveled.

Your eyes are conduit to the soul, a soul you do not own. Don't worry, my teacup, my buttercup, my poppy, neither do I, nor anyone else. The eyes are the rulers, whatever eyes you have that see. If you do not have eyes, the other senses might come forward and take the throne and crown—touch, smell, taste, sound. Perhaps you still could accomplish your search then, dear borrower of body. Except, of course, that without your eyes, nothing would be left that was yours.

Or, am I mistaken? I could be. Don't take all this the wrong way, my dandelion, my love, my wish, my dream, my stone.

You might have the last word after all, spoken with your borrowed, fleshly tongue. And punctuated with your eyes black as a river.

Other Americans
(in a Haibun)
By Ellaraine Lockie

The two hours early that would have been stolen by airport security sway noose-like in the draft over the train depot. Part of the $39 fare. I take on the job with x-ray vision aimed at passengers who wait on wooden benches.

A man with potato skin sprouting whiskers pulls up his stained pant leg. Scratches a scab. No baggage big enough to hold a bomb. The woman sitting beside me with missing teeth spreads like warm honey over the bench. Says I ain't givin' up nothin. Unzips her over-stuffed bag as though she senses suspicion. Points at each item to prove its necessity to her Eddie-Murphy-talking teenagers.

A kid with enough bottled water to blow up San Jose avoids eye contact through squint eyes. When he gives his seat to an old man in a walker, I ease out of national red alert and into local colors. Grab a cup of coffee percolated the old way. Drift along in the current of community.

A whistle crooks its sound waves toward the tracks to seats that could hold 300 pounds of honey. To a glass domed observation car where I step into the middle of America. A silent film surrounding a low buzz of reverence from the audience. Seats that face both sides of the panorama.

Patchwork of grassland
vineyards, barns, horses, dirt
roads An eagle circles

Hands champ at the glass bit that bars them from running fingers through fertile soil. America the Beautiful plays in the private rhythm of heartbeats. When a loudspeaker spills meals served in the dining car over the air, no one wants to leave the nourishment of this car.

The umbilical pulse of metal pounding metal. Embryos in a rocking chair of stop and go, switch of tracks. Of passengers unaware of a south slant until the birth of sunset over the Pacific.

A round of orange pours
into blue through the glass
frame Froth splashes the sand

Whistle, clang and squeal interrupt the reverie to announce Santa Barbara. I walk off and into a postcard picture.

Palms, flowers, sunshine
and harbor where mountains meet sea
Shadows of mission

Boutiques flaunt and exotic eateries flavor State Street. In Starbucks a woman wearing a multi-carat diamond orders a Venli Cinnamon Dolce Laite with sugar-free syrup no whip. Says to her Clark Gable-like companion, We'll take a bottle of '63 Rothschild to dinner. A pre-schooler at the next table plays on her IPOD while the mother reads Architectural Digest. Out front, a bronzed and buff teenager with a surfboard bleeps an alarm on a new Porsche with a U of Santa Barbara sticker. People who could pay $365 airfare to San Jose.

Armor of x-ray
Seat belts, clouds, distance, silence
A chill in the air

The Sea
By Margaret Vose

I lived my real life by the sea.
Walked windy headlands and forever beaches with
crashing waves and foamy surf, breathed salted air
and seaweed smells, made love in grassy dunes
as sea birds soared above.

Sunsets defined my days.
Summers foggy chill
and winters storms swept up my hill and
tore at the walls until
they trembled.
We went out to meet those storms when
life was real.

One day I finished with it all and left
my life beside the sea to travel
inward
where air is sweet and gentle, embrace my
memories,
and weep for those I cannot mend.

The Ditch-Rider
By Bernadine Fornesi

In the Mitchell Valley of western Nebraska, homesteaders were overjoyed when the Platte River was harnessed to bring irrigation to their acres. Ditches were dug around the farms in order to accommodate the flow of water for their plants.

A ditch-rider was appointed by the county. One of his duties was to notify each farmer the day and time of the water's release into their ditches. On the arranged day, he appeared with an iron tool that unlocked the sluice gate.

It was at one of these farms on his route, that the ditch-rider noticed when the sluice gate released the water; it was overflowing the ditches around the farm, and running onto the dirt road. With a quick leap into his truck, he drove down the hill, and pulled into the driveway of the farm. Two scrawny cats sat at the doorway of a tar papered shack. An old dog with black matted fur limped out to sniff at him before returning to the shade of a cottonwood tree.

Ralph, the ditch-rider, remembered this place. When he had come previously to notify the owner of his water allotment time, a bear of a man met him at the front door. The man had spoken in a rude, unfriendly manner.

The screen door rattled as Ralph knocked and hollered, "Anybody home?" Flipping open his notebook, he read the name of the owner of the farm, Elliott Lindstrom. "Mr. Lindstrom," he yelled, "I'm the ditch-rider; your irrigation water is overflowing your ditches and running down the road!"

The old, lame dog let out a yelp of protest at the loud voice, and the rattling of the screen door. Walking around the outside of the tar covered house, Ralph came to a root cellar with a wood door propped open. He called out, "Anyone down there?"

As Ralph turned to leave, a woman came up the dirt steps of the cellar. "If you're looking for Mr. Lindstrom, he isn't here. He went into Mitchell for some hardware, but he should be back any minute." The woman was dressed neatly in a cotton frock with an apron tied around her waist and Ralph noticed a bruise on her face and neck. Her eyes looked red and swollen. "Hello, I'm the ditch-rider. I've turned on your irrigation water, but it's all running down the road. Are you Mrs. Lindstrom?"

"Yes I am," she replied.

"Your husband must have forgotten about the day for the irrigation water. I'll turn off the sluice and we'll reschedule you."

"Thank you...you're very kind."

As Ralph left the farm of Elliott Lindstrom, he wondered if the surly man who had met him at the kitchen door previously was responsible for the bruises on his wife's face and neck.

Later that week, Ralph made another call to the Lindstrom farm to set up an appointment for the release of the irrigation water to their farm. He knocked on the screen door which hadn't been mended, so it shook and rattled with a great deal of noise. The old lame dog pointed his head upward and gave a mournful howl. After a time Mrs. Lindstrom came to the door "Can I speak to Mr. Lindstrom?" asked Ralph.

"No, he isn't here. He drove over to a neighbor." She crossed her arms in front of her apron. Mrs. Lindstrom had a short sleeved dress on, and the ditch-rider could see black and blue bruises on her arms. One wrist was wrapped in a bandage.

"Looks like you had a little accident," Ralph said as he pointed to her wrist.

"Yeah, I'm careless. I fell down the cellar steps."

Give him this note when he returns." Ralph scribbled on a page from his notebook. "This has the information of when the water will be released again."

That evening at supper, Ralph told his wife about the Lindstroms. "I think that brute is abusing his wife from the looks of her. She's just a little thing with lots of bruises. I'd like to give him a few bruises!"

His wife kept eating, but glanced at her husband as she spoke. "I think you better mind your own business. Don't get caught up between a husband and wife. They'll work it out."

Ralph frowned. "Maybe... I hope you're right. If I put bruises on your face and arms like I saw on that woman, what would you do?"

"I'd take that cast iron skillet over there on the stove and hit you a good one on the side of your head."

When water was released later to the Lindstrom farm, Ralph watched to see if the owner was diverting the flow into his crops. Water was going where it was supposed to go, and Ralph saw the big man out on the ditches shoveling trenches.

A week later, water was to be released again to the Lindstrom farm. Ralph had thought a great deal about the wife of Elliott Lindstrom. He couldn't get the picture of her bruised face and arms out of his head. With confused emotions, he pulled into the Lindstrom driveway. The farmer was standing by the front door with a leather strap in his hand. "What do you want here?" Lindstrom said in a loud voice.

"Just trying to sign you up for your next water allotment," Ralph responded. From the doorway Mrs. Lindstrom emerged. Her hair was tangled; the dress she wore was torn and soiled. On her arms and face were yellow and black bruises. A bandage was wound around her leg. Ralph's mouth opened with dismay. Elliott Lindstrom watched the ditch-rider with half closed eyes.

"What the hell are you looking at?" he growled. Ralph felt rage at the belligerent tone of the farmer.

"Did your wife have an accident?"

"Yeah...and she'll have another if she's not careful! Got in the way of me trying to hang that old crippled dog on the cottonwood tree." The woman at the door groaned as she looked at Ralph with pain and fear and hunched down in the doorway.

"I think you better get a doctor to look at your wife. The next farm over the hill has a telephone. I can make the call for you."

"She's my woman and I'll make the decisions about her. I don't want a damn doctor on my property! She'll heal up... she always has. You better be

34

on your way. I don't like the way you keep eyeing my woman!" The bruiser raised the leather strap and struck it rapidly against his leg.

Reluctantly the ditch-rider turned and walked to his truck. He knew he had to get help to the beat-up woman before the husband injured, and caused her death.

Ralph notified the sheriff in town. The next day the sheriff and a doctor paid a visit to the farm. They found Mrs. Lindstrom limping in the front yard holding a branch from a tree to help support her. The old black dog on his three good legs followed closely.

"Good morning Mrs. Lindstrom. I'm the sheriff, and I've brought a doctor. I think you need some medical help."

"Oh, please go!" she said in a trembling voice. "I'm fine. You better go before my husband comes from the field."

The doctor said, "Please sit down on this bench. I won't hurt you. I want to see if there's any infection in those cuts on your body." He removed the bandage from her leg, and pressed on the bone. She winced, but uttered no sound. "I think that bone is fractured. I'm going to make a support for your leg. Walk only with that stick you've been using. You need a crutch. I have one in my office. I'll get it to you as soon as possible."

While the doctor was administering to Mrs. Lindstrom, the sheriff drove out to the field, and talked to the farmer. "I'm the sheriff of this county. It looks like you've been using your wife for a punching bag. If this happens again I'm going to run you in. You're looking at jail time."

The farmer leaned on his shovel. His eyes narrowed to slits and his face turned beet red. The cords in his neck were swollen as he roared, "IS THAT SO!"

The sheriff raised his voice, "Yeah, that's the way it's GONNA BE!"

Each day Ralph drove slowly past the Lindstrom farm . Most of the time he saw the woman and dog in the front yard, and the farmer's truck in the dirt driveway, but never saw him. One week later, as he passed the farm the woman and dog were sitting by the irrigation ditch. She smiled, and waved to him. The old dog wagged his tail. He leaned his head out of the rolled down window. "Is everything all right with you, Mrs. Lindstrom? It's time for your water allotment, so I need to talk to your husband."

"Well, he isn't here."

"Are you expecting him to return soon?"

"No, I don't think so. He disappeared last week."

"Did he say where he was going?"

"No...I don't think he knew. Come into the yard. I want you to know about my husband's leaving."

The ditch-rider sat down upon the gunny sack at the edge of the irrigation ditch beside Mrs. Lindstrom and the old dog.

"Last week after the sheriff talked to my husband, he came from the field in a rage. He saw the brace on my leg, and started hitting it with a large stick. He whipped me pretty good. "He locked me in the root cellar. I was real scared. It was so dark and there was creepy things crawling around. He let me out long enough to cook for him."

Ralph could hardly believe what he was hearing.

"One morning when he let me out I tried to iron some clothes, and he came at me with a leather strap. He hit me, and I tried to move away. I had the flat iron in my hand, and I raised it and hit him on the side of his head. Blood came out, and he staggered out the door and fell by the lilac bush."

I tried to bandage his head, but the blood kept coming. After an hour I couldn't hear a heartbeat when I put my head on his chest... I decided he was dead."

After a few minutes of silence, Ralph asked, "What happened next?"

"I turned him onto a gunny sack and pulled him out here. I dug a hole deep enough to push him in and shoveled dirt to cover him."

Ralph had a sudden chilling thought that he was sitting on Elliott Lindstrom. Unable to speak he pointed downward, and the woman smiled and nodded her head. Ralph collected himself and stood.

"Mrs. Lindstrom, I think you did what had to be done. I see no reason for repeating this to anybody else."

"I won't forget you got help for me. You're the only person I could tell this to." The disabled black dog laid his head across the woman's legs as she stroked his gimpy foot and leg.

Ralph lit his pipe, and glanced back once as he left the farm. The breeze from the west rustled the leaves of the cottonwood tree where the woman and dog sat serenely upon the fresh, spaded earth. Buried underground was the pain and suffering of the past.

American Shakespeare
By Kevin Arnold

Last night we went to King Lear or Romeo and
Juliet or one of those martial tragedies named for
an obscure British monarch.

We were under the stars of the City of New York or
at Red Rocks or Ravenia near Chicago or at a bucolic park
in a smaller city where the Parks Commission bent

a few rules, the Arts Commission found some funds so the
actors could memorize those long soliloquies for almost
nothing, everyone dependent on volunteers

to keep the price down so we could fill the seats and blanket
the meadows where we laughed at the bawdy dialog and
shook our heads at the world's tragedies,

continually moved by the turns of phrase, while the
swoons we swooned when the lovers first kissed were
still held close in our hearts.

Brotherhood of the Midnight Snack
By Ellaraine Lockie

He makes it at midnight
An ensemble of garlic fried in olive oil leftover
rice and two eggs as top hats

An elaboration on the long-ago bread
fried in bacon grease
and dressed in Lawrey's Seasoning Salt
A rite he brought home from college into which
he initiated his little sister during summer breaks

When we'd eat in the breakfast nook
Lights out to watch fireflies spark the darkness
Curtains breathing in and out of the open windows after an
oven-baked day
Lilacs balming air that carried outdoor
conversations of mosquitoes and crickets

Inside, words sacred between siblings
What really went on at college
and in the fourth grade
Words that built the bridge that would
transport me out of farm life when most stayed

Now between bites of garlic fried rice
We talk of what really goes on in a marriage a
divorce, children, a job
Lights dim to see the bird bath outside the window
The water smooth, polished by the aged moon
An acorn plinks concrete and stills for the night

Purple lilacs shadow the surrounding peace and a
moth flutters a soft motor on the screen
Not a thing except thunder in the throat of distance to
warn us that this would be our last midnight rite

The Day Becca Found Courage in a Barbershop
By Judythe A. Guanera

It was tough being "Little Sis" to four big brothers. Mom was forever telling me they wanted to protect me because they doted on me. I didn't care why they did it; I hated being treated like a sissy.

"Boys are strong and brave," they kept telling me. "They have to be so they can protect scaredy-cat girls."

"I have just as much courage as you do," I would shout. At first I'd cry and run to my room, but after a while I'd stamp my foot in frustration—and then I'd run to my room, before they could see me cry.

The year I was seven my little brother, Danny, was born. I had desperately wanted a sister; I needed an ally so bad. But no luck. As he grew up, he began to mimic the older boys and loved to torment me about being weaker and less brave. I was sick to death of the teasing.

When I was little, my mom called me a tomboy, because I tried to keep up with my brothers. But, by the time I was 17, I began to believe what they'd been telling me. To be truthful, I was kind of scared of bugs and snakes and most slimy things. Still it was a shock the day I realized my sense of adventure, something I'd been so proud of, had totally disappeared. Maybe this happened because of my brothers' over-protectiveness or what they kept telling me, but I knew they were right. I was like the Lion in the Wizard of Oz. No heart, no courage.

"Becca, would you give me a ride to the barbershop?" Danny asked one day. "Mom says I have to go today and it's pouring outside. Please, Sis. Puhleeze."

With my newly-acquired driver's license in my purse, I was always looking for an opportunity to drive. So, I resisted the temptation to say, Danny you're a wuss. Are you afraid you'll melt if you get wet? Instead I said, "If you're ready to go in five minutes..."

He hurried to get his jacket.

As I parked in front of Beach Barbers, I could see the shop was full. "I'll go in with you, Danny. It's going to be a wait and it's too cold and wet out here." We found seats and passed the time listening to the other customers talking about the wall-to-wall antiques that Al, the owner, had collected. Mom was into antiques, but I liked shiny, modern stuff. I have to admit that Danny and I heard some good stories about all those old-fashioned things from men who seemed pretty close to being antiques themselves.

The door creaked open to admit an old couple, probably nearly as old as my parents. They stood inside the door, so still they might've been mannequins. Then the man reached over and patted the woman on the back. Two red spots appeared on her cheeks as she took a few steps toward Al, whose chair was closest to the door.

The woman cleared her throat a couple times before she spoke. "I want you to shave my head," she said in a shaky voice.

Whoa! I couldn't believe she said that. She must be crazy!

It got real quiet and I noticed a few other customers look up. Funny, because her voice was so soft. Maybe it was my imagination, but a feeling of suspense seemed to settle over the shop. You know, sort of like when you're watching TV and they play some scary music and you just know something weird is going to happen.

The two other barbers stopped cutting, their scissors and combs suspended above the heads of their customers. It was as though someone had pushed a pause button.

After what seemed like hours, the woman started to talk again. "You see, I have cancer." She reached up and tugged at her hair. A small clump of auburn curls filled her hand.

My heart stopped. I didn't know a lot about cancer, but I knew you could die if you had it. I didn't know it made your hair fall out, too.

"My doctor says I can be cured," she went on. "He's treating me with chemo and radiation. Nothing happened at first." She stopped and licked her lips. "But, then... my hair..."

By now I was holding my breath. I looked at Danny, who had slid forward in his chair. I don't think he even knew I was staring at him. I swear you could have heard the flutter of a butterfly's wings.

"I'm going to get well." The lady stopped and looked around the room. It was like she thought someone was going to challenge her. Maybe, all of a sudden she realized there was a shop full of people—all men, except me and her, just hanging on her words. Don't know if she even noticed me. But that didn't stop her. It was like once she got her courage up...

"I hate being sick." I wasn't sure what happened, but her voice suddenly got stronger. "Every morning when I wake up and see handfuls of hair on my pillow, it reminds me I'm sick. I thought if I got my head shaved, I could feel eccentric and bold rather than sick."

The man who had just sat down in Al's chair, jumped up and stepped to the side.

He moved his arms gracefully, like one of those bullfighters sweeping his cape. Al lowered his chair and motioned for the woman to sit. He wrapped her neck with tissue and then draped her with a cape. He looked real serious. When the other barbers finished with their clients, the men paid and then joined the others waiting their turn. It was like everyone wanted to share the moment with this lady...and she was a total stranger. Al began to clip her hair.

My scalp tingled as I imagined the little hair follicles hanging onto my head for dear life. (We had just studied about hair in biology class.) I swiped at the tears I couldn't hold back any longer.

The woman's partner stood close to the chair. I could tell he loved her— he looked at her like Dad looked at Mom the day Danny was born. But, I think he looked scared, too. I wondered if he had tried to talk her out of doing this.

If I had the guts to do what she was doing, I'd want to have it done before the shop opened—when nobody was around. And I'd go to a beauty salon, not a barbershop. Then it hit me. My grandma told me she used to get her hair done every Saturday so she'd look special for her date that night.

This woman knew she wouldn't look pretty when she was done. I decided if I was her, I'd go to a barbershop, too.

I didn't see any sign of a wig or a scarf or a hat. You can bet I would have had all three. I'd have been so afraid that people would stare at me and maybe laugh. I'd been so busy thinking about how humiliated I'd be if I were in her shoes, I had forgotten to watch her for a few moments. Just as I looked up, Al whisked off the cape.

The woman's chair had been turned away from the mirror. She stood up and I'm sure everybody could hear her take a deep breath. When she faced the mirror, she gave a little gasp. Then she patted the tops and sides of her bald head, and turned to face the other customers. I think I saw a tear glistening in her eye, but she was smiling. Everyone stood up and clapped, including Danny and me.

"Now, it's my turn," her husband said, as he climbed into the chair, and whisked off his baseball cap. Soon his thick, curly, gray hair lay with hers on the floor.

"Anyone else want to join ..." Al looked at the woman.

"Marjorie and Vick," she said.

"Anyone else want to join Marjorie and Vick?" he asked.

A man with a narrow fringe of hair walked toward Al's chair. "Don't have much to lose," he said, "but I want to support this brave lady. Boy, will my wife be sorry she sent me for a trim." People laughed, but they sounded nervous.

I could still feel the tingling in my scalp again and I think I heard a voice in my head whisper, "Don't even think about it." Yet something propelled me down the aisle toward Al. I heard someone gasp. I think it might have been Danny.

I reached the chair, just as Al finished the man with the fringe. They both looked at me kind of funny, but I climbed into the chair. My mind was made up.

When Al finished with me, everyone gave me a round of applause. It followed Marjorie and Vick as they left arm in arm. Marjorie gave me a thumbs up just before the door shut. I think I blushed.

I didn't dare look down at the floor for fear I'd cry. A couple of men patted my arm as I sort of dream-walked back to my chair. Danny stared at me, but I couldn't tell what he was thinking. Then he looked away.

Normal chatter took over, but it felt as though something had changed for me and maybe for everyone else in the shop. Danny got his usual crew cut, while I thumbed through a magazine. After a few minutes, I realized it was a weight lifting magazine. I hadn't even noticed.

As Danny and I walked out the door into the downpour, he touched my arm. "Sis, now that took courage. Maybe girls are tougher than I thought."

Best of Show: Poetry

Palimpsest
By Renae Keep
(after Vermeer's "Young Woman with a Water Pitcher")

Today, infrared scopes reveal the underpainting: how
the greenish sienna scroll on the wall, a map charting
the Netherlands' delta-flayed peninsulas, formerly
framed the lady's countenance
from wimpled head to draped shoulder like
a pensive cloud shadowing her reach.

Here, her southwesterly gaze met a Spanish chair,
twin lion finials roaring up at the Netherlands.
The Council of Troubles had made her grandfathers Inquisitors;
her Calvinist uncles, Sea Beggars;
her calm, gentleness, a surviving grace,
like the empatterned panes of an intact window.

Vermeer, son of an innkeeping art dealer, father of ten,
painting upstairs at his Catholic wife's mother's house,
erased the Spanish chair and shifted the map aside
so that the lady, hand tending the window frame,
looks serenely into an open space,
domestic jewels all insubstantiated by light.

The Call
By Kevin Arnold

Bradley was grading papers, the California sun shining on the small dining room table in his apartment, when Diana called from Dallas. Brad had married Diana almost three years ago, the second marriage for both of them, but they'd been living apart since winter. She sounded upset. "I'm sorry to bother you Brad. I waited until after breakfast."

"No problem, Di, I'm up. Life is good. Class isn't until one and I'm almost through my stack of essays. What's going on?"

"I'm afraid I'm calling with bad news. Dad had a heart attack. We were sitting around chatting at the club after dinner when he leaned over and grabbed his chest. He's in Intensive Care at Baylor Hospital."

Bradley straightened up in his chair. Of all the thoughts that ran through his mind, the one he was most ashamed of was that he hoped Diana wouldn't ask him to fly out there. He recovered and said, "He seemed so healthy. Vital."

Bradley asked about her kids, Beth and Robbie. He'd lived with them for two years before he and Diana separated, and missed them.

"They seemed more confused than anything. They're still sleeping."

"Oh, Diana, I'm sorry. Your dad will make it through, right?"

"Nothing's certain. Mom's a train wreck."

"It's hard to imagine her off her pins, she's such a rock."

The line was silent until Diana said, "Was it wrong for me to call you? We're trying to see how we can do apart, I know. But this is hard."

"No, I'm glad you called. What can we do for your Mom? Is she still upset I moved into teaching?"

There was another silence before Diana said, "Beth had shocked everyone at dinner by wearing a skimpy top. She has quite the cleavage now and, I mean, the spaghetti-strap blouse left nothing to the imagination."

"She wasn't showing any, you know, nipple, right?"

"Nothing like that, but a lot of flesh. Robbie kept sneaking peeks—I had to sit there watching him ogle his sister."

"He is a teenage boy."

"Don't go there, Brad. No one talks about nipples. Nobody I know of. Please. I had the nicest dream about you this morning. We were walking on the beach down in Carmel. And now you talk like that." She hesitated. "Do you guys talk about nipples?"

"No. No we guys don't, Diana. Well, not often anyway. It was a stupid thing to say. I'm still a little groggy." Bradley didn't like to think of the posh country club her father used to bring him to in Dallas, all those rednecks with law degrees. This small apartment he'd moved into in Sunnyvale, California, seemed right for him, the perfect distance from Palo Alto, the expensive town where he had lived with Diana.

"Should we ring off?" she asked quietly, tenderly.

"Are you going to be okay? What are they saying about your dad?"

"They won't say a word. No visitors, period. That can't be good."

No, Brad thought, it can't, but people come through heart attacks. "I'm so sorry, Diana. Call me if things change."

Bradley returned to his papers. Part of the draw of the job was that they let him create his own poetry curriculum at the local community college. He'd divided poetry into three time segments. He had them studying the period before 1850 first. In four weeks he'd move them into 1850-1950, the flowering that seemed to spring, in America, from Whitman and Dickinson. He would end the quarter with the myriad directions poetry has taken since 1950, which always made Brad think of the Louis XV's phrase aprè s moi le déluge.

He was grading their first papers of the quarter. He'd asked each of them for a short paper in which they printed out a pre-1850 poem and wrote a few words about it—"not a critique, but why it has meaning for you." Halfway through the stack now, he grabbed a new paper to see a poem from one of his favorite poets, William Blake, a poem Bradley hadn't looked at in years, "The Little Boy Found."

The little boy lost in the lonely fen,
Led by the wandering light,
Began to cry, but God, ever nigh,
Appeared like his father, in white.

He kissed the child, and by the hand led,
And to his mother brought,
Who in sorrow pale, through the lonely dale,
The little boy weeping sought.

If Bradley remembered right, a bearded young husband wrote the paper, which Brad enjoyed because his commnts were personal. The bearded guy saw himself as the 'God/father in white' of the poem, leading his son to his mother. The father had no idea why he chose the poem, nor why he saw himself in such a positive role. He finished his paper by saying "Even though I have no son—I have two daughters—to lead to his mother, the thought of being able to save a child like that keeps me coming back to the poem. I've memorized it."

Brad had to look up the word 'fen,' a bog, probably more familiar in Blake's day. Blake's biography said his life spanned seventy years, a long life two hundred years ago. The phrase "God, ever nigh," jumped out at Bradley, a notion more widely held then than now. After all that happened in his life recently—his neighbors divorcing after Brad had slept with the wife and Brad's marriage to, and now, separation from Diana—Brad was trying to work more in concert with God.

Bradley never felt comfortable around Diana's dad. An oil executive, her father had that Texas conservatism that made Brad so uncomfortable. He would take three syllables to pronounce Democrat's one-syllable names. He could stretch "Hillary" to five or six, and was doing so more now that she was the front- running Democratic presidential candidate.

About an hour later, as he was nearing the bottom of the paper stack, Bradley thought he heard a noise outside his apartment. He got up from the dining room table and peeked out a window by the front door. He had the fleeting thought it might be Cindy Montgomery. He opened the door, but no one was there. He walked around outside. No one, nothing. What had he heard?

More importantly, he thought, why am I thinking about Cindy Montgomery? She would be a handful, he thought. An intense, interesting woman, Cindy was one of his students, around 35, young for him but not absurdly so. She dressed more like a teenager, more like Beth, than her age. And the poem she'd handed in was "To His Coy Mistress" by Andrew Marvell, with its unambiguous couplet about coupling:

... The grave's a fine and private place,
But none, I think, do there embrace ...

Okay, Bradley my boy, he cautioned himself, supposing Cindy Montgomery had tracked him down to his nondescript apartment and appeared at his door? What then? The last woman who'd done that, the neighbor's wife, had ended up getting a divorce. Would he and Cindy share a pleasurable but fleeting coupling like that fateful night? Afterwards, what would they talk about? Could he tell her about his part in his neighbor's divorce? Absolutely not.

Would Cindy be interested in his ambivalence with Diana, or how he'd quit his technical job when the teaching gig opened up? No. Would she care that he'd chosen this apartment because it seemed unsuitable for hospitality, one that would lend itself to an intentionally monkish existence? That he'd specifically chosen a place from which he could ignore Diana and her horsey friends and teach poetry and even write a little? No, coupling or not, he'd probably find little to talk about with Cindy Montgomery.

Was he fantasizing? He looked back over her comments on Marvell's poem, which was well written except a sentence he circled: "This poem reaffirms my belief that life is meant to be lived, that one must, like that movie said, "seize the day." With that, Brad convinced himself he wasn't imagining that she had designs on him, but still scribbled "Awk—fix" in her margin.

"All I want is quiet, some quiet moments," Bradley said aloud to no one. Right then the phone rang.

It was Diana, crying. "He's dead, Brad. I know we're apart, but I need help with the kids and Mom. Can you come out? And I need you to hold me."

His mind rushed, thinking of that phrase of Blake's "God ever nigh." That certainly fit with Brad's experience as he questioned what he should do. The process of forming the question brought an immediate answer.

Diana interrupted his thoughts. "Please, Bradley."

He couldn't remember the last time she'd called him by his full name. As he did regularly, he imagined Diana's arms around him.

"Yes," he said softly. "I'll come out."

The Ass and the Hen
By Stanley Gedzelman

Every great story must illustrate a universal theme but have a unique twist.

Neither the ass nor the hen were aware that they lived on a very modest farm. The farmer used the ass for plowing, harvesting, pulling the carriage, and a variety of other hard labors. The hen had a much softer life. She was a prize winning egg layer. Her eggs were known far and wide for their size and quality. Every day she was sure to lay one of these eggs and the farmer always seemed to give her a smile and sometimes even poked her breast gently and lovingly.

The hen was not very nice. She was always provoking and taunting the ass. "It is difficult for me to live with someone so crude and crass as you," she constantly told the ass. "But you have the life you deserve and I have the life I deserve. While the master snubs you he is very loving to me. Just look at the difference between what he feeds you and what he feeds me. Your diet is full of thistles and thorns while I eat the finest corn."

This was partly true. The field was plagued by bull thistles and this vile weed comprised the bulk of the ass's diet. But the hen did not realize that she was fed inferior animal feed corn that the farmer grew around the perimeter of his field to discourage thieves.

The ass came to feel that the hen was right. "I do all the heavy work and he clearly dislikes me but he likes you even though you do nothing."

"Not so quick, Dense Head, I do the creative work around here. Can you lay eggs? You are just a brute so the master justly treats you as a brute. He can't stand your raucous braying - no one can - while he clearly likes my gentle cooing."

One day, the hen simply stopped laying eggs. It depressed her at first, but the farmer did not show any anger. In fact, he spoke gently to her, continued to poke her lovingly on the breast and to feed her as well as before.

Plowing time came and the ass knew he was in for arduous days. From dawn to dusk he strained at the plow tearing it through the clotted clay soil. Exhausted in the evening, when he was led back to his stall in the barn the farmer went to fetch his daily meal of thistles. There was a never ending supply of that harsh fare even though the dried thistle bulbs tasted like a delicacy after such hard days.

All this time, the farmer lavished ever more loving attention on the hen. She found that the corn had a new divine sweetness and that the farmer had increased the size of her portion. The ass smacked his thick lips at seeing and smelling the delicious corn and begged the hen for a taste. "You really don't need all of that. It would give me such pleasure to have just a few of the extra kernels."

But the hen, who had previously been something of a careless eater suddenly became an extremely fastidious eater, covetous of every kernel, and out of a combination of spite and jealousy, dropped not a single kernel, but gorged herself on more than she had ever eaten before to make doubly sure that the ass got nothing of her fare.

Through all the days of the plowing, the hen became absolutely intolerable to the tired ass, lording it over him ceaselessly. "Now the master has increased not only the size but the quality of my portion. It just shows how loved and honored I am for all my wonderful years of superlative egg laying. You were born a brute, you remain a brute and you will always be a brute, so your life will continue to be one of the travail that you deserve at the same time that I have grown even more beautiful and beloved than ever."

On the last day of the plowing, both ass and farmer returned to the barn exhausted and bathed in sweat but happy that the year's most difficult work was over. The farmer gently and lovingly poked the hen's breast as had become his habit but for the first time he went over and patted the ass, as if for a job well done. The hen was so astonished that she was speechless while the ass felt a pride he had never known before. "I am appreciated at last," he said to himself.

The farmer then went out to get the animals' feed. He quickly returned with the customary bale of thistles for the ass and the hen's large portion of sweet corn.

The farmer threw down the bale of thistles for the ass and then opened the bag of corn for the hen. Suddenly he chuckled to himself. "Oh me, aren't we all slaves to habit." Looking at the corn for a moment he poured it on top of the pile of thistles. "Well, well, as they say, waste not, want not."

Then the farmer lovingly picked up the hen and, with a unique twist, snapped her neck and carried her out of the barn for his family's feast.

The Notebook
By Elaine Mannon

Blank pages
Fall into the fullness
Of their emptiness

Repo Man
By Linda Brown

The phone rang as Frank was pouring Wendy's first cup of coffee. Frank gave Wendy a look of resignation, and Wendy jumped up to answer. This early in the morning before morning coffee, Wendy dispensed with business information and simply answered with a "hello".

"This is Jack Welles. Can I talk to Frank?"

"May I ask what this is regarding?"

"I'm in trial and I'm in trouble, now is Frank there?"

Wendy didn't like his manner, but recognized a job when she heard one. Frank had been a private investigator for a couple of decades, but things had been slow lately. Wendy had worked with him a number of years and hoped this call would get his detecting juices flowing again. She covered the mouth piece on the phone and hissed to Frank, "Jack Welles?"

"Yeah, I know him; he does a lot of defense work for different insurance companies."

"He says he's already in trial and needs help."

"Well, give me the phone so I can see what he wants."

Frank picked up a pen and pulled over a legal scratch pad to take notes. He took the phone and barely had time to identify himself, then spent several minutes scribbling down information from the attorney. After about ten minutes, Frank assured him that he and Wendy would get right on it. Then Frank asked him if there had been a neighborhood canvas, and Wendy could hear Welles shouting, "Yes! I've already done that, that's a waste of time! Just get me something on this guy and meet me at the courthouse at the noon recess!"

After he got off the phone, Frank threw the legal pad and pen on the floor.

"This guy is crazy! He's in trial, he's in trouble, and now he needs us to save his butt."

Wendy tsked, tsked, but was well aware that they had been painfully locked in the office for the last couple of days. Trying to get Frank to do paperwork was like having her fingernails pulled out with pliers. She knew repothat Frank would be happy to run after clues. So she diplomatically pointed out that they didn't have any urgent business and could always use a new case.

"What exactly is Welles hoping you can find?" Wendy gently nudged him.

As he poured the coffee again, Frank began to summarize the case.

"Welles basically has a case of 'he said, she said'. George Johnson, a Vietnam veteran, was suing "Antioch Slightly Used Cars" for repossessing his Porsche Carrera for the second time. Welles represents the insurance carrier for the dealership, Johnson was in default, but he claimed the repo man had pulled a gun on him during the repossession and had exacerbated his PTSD

(Post Traumatic Stress Disorder). He was suing for $2.5 million dollars. Welles is hoping we can find something on Johnson to discredit him with the jury."

Wendy harrumphed at this point. "That's gonna be kinda tough trying to dirty a Vet, don't cha think?"

Frank gave her one of his looks and said, "I think it's gonna be matter of showing who is closer to the truth of the matter. Of course the repo guy denied he had had a gun. And, yeah, I think it is gonna be tough to say anything against Johnson. Welles is right, the jury will be automatically sympathetic to the Vet, but we gotta try to find something. And, you know that's gonna be hard, cuz nobody likes repo guys."

"Of course, if Welles had done proper background on Johnson he possibly wouldn't be so desperate. Wendy, you get on-line, but don't spend too much time. In fact, maybe you should just go directly to the courthouse and see if Johnson has any criminal history or any other lawsuit activity. I'm gonna go canvas Johnson's neighborhood."

"Wait, I thought Welles specifically said not to do that."

"You know I'm not good about following directions. The Air Force would have never put me into cryptology if I didn't know how to think outside the box. I'm going to go door to door. When Welles wasn't shouting, he mentioned that the Repo Guy had taken his twenty something son with him; I don't think he had a gun, he wouldn't have taken a chance his kid would get hurt. I just have hunch, I'm going."

"O.K., O.K."

Wendy didn't especially like going to the courthouse to look up old records though conditions had improved. She used to have to literally go through the old records books, then used microfiche for records. At least now they had the last twenty years of civil and criminal records on the computer. She would have to enter Johnson's name in both data bases and if she found anything, she'd have to fill out a card, take it to the one lone clerk and wait for the clerk to try to pull the file. She thought she might have a couple of leads which only looked to be legal stuff regarding other debt collections and rental evictions, but sometimes one just had to slog through the details. But while she was still standing in line for her turn, Frank called Wendy about 11:00 a.m.

"Where are you?" Frank's voice was so excited; Wendy knew he had lucked out once again.

Wendy replied, "I'm in the courthouse; I have located a couple of minor things on Johnson."

"Go outside! You gotta hear this, you are never gonna believe it."

Neither spoke as Wendy hustled to get outdoors. "O.K., I'm outside and no one can overhear."

"That ineffective Welles! I went to Johnson's neighborhood and the third door I knocked on I hit pay dirt. Remember Aunt Bea on the Andy Griffith Show? Well, this woman who came to the door could be her twin sister. Anyway, she not only remembered the repossession from 18 months ago, she told me she saw the whole thing. And she had incredible detail. Plus, she lives directly across the street from Johnson.

"It turns out that Johnson's Carrera had a faulty loud muffler so whenever it started up it made a huge noise. She was on her porch to pick up her newspaper, when she heard the Porsche start up and saw a young kid in the driver's seat. Johnson pounded out of his house just as the car started to pull away from the curb. Johnson ran at full speed and dove head first into the open sun roof. 'Just like in the movies!' she kept saying. Anyway, they drove off down the street weaving back and forth with Johnson's legs sticking out of the sun roof. She said she could see Johnson pummeling the panicked young driver the whole time as the Porsche nearly collided with the parked cars on both sides of the narrow street.

"She yelled at her daughter to come quick to see this fiasco. When he turned around saw a second car, an older Cadillac, speed past her house being driven by an older man. The Cadillac pulled up next to the Carrera at the corner. She said she could even see inside the Cadillac. There appeared to be a heated exchange between the Cadillac driver and Johnson. She could see that the Cadillac driver was extending his right arm towards Johnson.

"Man, Wendy, I really got worried, maybe he did have a gun! But she said it was white and it fluttered when he waved it at Johnson. By this time, her daughter was outside too, and at the stop sign, they saw Johnson exit the Carrera and shuffle dejectedly back to his house. The kid in the Carrera roared off and the man in the Cadillac followed him."

Wendy was stunned, "So, no gun!"

Frank repeated, "Yeah, no gun, just paperwork!"

"Geez, Frank, you did it again. Welles is gonna be so happy."

"Yeah, you go meet him and tell him I'm going to Welles' office to get trial subpoenas issued. They said that they would testify."

Wendy dutifully drove off to the courthouse. And, when she strode into the courtroom, Welles saw her and called for a ten minute recess to confer with his colleague. The judge paused for a minute considering, but then announced it was so close to lunch they might as well break for lunch.

Welles was ecstatic with short report from Wendy, even though he reiterated that he had told Frank not to re-canvas the neighborhood. Wendy just gave him a knowing look and a slight smile.

Welles requested a side bar and revealed the new evidence. Johnson's attorney tried to say it was too late for new discovery, but the Judge ruled to allow the eye witness testimony.

Welles called "Aunt Bea" to the stand after lunch and everyone could see from the looks on the jurors' faces that they were impressed with "Aunt Bea's testimony. It took the jury only about 30 minutes to return a Defense Verdict in favor of "Antioch Slightly Used Cars" and the Repo Man and his son making Johnson's case over in a matter of minutes.

Wendy knew that Frank would endlessly repeat his success story for the next several days, but it would be better than doing office work. And Frank's bill would be paid with a smile from all except of course the plaintiff and his attorney.

The Buzz
By Evie Groch

The bee's chaotic flight brings it
to random landings.
How can it be called a beeline?
Pollen searches are arduous endeavors
rewarded by abundance
when petals unfold their secret stash.
The next buzz may bring us wondrous
nectar – near perfection.

In Hollywood the latest buzz is
attracted to imperfection.
Wagging, salivating tongues contort to
resemble the telling of truth
of which there is very little.
Gossip sheet scoopers with oversized ears
lean in to capture the perfect sleaze
in the buzz of the moment and
splat it on the front page of
their scandal sheets,
a blotchy stain for hungry eyes.

Carpentry mavens eye their joints
and miter them to create perfect seams with
their buzz saws --
evoke contented hums from clients. As
the buzz goes, so does the cut.

Pot smokers laze between their own joints
and stashes of hash.
Their next buzz brings them
closer to that hoped-for perfection –
the perfect state.
No buzz cuts for them.

I sit in my hairdresser's chair, anticipate
the final crowning touch, the sculpting,
before he sets
me free with perfect locks to
dazzle the world outside
his door. I prepare for it when I
hear Brian say: Perfection is just a
buzz away.

Closure
By Bernadine Fornesi

Out on the front porch
Granny falls
Over the railing
To the cement killer below

Neighbors shake their heads
And start to moan
Lordy, Lordy
Looks like ole Granny is dead

Over the still form a blanket is laid
Their ringside seats are gone
They wait for the worthless one
As the grits lay scorched on the stove

All blame is laid upon the hussy
Trudging home from work on the streets
Her hair is wild and her lipstick smeared
When she opens the wooden gate.

Oh Granny, Oh Granny I got no one that cares
Only the needle comforts me
Afraid of Granny's ghost she sleeps beneath the bridge
And soon forgets her former home

Propped against the garbage cans
In the alley where the rats run free
Her service of John's is brief
As she holds out her hand for pay

They fling her aside and hitch up their pants
And slink from the dark
To the lights of the street
No cover for the silent body by the garbage can

But a blazing light rips through her core
As she hears a wail from on high
Through a moving breeze a faint cry
Come Home, Come Home ungrateful one

Premonition
By Amy Kelm

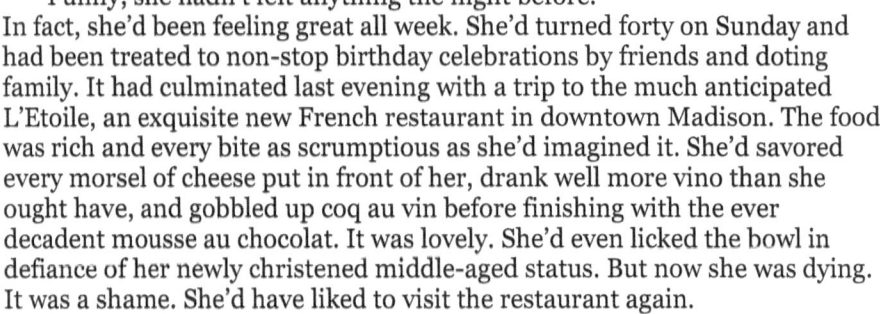

Mona Weekly knew she was dying the moment she opened her eyes. The pain that shot through her abdomen was sharp and specific. She grimaced in pain and tried to sit up. "Ouch!" she cried quietly, and doubled over pressing both hands into her stomach to ease the pain. This was it; the end.

Funny, she hadn't felt anything the night before. In fact, she'd been feeling great all week. She'd turned forty on Sunday and had been treated to non-stop birthday celebrations by friends and doting family. It had culminated last evening with a trip to the much anticipated L'Etoile, an exquisite new French restaurant in downtown Madison. The food was rich and every bite as scrumptious as she'd imagined it. She'd savored every morsel of cheese put in front of her, drank well more vino than she ought have, and gobbled up coq au vin before finishing with the ever decadent mousse au chocolat. It was lovely. She'd even licked the bowl in defiance of her newly christened middle-aged status. But now she was dying. It was a shame. She'd have liked to visit the restaurant again.

"Shit," she said to no one but herself. "Today of all days." It really was inconvenient. It was only Wednesday and there was still so much of the week ahead of her. She had to get the kids to school, run some errands she'd been neglecting over the past few days, and then tend to the never-ending series of her kid's activities. Both Susan and Cole had soccer and band practice that afternoon and she was on deck for the carpool. Why she'd ever agreed to this schedule in the beginning of the year was beyond her. But it was what it was – no sense in complaining now. How would she ever fit anything else in today, let alone dying? Plus, the forecast called for beautiful weather. And, no one should die on a sunny day.

She limped slowly into the kitchen and was relieved to find the searing pain that had just moments ago ripped through her pleasantly subsiding. What a relief. She needed the time to make lunches and get the kids out the door. She could die after she made peanut butter and honey for Susan, and grilled cheese for Cole. Then of course she'd need to put the dishes in the dishwasher and wipe down the counters. She wouldn't want to leave her house a mess. What would the neighbors think? People would certainly stop by to offer their condolences. Maybe even bring casseroles? She hoped there was room in the freezer. Of course, her dear husband Geoffrey would be too grief stricken to clean; so she might as well get it done herself. And maybe vacuum too. She wouldn't want people's last impression of her to be that she was a slob. Mona sighed. Dying was going to take more effort than she wanted to expend today. Too bad this couldn't have happened on Friday -- after the cleaners had come.

"Oh...," Mona gasped and doubled over. There it was again—the pain in her abdomen that was surely killing her. Cancer? She clutched the counter tops and momentarily held her breath. This time the pain was relentless. Her entire body stiffened and she held her breath for the roughly eight seconds it took to pass. Ouch. This pain lasted much longer than the one she'd had earlier that morning. It surely signaled the end.

"Are you ok, mom?" asked Cole, looking up from his toasted waffles.

Her ten-year-old was such a sweet and sensitive boy. He was always expressing concern while the rest of the family seemed indifferent to matters of health. "I'm Ok, honey. Don't worry about me. Just eat your breakfast," Mona reassured him. "I'm sure this is nothing. And chew those waffle pieces carefully. I may have cut them a little too big."

"Morning, honey," said Geoffrey, walking briskly into the kitchen. "What do you have going on today?" He paused briefly to kiss her on the cheek and then continued past on his way to grab coffee.

"Mom's sick" said Cole, drizzling circles of syrup onto his plate.

"Oh, it's nothing," Mona quickly responded, cutting him off.

"It didn't look like nothing. You were all hunched over," continued Cole.

"Don't talk with your mouth full, sweetheart. And wipe up that syrup from the table. You're dripping all over."

"Honey?" quizzed Geoffrey grabbing a bagel from the toaster. He sat down and began reading the paper. "I can't believe the Brewers lost again last night! I was sorry we missed the game but it looks like we didn't miss much after all."

"Oh, I'm sure I'll be fine," said Mona, referring back to their previous conversation. "It was just a crazy strange pain that stabbed me in the stomach. I couldn't really breathe for a few minutes. But it passed."

"Um-huh...," mumbled Geoffrey, continuing to scan the sports section. "With that loss they're now under 500! Can you believe it? Good thing the rest of the division stinks. They may still have a chance to pull something out before the All-Star Break..." And then he added, "I'm sorry, honey... you said your stomach was hurting? Do you think you should go see someone?"

"Oh, I don't know," replied Mona, finding comfort in her husband's remarks. It was validation that he would in fact miss her when she was gone. "I suppose I should. I have lots of errands to run though. You know how it is. Today after I get the kids off to school, I was supposed to get the dry cleaning, take those boxes to the post office, and I really should clean out the freezer."

"The freezer?" questioned Geoffrey without looking up.

"Oh, you know how overcrowded it can get. And you never know when you're going to need the space..." her voice trailed off. It was too much to think about. Plus, her family hated casseroles. What would they eat after she was gone and there was no one there to cook for them?

Geoffrey got up from the table. "Well, you call me if you need me." He bent slightly to kiss her on the forehead and grabbed his briefcase. "See you tonight," he said, waving over his shoulder.

"Yes," she called after him. "See you... um... tonight. And honey, drive carefully."

Mona finished shooing her kids off to school and then phoned her doctor. She knew calling for same-day appointments was frowned upon, but she hoped they would make an exception for a dying woman.

"Yes," she replied, "I'd be happy to hold." Mona sat at her desk and waited patiently to the sounds of elevator music. She opened her computer and pulled up the exercise schedule at the gym. It had been four days since her last workout. She really should try to get one in today–especially after last night's dinner. It might even take her mind off the impending doom; if anything could take your mind off something like that. Would the tumor growing in her stomach make exercise difficult? Thankfully she hadn't felt anything in the past twenty minutes or so. Maybe it wasn't cancer. If she chose a short class – or maybe one that wasn't quite as hard as her usual - she might be able to manage it. Water aerobics could be an option...

"Yes, thank you," Mona repeated when the receptionist finally answered the call. "I really need to see someone today. I'm having terrible pains in my abdomen." She listened and then began answering the questions posed her. "Yes. Mona Weekly. 5-30-73. My doctor? Dr.Gates. What time... 9:30am or 11:00am you say? Let's see... I'll take the 11:00am. Yes. See you then. Thank you."

11:00am was perfect. It gave her just enough time to get to the gym, shower and then drive to the doctor. "Owww..." she grimaced. There it was again. Death. It was back with a vengeance. Momentarily unable to move, she braced both hands against the side walls in the hallway and closed her eyes. When the pain dissipated, roughly five seconds later, Mona hurried back to her room and began changing. "Shit," she spat again. She would need to shave before putting her swim suit on.

Exhausted, and sporting wet hair, Mona rushed into the doctors' office at 11:02am. She had been in such a hurry that she even skipped grabbing a cup of free coffee at the gym. She hated to miss that brilliant jolt of caffeine. Normally, by this time of day, she would have downed three cups of the liquid gold. But today she hadn't even had the one. Dying will do that, though. It messes everything up.

Mona waited patiently until her name was called, and then walked into the exam room. Doing as she was told, she changed into the paper smock and crawled up on the table. Why was this happening? Why now? She was too young to die, wasn't she? It wasn't fair. How would she ever leave her beautiful children? They were still so small. They needed her. How would they ever get along without her? Geoffrey's temper was short and she knew he'd be a mess. Would he remarry? He should, the poor man. She must remember to tell him that he should remarry. Besides, the kids would benefit from having a woman in the house. But Geoffrey must be picky. Not just any woman should be allowed to care for her kids; and certainly not that divorcee from school, Lee-Anne. She'd have to remember to warn Geoffrey about Lee-Anne. That woman was trouble of the worst kind. She'd heard that Lee-Anne regularly sent her kids to school without a water bottle. And she never volunteered without being asked twice. Maybe Geoffrey could find someone from church; someone who would know how to French-braid Susan's hair. Yes, that was important. Her beautiful little girl... maybe she should take Susan to get her hair cut after school. A chin length bob would be cute. Susan could even manage that style herself.

The doctor's knock startled her. "Hello, Mrs. Weekly. How are you?" said Dr. Gates entering the room.

Mona tried to be brave but she heard her voice quiver. "Oh, you know... I'm not that great, actually."

"I see from the chart that you're having some pain in your abdomen. Please lie down."

54

Mona obeyed, and stared up at the ceiling tiles. Fear swirled around her head and coursed through her veins, grabbing every cell in her body. Tears began forming in the corners of her eyes. She didn't want to die.

Dr. Gates quietly pushed and prodded her from multiple angles before asking her to sit back up. "Mrs. Weekly, when was your last BM?"

"Oh," said Mona, startled and embarrassed by the unexpected question. "Um....maybe Monday... it could have been Sunday... or Saturday... but I think it was Monday."

"I see. Yes. I think that's it, Mrs. Weekly. You're constipated. I can feel that you're backed up in there," he said with a slight smile. "The pains you're feeling are likely gas pains. Have you had anything especially rich to eat in the past few days?"

"Um... well, now that you mention it..."

"Let's try a laxative, Mrs. Weekly, and lots of water." Dr. Gates stood and handed her a prescription. "Try this one. It's very gentile. And, if you're still having pain in 48 hours, give me a call back."

Mona sat dumbfounded as Dr. Gates closed the door behind him. Of course that was it. Why hadn't she put two and two together? She exhaled loudly. Her shoulders fell back to their regular position and Mona sat straighter than she had all day. She swung her legs over the side of the table and jumped to the floor. She dressed quickly and paused to admire her now dry hair in the mirror. She looked pretty good for forty!

Keys in hand, Mona whistled as she bounced towards her car. Life was good. No, life was great. What should she make for dinner? Fettuccini Alfredo? Or maybe she should try that new stroganoff dish she'd cut out of the magazine. Geoffrey would love...

"Owwww!" Mona Weekly stopped abruptly in the middle of the parking lot and grabbed her head. The dull pain she'd been feeling all morning behind her eyes had finally materialized into a full blown headache. She'd been too preoccupied with dying to pay it much attention, but now it was throbbing wildly across the very front of her head and impossible to escape.

She closed her eyes and rubbed her temples. "Oh, no! An aneurism."

An American Haibun
By Ellaraine Lockie

Mini-flocks of eight or ten wild parrots often emblazon the trees in my yard. A stopover en route to or from the Home Depot parking lot. As though picking up supplies for ongoing nest repair.

Green red and yellow packages
slur the airwaves Jingle of chatter

Today bells ring the sky from blocks away. The entire flock arrives as I close the front door behind me for my walk. The surreal surprise of sixty-some parrots. Bodies built for South America that have branched the skies of Northern California for thirty years. Their evolution from a few slave-traded rebels and rejects. And their sheer spirit for survival stops me mid-step.

Ornaments on palm filbert
cherry blackberry Breeze
of wings folding

I refuse to relinquish either the exercise or the parrots. So I walk fast circles around the driveway. Tree-to-tree talk, as affable as small town gossip over clotheslines. Drowning echoes of the morning's Mercury crime-corruption jobless-foreclosure-war News . . . and the crinkle of worry by fingers on fabric over a breast lump.

Beaks fill with nectar from
eucalyptus blossoms Bright pink
petals fall

Dizzy now, I switch to a house-wide back and forth stride. Envision that every Silicon Valley soul in torment could line up right here. Like the way back-to-belly cars parade slowly around this cul-de-sac to see Christmas lights.

Sprinkler shower play Parrots
groom one another The sun sends
glitter

Every feather a rainbow. Every squawk an upbeat, an hallelujah. An invitation to plan the next thirty years. Even the native crows acquiesce their territory to this gift. But it is I who am repaired.

Open Road
By Doug Baird

For a change of scenery I decided to take a different road back to my ranch. I was enjoying the windy clouds rolling across the big blue sky, typical for this part of New Mexico. My old Ford pickup wasn't moving fast and I was tired of all the big rigs honking and pushing me aside as they roared past in both directions.

Making a quick decision, I turned off the main highway at a remote spot that looked familiar. It turned out to be the old strip of road now invaded by weeds and stray tumbleweed, and seldom traveled since the new highway had replaced it. I steered passed the occasional potholes while enjoying the distant mountains, the warm desert breeze, and the sea of crickets all around me.

I felt almost hypnotized by the scenery. As my attention drifted out the window to savor the wide-open terrain, my old truck stumbled over something big in the middle of the road. The sound jolted me awake and I jammed on the brake. As the truck came to a stop, I pulled back on the hand brake and pushed open the creaky door, not eager to see what I had just run over.

Behind me was a craggy rock that no doubt had gotten the best of my pickup. Looking underneath, I saw oil dripping and the exhaust pipe bent out of shape. Back inside my truck, I noticed the gearshift was loose and realized the boulder had probably broken the gearbox and made a mess of the back axle.

A long look around made me realize I was miles from the main highway. I couldn't even hear the noisy big rigs. Shuffling through the glove compartment for my cell phone, I discovered I had not recharged its battery. I had very little water and a long walk back home. My side excursion down this old road suddenly made me feel stranded in my own backyard.

As I walked to the other side of my truck to check the damage, a distant object caught my eye. I couldn't make it out, but it looked like someone walking far down the road. The heat from the hot pavement made this person look wavy in the light.I moved to the front of the truck and squinted. Yes, someone was coming toward me, a couple hundred yards away.

Why would anyone be walking in this heat? Maybe someone as crazy as me!

At that moment I noticed I could no longer hear any sounds around me. No crickets. No running lizards. No hawks. No distant prop planes. Why this sudden silence? What was happening? The strangeness of the moment reminded me of my fears when I lived in the city.

I continued to stare at the body coming toward me. Soon I noticed another person farther down the road. Were they coming to help me? Was the heat affecting my eyes? My mind? Maybe I needed some water.

For some reason I turned to look in the opposite direction. What I saw rattled me — three or four more people were walking toward me. Surely I was suffering from heat prostration, I thought, and took another gulp from my water bottle. I felt like I was in a zombie movie. All these figures were headed in my direction. Had I received a bump on the head when my truck hit the rock that caused me to imagine all of this?

I grabbed my tote bag and water, abandoning my truck to whatever fate it was headed for. I ran, not walked, across the hot desert sand to get some distance from the road. When I turned around they were still walking. Some of the figures looked translucent. It was eerie. I stood still and waited for them to reach my vehicle. I even got down in the brush to hide, as if that would save my sorry ass.

From both directions they continued to walk at a normal human pace. Near where my truck was stranded, they converged. I expected something to happen, but they just passed each other and continued walking. No sound. No words. No reaction to the others around them.

I was afraid I might pass out from the heat if I continued to watch this parade of mysterious people, and decided to brave a slow walk back to my truck. The only sound came from my boots as they crunched dead weeds.

Getting a better look as I approached the road, I came to a quick stop — a shiver ran down my spine. These walking figures were definitely translucent, almost a mirage. They appeared to be humans, women and men. All wore thin, white garments that fluttered in the breeze. I felt like I was in a dream.

I stood without moving and hoped they would not see me. They seemed not to notice my truck or anything else. It was as if each one was on a private journey, deterred by nothing. I took a deep breath to check if I was still alive.

I watched these ghost-like beings move gracefully past me. There were many more now coming from both directions, all in a row, walking only on the old highway and no other part of the desert. They walked straight ahead with arms down at their sides. Some limped, some walked faster than others, with no sound.

I was shocked that I could see clear through them.

My curiosity suppressed my fear and I decided to move closer. I felt in another world watching the long line of glowing bodies. I could see their faces now, a diversity of age and nationalities. Some wore hats. Some were barefoot. Some had long hair, some short. All looked focused on wherever they were going.

Impulsively I reached out to touch one of them. My hand crossed their path, but it felt like I was touching air. They walked right through me, staring straight ahead. I quickly pulled back, stunned by what I had just done.

I held my hand as I continued to watch this procession of faces. I saw a sense of rest and peace in their hollow eyes, with no urgency or stress. They seemed to be traveling a path that was both planned and yet a routine occurrence. Perhaps it was a passageway. Maybe they were in transition. But I didn't understand why they would be going in opposite directions.

Suddenly one of the figures glanced over at me. For only a second, his eyes looked directly at mine. I was jolted back off the road, and I kept my eyes on the man as he continued walking. I grabbed my chest, my heart pounding. My mind raced with questions. Why was I here at this moment?

Was I meant to see them? Was I supposed to do something? And where were they going?

I lost all sense of time. As the long lines of people began to disappear into the horizons, I stumbled back to my truck. When I put my hand on the fender, I was startled to feel cold metal. I climbed into the truck and noticed that the leather seats felt surprisingly cool. When I moved around, my arm bumped the gearshift and it felt steady. I moved it again and it seemed in gear. I got out to look under the truck. I could no longer see the oil that had been on the pavement earlier. What had happened?

I started the engine, put it into first gear, rolled forward, and tested the steering. My old pickup had life again! I couldn't believe it. As I drove, the sounds around me began to slowly reappear. Still baking from the sun, I felt overwhelmed and exhausted, yet strangely calm.

They knew I was here, sharing this old road with them. Our paths had crossed, but I was not on their journey. I remained in this world, not part of theirs.

Boom and Bust
By Stanley Gedzelman

This is a story of how economics
Gets us in a fix.
The first generation built a pyramid
They loved what they did.
The second noted with alarm and regret
It was wracked with debt.
The third gazed up and asked with stupefied fear
How did this get here?
Some later generation will try again
To start the refrain
Of cycles that oscillate from boom to bust
From ashes to dust
So forget the debt –
Whenever we create
Debts evaporate.

One Slightly Weird Sister
By Robert J. (Jamie) Miller

I was settling down to a quiet night of reading my new Susan Dee mystery when it started. Her work is kind of spooky anyhow, so when I heard humming and drumming, I first supposed I was imagining things. No way, I realized. It must be those dang kids in the house behind mine, playing some of their weird music. I tried to ignore them, but I couldn't, so I stepped to the back door to tell them to cool it. But it wasn't those kids. What the hell was this? There was a fire burning right in the middle of my back lawn!

"Hey! You kids! What do you think you're doing? Put out that fire NOW and get out of here!"

The humming and drumming went on, and as I looked closer, I saw three figures dressed in black, and in the middle of them was the fire. Hanging over it on a tripod of sticks was a kettle. I recognized that arrangements of sticks: we used something like it in Boy Scouts to cook a stew. But in the middle of my lawn? NO WAY!

"You guys! Get out of here! That's my lawn you're burning up! What do you think you're doing, anyhow?"

"Shhh!" a voice said. "We're trying to say the sooth!"

"YOU'RE WHAT?"

"Soft! We're trying to say the sooth," the voice came back. It was gentle, feminine, seductive.

"OK, I'll be quiet," I whispered back, "but who are you and what are you doing in my back yard?"

"We are soothsayers." The voice was soft and tempting. "Let us say the sooth of the night, and we shall be gone, as quickly as we came. And..." her voice softened still more and I could feel it caressing my ears and my soul. "You won't regret it."

"I regret it already, but OK, do your thing, whatever it is. Just don't make a lot of noise or disturbance. We have a neighborhood association here controlled by a bunch of old grouches and complainers, and they'll be on my case if they catch you."

I heard them whispering among themselves. "Forsooth, they will trouble you no further. We shall disappear them, and then be about our magick."

"Can you really do that? Disappear them, I mean?" This could turn out really well, after all. "Would they stay disappeared?"

"We can, with succor from you, and they would. Can you furnish us a firkin of water from your well? We were unable to find it. The well, I mean." There was more whispering, and she said "Correction. We need not a firkin. A gill would be generous to our needs."

"I can do that. Now, how much is a gill?"

"Lead me to your well, and we shall drink deeply and sweetly." She stepped up under the porch light. She was beautiful! A babe! I'd drink a gill with her any time!

"Uhhhhh, OK. But, uhh, I don't have a well. Not here at least. But if you follow me, I will lead you to my... well... well, and there we may drink deeply. And you may have a gill for your friends. By the way, who are your friends? If I may ask?"

"Sisters. We are sisters, Eolinh, over there, Escrith, there, and I'm Oedrich. And you're?"

"Ed. Short for Oedward, I suppose. Oedward Oeastman. OK, let's get your gill of water."

I filled a pan from the kitchen faucet, and asked "So, would you like anything else?"

She returned to the shadows of the back yard which, somehow, stayed dark despite the fire burning in the middle of my two thousand dollar lawn. No matter. For a babe like her, I'd gladly sacrifice my lawn! She was back in a moment. "Our seeking for the sooth would be greatly aided if you were to come up with a few ingredients which seemeth to be in short supply around here."

"Well, yeah, this is Bakersfield, CA, and lots of things are in short supply here. Let's see the list." I looked it over. Things on the list reminded me of the spell cast by the three weird sisters in Shakespeare's MacBeth:

'Double, double, toil and trouble, fire burn and cauldron bubble...
Fillet of a fenny snake, in the caldron boil and bake;
Eye of newt, and toe of frog, wool of bat, and tongue of dog,
Adder's fork, and blind-worm's sting, lizard's leg, and owlet's wing...'

When Miss Martini made me learn this in ninth grade, I had never imagined that I would use it someday. The idea was gross enough to appeal to 14-year-old boys, but seriously, how often did she think this would happen?

"I don't think I can help you," I told her, looking over the list again. "I mean, you want a 'goat's beard'? And 'wool of bat'? And 'adder's fork'? If I didn't get butted by the goat or bitten by the adder, or get rabies from the bat, I'd likely be in trouble with the SPCA or People for the Ethical Treatment of Animals. Sorry, Oedrich, I don't think I can help you."

She laughed, a merry little laugh that seemed out of place with the black robe and hood. "Oh, Oedward, didn't they teach you anything in school? We don't use animal parts in our spells. Our spells are vegan!" She laughed again. "Competely vegan!"

"Then what...? Oh. You mean there are plants called by all the names in that spell?"

"Forsooth! Then you will help us find them?"

"Yea, forsooth. But how will I know them, even if we can find them in the dark? I mean, I don't even know where to start looking. And do they grow here? After all, Bakersfield is hardly the Scottish highlands."

"Hast thou not a book of plants useful in magick?"

"No, and I doubt that there is such a book this side of maybe the University of California. We could start with Google. People say you can find anything on the net."

"Then shew me now this net that holds everything!" I led her to my computer and brought up Google. "This is a net?" quoth Oedrich. "Seriously?"

"Yea, verily! Just watch. Let's start with 'adder's fork' and see what we find." It didn't take long to find that 'adder's fork' refers to a fern,

Ohioglossum vulgatum. "See, that was easy. I know where ferns grow, near here. We could go looking. But does it have to be that exact species? Maybe they don't grow here?"

"We can only search and hope. Now shew me the other ingredients." We recognized several of them. For the really weird ones we decided to look on the shelves of the local health food store. And then we were away to search for that Ohioglossum.

We drove to the edge of town and out to where the road crossed a sluggish little stream that rollicked more boisterously during winter, then parked alongside the road. Oedrich stretched out in the seat. "Nice wheels," she said. "Homely. Verily, a room fit for a palace."

"Thanks. Ummm, I've been wanting to ask you something. Do you come here often?"

"Where? The Baker's Fields? No, this is our first time. It's OK, but I really prefer the highlands."

"Yeah, I'm sure I would, too. And, uhmm... are you three guys like the 'weird sisters' that Shakespeare wrote about in MacBeth?"

"Oh, that story by Shak? Forsooth, it doth bedevil us whith ersoever we go. Aye, that was us."

"But people play it like the 'weird sisters' were old hags."

"Well, that was a long time ago, and we were much younger then. I'm cold. Woulds't thou not throw thy doublet over me for the nonce?"

I did, and we cuddled together for a nonce or two, but soon enough I said "Hey, shouldn't we go look for our ferns? We found some growing at the edge of the stream. The stream was hidden from the road and from passers-by by a grove of willow, and within that willow grove we disported ourselves for a goodly time. "Oh God, Oedward, that was good!" she said as we finished disporting ourselves. She lay back and purred contentedly.

"It was good! Stay with me. I would disport myself with you every evening, if thou wilt."

"I cannot, for I must away before the dawn, along with my sisters... OhMyGaahd, I forgot all about my sisters! They await our return with the adder's fork and the rest of the ingredients! Let us haste!"

We grabbed a handful of the first ferns that our flashlight revealed, then bolted for home. We parked in my driveway and kissed fervently, as my hand strayed hungrily over her tabard and kirtle... Or whatever those clothes were called... And then she dashed off to rejoin the other weird sisters. Then I sat on my back porch, listening as they chanted softly. Now and then, they did something to the fire and sent a cascade of sparks toward heaven, and finally the chanting stopped and the embers of the fire burned themselves out on the ruins of my lawn.

Oedrich came shyly to my porch. "Oedward, I promised you would not regret it if you helped us. I have seen the sooth, but I know not what it means."

"That's OK. I guess oracles never gave straight answers. Tell me."

"It said 'Sell STLD. It's going no place. Ditto HMC, HDM, and PWX. Put it all on TSLA, at market. But hasten! Within the week TSLA will begin a big move up. Buy and hold. It will top 200 ere long.' Do you understand these mysterious words?" Without waiting for an answer, she turned and ran back to rejoin her two sisters.

"Are you sure about this?" I called to the darkness. Then, "Yes, I do understand. I believe you. Hurry back to me, Oedrich! Please. Hurry back."

The pale light of dawn was outlining the mountains around Tehachapi pass, and my lawn was silent. "Hurry back," I said again.

And then, softly, almost to myself, "I love you."

To Rhyme or Not to Rhyme
By Ida Lewenstein

Doesn't anyone write poems in rhyme anymore?
Has rhyme gone the way of the dinosaur?
Where are the likes of Dickenson and Poe?
Where are they now....does anyone know?

There's a new generation of poets
Given to free verse
To them rhyme is restricting
Almost a curse.

Rhyming, they say, is simply 'passe'.
No longer the status quo
Try telling THAT to the devotees
Of Edgar Allen Poe!

Or ask a child jumping rope
How do you keep the time?
It's no brainer says the child
It's the rhyme....always the rhyme.

As for me,...
I'm going to keep on rhyming
That is how I am
Just think.......
If no one ever rhymed
There'd be no Mary
Or her little Lamb.

Link N' Milton
Greg Erion

"Might be about time to wonder down to the Saragossa, Link."

Link, shifting slightly in his chair, and squinting toward the sun spat bout' half a plug of Redman chaw at the scorpion. Stopped his wiggle up the steps.

"That's a far piece – been to the Saragossa afore, Milton?"

"Yup in '68. Was when that SOB Buchanan died."

"Buchanan who?"

"Ya know, Ol' Buck, afore Lincoln came in."

"Ah, you mean President Buchanan."

"One and only."

Another shot of Redman put the anthropod out of his misery.

"Milton, didn't figure you was one ta follow those politicians."

"Well, I twern't but that miserable so-and-so just riled me up."

"Hows that?"

"He pushed that Dred Scott decision."

"He what?"

"Ya never heard of it?"

"Can't says I had."

"Damn fool backed sayin slaves weren't citizens."

"So hows that to you?"

"Link, sometimes yousa damn fool. My mammy and pappy were slaves. What do ya think. I just get up in the morning and rub coal dust all over me? Sometimes I think ya fell off your horse oncet too often."

"Oh."

"Judas Priest. .. Anyway twas fixin to go down to the Saragossa. Spite your spurs bein' a bit dull could use the company."

"Dred Scott?"

@@$^^^%

"OK, I'll go. So whats in Saragossa?"

"My other ranch. Brother ran it but just found out he was killed. Gotta mosey down and sort things out.

"Sorry Milton."

"Mmm hmm. Maybe settle a score that needs settlin.' Say bout' time for supper. Cookie's set up some armadillo fricassee, glazed with a light cream tarragon sauce. Interested?"

"Iffn better N' his powder burn biscuits N' jerky count me in."

"Reckon we're about three days from the Saragossa, Link."

"Say, what's that up ahead. Looks like fellow travelers. "

Hmmm.

"Howdy. Well sayyy what do we have here – A $&*%^# N****. Now raise your hands slowly. Maybe a little neck-tie party? Heh, heh"

Milton raised his hands, his hips sliding to the right, his horse the same.

Milton's shirt tugs at him, as he watches the look of surprise on the sallow face going blank before toppling off the horse. Another shot, crossed eyes, slumping forward as a now useless left hand cannot prevent falling face forward onto the cactus bush – pain no longer a factor.

"Damn, Link, ya shot a hole in my shirt."

"Sorry Milton, should'a moved your horse over another step. And you mister can sit nice and easy, my finger is sorta itchy ya see."

"It was one of my best shirts."

"Reckon we can sew it up. N' you can grab a shovel – your pards look ready for a dirt nap."

"Why dja kill my brother?"

"Mister I don't know what yer talking about."

"His horse, his saddle. Was just up to my spread six months ago on whats underneath you."

Movement, yet another shot.

"He moved."

"Well ya told him to sit nice and easy. Some folks just never learn. Hell, now we gotta bury allm'."

"Nah, let the buzzards do their job. They got time."

"Ya know, Link, yer spurs are getting sharper all the time."

"Figured youd' sorta mosey in that direction."

"Be in ta the Saragossa bout' evnin tomorrow."

"Whata we got for fixins?"

"Oh, powder burn biscuits N' –"

So, really whos' Dred Scott?

"%@#$@^^%%^!"

Homecoming
By Margaret Vose

Grace Godfrey looked up from the scarf she was knitting and checked her watch once again. She sighed and reached over to turn on the lamp. Daylight was almost gone. Large fluffy flakes were gathering in the corners of the front window. Snow had been coming down all afternoon and showed no sign of stopping.

"For gosh sakes, Gracie, the kids will be here when they get here. You always get so jumpy before they come," Hal said, looking over the top of his newspaper.

"I don't understand why they didn't fly instead of drive. They would have been here yesterday."

"It's cheaper to drive."

"Serena never worried about that before, Hal."

"Now, Gracie, don't start that. Besides, they have all those presents to bring."

"It's a wonder those children have any Christmas at all. She is the most disorganized young woman. I don't understand how our son copes with it all."

Grace watched as her husband slowly got up and wedged the Want Ad section under the logs in the fireplace. The paper caught quickly at the touch of the match. They watched the flames move to the dry kindling that Hal had cut from the brush on the slope in back of the house. They listened to the crackling fire as it caught the larger logs. Grace frowned, picked up her knitting and Hal returned to the sports section.

The insistent ring of the telephone startled them both. "Oh, my, I'm all tangled in this yarn. Will you please get that, dear?" Hal struggled out of his easy chair again and hobbled into the kitchen to answer the wall phone. Grace strained to hear his clipped responses and anxiously watched him resettle himself in his chair by the fire.

"Well...who was it?"

"It was John. They're on the river bridge and traffic is pretty slow in this storm. They should be here in half an hour."

"Those poor children must be starved. Little Lilly and Sean are probably full of rice cakes and soy beans and ready for some real food." Grace hurried into the kitchen to finish dinner.

Hal put another log on the fire and tried to remember the last time John and his family had come to Keokuk. Probably when I had my hip surgery. Or was it when Gracie came down with the pneumonia and Doc put her in the hospital for a couple days. I'm so proud of John, I really am, receiving a scholarship to the university, and now, a full professor of business with a smart, pretty wife and two great kids. Grace never understood why John didn't take over the hardware store and settle down right here in Keokuk. She can't get over it and it's been over ten years.

In the kitchen, Grace checked the meat thermometer in the rib roast and the mashed potato casserole and turned the oven to low. A green salad was crisping in the frig and the chocolate cake was in the cupboard. She was pleased with her work – all done and ready to go.

Car lights swept the driveway. "They're here, Gracie!" Doors slammed, voices called, "Hellooo, Merry Christmas !" Snowy boots stomped up the wooden porch steps and the door swung wide.

"Take your boots off and come on inside. Your dad has a fire going."

The initial excitement of the homecoming ritual played out with plenty of hugs and handshakes, smiles and kisses. Duffels and bags of gaily wrapped presents were dropped in the hallway and coats were hung on wooden pegs by the front door.

"I'm so hungry, Mom. When can we eat?" bellowed Sean.

"Just as soon as I can unpack your food and warm it up a bit, honey."

Hal and his son moved to the front room while the women and children headed to the kitchen.

"Grace, did John tell you, Sean and Lilly's allergies have almost disappeared since we put them on a gluten-free, vegan diet. John and I are moving in that direction, as well."

"Oh."

"It's easier to prepare the same meal for everyone. We've eliminated most fats, carbs and sugar from our diets. I will say it's more expensive to be vegetarian and buy organic, but I'm back teaching modern dance at K-College which helps with the budget and I love it. It's so fulfilling to be with young, creative students again."

"Oh," nodded Grace. She suddenly felt very tired.

The family dinner table was politely subdued. John gamely approached the edges of a slice of perfectly pink-in-the middle beef with caution, while Serena gingerly cut and moved the food from one side of her plate to the other.

"Such a lovely tossed salad, Grace. If it wasn't December I would guess these greens were right out of the garden. John and I planted our first kitchen garden last spring, all organic seeds, no pesticides. It is such a relief to know where your food comes from, don't you think?"

"Oh, yes," responded Grace. She was beginning to feel a little dizzy.

The chatter of the children kept the table conversation light until they were excused to watch a PBS Christmas DVD their mother had brought for them.

Serena cleared the plates while Grace poured coffee and decided not to mention chocolate cake. "Well, John, did you root for the Yankees in the Series this year? That Derek Jeter is the world's best shortstop, isn't he? Never saw anyone like him! " Hal beamed at his son.

"He's the pride of Kalamazoo, Dad."

"C'mon, John. Let's you and me let the girls finish up and we'll go in the other room and solve the problems of the world. I've got some good brandy your Uncle Bob sent me for Christmas I'd like you to try."

Grace and Serena finished their coffee, exchanging pleasantries and wan smiles across the vast prairie of the dining table.

Finally. "Grace, John doesn't know how to talk with you about this. He knows how you and Hal love this place and all the memories and he can't think of you not being in Keokuk. But, we both worry about you in this big house with no family near."

Grace shifted in her chair, "We're just fine, Serena."

"We would be so happy to have you closer and the children would love seeing their grandparents more often." There. It was out on the table for Grace to contemplate, for her and Hal to discuss, face-to-face. Serena had to proceed. "John and I have noticed several nice senior housing developments going up around our area and ..."

"Excuse me, Serena. I'm not feeling so well. I'm going to take some aspirin and go to bed. Good night."

Serena watched her mother-in-law slowly make her way up the stairs. It had not always been easy with this woman over the years, but a benign truce had developed between them. Grace was known as the strong one in her family. Hal depended upon her at home and had relied on her in the hardware store. She had always been overbearing and critical which, Serena had told John, just shows how fearful and vulnerable his mother really was.

Serena's attention returned to her children and rounding them up for bed. She heard the low, measured voices of the men, as she passed the front room.

"Well, Dad, it's been a long day. I hope you will think about our talk."

"Oh, sure, John. See you in the morning."

Hal stared into the dying embers of the fire. He was surprised and taken aback to think his son thought he and Grace couldn't look after themselves anymore, were getting old and needed help. He wasn't prepared for this discussion. Not yet. But, it was true. Simple tasks were harder now – things always breaking down in the old house— like me, he smiled. I really would like to be around those kids more. How will I ever bring this up to Gracie? Finally, he got up and placed the screen on the hearth.

Sure glad to have John and the kids to shovel us out in the morning, he thought. He unplugged the tree lights, turned off the lamp, and made his way to the stairs.

Soon, all was quiet, except for the last gusts of the waning storm outside.

Oysterville Fame
By Renae Keep

The city of oysters, typically a tightwad set,
Opens its briny-spined purses and spends
Its pearls, its mothers, the barnacles off its backs
To purchase my dainty little volume.
They chant about it as they fold their wash –
How its history, bearded yet slick,
Somehow speaks to them in their own tongues
For the first time, not in recipes.

Ghostly Messenger of Truth
By Cheryl Levinson

George sits on one end of our living room playing his harmonica, accompanying a Bob Dylan album. "On your own/ A complete unknown/ No direction home/ Like a rollin' stone." I sit on our old couch, which is dressed up in an orange-red Indian cloth, and observe my husband – his large brown eyes, with their long lashes, his full mouth that tends toward a perpetual pout. I'm always surprised by his occasional sunburst smile. Even then, his eyes are not mirthful.

I move into the kitchen to prepare a simple meal of basmati rice with broccoli and lentils. I work quietly, so I won't interfere with the music. Fill the rice cooker, add three pinches of curry; chop scallions; slide the already prepared lentil-carrot dish out of the refrigerator.

George comes into the kitchen just before dinner is ready. "Hello," he says kissing me lightly on the cheek. I put my arms around him, draw him into a hug. He doesn't resist, but his hug energy just isn't activated. "How much time before dinner?" he asks.

"Five minutes" I say cheerfully. "I'll be right back, then," he says, and I'm left standing in the middle of the small white room, with its avocado-colored stove and the window that looks out onto a grassy, green empty lot. Like a rollin stone.

I hope he'll feel like doing it tonight, even though it'll be late by the time he gets home. I imagine him moving close to me in bed, spreading his body over mine. I feel his full weight sinking me deeper into the mattress. I look into his eyes, which look into mine. Our bodies and moans combine until there's no space between us. In the distance, I hear the swish and sway of the waterbed making its own love sounds.

Rarely do we have sex. Sometimes, in the middle of the night, we have reached out to find each other. We've made love in the darkness, rolled and kissed as if in a dream, then slid into sleep again, sighing and satisfied. We never spoke about this in daylight, never smiled at each other over the memory of our encounter, never touched hands in remembrance of passion. Always my husband's sullen silence. Always my expectant heart shutting closed like a poked sea anemone.

We were twenty and in college. We first met through a mutual friend, Stuart, in the campus cafeteria. George appeared at the large round table wearing a tweed jacket and a beret cocked to one side.

"Hi, Georgie – grab yourself a chair," Stuart said in his cantor-like voice. George took his seat across from us. Over lunch, he talked about Bob Dylan as the poet of our century. I fell into his eyes and the way he put words together. He must have noticed and been quite flattered.

"What are you doing Saturday night?" George asked, cutting away from Bob Dylan and standing up to go to his next class, books under one arm, white teeth showing as he smiled.

"I have plans," I said, "with a girlfriend."

"Well," he said, "just call her and tell her you're going out with me."

My knees went weak and a whirlpool spun in my belly. I knew I had been touched by the dark and light of all things.

Those were the days of Vietnam, demonstrations, and flowers in our hair. Love-Ins graced our city parks, while longhaired men played tambourines, and women in diaphanous blouses twirled barefoot in the grass. The scent of patouli oil mixed with marijuana was intoxicating. Free love permeated the air as if there would be no cost.

"I'm applying to be a waiter at Grossinger's in the Catskills – in New York," George said. "Just for the summer." We were sitting on the scratched, unevenly stained hardwood floor in his one-bedroom cottage.

"Why?" I asked. My heart beat wildly at the idea that he would leave me for even a minute.

"I need life experience. It's either that or settle down." He looked at me sideways, the same way he looked at pretty women sauntering by when we were out together.

Janice Joplin's raspy voice came from the radio. "Freedom's just another word/ for nothin' left to lose . . . Me and my Bobby Mcgee."

My heart picked up speed again. In the end, we lit candles and incense, took a few tokes of grass to relax and threw the I Ching, better known as the Chinese Book of Changes. Three pennies substituted for the yarrow stalks that ancient Chinese prophets used to probe the future. While concentrating on the all-important question, Should We Get Married, we threw the pennies and came up with numbers, which corresponded to a page that gave us an answer.

George read the prophecy while I stopped breathing. "Bad beginning, good end," he pronounced as if they were sacred words. Then he read something about the mountain coming to meet the river.

"Well," I said.

"Well," he said, "I think it's time for me to commit to something. I've always known it – you are the wifely type, so let's do it. Let's get married." With those three words, his lips barely moved. He was sitting on a low second-hand couch. I was sitting on the floor looking up into my beloved's face. I grabbed his knees and hugged them in gratitude.

A week before the wedding, my parents invited us over. "A serious discussion," my mother said sotto voce, into the phone. She served honey cake and tea on her best dessert dishes. My father eyed us over the chasm of a salmon pink tablecloth. His glasses rested on the bridge of his nose.

"A Jewish man doesn't take his bride back to a hovel," he said. "Please, George. I'll pay your rent for six months so you'll take my daughter to a nice apartment. You can pay me back after you both get better jobs."

"We don't want to live that way," George said.

Somehow, I found my voice. "Material things don't matter to us," I said, sitting shoulder to shoulder with my husband-to-be. "Dad, stay out of this."

I mistook his offer for meddling, for skewing my dreams in the direction he wanted them to go. I wasn't capable of understanding my father's love for me then, the pure desire for my well-being that filled the syllables and corners of every word he spoke.

It was a small wedding. At the reception, 40 friends and relatives nibbled on petite hors d' oeuvres, and drank the expensive champagne my parents provided.

Arm in arm, with mask-like smiles, my mother and father circulated between the four round tables, greeting people and chatting. George's parents, long divorced and re-married to more suitable mates, blessed us by speaking civilly to each other. The rabbi stayed long enough to join in the toast.

"I was there when you became a man at your Bar Mitzvah," he put a fatherly hand on George's shoulder. "It's such a joy to be here for your wedding, too." He touched my cheek gently. "Mazeltov, good luck to you both," he waved as he made his exit.

Soon after, George grabbed my hand and pulled me outside to the back of the synagogue. There we stood amidst the trash cans, me in my mini-skirted white sheath and borrowed veil. He in the rented blue suit which hung awkwardly on his stocky frame.

Ha-va Nagila, Ha-va Nagila, I could hear our guests sing in the background while dancing the traditional Hora, and clapping in time to the beat. Let's all be happy. George cried quietly at first cupping his face with his hands. Then he put his head on my shoulder and sobbed into my dress. I held him wordlessly, believing with all of my young heart that he was crying from joy.

I can still smell the steam from the iron, still feel the motion of my arm as I pressed out the wrinkles in George's white cotton Nehru shirt that Saturday morning. The front door slammed shut. I ran outside in time to see George walking up the street. Our mutt, Jessie, whom we rescued from a bus stop in a bad neighborhood, followed at his heels.

"What's wrong. Where are you going?" I asked catching up to him, my breath caught in my chest.

"Leaving," he answered.

"Why?"

"Because you iron my clothes, and cook meals, and hold down a job. And you love me too much." He kept walking, looking straight ahead. I walked too, staring at the side of his face.

"It's been a mistake," he said.

"Please don't leave," I begged. I cried. I scooped up Jessie and held on tight.

"It's a mistake," he said again. "I don't want it anymore."

I stopped in my tracks suddenly aware that several residents on the block must be peeking out from their curtains, watching the drama of a young pitiful woman without pride.

"All right GO!" I yelled hugging Jessie, watching George's back get smaller and smaller until it was a pulsing gray smudge on the movie screen of my life.

I knew he'd come back. I knew it while I spent the first empty month in bed at my parent's house. I knew it when I finally got myself out from between the sheets, marched myself to an interview, and got a decent paying job as a Social Worker. I knew it when my father said I could get any man I wanted, and my mother looked into my eyes with pity in her own, and kissed me on the forehead. I knew it when George's brother came back from tracking my errant husband down in Berkeley and reported that George was a bona-fide hippie who no longer wanted a traditional marriage. In the end, I was right. It only took him six months to call.

"You sound so far away," I said when I heard him say, "Hello, Boo," and could, at last, wrap myself in the affectionate name he always called me.

"You're my anchor," he said. "Without you, I'm just drifting."

Feeling powerful, I meted out conditions – we get into marriage counseling, and he goes back to college to get his degree. "You've a brilliant mind, and you quit one semester before graduation," I reminded him. "I stuck it out and got my BA. I don't want a husband who won't complete what he starts."

"OK," he said. "OK. OK."

I noticed the book on his nightstand. I had seen it there many mornings with its paperback cover curled at the edges from use. It sat there innocently, yet emanated the forbidden. I didn't want to pry, or discover truths. George had come back to me and that was all that really mattered. One morning though, in a brazen moment, I let my eyes fall on the title. Hidden Passions. I picked up the book and ruffled the pages as if I was shuffling a deck of cards. Finally, I opened it and read. Leather and handcuffs. Lesbian love. Man to man raw sex. A virtual arsenal of fantasies, described in erotic detail.

My life with George flashed before me. His rejection of my sensual offerings. His suggestion over dinner one evening, that we engage in a menage a trois. He and I would do it together, be together, experience it together, he insisted. We'd simply add a third element, man or woman, it didn't matter.

"Everybody's doing it," he said, noting my shock and recoil. "This is our chance to challenge the bullshit of our culture's puritanical standards, to release inhibition, to BREAK FREE!"

I shook my head and said no that wouldn't be all right with me while feeling dull and prudish, too cowardly to welcome a third person into our bed. The bed that stood between us, impenetrable as the Berlin Wall.

In spite of the past, we've stayed together four years now. We live in an upscale apartment that especially pleases my parents. It overlooks the Silverlake Reservoir, surrounded by evergreens, which gives it the appearance of a real lake. After accompanying Bob Dylan on the harmonica, and eating the simple lentil and rice meal that I prepare, George leaves to lecture to a group of budding therapists about the theory of Symbiosis in Couple Counseling. We spend much time separately and together in therapy. We like it so much that we're training to become therapists ourselves. George is the gifted one. He catches on to the concepts quickly and applies them in an exquisite way to real clients.

Therapy has helped us face many truths, the main one being that George loves me, but is not sexually attracted to me. I've learned that the constant lump in my throat and the frequent welling up of tears for no apparent reason are valid. My therapist points out that I've suffered a great loss – the romantic dream of what marriage is supposed to be has dissipated into thin air. I've learned, too, that I can be the one who holds the flame of love, and that this relationship can be the vehicle for me to work out my own childhood issues.

"It's healthy to stay and not run away," my therapist says, until those words become a mantra that I chant to myself on the days when every chip is down and I can't spot even one flower. So, I'm home alone tonight and I watch the sun set over the fake lake. The water turns dark blue, then black. The streetlights come on; the phone rings.

"Is George Epstein there?" a deep voice asks.

"Not at the moment. Can I take a message?"

"Are you his wife?"

"Yes."

"Well, I sure hope I can talk to him soon." The voice is irritated and pushy. "Four days ago he exposed himself to my seventeen-year-old daughter. He was sitting behind the wheel in broad daylight at the corner of Highland and Vine, with everything hanging out if you get what I mean. The world was walking by. Then he tried to lure her into the car. She had brains enough to take down his license."

I put my hand over my mouth to stifle a denial. I manage to recollect facts. How George frequently goes out for a drive alone. How he returns home with a glassy look in his eyes. How I've sensed that something was very wrong but never said a word. Pieces fall into place in slow motion. A tiny part of me fills with the cool, calm truth.

Yes, he was in our blue car. Yes that is the license number. Yes, I had switched cars with him that day for a reason I can no longer remember. Yes.

"I'm sure George will want to talk to you," I say, every inch of my voice polite, respectful. "He should be home by ten."

"My name is Robert," the voice volunteers. I detect a softening. Maybe he feels compassion for a wife who just this minute learns that her husband is a pervert. "I'll call back at ten, and if he's not there, I'll have to go to the police."

"I understand, sir. When you call back, George will be here."

I place the phone in its cradle. My hands are shaking, butI see it all. The rejections; the porno book on the nightstand; the solo daylight drives. Nausea takes over. I lean against the wall for support.

I know where George is and I call. "Family emergency," I tell the woman who answers the phone.

"I'll get him quickly," she says and lays the receiver down on the desk. Her heels click on the floor as she leaves wherever she is to get George from the conference room.

"Hi, Boo," he finally says, concern in his voice. "What's wrong?"

I breathe deeply. It seems I've been waiting on the phone for years. I tell him without mincing anything.

"Was it you?" I ask, knowing what the answer is. He says it was. He says it could have happened anywhere, anytime. He says he couldn't stop himself and that he needs help.

"Come home," I say. "Robert will be calling back at ten, and you need to be here."

"You'll probably leave," he says, genuine sorrow in his words.

"I'm not sure what I'm going to do," I answer. But in my heart I know. I close my eyes for a few seconds. I imagine a butterfly alighting on a stalk of tall meadow grass, then fluttering to some yellow wildflowers. The creature is happy in its freedom, as I will be soon enough. Right now, though, I'll see George through this dark time, good anchor that I am. We sit, he and I, on the couch that's covered in the orange-red cloth, our thighs touching, in a way they've never done before. Our clasped hands form the warmest home we've ever known together. Janis Joplin's voice drifts in from the radio. That Bobby McGhee song again. We listen to the sweet and bitter tale she spins, as we wait and wait for Robert, the ghostly messenger of truth, to call.

Sounds of August
By Evie Groch

Summer exhales in tiny hisses – Aspens
let out sacred sighs that escape through
transparent clouds.
I listen and salute them.
Amber and ocher drip from
auburn leaves to stain
the earth in matching colors.

Retiring leaves drop to pave
the footpaths with pop and crunch.
Chirps signal a return to home in
fledgling and empty nests.
Iridescent wings flutter as Monarchs cease their
rule and migrate in swarms.
I accept the farewell.

A crisper breeze sweeps through the
brittle boughs
as the season tiptoes away
on bare feet.
I bend with the boughs – to do
otherwise would upset season and reason.
Autumn
is on the horizon.

Forms of Address
By Evie Groch

Edyth's body, with support from the hallway wall, slumped down slowly and with great weight until it hit the floor with a thud. Her disappointment and frustration were so tangible, she could see their smudged tones of dark brown and stench-filled grey permeating her senses. She no longer knew what to think.

About a year ago, she had been eager to enroll in an art class near the school where she taught middle schoolers science. After a challenging day of teaching, she could let her concerns fall aside like dirty clothes before a bath and immerse herself in the arts, a passion she had denied herself for years due to lack of time. On her 30th birthday, the decision was made. She would wait no longer. After day one at the water color painting session, she went to the art supply store and trying not to see how much she was spending, bought the items on her teacher's itemized list. Like a child in a candy store, her eyes opened widely at every choice she had to make – exactly which brush, which manufacturer, how much of each paint color to buy.

Her art teacher was a slender and tall figure of a woman with gray flowing locks, a true free spirit who always dressed in black for the class and used her clothes to help absorb some of the excess water on her brush by flicking it against her thigh. Edyth wouldn't be trying that. They were so different, Edyth and her teacher. Her teacher had been a child of the sixties, open and at peace with everything, letting things take their course and being patient to a fault. Every question raised in class deserved a thorough and lengthy reply embellished with examples.

Many times this would slow the class down to a standstill. Edyth's A type personality found this hard to accept, but just like she was learning to let go of control and cede to her water colors the right to lead her outside of the lines, so too was she learning to appreciate her teacher's support of each student's needs and curiosity. She was learning exactness was not required.

After each class, Edyth would reward herself with a latte from the nearby Starbucks. She would bring in the painting and debrief it in her mind while sipping her drink and making notes about where she would take the painting next.

After months of visiting Starbucks after class, she noticed a professorially dressed man working on his laptop always in the same seat in the corner not far from her. No one wore corduroy any more, but on him it was fitting and made him looked distinguished, like an architect in his den.

One day, he begged her pardon and asked her to plug in his laptop cord for him into the plug near her feet. She did so gladly and then asked what he was working on. He deliberately took his eyes off his screen and made a point of looking at her directly, taking her in with his scan. At first she felt uneasy, like being x-rayed in an airport checkpoint, but soon his face softened and with a smile, he told her he was preparing his next lecture for his philosophy class. She could have asked many more questions, but felt she had in terrupted him long enough and let him return to his work with her comment of how interesting that must be.

Week after week, Edyth saw the professor at his usual seat at Starbucks. One day, she got up the nerve and asked if she could buy him a coffee refill when he was ready for a break so he could tell her more about the kind of philosophy he taught. He caught her off guard and offered to buy her a drink and take a break right then. She almost blushed. She knew full well that this was not a pick-up bar, but it made her feel giddy all the same. They sat for a while and talked about all the classes he taught at UCLA, among them Philosophy of Language, Ethical Theories, and Theory of Knowledge.

While he spoke, she glanced over at his screen and found the shorthand he was using incomprehensible. She didn't want to be caught spying, so she let it go and admitted to him (she finally learned his name was Sean) that she found all this fascinating and wanted to know more. Edyth felt, however, that she had to go slowly.

This weekly meeting became an expectation of hers, and she looked forward to it with as much eagerness as she did her painting class. She had been dressing in painting clothes for her class, old jeans, discolored Tees, tennis shoes. She was now starting to pay more attention to her apparel and even brought a change of clothes to slip into before entering Starbucks for her Wednesdays with Sean. Sean even ventured to ask her about her painting class and made complimentary statements about her work which so far consisted only of still life compositions and negatively nuanced geometric shapes. She surmised he was slow to open up and maybe a little awkward where women were concerned, but she found him charming and a delight. He couldn't have been more than 40, with greying streaks starting to frame his temples. At times he left his corduroy jacket at home and wore a Docker's light jacket, for her benefit, she chose to believe. They talked of the idea of being able to explain people's behavior, the writings of Kant, the meaning of morality, how one person comes to believe and know anything about what another person thinks and feels, and how language and communication relate to the world.

Their discussions were incredibly deep and all consuming. After a year of meeting at Starbucks, Sean invited Edyth to dinner at his apartment. He offered to make an Italian meal for her after learning she had been to Italy and loved pasta. She accepted. He jotted something down on a slip of paper and handed it to her, mentioning that on Friday she should come around 6:30.

"LA 43, Brentwood apt. 4" was on the slip of paper Sean had passed to Edyth. She hadn't looked at it earlier, but after putting on a bright red long-sleeved top and silk black pants, she read it and ventured out to find Sean's apartment using her GPS. Her Honda Civic pulled up to the indicated address, and she took the elevator to the second floor, a bottle of wine in hand. She knocked on the door and waited. No response. She rang the bell. No response. He's probably in the bathroom, she figured. She looked a gain at the address. She had parked on Brentwood Ave. in L.A. and this was apartment 4. She waited and then knocked louder and longer. Still no response. After about ten minutes, her heart sank as her body slid downward, bottle of wine still in hand. Why had he deceived her?

At the same time, Sean's dinner was getting cold as he waited for Edyth at 43 Los Angeles Street in Brentwood near the UCLA campus.

Fanny's Freedom
Cheryl Levinson

"Hello Sonny Boy, hello," she cooed, stretching slender fingers through the door of the cage to stroke the parakeet on its breast. "I can talk, can you fly?" She pursed thin lips and whistled.

"I can talk, can you fly? Hello, Fanny, hello Fanny," a raspy voice answered.

"No, I can't fly. Come here, you silly bird." Fanny wrapped her hand around the small chartreuse body, took Sonny out of the cage and set him on the floor. He jumped onto a miniature swinging bar, and then hopped to the top of a little wooden ladder.

"You play on your swing while I garden," she said as she walked out the back door, making sure to shut the screen behind her.

The flowers were profuse this spring. Fanny touched the light purple rose, felt its velvet petals, and brought it to her nose. Its fragrance brought up familiar sadness. Flowers fade. By tomorrow, their petals will be wilted and their edges brown. Fanny spread out her hands, palms down, and surveyed her own brown age spots. With a grunt she knelt on the walkway and wrenched a weed from beside one of the rose bushes.

"Oye vey, my creaking bones," she said aloud, forcing her upper body to stretch forward and pull more weeds. She had to win the weed war or these monsters would take over her entire garden.

While she worked, Fanny heard Sonny Boy chirping and squawking as he flew around the pantry and played on his swing.

That bird! What a character. He sure was a happier bird when he wasn't caged. What bird wouldn't be?

So Fanny usually closed off the pantry from the rest of the house to give Sonny freedom of flight in his very own space.

Swanee peeked her head over the fence. Her gray hair stood up in thin wisps. "Hi, Fanny. Gorgeous day, eh?" She smiled widely, not caring a whit about her missing front tooth.

"Oh, Swanee. You scared the daylights out of me!" Fanny turned back to her garden and continued to pull and yank, throwing weeds into a green garbage bag.

Swanee chuckled. "Are you at that garden again?"

"Of course, of course," Fanny said, feeling her neighbor's eyes on her back. She wished she could wave away this witch-like invader. Fanny doubted that Swanee ever took a bath. There was a year of dirt under her fingernails, much like the disgusting fingernails of the homeless woman who walked up and down the street wheeling a shopping cart full of paper bags.

In spite of Fanny's lack of neighborliness, Swanee didn't budge. She had the nerve to give a loud whistle that coincided with Fanny's pulling out a particularly stubborn weed.

What a busybody, Fanny thought. Nothing better to do than make sounds. Why is she hanging around so long? Like she's stuck in cement. Probably enjoys annoying me and breathing down my neck.

Reminds me of Mama. Any little thing I did she'd be there, pointing a finger. I'd call her "Mama" to her face, but she wasn't a mother. She was "Sarah" to me – Sarah the witch. One time I was sitting in a rocking chair, embroidering. She walked across the living room just to look at my little swatch of needlework.

"See this stitch? It's wrong, stupid girl. You and your sister – good-for-nothings. Boys at least get a job and bring in money," Sarah said in Yiddish. I remember. It felt like she slapped me across the face.

Can you hear that crazy bird?" Fanny shouted in Swanee's direction, trying to break the bad memory as if it were glass.

"Yeah. Crazy bird. Makes crappy noises."

"You know that a woman once offered me a hundred and fifty dollars for him? She couldn't believe how Sonny Boy talked."

"If I were you, I would've took the money and run," Swanee said with a laugh that came out more like a snort.

"Never, never, never! Do you know how long I spent teaching that fella to talk? Day and night I stood by his cage saying 'Fanny' or 'hello' over and over. And you come along and say I should've sold him?"

"OK, OK," Swanee dipped behind her side of the fence, mumbling. Fanny kept her head down. Relief finally. Alone with herself and her flowers. Her thoughts drifted like wisps of clouds in the sky.

Sarah wore her long hair pulled back tight and knotted at the back of her head. I didn't think she was a handsome woman even though a lot of people did. She'd walk into a room and the butterflies would start in my stomach. I shivered and shook even on the warmest day. Sarah's mouth never got soft. Not even when she slept. I watched her napping on the couch, and prayed that God would turn her into an angel. Of course, I was a young girl then and believed in things like that. Now I don't even believe in God, so I won't leave my house. It's gotten that way over the years. I could fall down in the street and who would help me? Not some man up in the sky that religious people call "God," that's for sure. All the bustle and movement out in the world.

Everyone walks fast, talks loud, drives with such speed. They make me nervous . . . is that the phone ringing?

Fanny pulled herself to her feet and rushed into the house.

"Hello," she said into the receiver. "Oh, I figured it was you, Sidney. Yeah. I have enough groceries. You don't have to get me anything. I was just gardening, and so many memories about Mama came back to me. She was a terrible mother to me, Sidney. She was a terrible mother to all of us."

Fanny listened while Sidney told her that he didn't want to hear anything bad about their mother. He always said this, while pointing out how hard Sarah worked to raise six children and put food in their mouths; what a wonderful seamstress Sarah was, and such a great businesswoman for someone who came from Lithuania and could barely speak English. And she did all this without a husband.

Fanny didn't argue with Sidney. He shopped for her, fixed her leaky faucets, and just last week, he climbed on her roof and patched it. Her brother was a gem. What would she do without him?

Today, even after she said goodbye to Sidney and hung up the phone, certain memories floated up to the surface though she wanted to force them into a sealed box labeled "forgotten."

Usually being among flowers soothed her; still as she went back to the garden to cut roses for a bouquet the past pestered her and pushed its way upward.

That day when Sarah took me shopping for fabric to make Mrs. Clansky a dress. We were walking near Grand Street on the lower east side. A little girl, maybe she was three or four, ran up to me with her lollipop. "That lollipop is beeeeeeutiful," I said. "Such a bright red!" Before I got another word out, Sarah yanked my arm.

"Stop with this foolishness. Can't you see I'm in a hurry? Don't get too friendly with the girl. You might decide to have one, God forbid. Then what? You wouldn't know what to do with a child."

"Don't worry, Mama. I'm never going to have children," I said.

Sarah stood in front of me, hands on her hips. "What if I marry you off and your husband wants children? What will you tell him?"

"I don't even want a husband. I don't want a man to touch me like Norman does." I said in a loud whisper.

"Norman down the street from us?" Mama said, and then she slapped me across the face. I touched my cheek. It was hot and I knew it was as red as that little girl's lollipop.

"Norman with a wife? Norman, old like a grandfather? That's a terrible lie, Fanny. Do you think an old man would want a homely freckled girl like you?"

She grabbed my arm and I marched alongside her to the bus stop, my chest bursting with tears that I wouldn't dare shed.

As this memory flooded back, Fanny's heart seemed to open. She cried as she never had before. Tears fell on her lavender and yellow roses as she cut and yanked them from their bushes, petals dropping to the walkway. Her life had been a prison. Now she was old, and it was too late to break free.

But I have children, she thought. That's why I love growing flowers. They bloom with just a little water and the right amount of sun. I plant and prune, and make them beautiful. Sonny Boy is my child too – a smart and special one. When I think about it, I've raised a lot of kids. If only Sarah were alive now. She'd see what I've done without even a husband to help me.

She listened for Sonny Boy's squawking as she walked toward the pantry. "Hi, Fanny, hi Fanny," he said as she opened the screen door. Then, in a flash, in spite of his greeting and before she could blink, Sonny Boy was out the door and flying, flying into the seamless sky.

At first, Fanny cried out, arms flailing, "Oh, no! Oh, no!" She watched helplessly as he became a speck, one hand shaped like a visor shielding her eyes. She held the other hand up, motioning him with waving fingers. "Come back, come back," she yelled. She meant to clip his wings, but the truth was she liked watching him fly high around the room, enjoyed his love of freedom, laughed at his excited bird sounds.

Fanny stood forlorn in her garden, keeping her eyes on her bird-child until he became the tiniest of dots. She hadn't yet grasped that he wouldn't survive for long in the outdoors. Later, the knowledge would hit her like lightning. But now, in this moment, a strange excitement rose in her, an excitement she would have been unable to explain. It was as if her Sonny Boy, this bird that made his way skyward, was loosening something inside of her, freeing her from invisible chains that bound her to her life.

"Go Sonny Boy, GO!" she shouted as if out of a dream. She ran forward, young again in that instant, to glimpse the very last of him. Her heart pounded with a strange and glorious joy.

Treasure of Words
By Bhawna Panwar

Wrapped behind a thin plastic cover
Stood a stack of pencils lined up standing tall like proud swords.
Some of these pencils sprinkled with stars, ready to fly away like clouds and march amongst the paper sky.
Before it all began, each twist and turn took away the layers and paint as they fell like the scrub of time, baring the tip free.
Taking the graphite point, carefully mastering the technique
To trace the curvy ridges and outlines of small and long words without fear.
Gently touching and absorbing the meaning of each letter
How it is like to have no words to describe what his young heart can feel.
This wooden stick bears the weight of his tiny fingers and the paper opens like a treasure box
To carry in his words slowly one by one,
To string together his heavy heart's voice of a sentence.
Such a simple instrument for his everyday life's battlefield of words,
Giving his two glowing eyes hope on the wings of a shiny sweet yellow coat.
So the words can spread over and around his limitless space
And give him his liberation.

Cliff Soaring
By Robert J. (Jamie) Miller

"Luke, this is crazy! You cannot fly a hang-glider in this weather. This is IFR, Instrument Flying Rules! And you have no instruments. The base isn't more than 100 feet above the beach, and you'll be totally in the fog with this onshore wind."

"Naah! What's to worry about. There aren't gonna be any power planes flying down in this stuff, not down around these cliffs."

I was busy buckling into my hang-glider harness, and didn't want to stick around and listen to Matt hassling me. The breeze was picking up and I sensed a great flight. "So maybe I get vertigo. Hey, this is a hang glider! It's stable. I just hold it steady and ride it down to the beach. What's the worst that can happen?"

"What can happen? You bust your ass, that's what. You turn into the cliff and I'll be identifying you by tattoos and teeth. After someone scrapes up the remains, that is."

"C'mon! I don't need instruments. You know I can feel altitude change in my ears, and I'll hear the surf at the base of the cliffs, so it's gonna be cool."

I rechecked my harness and jumped up and down a couple of times to make sure that everything felt right, then took a few steps toward the cliff and stepped off. "I'll send you a postcard!" I yelled as I turned parallel to the cliff to pick up the lift from an on-shore breeze turned abruptly upward. I knew my hang-glider. In calm air, we would descend about 300 feet per minute. These cliffs, towering above the Pacific and barely inside the San Francisco city limits, were nearly 300 feet above the beach. The slope-lift should be good and strong. But even if it wasn't and the lift was dead, I could glide northward and settle gently onto the sand. It would be a long walk back to where I had left Matt and the car, but I had my cell phone. What could go wrong? Matt would pick me up. That's what friends are for. Right?

I had plunged into grey, indecipherable stratus. I had never flown in anything like this. Hang-gliders never go here, but here I was, floating in a world that was invisible, marked only by the muted sound of the surf below. I turned carefully, guessing what ninety degrees would be, and for the first time, I felt fear. The cliff face should be to my right, but where? My world had shrunk to a small white luminous ball with me in the center. I worked north along the unseen cliffs, feeling the altitude in my ears and sensing, rather than hearing, those cliffs alongside. No, I was hearing the cliffs, the sound of the surf below to one side, soft and diffused by the cloud, and the hard-edged echo from the cliffs on the other. As I worked north and south, sensing altitude change by the faint pressure in my ears, I suddenly heard traffic sounds. Highway 1! I was above the cliffs. Yes! This was working! Where is the borderline between exhilaration and madness? I was riding it.

Enough. I was shaking from the tension. This was enough. I turned seaward and let the altitude play out for a moment, while I regained my senses. I would fly a "racetrack" pattern and relax for a few seconds. The grey fog below darkened and shapes flowed by.

A ship took form out of the mist. A sailing ship, a square-rigger, four masts. Sails set but damp-looking and hanging limp. It was stranded on the narrow beach, listing to seaward, hull already settling into the sand. "Hello!" I called, but the sound was swallowed by the fog. There was no answer but the restless surf. "Hello!" I called again.

Time to turn back to the cliffs and their lift. Forget the ship, I didn't want to land on the beach. I turned parallel to the cliffs and the changing pressure in my ears confirmed my ascent as I worked back and forth, north and south, there in the stillness of the fog. A half-dozen passes along the cliff and I could hear the traffic on highway 1, a couple more and I was sweeping down the headland looking for Matt and the parking lot. There they were! I turned a graceful circle, killed some altitude and settled to the ground.

"Where the hell have you been?" Matt asked.

"Where can you go in a hang-glider?" I answered. "Seriously, I saw something. There's a ship down there. Stranded. Like something from a 'Tall-Ships' event. I need to tell the Coast Guard."

A steady, unhurried voice listened, then passed me on to the next level. "Yes," the voice said. "Sounds like 'Carrier Pigeon'."

"Huh?"

"You're lucky. She's seen rarely, maybe once or twice in most years. Usually in foggy conditions. But seldom this far north."

"Wait, what...?"

"Sails set, but no wind filling them? Right. Anchors stowed? Was anyone on deck?"

"Yes... No... I don't know! Shouldn't you go rescue them?"

"I'm guessing it's clipper ship 'Carrier Pigeon'. It went aground in a heavy fog in 1853, 129 days out of Boston. Pigeon Point lighthouse was named for her."

"1953? Like 60 years ago?"

"Eighteen-fifty-three."

"But... But it's there now!"

"Yes, sir. In a heavy fog, your eyes can play tricks, right?"

"No, it was there."

"We'll wait to see if there are other reports. Thank you for your report. Is there anything else?"

I slipped out of my glider harness in a daze, and stumbled to the edge of the cliff. The fog was clearing. The beach was empty, except for the driftwood and kelp fronds thrown up by the last storm.

"Well?" Matt asked, as he caught up with me.

"You were right. You can't fly a hang glider in a fog like this. A person shouldn't even try. It's the fog. The fog plays tricks on you, you know. I'm through for today."

Elegy to a Beloved Colleague
By Jo Carpignano

(Charles "Chuck" Frost 1929 to 2012)

His voice was soft, and spoken words were few,
"Hi there." or : "How are you today?" he'd say.
While every story brought to us was new,
he read it softly in a whispering way.

Wiry and slim, he moved with quiet grace,
a bit of Gary Cooper in his loping stride.
His walk deliberate, with a measured pace,
the unimportant wanderings set aside.

He knew specific rules for every word
semantics and italics, well he knew
From him, exacting use of language heard,
"A better way," he'd say, "for clearer view."

Aware of evereley writer's fragile mood,
with tender ear, corrected written word.
Used prudent caution, as all critics should,
caught deeper meanings, others found absurd.

Wrote of his travels in far distant lands;
visiting China, exploring in Spain,
sailing the high seas, and walking white sands.
He studied life's joys, examined its pain.

We heard the roar of untamed winter storm,
felt cold blustering winds, smelled salty sea air,
savored sweet fruits, tasted fresh bread still warm.
"Use all senses," he'd say, "Give words some flair."

Before final days, time started to shrink, when his
finished work, in published form came.
The long labored book, not quite dry of ink, in hard
cover bound, displaying his name!

Chuck lived life strong, leaving us simple rules. This
wise, knowing man, who seemed a bit shy, might say,
"You're all well schooled, you have the tools –
I reached my dream - You can too, if you try."

Well written book confirmed this writer's care, in
printed form, Chuck's words will long survive.
Abundant written guides he left to share, and
with remembered voice, remains alive.

83

Who Are We?
By Pat Callaway

Who Are We? What is life?
What is death? Is there a God?

How can something as complex as a human being exist without some powerful, creative force behind it? What are humans? So complex: cruel, yet compassionate; loving, yet hateful; forgiving, yet intolerant; wanting what we don't have and accepting what we don't want; often lonely, even if surrounded by people; believing in our self-righteousness; habitually imposing our values on everyone else; so critical of others until we are reminded ever so often that everyone has importance in their own unique way—EVERYONE!

Sometimes It Takes a Great Loss To Find One's Way

Does our God exist in our imaginations because we need Him to make sense of our world?
Would He exist though primal instinct without ever having been told to believe?
Haven't all cultures had some form of instinctive belief, all of which focuses around the same philosophy--the golden rule?

Is our universe infinite?
Is there more than one dimension?
Is there more than one "source"?

Is our existence a game between the gods of the universes? A puzzle....about what works best?

So complex: diversity in nature; evolution; skin that heals itself. If we first discovered the fluidity of water as an adult, would we not be in total awe?

In our own limited area on planet Earth, we concede an exaggerated importance about ourselves. Yet, in the framework of this vast, yet to be discovered cosmos, are we not simpletons?

Short Story: Best of Show

Cassie's Valentine
By Valerie Stoller

Saturday night. My favorite part of any week. Man, I can't wait for Billy to pick me up and take me out for some tequila shots and sweaty dancing. Friends with benefits, that's what Billy says we are. Meaning sometimes we end up in bed. But no strings. Me, I'm pushing forty, but not dead yet.

Been putting in sixteen-hour days for the past two years, getting my B and B fixed up. Used to be our B and B. Jake, my ex, convinced me that buying a run-down motel in the Joshua Tree desert would save our marriage. Then he ran off with a waitress from the health food café. Some save that was.

Well, I showed him. Picked out everything from the paint to the turtle soap dishes in each guest room. Spent hours stripping wallpaper, nailing up desert art. Made this place into a thing of beauty. Turned out to be the best divorce therapy ever.

So, where is Billy? I'm ready for my night out.

I duck into the bathroom, check myself out in the mirror one last time. Love the bleached blonde streaks I've added. Kind of a punk look. Barb-wire tattoo on my bare shoulder. Got that a month ago. Don't mess with this gal.

Ding dong. Billy finally. Why is he ringing the doorbell? Usually just comes right in. I pull the heavy oak door open. Oh rats. Not Billy. Two men with luggage. Must be the last of my weekend guests. They'd called to say they got stuck in LA traffic. Duh. What do you expect if you leave the city on a Saturday afternoon heading out to the desert? A fast cruise, just you and Jack Palance riding high into the sunset? No way.

I plaster on my hostess smile. I know what's coming. Listen to them complain about all the traffic, how long it took to get here. Blah blah blah. Then the questions. Did you decorate this yourself? What is there to do out here in Joshua Tree? Can you tell us some good places to hike? Good places to eat?

Sometimes I just want to shout: "Read the damn guide book. I'm not your mother." So tired of taking care of everyone. No one takes care of me anymore. And I'm doing just fine. Well, most of the time.

"Howdy. You must be Cassie. I'm Tyler." This guy towers over me, looks like an up-ended tree stump. Gray straggly hair pulled back in a sad pony tail. Fat suspenders holding up jeans below his chamois shirt. A lump of a man.

"Yes, come in." I start into the living room, but the other guy stops me, puts his hand on my arm.

"I'm Karl," he tells me.

Like I need to know this. He's real skinny with a groomed salt-and-peppered beard. Are they a couple? I'm curious but don't say anything as I lead them inside.

"Gosh, this place is very pretty." Karl makes eye contact. "Did you decorate it yourself?"

He walks over to the stone fireplace and touches the Mexican crosses I've nailed up. What does he think? I hired Martha Stewart to be my personal decorator? Like I have that kind of money. Men can be such idiots. At least with Billy, I can count on a fun drinking partner and good sex. Works for me. Relationships are over-rated.

My cell phone buzzes in my pocket. Billy calling to ask where I am. He's been waiting for me at the honkytonk bar up the road. Oops. I thought he was picking me up. Then he offers to come and get me. Good, 'cause I plan on getting pretty drunk.

"Are you a scotch drinker?" Tyler pulls an unopened bottle out of his duffel. "It's single malt." He waves the bottle. "Brought back from Scotland."

Never turn down a free drink. Maybe it will take the edge off. Tomorrow, as it happens, is Valentine's Day. Also my anniversary. Seven long years ago, my ex and I figured we'd drive all night and land in Las Vegas just in time for sunrise. Got married in an Elvis Chapel, complete with a pompadoured preacher. Should have known better. Elvis wasn't exactly a great role model for marriage.

"Sure," I tell Tyler. "Why not?"

I bring out three shot glasses, but he insists we drink the Scottish way. Whatever. Eight-ounce glasses, one ice cube. He pours in a good splash, then one ounce of water. Says some Scottish version of "Cheers." Down the hatch. Damn. Burns all the way. Nice.

"So, Cassie, tell us about you." Tyler pours himself another shot. "How'd you end up here?" Gives me a nod and gulps his drink. Is he hitting on me? Jesus, just another dirty old man.

"Gee, it's a long story." I'm sick of doing this with every new guest. Change the subject. Get him to talk about himself. That usually works. "How about you two?"

"Hmm...let's see...where to start?" Karl reaches for the bottle of Scotch, pours himself a drink. He leans back on the couch and smiles at Tyler. His eyes are bloodshot. Probably started drinking on the way out here.

"Tyler and I met almost thirty years ago." He swallows the Scotch.

Oh, great. Now I have to sit through The World's Greatest Love Story. I wish Billy would hurry up. I hold my glass up and motion to Karl to pour me another one. Might as well make it worth the wait. I run my hand through my hair and watch Karl pour my drink. I sip it this time and let him tell his story. The Scotch's fire spreads its glow.

Karl tells me they met in college. Went separate ways but meet up every so often for vacations. Huh? What is this, Brokeback Mountain? I mean, I

86

don't care if they're gay. Whatever. Just kind of a sappy story. I glance at Tyler. His cheeks flush, and he excuses himself to go to the bathroom.

Karl sighs and puts down his glass. His fingers tremble. No, his whole body is shaking. Oh my god, he's crying. What the hell? Where's Billy? Get me out of this drama. I just want to have a fun night out.

Tyler comes back in and walks over to Karl. He sits down next to him on the couch, and puts his big tree limb of an arm around Karl's shoulder.

"Sorry about all this, Cassie." Tyler holds on tight to Karl, gives him a squeeze. "Must be the Scotch." He smiles at me the way my dog does when she's left a puddle on the rug.

"You see, Karl and I made this promise to spend the weekend out here together. Tomorrow will be the first Valentine's Day since Karl's wife died last year."

Karl looks up, his cheeks wet. My hand tightens around the glass of Scotch. I can't breathe. Damn it. I don't want to care. I don't want to feel his pain.

"Oh. I'm...so...sorry," I stammer. My eyes hurt. Please stop. I don't want to hear any more. But Tyler goes on.

"I lost my own wife five years ago." His cheeks glisten. He won't let go of Karl. Now I'm crying too.

"So Karl and I decided we shouldn't spend this Valentine's Day alone. We'd rather be with each other." He hugs Karl again. "That's what good friends do."

I can't seem to stop crying. I rub my tattooed shoulder, embarrassed. No one says anything for a while. But somehow I feel so close to Karl and Tyler. Maybe Billy won't show. I just want to stay here, full of scotch, broken open by the love of strangers.

Late Quarter Moon over San Francisco Bay
By William Baldwin

Huge and red, like a slice of blood orange,
You float up behind the Berkeley hills
As if just wiping your own blood,
Fat scimitar,
Warning of holocaust to follow,
Universal disaster,
Coagulated over the black bay

A Seal
By Jamilla Marie Skalna

Sunday morning in Carmel was misty and moist, verging on rain. After Jim's mother passed away, he went down every other weekend to fix up the house she had been living in. He didn't want to sell his mother's lovely house, which was only a short walk from the Carmel River Beach.

He was just starting to install a new hot water heater in the corner of the kitchen, and sometimes would peek out the window at the overgrown garden where hummingbirds fed on the large flowering fuchsia.

Suddenly, he remembered that the day-old bread and muffins at his favorite bakery might be sold out if he didn't hurry. He put on his blue and yellow checkered jacket and his blue hat with a cowboy string, and set off in his blue van.

Muffins at half price were gone, so he bought scones and bread. In the grocery next door, he bought some grilled chicken, baked potato wedges, chocolate milk,and bananas.

"What a nice picnic!" he said to himself. "Who needed hot water today anyway?"

He headed south, down the coast. The sun started to come out halfway, and by the time he reached the ranger's station, the sky was lovely blue.

He went into the new building full of maps, postcards, pictures, and displays.

"Hi," he said loudly.

"Hi. What can I do for you?" a young ranger asked, doing some paperwork.

"Well, my friend's coming to visit me from the east coast in two weeks, and I want to take him on trails into the Ventana Wilderness Area, east of Big Sur, so I'd like to check on some possibilities."

Jim unfolded the map of the area he had brought with him. The ranger leaned over the map, studied it for a moment, and pointed to a spot.

"Here's the best place to go," he said. "I went there recently with some friends."

"When did you come here?" Jim asked. "I haven't seen you before."

"This month. I just graduated from Pacific Grove High School."

"Really? I graduated from there, too!"

"When?"

"Oh, a long time ago. In 1951." He was a little surprised by his own statement. "I guess things have changed a lot since then. But I'm looking forward to going to my fortieth reunion this fall."

Just then, a young couple came in.

"Hi," the wife said. "We saw a stranded baby seal near Pfeiffer Beach. Can you do something about it?"

"Really?" the young ranger said. "Poor baby! I'll call Monterey for help."

When he called the station in Monterey, the ranger said, "We're busy right now, trying to rescue two seals at Pebble Beach. Can you rescue the seal pup by yourself? We'll come to your station to get him later."

"Jim," the ranger asked, "would you like to come with me?"

"Sure," Jim answered, a bit taken aback.

The ranger took a blanket and a cardboard box out to his green jeep. Jim followed in his van, and both headed down the narrow road that went a few miles through a small wooded canyon to the beach. The ranger drove fast and soon disappeared from Jim's view.

Halfway to the beach, an affluent-looking middle-aged hippie, in a fancy colorful patchwork outfit, stopped Jim to ask, "Are you a fairy for the festival?"

"What festival?" Jim asked.

"It's by invitation only," the hippie answered, laughing.

"No, I'm going to rescue a seal."

"Anyone can say that. This road is open only by invitation."

"You're kidding me. It's a free road, and you don't have any right to stop me."

"You're not listening to me, old man. If you don't have an invitation, turn your car around."

"The ranger's waiting for me at the beach. He must have driven by here just a few minutes ago," Jim said angrily.

"Are you kidding, you marmot! I would see someone driving down here. And I didn't."

"You have to believe me. The ranger is waiting for me."

Jim was getting angry. He turned off the engine, got out of the van, and charged into the hippie, knocking him to the ground. Since the hippie was "high," that was the end of the fight.

Jim jumped back into the van and headed for the beach.

When he got there, he found the baby harbor seal, whimpering and huddled in a ball. The ranger had already scooped him up in a blanket and put the yelping, squirming little fellow in the box.

The seal was gray and black, with an almost doglike face. A bit of umbilical cord was still attached to him. "He's about twenty pounds," the ranger said. "Obviously, he's not very old."

Jim petted the pup's soft wet head as he said, "You're gonna be alright, little fella." The ranger looked warmly into the pup's bright black eyes to calm it.

"Do you think he was born here?" Jim asked.

"They're born on the beach in the sand," the ranger explained. "Their mothers leave them here while they go back and forth to feed. If people are around, and especially if the pups get touched, they may abandon them.

Probably those hippies who were here scared her away. They're hiding here somewhere. I can feel they're around."

The pup ceased struggling, but continued to shiver and sniffle in-between breaths.

Occasionally, it sneezed like a dog. But it seemed to trust Jim and the ranger.

"What will they do with him in Monterey?" Jim asked.

"They'll nurse him and train him to go back into the sea." They dragged the box to the car, and the ranger drove off.

Jim stayed alone on the beach. He didn't hurry, even though he knew it was time to go back and get work done on the house. He unpacked his lunch and ate it all. Then he lay down on the sand and closed his eyes.

A moment later, two barefooted hippie girls emerged from the nearby dunes and walked up to him. He was impressed by how pretty they were.

The taller and more beautiful one was wearing a light blue silky dress covered with small white stars. Her long red hair was tied in a headband made of blue and white flowers. She beckoned for Jim to dance with her.

As they glided on the surf, the other girl danced around them, tossing sand in the air like fairy dust. Then she picked up a sand dollar from the beach and placed it in Jim's hand.

Jim opened his eyes. The beach was empty. But in his open palm, there was a sand dollar.

Bookwus
By Robert J. (Jamie) Miller

HONORABLE MENTION

We heard about the earthquake as we sat down to dinner. Lindsey reacted like the Californian she is, radiating a well-practiced calm.

"A seven-point-four? That's pretty good. Did they say where it was?"

"Shh. Not yet." I was reacting like a Nebraskan feeling his first quake, waiting for the buildings of the college to crash around us. "Something about the juncture of the Pacific and Juan deFuca plates. Should we get under the table?"

"No! C'mon, Nick, it's over. Ten minutes ago. Relax."

"The news anchor mentioned a tsunami warning. What do we do about that?"

"Oh, I don't know. Go over to the beach and go swimming?" She laughed and leaned over to kiss me. "We stay right here. Portland's seventy miles upriver. And I have homework."

I tried to study but found myself drawn to the TV and the latest reports on the tsunami. It hit Vancouver Island with a five-foot surge. I had grown up as far from the ocean as you can get, and found its moods endlessly fascinating. Lindsey, on the other hand—. No, Lindsey was staring at the TV too, ignoring her books, as fascinated as I was.

"Hey, Lin, you want to drive over to the beach? Tillamook Head, maybe? I'd like to see this thing hit."

"I thought you were scared."

"Yeah. But—"

"But drawn toward it? Drawn toward and warned away. You've seen the Bookwus."

"The What?"

"Bookwus. It's Canadian Indian mythology. A sort of death-spirit that comes from the sea to lure you to his domain. He beckons you closer with one hand and warns you away with the other and he dances. He dances two-steps-ahead, one-step-back, two– ahead, one-back, two-ahead…" Lindsey's eyes were closed and she was nodding her head to a beat only she could hear.

"Lindsey?"

"Oh, sorry. Anyway, the dancer in this ceremony wears a sort of weird human-like mask with huge eyes and a nose that's kind of like an exaggerated hawk's beak, all painted up in black, white, and red. If someone was seeing it for the first time in a dark lodge, with only a fire in the center, it must have been pretty terrifying. I saw one of these dance masks in the museum at Vancouver, British Columbia, when I was in high school. It was so fascinating, it actually got me interested in studying the native cultures."

"A dance mask? Seriously, Lindsey? And now you're into some kind of paganism?"

She moved behind me and kissed me on the neck. "Yeah! Lets go do a pagan ritual right now!" She laughed again. "You Bible-belters are all alike! Get a girl excited, then run away at the last minute." She studied the TV again and turned serious. "Let's go see this."

We headed west on highway 26, driving too fast for the narrow, curving road, then parked overlooking the Pacific.

"This is the place I was thinking of," Lindsey said. "The cliffs are 30 feet high, here. We'll be safe." She climbed out of the car and walked to the very edge of the cliff.

"God, it's beautiful here! Look! Look down there!" She was pointing toward the edge of the surf.

"Lin, please! Don't get so close to the edge. You scare me!" I may have been frightened, but I couldn't help thinking that she'd never looked as beautiful as she did at that moment, with the late-day sun lighting her face.

"OK, I'll back up, but come here. Look, down on the beach. There's Raven!"

"What? That bird?"

"Yeah. Maybe it's Raven, himself. Did you know that some of the native peoples' legends say that earthquakes mean Earth is in labor, trying to give birth to new lands, new mountains, new islands? Now we know it's true."

"Yeah, cool, but what did you mean 'Raven, himself'?"

"Another native myth. Raven, the immortal spirit-creature. He loved playing pranks, but as he did, he made the world what it is. It's like there weren't any people until he went walking along a beach like this one and found a huge clam-shell. When he pried it open, these tiny people spilled out and started growing until they got to be the size we are now. Then he—"

"Seriously, how did you get so into this weird religion?"

"Remember my major, Nick? American Studies? Hel-lo! 'Issues of Church and State' covers more than Salem witches and parochial schools. This is America, too." She sat down on the cliff, wrapped her arms around her drawn-up knees, and watched the restless ocean.

A Dead Friend
By Linda Marie Pillay

I bundled up and made my way through the fog to the bus that took me to her bedside. She was so long and thin. The machines huffed and puffed-swish beep-swish-beep. The Lilliputians dressed as nurses pulled and pushed and arranged and rearranged the various tubes and bandages connected to her body. I barely recognized her as the same person who had been my friend from so long ago. Should I say good-bye? Or wait to see what happens next? I remembered when.....

The time we found a $10.00 bill on the street and fought over it. I was not as generous as you know—when the raggedy man suddenly appeared from nowhere and asked if we had money so he could buy a coat—you gave him the $10.00. I said what a waste he is going to buy drugs or alcohol. I'd don't know if you gave him the money to spite me are that you really did feel sorry for him. We had lunch at the Mexican restaurant and when we left there he was thanking us for the warm coat he had just bought from the salvation army.

Your eyelids move now. I wonder if you are waking up to this mess they've confined you to.

Your beautiful lashes still so striking and dark fluttering- from what? What are you seeing in your coma? Who are you flirting with in there?

The muses own me...

I remember when you would sing in the cabarets and your voice carried to the streets. Your lovely voice was music to my lyrics. My poetry your songs -only then were we made in heaven. Then came the chorus and the musicians and I moved further and further from the stage. Sometimes you even forgot I was there—speaking past me—beyond me.

The tiny nurses from far away countries-that roll their Rs when they speak have returned to fuss over you again. They have asked me to leave so they can change the waste that comes from your body. There is no dignity in being this ill. The smell from your near lifeless body floods the room and carries to the hall like trails of smoke from a fire.

I can take no more - I leave wrapped in my coat, headed for the bus home.

Remembering---

Crossing the street with a child in each hand-you with yours and me with mine. Back and forth each day from the apartment complex to the park and back to fix dinner for them and husbands. It was so comfortable then. So when did it change? When did bliss become knowledge? We didn't know things would be different did we? We were going to be frozen in time—no beginning no end...

Exactly like the nuns told us in school who God was—what heaven and hell were. We rushed our babies to be baptized so they wouldn't be left in limbo. We drag them to church every year so crosses made of ashes could be slashed across foreheads.

I've returned to the hospital to watch you die. I don't feel you anymore. I don't wonder why you haven't called or visited me—when did we stop going places together—when did the laughter stop?

Your children and grandchildren gather around the bed. They let me know the priest has come to perform the ritual for the sick and dying. They whisper—how old I look. What did they expect at my age? I want to pull off my clothes and scream—look closely my dears and view your future!

A year after my husband died and two years after yours left—we sat quietly on my couch listening to music. The kids were gone. The room was covered in empty shadows. I decided to confide in you... Maybe it was to stir up trouble... Create a volatile energy field—I slept with your husband... I confessed—I had sex with your husband too she said. We laughed and the sun came out through the clouds.

AND

Should I tell the kids? We made love over and over and it was beautiful until it wasn't any more—no need to be physical or to give it a name or to define or join us. We had no need for descriptions like a botanist in a garden with two names for every plant or doctors with the same labeling only with behaviors and diseases. We grew apart and grew into other friends and lovers.

I slip past the sentry guarding your bed to see you late—after visiting hours after grown children and half grown grandchildren left.

Your face is more anguished than peaceful and the rhythm of the machines keeping you alive are hypnotic. The night shift approaches me and wants to know if I'm a relative.

Yes. I have just flown in from Europe and I'm her sister. After all, I'm not under oath. Someone looks into it—we were not aware she had a sister Someone said. I looked aghast—bewildered sitting up straighter in my chair I demanded to know whose oversight that was? We were left alone for the rest of the night.

Was she still there under all the tubes and hisses and dings?

Now I remember...

Your music was so beautiful. At first you sang other people's songs. I listened in awe. I couldn't believe I was so close to someone with such a powerful gift. I dared to show you my poems and your praise was Nobel and Pulitzer worthy. Our collaboration made us a wanted product all around the town's bistros and cabarets. I sat in front near the stage with a glass of red wine and breathed in your essence. Our songs filled me with odes of joy. I loved you like I had never loved before.

We were in the here and now for a long time or maybe not long enough. Can you hear me? My friend—you are so close and so far away. I see you sinking into the next world. I'd drift off to sleep while resting my head on the edge of the mattress. When I awake the sun is shining through the window.

You had left this world while I slept. The nurses are pulling tubes from orifices attached to your unmoving body. I put my coat on and walk out.

Someone follows me and wants to know how I feel if I am all right. I feel fine—she's dead and now I'm going back on the bus and have breakfast at home.

Survivors
By Maria Barr

Remembrance of San Bruno Fire September 9, 2013

Survivors coming home, to a new life, and some of you to a new home rejoice. When you arrive and sit down at the celebration table and see the empty chair, remember me. You see, except for cruel fate, I too would be there; family, friends, and neighbors to greet, and in peace and serenity live out my life.

Remember how on that fateful sunny morning, I happily waved, not knowing that would be good-bye forever. Oh, how I too fought to stay. Alas, my valiant effort..futile, leaving only whorled foot prints in the ash of the hot cinders of that horrific day. Because I can never come home; incorporeal, faceless, bodiless, I linger, and like a soft and gentle breeze I touch your brow to whisper, 'do not burn in ashes again my memory.'

As a traveler after a long and arduous journey who is happy to return, let me embrace and welcome you home, then together let us pause for a moment of silence, to speak with the voice of memory and herald to all that I too lived, that I too once was. Because a memory cannot be burned, so let me live in your hearts and in your minds as a sweet reverie to save me from the more devouring fire of....Oblivion.

Landslide
By Jeannine Gerkman

March 25, 2014

Too much rain and too much thunder Sturdy
bones sawn asunder
Sinews ripped and strewn above
Boulders tumbling under grass, roots aloft
Majestic trees shredded and torqued
Dirty rapids running filthy
A mountain splintered and twisted
Homes entombed, lives lost
Clouds dripping, heavy with tears

Nestle
Jeannine Gerkman

I have a friend named Hannah,
She's tiny but she's bright,
She a wrote a poem inside her head,
The other Tuesday night

She used "nestle" without blinking,
I delighted in her words,
And it got me thinking,
What is Nestle?

Babies nestle in mother's arms.
Ceramics nestle in straw Russian
dolls nestle in each other
I simply am in awe.

Dew nestles in rose petals,
Eggs nestle in nests.
Jewels nestle in velvet,
Breasts nestle in vests.

Saddle on a horse's back,
Cell phone in a pocket,
Books in a backpack,
Picture in a locket

Pearls on a necklace,
Garlic on a string,
Pancakes at breakfast
Feathers on a wing
Flowers in a vase,
Pillows on a bed,
Crayons in a case,
The brain in my head

Nesting dolls, tennis balls, gears in watches, bears in dens, shirts
in boxes, pigs in pens, nursing pups, even teacups....
They ALL Nestle!

Visiting the Farm
By Linda Brown

I can't remember the first time we went back to Iowa to visit the farm where my mother had grown up. I suspect we stopped when we were going across country from California after my father was transferred to North Carolina; my father was a pilot in the Marine Corps. I was in the first grade at that time.

But I am certain we stopped there four years later when we were going back to California. I would have just turned 11, my brother, Rex, was turning eight, and my brother, Garry, and was just four.

My cousins who lived on the farm were Joyce, who was my age, and Lois, was a much older and more sophisticated 15-year-old.

Having only lived in military housing tracts my whole life it was amazing to me that they lived on land that was theirs as far as our eyes could see.

I wanted to see and explore everything and was eager to listen to any family stories my prying ears could hear when the adults talked.

My uncle Earl proudly showed off his barn which his Grandfather had built and proudly bragged about all his livestock. My dad had been raised on a farm in Missouri so he knew all the terminology and asked right questions. We saw cows, horses, pigs and all the other animals on the farm. Uncle Earl teased us saying if we could catch a baby pig we could have it. But the pen was very muddy and it was a difficult choice whether to jump in and try to grab a pig of our very own or risk our mother's ire at getting muddy. Instead, we clung to rungs of the pen and dreamed big dreams.

I was impressed with my girl cousins who also seemed to know so much, I begged my cousin Joyce to show me the horses out in the pastures. We walked and walked, when suddenly she turned around and began walking even faster. I was so disappointed.

"Where are you going, Joycie?"

"I have to go visit Mrs. Jones."

"Now? I'm not going to be here very long. Where is she?"

Joyce gestured in the general vicinity of the farm buildings. "Yes. I go every day about this time," she explained.

"But won't she understand that I'm only here for a little while? You can go visit her any time."

"I know I can visit anytime, but now I have to visit her right now. I'll take you to see the corn crib after I'm done with my visit."

I was very upset that she had to go right then, we hadn't even gotten to see the horses in the far pasture.

Later, the entire family got a good laugh out of my not knowing that "visiting Mrs. Jones" was a euphemism for going to the bathroom.

We did get into the corn silo. It was dried corn and we got all dusty rolling around in it.

We also got a stern talking to about the dangers of possibly suffocating in it. But it was worth it.

Afterwards, we had to wash at the makeshift sink behind the cold house. It had an old chipped white enamel bowl instead of a sink which we poured water into. We scrubbed our wet hands, arms, and faces with a big old piece of homemade soap and dried them on an old towel hanging there.

The adults were lounging in the shade under the trees and the family dog, a cross between a German shepherd and a collie, was bouncing around trying to get anyone's attention.

I knew that by some strange coincidence his name was Rex, but I don't think my brother had realized it.

So when Uncle Earl finally lost patience with the dog, he hollered, "Go lie down, Rex! And stay!"

My brother hid behind my mother's skirt and plaintively asked, "What did I do now?"

Whenever we get together, our family still laughs with my brother Rex when we recall that dog and our memorable visit to the Iowa.

Beginnings
By Don Rogers

Beginnings... a new year...
A new start... a new...?
Questions mixed with hope.
Will this year be better than the last?
Will newly made resolutions find fertile ground? Or
will the year of the horse race on ahead... Leaving
the dreams of many behind?
Beginnings... new year
Pregnant with promise
Hopeful of delivery...
From choices and circumstances... That
could have been better.
Woulda, coulda, shoulda, If
only I had...
Beginnings... a new year
Hopeful expectation and... for some...
Determination...to make a new start.
To leave behind questionable choices.
To get past some circumstances... And
not be left behind as...
The year of the horse races on... But
to take the reins and...
And grasp the promise of beginnings.

Tea Ceremony
By Jo Carpignano

Zen Master smiled, spoke cheerfully explained, this
tea was made with powdered leaves
more potent flavor in this form, a
better taste, he said

Inscrutable assistant poured the heated brew but
Master placed each cup in waiting hands
receiving with the left, then clasping with the right

Listening well to Buddhist priest instruction
I stared fixedly at plain, brown cup now drained and
into it I emptied the contents of my mind

Intensively I gazed at my brown bowl wondering
if it portrayed what I've become depleted,
colorless, and bland

Rough and lumpy at the rim, bleak inside without
the graceful patterns on others' cups devoid of
brilliant glaze and intricate design

Continuing to study the inside of my cup
I thought – perhaps *not* empty, dull, and colorless but
free of superficial shine, and bright design

Polished with age instead, and smooth, with not
too many flaws
lacking flair and ostentation, but serene and calm like the
tea that I'd consumed; clear,
strong, and warm

Tommy's Story- Discovering Dyslexia
By Michele Jessen

To the Application Processing Coordinator,

For many years our son Tommy served as our family ambassador. He was naturally joyous and smiled easily. But during reading time at school we noticed he had an aversion to books. He avoided reading by implementing charming and often distracting behavior. Reading to Tommy was a nightly routine at home, but at school it was of no interest, as he loved movement more than stories. Early in school his peers began to sound out words. He could sing the abc's but not recognize one single letter. After many years of repetition of the alphabet he still had not mastered sound and letter recognition. As a credentialed teacher, I thought I could help him to learn to read at home. I was wrong.

In kindergarten he seemed to retain nothing about phonemes and sounds. Listening to stories was fine. But his reading comprehension was deficient. The strange thing we began to notice was his way to name something. He used descriptions to make himself clear. He could not recall or bring up the words that eluded his memory. It was like describing an elephant to someone who had never seen one using multiple sensory phrases, leaving out the one concise word to describe the creature...elephant.

Year after year he developed in every other area: math, art, music, PE, and science. Finally, at the end of first grade his teacher had him 'read' a story from the grade level anthology. He did it perfectly. I did notice that he followed the teacher's lips and cues as to each line. He did not seem to need the book in front of him. His proud instructor had tears in her eyes and proclaimed he could read. I felt something wasn't quite right after this strange parent/teacher conference.

To appear to fit in, he developed strategies to get through his classes. He seemed to fly under the radar. No one knew exactly why this apparently intelligent boy could not read. One of the ways he eluded detection was with sight words like stop, walk, McDonalds, etc. The symbolic pictures allowed him to imprint the word, which then he used to memorize when naming that word. When reading a story, he again could memorize it by the first letters, then use picture clues and context, along with repeated sentences to comprehend a few parts that made sense. Strangely, with each story, he had to start at the beginning, not the middle. I knew something didn't feel right.

It may seem that at this point in my story that I would have caught on or figured out the truth about Tommy. Yet I trusted the teachers who simply said he would eventually get it. We were all mistaken. Time and years passed by without progress.

My mother and I confirmed our suspicions when she read a story about the Titanic from the fourth grade anthology to him. She told him to remember the main character's name before starting to read to him. After she finished reading, he not only couldn't name the main character, but had no idea what the story was about. He also could not recall any part of the plot, setting or people. We began praying for a solution to this mystery. Then I read a book called Overcoming Dyslexia by Sally Shaywitz and many of the pieces of the puzzle fit. The markers gelled with the patterns my son displayed.

After meeting many reading specialists and veteran educators we came upon a recommendation to have him independently tested. His scores showed he was intelligent but unable to pull up vocabulary. Academically he read below a kindergarten level. We pulled him out of school for three hours a day for ten weeks to work on reading. He started a specialized intense reading program in October and ended in December. We saw a change in just a few sessions.

He responded well to their methods and found a way to circumvent the typical reading processes for one that worked with his type of brain. I was amazed. He was such a joyous boy, we all celebrated. We had a party with the theme from his first book called Sailing.

Presently in school at 5th grade this year, he is able to spend approximately half the day in regular education and half in special education. He still labors very hard to read. With reading being a major part of nearly every core subject, the struggle is far from over, but at least he is on his way.

Now it is time to delve into what he is really capable of doing. The public school system did not recognize what was going on with a Tommy for many of his formative years. It was only after we nearly completed the sessions at age nine with private specialized instruction, that his regular school began to address his reading problems. (In his current public school, Tommy had to train his special education instructors how to help him to read.) Consequently, we now recognize how vital a professional staff of qualified teachers can be in our son's education. With each new hurdle there are small moments we stop to breath and to cherish. My favorite quote from that time in our lives was when Tommy proclaimed, "I am just like everybody else, I can read!"

We come to you at this pivotal point in Tommy's development to guide him into what is a promising future. Our son will succeed wherever life takes him. I know this because I have seen him overcome great academic adversity. We wish for your school to become part of his journey as he develops into the extraordinary young man he is meant to be.

Please let us know what to do next. You mentioned shadowing in your last communication. Tommy is more than ready, so please call me at your convenience.

Sincerely,

Tommy's Mom and Advocate

Time's Line
By Beth Mostovoy

caveman scrawlings on the wall
disciples answering the Lord's call
from the light of truth to the most absurd
our existence measured and bound by words

a writer's tool a
dunce's stool
Shakespeare's Fool
an inkblot's pool
a ghetto's school
a drabble's drool
a kingdom's rule
a lover's duel

words that weave from life's vast spools
world's glittering array of jewels
stitching history's needlepoint of Time
inks of our labors bear fruit on the vine

a woman's coy
politician's ploy
Helen's Troy
a ship's ahoy
a mama's boy
a preacher's toy
an artist's noise
an athlete's poise

our candle, our light, our guiding flame
where all is different and all the same
heard or unheard, life's beginning and end
lie in the strokes of an inauspicious pen

The Twenty-Six Cent Message
By Judythe A. Guarnera

Ten years ago my brother Joe called from Ohio to tell me that Dad was seriously ill. After what had been labeled a successful back surgery, he had slipped into a coma. He was in intensive care and his prognosis was poor.

In California I made plane reservations, packed my bags and left for Florida. A dusting of snow on the tarmac in Denver delayed my landing and I missed my connecting flight. The next one wouldn't depart for ten hours. I desperately needed to be at Dad's bedside. Ten hours! I felt trapped in the vortex of a tornado with no possible escape.

With my thirty year marriage in chaos, I depended on Dad, my staunchest ally. Suddenly I remembered the book, "Peace, Faith and Healing, I had impulsively jammed into my carry-on. My breathing eased; something told me it would offer the lifeline I needed.

When I had first noticed the title in a bookstore, the information on the jacket intrigued me. The author, Dr. Bernie Siegel, believed that because he and other physicians focused on 'curing,' they felt personal failure if their patients died. To avoid burnout, he knew they had to change their thinking. Siegel's goal was to convince doctors to help patients find peace and quality in their lives, to help them "heal" rather than cure them.

I found a seat in the terminal and plunged into the first chapter. To fulfill his mission, Dr. Siegel traveled throughout the U.S. to share his message. In cabs from the airport he would often find a penny, which he saw as a sign that he would encounter an interesting person or event that trip. He was seldom disappointed.

Siegal's philosophy propelled him into new adventures. To celebrate turning fifty, he began training for a twenty-six mile marathon. On the day of his race, he felt nervous, but exhilarated. Halfway through he "hit the wall," the point at which long distance runners feel they can go no further.

I imagine he questioned his sanity, wondering why he thought his fifty year-old body could run a 26 mile marathon. Ready to quit, he saw a penny in the road. Just as he did when he found pennies in cabs, he took this as a sign and stepped to the side of the road. When it was clear, he darted out, scooped up the penny and continued running.

Before long fatigue returned; his resolve dissipated. Scanning the road for another penny, he spotted a quarter. Without breaking his stride, he picked it up. The proverbial light bulb went off. He had found coins totaling twenty-six cents; he was running a 26-mile marathon. Dr. Siegel had his message: he completed the race.

As I sat in the airport, I needed that kind of message. After an hour of waiting and no epiphany, I was back in the tornado vortex again. Thinking coffee might help, I joined the line at Starbucks. Someone jostled me and I dropped the book. As I bent to pick it up, I saw a penny, which I scooped up with a rush of elation. Coffee forgotten, I hurried back to my seat to continue reading.

For the rest of the trip, I read and re-read, looking for inspiration. Eighteen hours after I left home, my plane finally landed in Florida. Joe picked me up and we rushed to the hospital.

Once there I located a phone booth to let my kids know I had arrived and their grandfather's condition hadn't changed. As I deposited the coins, I noticed a quarter in the slot. Startled, I grabbed it, pulled the penny from my pocket and stared at the coins. I had found twenty-six cents, the same amount and in the same order that Dr. Siegel had. Just as he chose to believe the money was a sign he should complete the marathon, I chose to believe, since Dad was still alive, that somehow my presence would be instrumental in his survival.

In his book Dr. Siegal stressed the difference between curing and healing. If Dad had been cured, he would have arisen from his bed, dressed and gone home to live out his remaining years. Instead he spent the next eighteen months in hospitals and nursing homes. During that time I believe our family helped him to heal and to come to peace with this challenge life had given him. And that journey began in the hospital in Florida that winter day.

Dad watched his family grow in appreciation for each other. "I love you" took on a new significance, when we realized we had been given precious months to "heal" wounds, physical and emotional. Just before he died, Dad told my brother that now he was ready to go. This feat in itself was amazing, because Dad's ruptured esophagus had ended his ability to speak. Our family can verify that speaking is not the only way to communicate.

To this day, I enjoy finding pennies, which always gives me a thrill of excitement as I look for the special person, event or message that might be coming my way.

The Purple Paper Clip
By Elaine Mannon

Gathered images
Moments of unruly thoughts
A poet's harvest

The Reset Button
By Sally Shuncky-Hernandez

It is 7 a.m. and I am still pondering the topic of what I waste in excess. Oh, sure, I waste my extra cash on sale items such as seasonal chocolates and large bags of Doritos which I quickly devour but my biggest waste is TIME. I sit and think about many things and reach no conclusion while losing another hour of precious time. That is my resolution for this year – stop thinking about everything and take action!

Four years ago, Becky, a dear friend of mine moved from Millbrae, California to Atlanta, Georgia. Saturday, January 4 was her 90th birthday. Her wish was to celebrate with all her friends and family in one location. She wanted her grandchildren, the cousins, to know one another; her friends to meet her relatives and she wanted everyone to celebrate her wonderful life. The weekend party in Atlanta was a success; people came from California, Iowa, Nevada, Tennessee, Texas, and Georgia. There were 35 people present at the main dinner party on Saturday night and the toasts were numerous but each person mentioned Rebecca's ability to live life to its fullest each day. Her widowhood began forty years ago and she was forced into the work force after years of homemaking. She made a new life for herself and gathered more friends. One day, she told me that it was a good thing that she was forced into a new lifestyle.

The main thing I learned this weekend was that everyone loves her for her positive attitude and her active life style. She was born in Oklahoma, married a man in the Navy, and had three children in Florida and Washington DC. Then, she lived 48 years in California and now she is experiencing life in Georgia. Who knows what the next phase of her life will bring? She had a wonderful time celebrating her first 90 years. She sang, she danced (even twerked) and reminisced about some of the things she has witnessed over the years. It was a joyful evening and our happy noises brought a strange man from the bar into our private dining room. He introduced himself to the birthday girl. He was only 72 so she turned him down because he was too young. He didn't give up and returned once again before we left the restaurant at midnight. She has always been a magnet for people who want to share her joyful life. I have only known her for 20 years but we have shared many happy times at San Francisco Giants' games, traveling around Northern California, celebrations at the churches or in the local community. She encourages people to take positive actions even during funerals and memorials.

When I arrived home from the weekend trip, I immediately unpacked and began to straighten up some areas in the apartment. (One thing that keeps our friendship strong is that Becky and I both tend to be messy.) This weekend, a ll the guests stayed in a hotel but it warmed my heart when I visited her apartment on Friday and saw the messy floor that she left there before she moved into the hotel. Neither one of us is a neat freak. The floors of her house in Millbrae were never neat and my floors will never possess that quality either. This trip encouraged me neither to waste time cleaning nor waste time thinking about it but I will become more active with family and friends – the important things in life.

It is now 11 a.m. and time for me to begin my daily actions. Off to the library I head to print this tale, then to the post office to pick up the weekend mail and hopefully, I will arrive to class on time. For the next 357 days, my motto will be – don't think about doing something – do it!

My Life
By Ryann Murrin-Desouza

Life is hard.
You try to understand.
When you think you know what it's all about,
You're wrong.
You try to do something right,
And it ends up hurting someone.
All you can do is hope for the best.
Sometimes it works,
And other times it doesn't.
Life is just hard,
Look deep into life,
And do you really see what life is really all about,
No, you do not.
Understanding the way people are,
And the way they act.
Will take more out of you,
Because you're the only one that can understand you.
I hoped at times that things would start coming easy for me,
But all that happens was more problems are just up ahead of you.
Waiting for that special moment,
Wondering,
Hoping,
And understanding that one-day you will know what life is all about,
Heartache,
Problems,
Prejudice against anything that lives in this world that we call home.
Just be patient,
And what you've been looking for,
Will be right in the palm of your hand.
Where it has been all along.

Monologue After the Moon
Ellarine Lockie

> There fell a silvery-silken veil of light,
> With quietude, and sultriness, and slumber,
> Upon the upturned faces of a thousand roses . . .
> --Edgar Allan Poe

Queen of the Night, where
are you Goddess Luna
who used to slide
the silk of your arm through the
window across the bed to
massage stress into rest You who
can beacon a safe path for sailors
and nocturnal animals
Your knights of shining armor
in the sky echoing every epical act

Five nights straight now
your ghost steals the
sleep from my eyes
It stares with its own
anemic eyes and mocking smile
It slithers through the stars
A voyeur who can't
but watches others make love

Great Bear in Swedish folklore
says the dogs up there are so
afraid they bark
Even brilliant Sirius dims when
your imposter lifts its bald head
out of the darkness
Creeps under trees,
haunts houses and roams cemeteries
And then sheds its rotted rays over
the earth like a shroud

I would welcome even the
sinister dreams it whispers in my ears
rather than this offspring
creature Cannibal who rattles
the cage of my mind Swallows
the flesh of my sanity
The iron from my blood
Weariness which doesn't cease when the sun
god awakens the eastern sky

Come back Rishima/Mahina/Mizuki
and honor your eternal commitment to my
gender with your regal crown of light
You who govern the ocean's cycle along
with ours It's time—the creature is drooling
The red petals on the roses are dropping

Timeless Tear
By Carolyn Donnell

I sat upon a grassy hill, beneath a spreading oak
and watched as autumn sunlight turned green leaves to
         burnished gold.

A bubbling stream ran at my feet, its soothing sounds did flow.
The cool clean air did fill my lungs, refreshing flesh and soul.

A crackling in the brush did cause the reverie to end.
My eyes sought out the noise's source and spied the russet skin.

The Lord of forest dark and deep did pause to view his realm.
He turned and contemplated me with head, imperial.

I gazed into his sable eyes and saw my own face pale.
He showed me then the hunters' guns defaming glen and vale.

I shed one tear, and as I stared into those regal orbs,
I swear to you, I saw there too, a drop in his eye form.

And for one timeless moment two united in that wood.
Our minds, our hearts, our souls did blend. At last, I understood.

I heard a shot ring from the west. "Go, run the other way."
I shouted, pointing to the east to try to aid escape.

But sportsmen had their way today. Mere contest was their goal.
Those antlers, just a prize to place for viewing on a wall.

I went to see that royal head, to pay my last respects.
For one brief instant, I did wish the hunter's there instead.

The Café
Lisa Johnson

In the early nineteen fifties my mother had a café in a small town in Mississippi, on the main street, next to the garment plant. I don't recall the name or even if it had one. She borrowed the money to start the café from her father, an ex-farmer business-man, who had owned and run a couple of cafes. My father was a farmer, with no leaning toward business at all.

The drive to town from our farm took about fifteen minutes. On Saturdays Mother took my little sister and me to the café with her. We'd hang out there until early afternoon when it was time to go to the double feature at the Ritz Theater, a few blocks walk up town. Mother would give us each of us a dime and off we'd go. I looked forward to it. Movies were my favorite thing.

While we waited for show time, my sister chatted and charmed the customers in the café. She was an exceptionally pretty child with blonde curls and big blue eyes. At eight, she wasn't shy or withdrawn, as I was, at eleven. She was friendly and funny; she made fast friends with several customers, one of them a man who, years later, would become our step-father.

The café was large and square with wooden tables and chairs and a counter with stools. A big juke box against one wall spewedout melancholy country and western songs. At the front, near the windows that overlooked the street, stood a freezer filled with ice cream treats and flavored ices. One popular item was chocolate covered bananas that I remember especially, because one Saturday I ate so many of them I threw up on the ride back home tothe farm.

My mother had a cook named Annie, a pretty, light skinne Negro woman who made the best barbecued pulled pork on a bun, the juiciest hamburgers in town. Each noon Annie produced a special, like country fried steak with mashed potatoes, that sold out to the garment plant crowd. Sweet iced tea with lemon wedges was popular with that crowd; no hot tea drinkers that I recall. Of course, there was coffee. Not fancy coffees with a variety of names and brands, like we have today, just plain coffee served in a plain white mug or cup that went well with a slice of Mother's 's apple or pecan pie, peach orberry cobbler.

The café was open six days a week, closed on Sundays for rest and church going. My mother had a good little business. People liked her, her sweetness, her openness. She'd call out, "Come back now, you hear?" An expression that sounds corny and phony today, but back then it sounded, as she meant it, sincere and grateful.

And yet, she walked away from it, her thriving little café. She left the area late one Saturday night. Drove away with her daughters and refused to return. I suppose it's because she felt sad and trapped and didn't know what else to do but run. Her father and one of her brothers took over the café until it was sold.

On one of my trips back to the South as an adult, I drove slowly through town, straining to see—what? A memory come to life? I parked on Main Street, stepped up on the old high sidewalk. I walked past the section the locals used to refer to as Dago's Fish Fry, or the Eye-talion's place, run by one of the few Italian families in the area. They had olive toned skin and were a rarity: they were Catholic. I used to smell the fish frying half a block before we passed it on our way to the Ritz Theater. It's a second hand furniture store now. No scent of fish frying or any other food. In fact, most of the eating places in town are now fast food franchises.

A little further on I stopped where my beloved old Ritz Movie Theater stands, all boarded up. If you want to see a movie in a theater now you have to drive half an hour to the nearest town. I crossed over to the other side of Main, headed toward where the old garment plant used to be. The Big Yank Clothing chain took over, but later moved out of town. The old building was razed and in its space stands the Jitney Jungle Grocery Store.

Next door, in the building where my mother had her café, is a Laundromat. One of the locals informed me that no decent white person went in there to do their laundry. The following day I returned with my dirty laundry and went in there. I waited among a scattering of poor black people for my laundry to go through its cycles, trying to conjure up how this used to be a café.

The Children
By Margaret Vose

HONORABLE
MENTION

On a jewel-lit night
The bullet hit its mark
In the skull of Amoud
Nine-year-old dreamer
On the roof of his steamy house
                    in Baghdad.
In East Oakland
"Cha-Cha" smeared his face
With chocolate cake
On his third birthday.
He did not survive the daily abuse
                    and beatings.
On a corner of McArthur Boulevard
A tiny girl stood in a new dress and shiny shoes.
The Chevy plowed into Aliya
Her small lifeless hand
Held in despair by her mother
                    on the first day of school.
Oh, come broken children
To a room within my heart
Come rest in the soft light of love.
Outside my room grows a garden
Watered by my tears, nurtured by hope.

Come play in peace.

Social Insecurity
By Rudie Tretten

Two people – 200 years.

There they were seated in the back seat of our car as we drove from San Francisco Airport to Judy's home in the City.

And there on Judy's lap was Bill's light weight wheel chair. It couldn't fit in the trunk with Bill's very large suit case and carry-on bag.

Not our usual Monday evening, which is the way it should be when you are relationship facilitators for a 102-year-old man and his 98-year-old girl friend. In their own very personal way they provide confirmation of that advice I've heard from doctors over the last few years: "Keep on living."

They're doing it. Our two friends both graduated from Whitman College in Washington but he was several years ahead of her. They met 15 or so years ago at an alumni reunion. Since then they have been doing the San Francisco-Honolulu commute a couple times a year.

These are extraordinary human beings. Bill was early-on a successful inventor and manager. He has run several resorts in the Islands and has real estate and other investments. Whitman College has benefitted from his success. He is a widower with two children.

Judy's range of experiences include teaching on an Indian reservation, service in the Red Cross in World War II, modeling, teaching drama in a high school, and three Peace Corps assignments. There's more too, but the above makes the point. Both Judy and Bill are still sharp and clear thinking.

So Judy wants Bill to come and live with her in San Francisco. "Too cold," says Bill.

Bill wants Judy to come and live with him in Honolulu. "Too warm," says she.

Thus, the commute was born.

This time his arrival was set for March ninth. Then itwas changed to March fourteenth. Then it was changed to March twelfth. Flight 12 Hawaiian Airlines arriving at 10:00 PM.

We were there seven minutes early. The flight was 15 minutes late and the passengers did not begin to appear in the waiting room until 10:50.

Then off to the right coming from the elevator, he was rolling in our direction pushed by a porter. Judy saw him and bent by osteoporosis, cane in hand, she moved to greet him. And she did with a big hug while he rose a bit from his chair.

Two happy people. Two hundred years. Shirley and I walked over and shook hands with Bill in a somewhat more subdued welcome to the mainland.

On our way home from Judy's, we marveled at our friends.

"We're really lucky to have this experience," we agreed. "How many other people could have had a 200-year back seat with just two people?"

So a week later our financial advisor tells us that his wife's mother, age 93, has a boyfriend 103. Both still drive and have very active social lives, and attend a variety of shows, films, and multiple other events.

But all of this poses a problem for us. Longer life requires longer term financial planning. Social Security is not just a federal program. It is an effort to provide security for individuals and families who attain old age or suffer disabilities en route. This thought leads me to why 65 was selected as the retirement age that millions now surpass.

It was Otto Von Bismarck, leader of Germany in the 1880's who chose that age for retirement, in part, because few people lived to that age. When we created our system, 65 was still not a widespread attainment. Thus, the two hundred year back seat phenomenon brings us to an American dilemma. How do we make Social Security viable in a world of 90-plusers?

When Autumn Leaves Fall
Derrick Chinn

When autumn leaves fall, I dream of the wind in silence and all

The leaves were swept and held by the breeze
These leaves had fallen from old branches of trees
From roots well grounded in the soil of years
Before falling to earth as raindrops in tears

They climbed and rose and escaped with the wind
And twirled and turned and sank as they spin
And spun, around and around the skies and the ground
And sang with the stars without making a sound

One autumn day, she entered my eyes
Her beauty, so beautifully, rose as stars rising high
The moment I saw her I knew she was one
The one and only, for my clouds had parted
And gave rise to the sun

There were days and months and even a year
With her, I dreamed, a dream I held dear

The fall that came had gone away
With days gone by as a pendulum sways

San Bruno Centennial
By Maria Barr

March 23. 2014

On September 23, 2014, San Bruno, The City with a Heart, will be celebrate it's Centennial. A 100th anniversary is a very auspicious ccasion if one can imagine an hour glass counting the hours, days, years. Much has happened in those 100 years and, one cannot but wonder, what is in store for us in the next hundred years. Will we be living in cities here on earth...or in outer space? Sounds pretty far fetched, but with technology advancing so fast it could be a possible, especially since we will soon have a space station conducting a six month study on outer space habitation. Where ever we live in the future we should remember our great little city, as Aristotle said, "a great city should not be confused with a populous city." San Bruno as everyone knows is small, but it is the people and the unique beautiful area that inhabits our memories and makes San Bruno a great city.

Memories, stories, photographs have an important function in keeping alive the story of the people who settled here. Because there are so many people and so many things to remember I will mention only a few, starting with the Ohlones. Peace loving Indians who at one time, lived, loved, worked right here in the back yard of this Senior Center we are standing in today. The idyllic Indian life changed forever one day in 1769 when Gaspar de Portola stood on what is now Sweeney Ridge and glanced out at the mountains, the bay, the ocean and knew that this was a special area to claim for his Spanish king Carlos III. The area he saw before him was abundant in natural resources making it an ideal place to settle. In order do so, the land had to be surveyed and roads laid out. Bruno Hecate a Spanish surveyor looking up at a tall nearby mountain decided to name it after his patron saint, San Bruno, which is how our city got its name.

Of the early settlers Jose Antonio Sanchez, is important to our city's history because in 1835 the Mexican government granted him Rancho Buri, Buri, consisting of 15,000 acres which includes the area from San Bruno Mountain to San Francisco Bay. All this land at one time belonged to him and his family. Unfortunately, Sanchez died in 1845, and the land reverted to his nine heirs, however by the time the case was settled in 1872 not much land was left in the Sanchez family. To complicate things, in 1850 California had become part of the United States. The legal process was long and extremely costly, and the heirs lost most of their land to sheriff's auctions. Some of the land was sold to wealthy local men, who in turn sold at a profit to others who in turn sold it to someone else for even more profit. D. O Mills and Charles Lux bought large portions of the Sanchez's land and became very prosperous ranchers in the area. Custodio Silva who who was employed by these two men saved his money and in 1871 he purchased 29.21 acres near interstate 380 on the El CaminoReal from a descendants of Sanchez for $ 5000.00 in gold, land he used to buy, break and sell horses.

By 1887 the area had changed dramatically as people bought, then resold and consolidated the land into various parcels. San Bruno was now owned by several hardworking pioneer families who were the real architects of what we see today. In the early 1970s it was my good fortune to work with Gordon Silva a grandson of Custodio Silva, when I worked for Pacific Bell on Montgomery street. Gordon had lost a leg when he served in WWII, but people would not know it by looking at him, tall and dignified. He never mentioned his mishap to me. What he did talk about was his recollections of his grandfather's ranch, about horses and about his home on San Luis Ave. Years later at the local library I discovered a book, images of America, San Bruno, written by a local historian Darold Fredrick's where I found a photograph of Gordon astride a mule on his grandfather's ranch, taken in 1916. There is another photograph of a still young and handsome Gordon taken at a formal dinner at his family's home. This same home he offered to sell to me around mid 1970s, when he was getting ready to retire, but of course I could not afford it.

In 1976, however, I was able to afford a home on Concord Way in the community of Crestmoor Park where my husband, my daughter and I lived happily for many years. Our daughter Desiree, attended Engval and Crestmoor schools and later Capuchino High School and is now an educator. We lived an idyllic life until I lost my husband in late 2006. My loss devastated me, so I joined the San Bruno Creative Writers Group. I started writing to help me cope with my grief and to rebuild my life.

One day while sitting in the middle of my family room I heard a loud boom and felt my house shake. I thought it was an earthquake. When the loud rumble and tremendous heat wouldn't stop, then I thought it was an airplane crashing on my roof. It was hard for me to breath, the heat kept getting hotter and hotter and I started to loose consciousness. By the time I realized I was in danger of losing my life I ran outside, after several attempts I was able to climb my back yard fence only to be trapped in some bushes. A young man chasing a dog on their deck saw me, he ran to lift me up out of the bushes and he and his girlfriend drove me to safety. Because my neighbors cared to help me, I survived the San Bruno Explosion of September 10, 2010. This explosion ravaged my community. During this devastation I was helped by many of my friends, neighbors, even strangers as far as Japan. What I learned from the experience is what had made San Bruno great—common ordinary people, people who had stayed to become family, friend, and neighbors who helped people.

I regret that at the time I worked with Gordon Silva, I did not write down his stories, because now working by memory I know that I missed out on capturing more of his knowledge of the history of San Bruno. Fred Beltramo, a local photographer, on the other hand had the presence of mind in his lifetime to take many pictures of early San Bruno that captured some of the people who made San Bruno a great city. In retrospect I believe it was not the leaders, who worried about votes, preoccupied with agendas, or the wealthy who bought and sold at great profit, but the common ordinary people who loved, lived and stayed to raise families whom we remember. They were the people who settled here, built businesses that sustained their families, friends, and neighbors. They were citizens who carried out the vision of the city, who worked to make our community, our churches our schools efficient, effective places where their future generations learn to persevere the landmarks of their elders and continue to strengthen the roots of home.

In the next hundred years even if outer space is the new home, we should remember the people who touched us. The people then and now who dwell in our memories. The community lucky enough to call San Bruno home and has every reason to be proud. With pride we offer thankful salute to our, City With a Heart. Long Live SAN BRUNO.

Clean-Up in Rwanda
By Ellaraine Lockie
(in a Villanelle)

Outside the church, bodies stack waist high
Draining fluids flood ankles as you wade
Only bee hum and birdsong to ask why

You can't because maggots, bloat and flies have
conspired in your throat to blockade
Outside the church, bodies stack waist high

You can't breathe either, as there's no good-bye
to the putrefied stench that invades
Only bee hum and birdsong to ask why

Dogs cleaned first with teeth like Samurai
Trench rats assemble in banquet brigades
Outside the church, bodies stack waist high

Cows, pigs and chickens meander by corpses in
a role reversal parade
Only bee hum and birdsong to ask why

Everything on the ground wrapped awry
The bombshell of shock a silent grenade
Outside the church, bodies stack waist high
Only bee hum and birdsong to lullaby

Our Past Is Made Up of All Our Best Efforts
By Judythe A. Guarnera

The door slammed. I yanked it open and watched my husband of almost thirty years, tromp across the front lawn. As he opened his car door, he looked back as I stood silhouetted in the doorway.

"You're wrong you know," he said so quietly I had to strain to hear. "There was never anyone else, but you. No one. Ever." With those words, he disappeared into his car. Perhaps symbolically, the car sputtered and shook before the engine turned over and he pulled away.

Tears cascaded down my cheeks. I was once again the twenty-year-old who had fallen in love with the slender young man with curly black hair, soft brown eyes, a tender, but tentative smile, who was exactly one year older than me. A birthday wasn't the only thing we shared. We both worked hard, loved our families, espoused similar political beliefs, loved children and knew how to live within a meager budget.

In four years we had bought our own house, had three of our four children and established a comfortable life style. Our frugality all owed me to be a stay-at-home mom and him to be the bread-winner. We made a good team. On our ninth anniversary we conceived our fourth child, who appeared nine months to the day later on our shared birthday. Fate seemed to be giving our marriage a stamp of approval.

My husband gained prestige and acknowledgement at his job while he pursued a college degree. He became the first college graduate in his family. When I expressed pride in his accomplishment, his eyes flattened and darkened with something I couldn't identify. I believe this was the first time I suspected all was not well. Later I realized there had been other signs I'd ignored.

Our children and their activities kept us busy and distracted us from working on our relationship. We became more financially secure, but failed to notice the seeds of discontent threaded throughout our marriage. Once the children completed their education and secured jobs, I had more free time than I wanted. I decided to step back onto a road I had abandoned when I married and gave up my dream of a college degree and a career. I found the challenges of college stimulating. Although it wasn't my intention, my choice to complete my Bachelor's degree had a profound negative effect on my marriage.

Once begun, there seemed to be no turning back. Again, relying on hindsight, I wondered that fateful day as I stood in the doorway, watching my husband drive away, how we had ever fallen in love and why we had stayed together as long as we had.

To understand how this dilemma developed, I must point out where our paths diverged. I was gregarious, outspoken, loved a good conversation, especially one with a suitable amount of controversy to jack up the interest level. Quick to say I love you, never able to stay angry, optimistic to an annoying fault, my husband, was my polar opposite—quiet, introverted, someone who refused to discuss religion or politics, content to sprawl on the couch and watch TV during the few hours he wasn't working, going to school or playing sports. I found itour difficult to engage and sustain him in a conversation of any length.

John had a guttural laugh that seemed reluctant to emerge. I tried to make him laugh, but he withheld his laughter and I began to wonder what else he withheld.

We argued about disciplining our children, what they should and shouldn't do. And we blamed each other when we didn't approve of their behavior. The tenuous thread that held us together showed serious signs of fray. Angry words replaced words of love.

We made deals to get through activities. When days had gone by without any significant words passing between us, we'd turn on the smiles when company came or a work-oriented event required us to attend together.

My studies intensified as I neared graduation. When I began working, I switched from roasts and potatoes to microwaveable meals. But we ate separately. I began to wonder if he had found someone else.

"Are you having an affair?" I asked one day, my gut wrenching.

"Yeah. What's for dinner?" he replied, head buried in the refrigerator. I never knew if his answer was fact, but I realized later he was trying to tell me our relationship was over.

When we separated, angry words became the tone de jour. We battled endlessly through the long divorce. Each of us took steps to move on and our new lives fleshed out. But the infrequent contact we had continued to hit the near-explosion range.

All the paperwork that accumulated in our divorce, served as one big tally sheet of wrongdoing that I carried in my head, long after the decree was final. That tally sheet created a major roadblock preventing me from moving on.

I joined a divorce support group. Although the support helped, I felt stuck. The group featured speakers and therapy to help us begin to rebuild our lives. What one speaker said grabbed my attention.

"Repeat after me," she began, 'in my marriage I did the best I could.'" I did as requested and heard the words echoed by others in the room.

"Now," she added, "say, 'my spouse did the best he or she could do.'" This time there was an audible silence.

The heck he did, I thought, and imagined others thinking the same. Because she had oozed compassion and understanding when she began her talk, the occupants of the room stayed in their chairs, albeit still in silence. She continued to make the case that, up to that moment, all of us had done the best we could. "After all," she asked, "who would choose to do the worst?"

I left the room that night, intrigued, but not convinced. It took a while before I could embrace that idea and forgive myself and my husband. He wasn't the best husband for me and I wasn't the best wife for him. But I had loved him and had intended to do my best. And I believe his intentions had been the same.

Only when I acknowledged that did forgiveness become an option.

And my past, sorry as my efforts might have been, was the best I could do at that time.

The speaker reminded us not to use the past as an excuse for poor future behavior. Seeing the limitations of my past is a strong motivation to do better in the future. My past is indeed, made up of all my best efforts.

Mystic Grandma
By Elizabeth Fajardo

Every visit from Grandma Ester was as magical as the illumination of the full moon over time and space-electric, captivating and enduring. Within seconds of her auspicious arrival from distant realms, Abuelita, as I called my maternal grandmother, would transform a humdrum day into a world of wonder. Words uttered with an unquenchable spirit by a woman who seemed ageless, became vibrant lyrics enticing a little girl to grow wings and fly across the shoulders of trees too large to climb, yet close enough to touch in dreams. The stars were no longer remote sparks, but rather stepping stones to Heaven, reachable at a moment's notice by just believing. During my darkest days, in the wake of my father's passing, the memories of my precious, unconventional "granny" kept me warm, for it was her perpetual optimism that gave my life purpose.

Ester's own history—a fairy tale in the making—was eclipsed by the murder of her "amor verdadero" or true love. Adolfo, her first husband. The unrelenting grip of this tragedy would impact all future decisions made on behalf of the family. It was as if the fatal bullet had severed two hearts, leaving behind a chokehold of anguish in the excesses of her unsettled mind.

Statuesque and slender, easy to smile, sporting a bob haircut in shades of cinnamon brown, and an olive-skinned face graced with great almond eyes and cheekbones high as the sky, she was a ravishing beauty from head to toe, in her prime. Born to the limelight, Abuelita's every step was framed with a demure demeanor. The flexibility of movement and poise alone could've propelled her to prima ballerina status. Instead, these attributes fueled the passion behind a single mother of two girls.

When Abuelita was present, my vision was directed at her hands—delicate fingers meant for dropping hankies in the company of chivalrous suitors—but ultimately obliged to carry the load for three generations of women. Moreover, she possessed an unflinching look of mischief, so often masked by polite chitchat and attentiveness. Though able to emerge in any walk of life as refined as a royal, there was something about the way Grandma glimpsed at onlookers or out at the world in general. On the surface, in bright sunlight, her eyes appeared lucid and enchanting. In the dead of night, an irrepressible melancholy overshadowed her previously opulent aura. Only the recitation of Adolfo's love letters could serve as consolation.

The black turban should've been the tip-off that Abuelita was no ordinary elder. My avant garde grandmother was a force of nature with a gypsy soul who yearned for adventure. Throughout my childhood, she would leave for months at a spell en route to El Salvador. To my delight, Grandma handily came home to attend my first wedding. Her advice before I walked down the aisle, articulated in Spanish, was, "Sigue tu corazon,"or simply, to follow my heart.

I was intoxicated with anticipation as the Matriarch of Wishes drew on her colorful background to charm me with tales of days gone by, describing scenes encapsulated within a crystal ball, visible only to a believer of the unforeseen. Paths of soft pink rose petals doused the countryside with hypnotic perfume, while handmaidens frolicked nearby, in perfect view of a glorious castle. Luminous dawns out of the mists of time created opportunity. I held fast to every new account, awaiting the outcome. Time after time, the resolution remained the same, either the boy won the gal or a wedding ensued. Even so, I deemed each narrative to be fresh, which in the best-case scenario, continued way past bedtime. Mostly, I was entranced by the card readings.

Some say, immediately following the killing, the search for answers acquainted Grandma with the ethereal. Early on she was known as the mystic, or in close circles "Senora Ester, la Magnifica." The title was given in jest, and was rarely referred to outside the premises. Yet, her reputation preceded her. It took only a simple request by visitors and Abuelita was always game. With a twinkle in her eye and a quick shuffle of the deck, the code for all takers was revealed. Spoken discreetly within the language of love, our resident fortune teller's answers were revered in the court of the faithful.

Amid the scent of Mom's mouthwatering flan pervading the entire house and cards dancing on the table like flickering fireflies, I was bewitched beyond imagining. The instant the King of Hearts landed alongside his matching female counterpart, it was made known that a betrothal was about to take place. Upon hearing this news, the correspond ing recipients, waiting with bated breth, erupted into cheers. I turned to see the expression on Abuelita's face and elicited a wink for my efforts. It was just another Saturday afternoon.

Sundays were reserved for church. Senora Ester shed the mystical veneer and the turban for a mantilla and the tempest of desires became subdued for the religious services. I never questioned the motives or the enactments I was privy to on the weekends. My thoughts were, "Didn't everybody's grandma read cards?

However, my doting grandmother had less of a mind for business and inevitably lost the family fortune. She remarried, gave birth once more, and divorced. After scraping together her meager savings, this ingenue turned survivor, entered San Francisco by bus in 1945 as an unemployed, unaccompanied young lady with two daughters in tow. Due to Grandma Ester's perseverance -acquiring nanny job after nanny job, and pinching pennies-the tiny family of three would come to live the American dream.

In Grandma's eulogy, I reminded loved ones to follow their hearts, as she advocated. Through Abuelita's experience and subsequent stories, I learned to construct meaningful phrases, and to evoke indelible images, inspired by the visionary who brought them to life. What I discovered, best of all, was to let go of fear because no matter what the cards hold, if you believe in yourself, anything can happen.

If It's Good, It'll Find a Home
By Kevin Arnold

For those who weren't writing back in the nineteen eighties, it's hard to imagine what a broad shadow Raymond Carver cast across the writing world. His work and articles about him seemed to appear everywhere, including The Paris Review, Atlantic, Poetry, and The New Yorker. In his final year, 1988, he was in inducted into the American Academy and Institute of Arts and Letters.

Ray's respect for the poor shone through Bruce Weber's New York Times Magazine profile: "Until I started reading these reviews of my work, praising me, I never felt the people I was writing about were so bad. . . . The waitress, the bus driver, the mechanic, the hotel keeper. God, the country is filled with these people. They're good people. People doing the best they could."

He showed up at the summer fiction class I was taking at Stanford. Over six feet but with a markedly gentle presence, Ray seemed reclusive and confident at the same time. He had recently broken into Esquire with a short story called "Neighbors," which he read for us from the freshly printed magazine with a slick cover.

The story is about a couple who, when asked to look after an apartment across the hall, enjoy separate, secret erotic lives there. The man tries on women's clothing; the woman returns with suspicious lint on the back of her sweater. The sentences were like Hemingway's, short and declarative, subject-verb-object, but there was warmth that belied the tale he was telling. Sex was approached in a non-judgmental way, yet without titillation. It was unlike any story I'd heard before.

After his reading Ray sat on a desk in the front of the class and talked to us. He seemed to have done everything in the writing world—attended the renowned fiction workshops at Iowa before his Stegner, edited a literary magazine, and was charming, accessible, and encouraging to boot. If Ray Carver could go from articles in Popular Mechanics to a story in Esquire, he told us flatly, any of us could. He felt indebted to the writing life and wanted each of us to experience it firsthand. Back when stories were sent through the mail, he said, "Send your stories off and when you get them back re-read them, fix them up and send them off again. But do a favor to whoever has to open the envelope. Pass up those metal clasps, they ruin our fingers."

He told us he sent his stories out not when they were finished, bcause they never were, but when he just couldn't stand to have them around any more. I -hadn't yet heard Leonardo Da Vinci's pithy, "art is never finished, always abandoned"; I sat wide-eyed. Ray noticed one sign that he was getting close to sending his stories off was when he found himself revising a word change back to his initial choice.

He was convinced good work would be published. "You hear about editors publishing each others' work, and that you have to have gone to a certain school or whatever, and that's not a good way to think. It can become an excuse. Do your best work. That's where to spend yourself. Then send it out. If it's good, it'll find a home."

We adjourned to a bar, the Winery, at the corner of El Camino and California Avenue in Palo Alto. Chuck and Ray knew the bartender, and quickly they had hard liquor drinks in front of them at the bar.

Soon I was introduced to Maryann Burk Carver, Ray's wife. I surmised she must have come in from a nearby town to join her husband, but after they said hello with a light kiss, they didn't sit together. I ended up chatting with her at a little table in the corner. Later I would learn this was the woman who went to the head of the Iowa workshops to say they were dismissing Ray's work too easily, the same Maryann who this seemingly gentle man would physically abuse. She was also the woman who, more than thirty years later, would write a well-crafted, generous memoir of her life with him, What It Used to Be Like: A Portrait of My Marriage to Raymond Carver. The title would have seemed absurdly pretentious back then. Except for the enthusiasm the instructor showed about Ray's arrival, neither I, nor anyone it seemed, knew Ray was someone who would eventually be referred to as the American Chekov.

Maryann was attractive, and as unprepossessing as Ray. If I had to characterize her in one word, it would be "genuine." I was immediately drawn to her and my respect for her has grown through the years. As her bushy-haired husband knocked back drinks at the bar with the sun still bright in the window behind him, she thought this was great, this writing life Ray was living, something to which I should aspire.

Ray's life started changing, dramatically, not longafter that. Probably the biggest change was that he quit drinking at the same time that his national reputation grew immensely. He was widely published. For example, inone year, 1981 he was published in the Atlantic, the Hudson Review, the LA Times Book Review, Nation, the New Republic, mentioned in Newsweek, New York magazine, written up in the New York Times, Saturday Review, written up in Time, published in Washington Post Book World, and anthologized with a Pushcart Prize.

When we learned he would be teaching at Centrum, a summer workshop at Port Townsend, Washington, my wife and I put in applications and were accepted. She drew Gordon Lish as her workshop leader. Gordon was cutting quite a figure in New York, calling himself Captain Fiction. I requested, and was assigned to, Ray's group.

I bought two of his books, both collector's items now: Put Yourself in My Shoes (Capra, 1974) and Furious Seasons (Capra, 1977). I didn't spend much time with Furious Seasons, which seemed to be too much about fishing for my taste at the time, but the latter book fascinated me; I read it over and over. It was a chapbook with only one story, that of a man who leaves his day job to write, and the strange way people react to his decision. The host and hostess recited bizarre stories, tales that they think the newly liberated writer should integrate into his work, each trying to outdo the other.

In addition to our morning seminars, each participant had a private meeting with their workshop leader to review our manuscripts. A few days before the conference I had typed out something completely new, some wet clay that Ray Carver might sculpt into greatness. He'd had it for a few days before I visited him in his apartment in officer's quarters.

I still remember the bay view from the kitchen table where we worked. He started right in on my manuscript. I would have been devastated by even one word of Carver's criticism, but he never gave any. Instead Ray was overwhelmingly pleasant and curious about my work, which I was busily dismissing with talk about the overcast Port Townsend weather. He'd taken my work much more seriously than I'd taken it myself. He examined every sentence to see if it was doing my bidding. He'd lectured on how sentences must do what the writer wanted them to do, and not anything else. The problem was I wasn't sure yet what I wanted of the poor sentences. I think he must have noticed my reticence to defend the text, because it seemed that a light went on for him.

"So, [my first name]," he asked. "How many times has this been through the typewriter?"

"It's pretty much a first draft," I said. "I wish I'd brought something more finished."

Almost ten years had passed since our first meeting; his life had changed dramatically. He'd joined AA and opened up to the existence of God. His stories took on a more hopeful tone. He'd separated from Maryann; a divorce was rumored. I worked to discuss some of these things rather than my dashed-off manuscript.

He told me he was headed to Tacoma the next day to see Maryann and the children they shared, a trip he didn't seem to look forward to.

"I read a bit about your father," I said. "My Dad's broke too. It's been a little different, because he had an education and some money once, but he's broke now. I'm sending him small checks."

He nodded sympathetically. "Raymond [his father] didn't have a suit for his funeral. They put him in someone else's sport coat."

My situation quickly paled. "Fathers." I shook my head. "We work so hard to go further than they did. I guess we have, though."

"Don't concentrate on how you're doing better than your dad if you want to write. A writer has to write from . . ." He raised his hands as if they were growing out of the earth, with open palms and fingers spread. " . . . from, you know, from underneath." He whispered the word as if it were a secret, in a way that didn't invite comment.

Besides the organic connotation, I think Ray meant sociologically from underneath as well. He didn't have much interest in characters "on top of things." Ray ended the session with a bit of generosity that can best be described as breathtaking, especially considering the quality of the work I showed him.

"When you have a story really, really ready, you can put my name on it," he said. "Tell the editor Ray Carver wants him or her to look at it. Only use my name with something finished though, twenty or thirty times through the typewriter at least. And get the editor's name right, even if it takes a phone call."

I never took him up on it. When I finally had a few things possibly worthy, it was a little late. I smile when I imagine an editor today reading a cover letter inscribed, "Raymond Carver thought you might be interested in this."

I took a snapshot of him that day, which I framed and mailed to him. He responded with a typically effusive thank you note.

When I met his second wife, Tess Gallagher, about a year after his passing, she told me the photo now sits on the bureau in her bedroom.

Six or seven years after the workshop, shortly before Ray died, he was invited to Stanford as part of the prestigious Lane Lecture Series. He looked a picture of health in a beige-colored suit with a blue shirt and tie, ready to address the thousand people gathered in the lecture theater. There were those in the audience who knew, despite his appearance, he was facing the tough odds of lung cancer. He read two stories from his later, fuller work that night.

First he read "Cathedral," the title story to the volume that brought nominations for the National Book Critics Circle Award and the Pulitzer Prize. Then he read "Elephant," a story about a middle-aged recovering alcoholic. The narrator, who finally has his financial act together, finds himself sending checks to his kids, his mother, and now his brother. At the end, the protagonist saves a few pennies by walking to work. A fellow worker comes by and picks him up in a late-model car he's just bought on credit. In this complexly crafted story about lack of money and redemptive trust, Ray Carver ends with having the two characters "[screaming] down the road in his big unpaid-for car."

Carver's last few years were filled with fame and fortune. Ray won big awards, most notably he was the first winner of the Mildred and Harold Strauss Living Award that gave him $35,000 per year tax free back when that would go considerably further then than today. The awards allowed him time to write; he found a solid partner in Tess Gallagher, whom he married five days before his death; his stories were published with some regularity in The New Yorker and translated around the world; and he was lionized whenever he read, as he was that night at Stanford.

People grew quiet as he read "Elephant." When he read its last line—that unpaid-for car—the auditorium was completely silent, stunned as if we knew what a presence we might lose. He laid the book down on the podium and looked up into the crowd of faces, a long, quiet moment, and then the room burst into applause. We rose to our feet. I'd heard he'd received scant attention when he'd been a student at Iowa or a fellow at Stanford, so it was wonderful to see him in such glory now. Ray made a purposeful exit, row by row. When he saw someone he knew, he would wait at the end of the row and his friend would come out for a hug. When he got to my row, he looked over invitingly as if to say, Kevin, come.

My wife, who would later earn a Stegner fellowship herself on her way to becoming a successful novelist, encouraged me to stand. In the intervening years we'd had two kids. I'd taken on more responsibility in my corporate job and published my first short story and two poems. Still, standing up just seemed too forward to me. Except for the photo and a note or two, Ray and I hadn't communicated in years. So I remained rooted to the chair, smiling shyly. Ray shrugged and moved up to the next row, where a woman in a black dress and jangling silver bracelets leaped up to hug him. I watched him—

kind, generous, grateful—and I felt like one of the tongue-tied characters of his stories, incapable but aware.

Note: Publication dates were taken from http://www. poetryfoundation.org/bio/raymond-carver#poet

Fixing Flipper - The Journey of a Dolphin Activist
By Erin Dienzer

It's hard to imagine it now, but 40 years ago some of the only "interaction" we had with animals (other than the family pet) was via television. And in many of those TV shows, animals like Lassie and the equine Mr. Ed were anthropomorphized into our collective vision of how we thought they felt.

Back in the 1960s, Richard (Ric) O'Barry, working for the Miami Seaquarium, took several dolphins from the wild and trained five of them to play the role of "Flipper" in the popular television series of the same name. The show, and the five dolphins who played Flipper, were an instant hit.

Flipper swam "his" way right into our hearts as week-after-week we watched the loyalty, bravery and humor he brought to the lives of his adopted TV family.

But something happened along the way: O'Barry began to notice an unhappiness amongst his animal actors, culminating in what he believes was the suicide of Cathy, one of his trained dolphins.

"You have to understand," said O'Barry in a 2009 interview," dolphins are not automatic air breathers like we are. Every breath for them is a conscious effort. She looked me right in the eye, took a breath, held it — and she didn't take another one. She just sank to the bottom of the water. That had a profound effect on me."

On the first Earth Day in 1970, O'Barry found his second calling: creating The Dolphin Project, an organization dedicated to freeing captive dolphins.

"Dolphins are free-ranging, intelligent, and complex wild animals, and they belong in the oceans, not playing the clown in our human schemes," notes O'Barry on The Dolphin Project website. So over the course of several years, he felt compelled to free 14 of them living in captivity.

As you might imagine, his actions weren't always greeted with an enthusiastic welcome. Many people in the billion-dollar animal entertainment industry were openly hostile towards him and considered his tactics illegal and threatening. To that, O'Barry has responded, "They're in this for the money. Take it away, and they'll quit."

But as O'Barry was soon to discover, another more insidious story lay behind the trade and trafficking of captive dolphins. And once O'Barry realized what was going on, he founded a different organization with the purpose of not just releasing captive dolphins, but to keep them from ever being taken from the wild in the first place.

Save Japan Dolphins (SJD) is the result of that desire. As its Campaign Director, O'Barry undertook the challenge of stopping the kidnapping of dolphins from the wild (in a remote part of Japan called Taiji) for sale to amusement parks, and the subsequent slaughter of those that weren't wanted. As he notes on the SaveJapanDolphins.org site, "Most people in Japan don't have any idea that (a) dolphin slaughter is even happening. If we can spread the word around the world — and especially in Japan — we can expose the secret of Taiji and force the Japanese government to stop it."

Exposing corrupt business practices (or the inhumane treatment of others) is best achieved via vital media outlets, and one of those outlets is the movie theater. O'Barry partnered with Louie Psihoyos, executive director of the Oceanic Preservation Society (OPS), and the rest is cinematic history. Working covertly (and with the looming possibility of arrest and imprisonment) to film the rounding up, selling off and slaughtering of bottlenose dolphins in Taiji, the movie that resulted from their undercover trips to Japan was The Cove.

The Oscar-winning film has raised public awareness on a host of issues: the 'dirty side' of the captive dolphin business; mercury poisoning in marine mammals and where the butchered meat ends up; the health of the world's oceans; and the annual dolphin slaughter in Taiji.

The Cove started reaching bigger and bigger audiences, and — with petitioning efforts — was also screened at the Tokyo Film Festival. As a result of the increase in media attention, as well as the support that OPS and SJD have received, The Cove had the positive impact resulting in the city of Taiji calling for a temporary ban on the annual dolphin drive off their coast. But that was only a temporary reprieve; the capture and slaughter of these magnificent marine mammals continues. So, in turn, does O'Barry's fight.

What began as one man's relationship with five trained dolphins in Florida continues today with his crusade to end our view of these magnificent beings as animals simply put here for our collective amusement. For many of the world's dolphins who would otherwise have no voice, they have Ric O'Barry.

Dotted Swiss and Cookies
By Louise Lenahan Wallace

Why are you involved in the American Cancer Society's Twenty-Four Hour Relay for Life? The question put to our County's relay board members several weeks previously whispers into my memory.

Friday – 6:00 p.m. This early June evening, the sun has not yet set over Civic Field, but a brisk breeze blowing from the Straits causes both the American flag and the Cancer Society's flag to whip out at the top of the flagpole, and creates a flurry of jacket- and-hat seeking. The first hour of our Twenty-Four Hour Light of Hope Relay for Life has just begun with a "Survivor's Lap." All participants on this round have battled, and so far won, their personal fight with cancer. White-haired, middle-aged, and young, each knows with heart-deep knowledge why he or she is involved with the Relay. They complete the route and depart the grassy path, some slowly, some exuberantly, all with an inner triumph only they, the survivors, can know. The rest of the assemblage steps out to take their turn about the white-chalked oval. For the next twenty-four hours at least one member of each of the thirty teams present will circle the one-sixth mile track to raise money for fighting cancer.

The area inside the track looks like the aliens have finally landed. Where earlier in the day the only inhabitants were quarreling crows and speculative seagulls, tents have sprung up like dandelions after rain. Large, small, sturdy-enclosed and open-air drafty, each dwelling's décor is crafted to reflect the personalities of those making their statements against cancer.

The outpatient clinic's team has taken up residence in a "M*A*S*H" tent, complete with red cross, camouflage, and "Best Care Anywhere" sign. Their recruits have donned scrub gowns and caps for their trek around the track.

The realtors display signs advertising their space as "For Sale"; "To Rent"; "By Appointment Only." Mouth-watering aromas drift from this area. Joe is once again barbecuing hot dogs and hamburgers for all comers.

Twilight drifts over the field. Teams circle. The full moon rises. Clouds scud across its silver expanse so the area below is now brightly lit, now shadow-muted.

11:00 p.m. The "Candlelight Memorial" Ceremony temporarily displaces the circling routine. Individuals remembering a loved one who died of cancer, or celebrating the victory of one who battled and survived cancer, purchase candles in white bags marked with the loved one's name. These bags are placed around the track and the candles lit. Tonight 768 candles glow as the stadium lights are extinguished and sixty seconds of silence is observed for the persons so remembered. Each relay participant then walks the track, paying respect to the names shining there. The trek begins in almost- silence. Only the whisper of feet passing on the dew-damp grass and a heart-torn sob are audible. From the stadium above, lit candles in white bags spell out CURE. Our goal. Our hope. Down below, in the circle of shifting light, people walk silently, each one caught up in thoughts and memories, each one powerfully contributing, in a very private way, to the quality of the dream that one day cancer will be eradicated.

In the quiet, with the earnest dedication of the relayers warm upon the cool night air, the question once again rises from deep within me: Why are you involved with the Relay for Life?

The answer floats up on a patchwork quilt of memories. I am here for Vicky. And for Lee ...

Vicky. Kindergarten forty-five years ago. Of all my classmates, Vicky comes clearly to mind. White-blonde hair, wide blue eyes, a pale, heart-shaped face. She frequently wore a dress that was her favorite, and mine, too. Red, with a big sash and raised white dots scattered over its surface—dotted Swiss, I know now, but not then. I only knew how lucky Vicky was to wear a dress like that.

Occasionally absent from class, when Vicky came she often slept long past rest hour. Miss Adams always let her sleep, and made sure that we didn't disturb her. During recess, the rest of the class released outdoors, Vicky sometimes stayed inside and I—treat of treats—was allowed to stay with her. Both painfully shy, we had a grand time standing on chairs to draw on the blackboard, giggling, content in our world of two while the rest of the class rampaged outside.

Vicky's absences became more frequent. When she came, she slept nearly the whole time. Her mother, picking her up after school, talked to Miss Adams, their murmured conversations including a funny long word beginning l-u-k-e.

One day Vicky left school and didn't come back. I never saw her again. No one ever explained why. Years later, I learned the funny word spoken by her mother and Miss Adams. "Leukemia." I finally knew why Vicky left school and didn't come back.

In our kindergarten picture, Vicky smiles shyly at the camera. The black-and- white print does not pick up the color of her dress, but I know it is red with raised white dots, and I remember how lucky I thought she was, as we giggled and drew pictures on the blackboard.

Lee. My mother's friend, confidante, and bridge partner. Health-conscious before it was fashionable, Lee watched her diet carefully, even refusing dessert cookies offered by the bridge party hostess.

Stricken by an inoperable brain tumor, her health deteriorated rapidly. Mom visited her daily in the hospital. The last time, Lee—fragile, exhausted, bald—took Mom's hand. "You know, Della," she whispered, "if I'd known it was going to turn out this way, I would have eaten the damned cookies."

Why am I involved in the American Cancer Society's Relay for Life and Memorial Ceremony? For two shy little girls, who agreed to be friends for life, and for the giggles they shared forty-five years ago in a kindergarten classroom... For two bridge-loving women, whose friendship reached across many years and many card hands, and of whom my Mom says softly, "I still miss her...."

Ode to a Canyon
By Hannah Giarrusso

A desert canyon
All to myself
Red walls shining away
It's a different kind of wealth.

Some green-red-blue beauty
Mixed in the heart
It's something you just can't buy
All in a shopping cart.

And when I look at those walls
In midst of that heat
I hear the bird call
Oh, that chirping so sweet!

I still see those trees
That God tinted green
And I wonder oh how
Could He have made such a beautiful scene?

I look up at those clouds
Those puffballs snow-white
And the shadows they make
They dance like a kite.

The train toot-toots
As it pulls into the station
The owl hoot-hoots
Throughout the whole nation.

As the sun comes up
And the tumbleweed blows
The walls reveal the secrets
That nobody knows.

The place where death can be a step away
Or where it can be a million.
The place where I oh-so want to stay
For many years - a billion!

Up to Hermit's Rest
Sometimes on the bus
We hike up there with zest
We hike up without fuss.

Those majestic walls and mesas

The crevices and buttes
I look out at the sun
As I'm warmed by its rays.

In the lodge and by the fire
In the gift shop with those books
I have such a desire
To discover the Canyon's nooks.

The sun sets in the Canyon
Leaving just a small trace
Of the red on those walls
And a hint of white lace.

Leaving the Land of Wonder
I look back at the sky
I see the last condor.
He takes off to fly.

And then I know
That in the Grand Canyon
Although I may leave
My spirit will remain
Here, on this very eve.

Is it Too Late?
By Jo Carpignano

Why do we shrug
when nature's patterns change?
How can we be so smug while
Curiosity on Mars explores where
former streams and seas reveal that
Mars was wet before?

Why is it that we fail to see
Our future thus revealed.
Our numbers grow - resources go

Build a pipeline, wash the sand,
Cut down trees that save the land
Drain the seas, ignore the spoil
Crowd the cities, rape the soil

Is it too hard to find a way
to change the rule:
"Live for today."

Can we not tackle problems now
To save us from impending fate?
Did Mars have warnings too –
was it too late?

Disasters? Vs. Hope
Rudie Tretten

Given the disasters we're living through, the disasters we should be expecting, the disasters the scientific, economic, and political pundits can conjure up to befuddle the citizenry, there is still hope to be savored.

Today, the simplest kind of hope was induced as I looked out from our hilltop aerie at 7:00 a.m. The ocean's blueness was topped by a sky with a tinge of orange. No clouds. No wind. Beauty producing calm, and leading to hope.

Yesterday I had the bimonthly appointment with my radiation oncologist. Next month it's my surgeon. Having these two to meet with regularly is a source of hope. When the news is good – voila a joyful trumpet sounds. But it was more than the news that filled my hope cup.

It began with the receptionist. "Hi, Rudie" and a subsequent conversation. A couple of attempts at humor by both of us. Then the light-hearted me could sit down to await the summons from my doctor.

Before my scheduled conference there is the weighing routine with the chief technical assistant. Another warm smile and welcoming remarks. I'm really beginning to like this place and its inhabitants.

I have noted in a previous essay my dread of his title – Radiation Oncologist. I also wrote that his practice of his profession makes my dread seem foolish. Straight forward, honest, a pleasant temperament, and a sense of humor destroy my clichéd response to his professional moniker.

In keeping with the day, still sunny and a lot warmer, we chat about my current condition and any possible problems related to my 33 doses of radiation. He does some bodily inspection in the course of which I tell him that my dermatologist had done some biopsies and discovered a basal cell skin cancer I should have removed.

He checks out the spot and tells me what I should have known. She had recorded the biopsy results onto my record. He had some questions about a possible surgical procedure and we spent several minutes looking at my skeletal head on the computer screen.

I mention that his and the staff's positive welcoming remarks made me feel good, building on the gorgeous sunrise I had experienced earlier.

More discussion and he decides to check with two of his colleagues about his judgment on next steps since surgery on a heavily radiated area can cause problems.

He returns, and after affirming the surgery decision, I leave the office with him. At this point two other staff greet me with big smiles telling me they were glad to see me and that I was looking good. I thanked them for boosting my hopes.

So it's into the car for the 25-minute drive home complete with another look at the blue and peaceful Pacific.

Desperation? No, hope for a better world. A day later the hope bug is still with me reinforced by my attendance at my fraternity's Big Game Banquet (Cal vs. Stanford). No one of this Cal Bunch has any hope for a big 2013 upset victory. I sit with the group dating from the '50s and we enjoy the camaraderie. Most of us have had some sort of medical/physical problem but we're together again – 60 years after the two-bit martini. We hope to meet again in 2014.

On the way to my Pacifica home down Highway One overlooking the ocean, I spot another phenomenon that pushes the hope button. There spread out at varying distances from the shore are the lights of well over 25 small boats launching the crab season. Because of the darkness of the night and the clear atmosphere, the sight is particularly sharp. Man and nature interacting – for me a calming moment. There is hope. For, the crabs? Probably not.

Perlacher Forest*
William Baldwin

(* Perlacher Forest is a mostly coniferous forest on the southern edge of Munich)

We walked through the forest,
You and I,
All those years ago.
I sang Wagner to you,
Tristan,
For forty minutes,
Until the night absorbed us,
And we were finding our way back
By instinct:
The sense of our feet
That we still remained
On the dirt path.
And when we were back on the campus,
And reached the door of your dormitory,
And I asked if I might kiss you,
You said no...

Well, so here we are,
Forty-three years later.
I haven't seen you for forty-two.
And we're still two thousand miles
Apart,
And only "talking" by email...

Closets
By Ruby L Johnson

In the house where I was born there were no closets and no bathrooms. It was 1940 and our farmhouse was already old. When I was around nine or ten we had a bathroom installed on the screened in back porch. But we never had a closet; most houses back then didn't have closets. Houses in the South were taxed according to the number of rooms and closets were considered rooms. I've toured huge, antebellum houses that didn't have closets.

Our house had high ceilings and tall windows, with three bedrooms. Two at the front of the house, separated by a narrow living room (or parlor), and one at the back of the house. My parents shared one of these front bedrooms, my little sister and I shared the other, which was referred to as the North Room. It had a fireplace and a nice, wooden chifforobe. This chifforobe was a tall, free standing (portable) closet for hanging our better clothes. My sister and I clearly had the best and largest bedroom in the house with the nicest furniture. I don't recall there being a chifforobe in my parents' room; I think we all shared the one. There were, after all, only a few church going clothes between us; the rest of the clothes, our everyday clothes, could be stored in dresser or bureau drawers. My mother had pieces of cedar wood in the chifforobe that gave it an intoxicating scent. I opened the door of the chifforobe and took deep whiffs.

The back, smaller bedroom belonged to my mother's younger brother, Carey, who lived with us for awhile. There was no chifforobe in Carey's Room, only a wooden rod to hang his better pants and shirts. Even after Carey had left for a life in the Army, we still called it Carey's Room.

Carey's room opened out into a small, screened in porch where my mother stored colorful, handsewn quilts in a big, green metal trunk. I happened upon her one day, kneeling and staring into this trunk, cloaked in the sharp smell of moth balls, with quilts stacked on the floor beside her. She was holding a small ring box, when she noticed me out of the corner of her eye.

She could have quickly hidden the ring box back in the trunk, but she didn't; and as I've thought about this, looking back, I've come to the conclusion that she needed to share it and its story. At ten I was a dreamer and a weaver of romantic tales. I'm sure she sensed I would be sympathetic to her story. More importantly, I was totally devoted to my mother; I felt slightly alienated from my quiet, distant father. That's the only reason I can think of that I didn't consider her confession a disloyalty to my father.

Inside the box was a silver (or white gold) ring, with a diamond in the center that was not much bigger than an engorged flea, yet it was lovely in its simplicity. It had been given to her as a promise ring from her first love, Dan White. Their secret plans to run off and elope had been discovered and crushed by her father, who didn't approve of Dan White, and especially his family, which was considered lower class. Lower class was perhaps not what people said; they used words like "sorry" and "no good". Back then a person didn't marry a person, a person married a family. No father of honor would allow his daughter to marry into a trashy family.

My grandfather was an honorable man but he was far from wealthy, so he wouldn't have bought off Dan White. He wasn't a thug so he wouldn't have threatened him with bodily harm. Yet, somehow, he must have persuaded him to leave the area. My mother said Dan moved to Alabama. For years I secretly held my grandfather's heavy handed, narrow minded ways against him. He had caused my mother grief. I didn't credit my grandfather's approval of my father and the Gates Family. It wasn't until after my mother left my father, ran off and took up with, and later married my step-father, a man who came from a nearby community, a man and his family my grandfather bitterly disapproved of, that I realized my old, narrow minded grandfather knew what he was talking about when it came to marriage and families.

That day my mother gave me her cherished Dan White ring, knowing I would take care of it. And she was right; I kept it until I was an older teenager, when I started to wear it. I don't know if I wore it as a tribute to unrequited love or because I knew it pleased my mother or if I just liked its simple beauty. But when I lost it I never told her. I felt careless and neglectful, after all she'd been through. I spent a lot of time searching for it but it was lost.

A Big Fat Rat
By Ida Lewenstein

A Big, Fat Rat Sat
alone on a mat
Passing the time away.
A Lean, Mean Cat Spied this
rat.
Said he--
This is my lucky day!
The Lean, Mean Cat
Pounced on the mat
Devoured the rat.
And THAT was THAT!
Now a Big, Fat Cat Sits on
this very same mat,
Purring the time away

Creative Pursuits
Theresa Harbin Lebeiko

Best of Show: Essay

At Chicago's Illinois Visually Handicapped Institute in the 1970's, I was attending a staffing of students. I then taught creative writing and mentored students preparing for their G.E.D. Salient for me in that meeting were parallels that I heard in the progress review of two of our students.

Margaret, the first of those, was a 57 year-old female whose love was art. Her psychologist reported that she was intensely grieving the progressive loss of her sight and was suicidal. Another was Ian, a 19 year-old male. Intending suicide, he blinded himself playing Russian roulette; and before pulling the trigger, he wrote a poem. More important than the content of the poem is that the events occurred side by side.

In each instance, I considered their creative pursuits highly significant. Margaret's art had been central to her life, and she found her loss of sight devastating. Ian's poem, just before his suicide attempt, reflected his own creative impulses. As I heard these details of their lives, I imagined creative-destructive forces at two ends of a continuum, pulling in opposite directions. Beyond my imagining, I wondered how I might work with them.

In addition to their other work with the educational and clinical services staff, I wondered, How might I introduce creativity as an engaging, positive force in their lives? Might it also help them counter their potentially destructive pulls? I had the freedom to design curriculum to help them to address their needs. I also knew that guidance and support were critical components of whatever we decided, together, to do. My next steps: to explore with them, separately, what creative pursuits might be a match for them.

Before meeting with Margaret, I learned that her psychologist had said, "Even if you can't paint, you can always write." Amending that is where I started. "It's not possible to substitute one art form for another," I established at the beginning of our first meeting.

"That's what I thought," she responded, quite emphatically.

"However, the creative impulse is important. Even vital," I added. "And writing can be a way of channeling your creativity. Are you interested in exploring that with me?"

She was willing, so our work began. I initially brought in poetry and music for input. "Mending Wall" by Robert Frost was one of her favorites: because of its strong visual imagery and its easy movement from image to meaning. Another favorite was an uplifting album of songs based on the

133

writings of the philosopher, Teillhard de Chardin. I, further, introduced a tape recorder for note-taking and journaling; the taping was important to help with the frustration and despair she felt when, as she said, "Some days I can't even see the page that I'm writing on any more."

For Ian, I proposed a creative writing option. However, our real work together began with his question, "How can I write when I can't even see the page?"

"Talk to me, and I'll write down what you have to say."

"Then what?"

"Well, we can also tape record what you say."

"But I can talk to you first?"

"If you prefer it that way."

"But I need to walk when I talk. Not just sit still."

"We'll go to one of the meeting rooms and clear the furniture, so you have space to move around."

"Okay," he said. "I'll give it a try."

Margaret was delighted with her ability to express herself in new ways. She savored, for instance, her insight that the two figures in Frost's poem could represent conflicting parts of herself: the self that questions why versus the self that relies on the way it's always been. She also looked radiant when she experienced confluence between the ideas of de Chardin and her own that she had never articulated before. Another time she was relieved that she "wrote"— that is, tape recorded—her thoughts the night before when she was troubled and couldn't sleep. Her writing, she said, helped the "flotsam and jetsam" to clear so that she could be more peaceful.

As Ian walked and talked, I took notes and tape recorded what he said. Then he began to record on his own. I remember the satisfaction that I felt when I saw him at one of the center's typewriters, typing from his own recording. That was also the first of many other times I saw him there transcribing his own writing. I don't know what happened with Ian after he completed his term at the Institute. But I do know that he was more empowered to engage his own creative forces, as a blind man, because of the work that we did together.

My work with Margaret and Ian followed four years of teaching and was concurrent with completing a Master's Degree in English. What stands out most, however, is what a creative endeavor the work itself was for me. It began with the observation of competing polarities; was based in the belief that literary arts can be intimately aligned with our lives; and informed by my willingness to hear and address the students' own issues.

Our work together confirmed my belief in processes that engage students' creativity and empower them to resist destructive forces. When I've taught academic subjects, that belief has extended to assigning literature that is relevant and challenges critical thinking; listening to what students have to say when they have difficulty with writing; and taking notes myself when they tell me that they can talk more easily than they write.

"So talk to me," I've sometimes said in conferences with students, "and I'll take notes." I've then experienced the pleasure of hearing them express themselves orally, knowing that too as part of the creative process. And their question at the end of conferences "Can I have those notes?" suggests that the intervention provided the beacon of light that they needed.

Nancy's Poor Cats
By Stanley Gedzelman

September 2013 then 01 October 2013

When springtime came to Strathmore Road
I found the subject for this ode.
Nancy and Wendy often had spats
She then would visit us with her two cats.
I liked them one notch less than rats.
But their actions quickly changed my mood
It was time to form a feline brood
The male was yearning to penetrate
But he was going to have to wait
The female focused only on food
And did not want to be pursued
She did all she could to avoid
The ardent male. She bit, she clawed
She hissed, she spit; was she annoyed!
No matter his whole frame was taut
His finest efforts summed to naught.
A few days later the male looked bored
The female's wiles he simply ignored.
Her body quivered with reproductive fire
She couldn't have arched her back half higher
She traversed the room in high gear reverse
Trying to back right into his face
Her timing could not have been any worse
He yawned and sought out some safer place
He clearly did not want the female there
In the end her unfilled womb stayed bare
Wendy moved out, ending those spats
The new roommate was allergic, so goodbye, cats
Nature and nurture are seldom fair.

A Little Water Goes a Long Way
By Ellen Six

Letters from Lithuania were rare but always fascinating. From the time I was a young child, I would listen as my mother read these letters to my father after dinner or by phone to her sister in Wisconsin. This is the way that I got to know my Lithuanian family.

Mother was one of 12 children, six had lived and six had died. I had a Grandmother and four aunts in Lithuania that I would never get a chance to know except through letters. I heard stories about the farmhouse that needed a new roof and the cow that had stopped giving milk. There were profuse thank-yous for the packages that Mother had sent with yard goods for new dresses and the brown wool that would be perfect for a burial dress for Grandmother when that day came, in God's good time. The scarves would bring a good price and the money could be used to pay to patch the roof. A goat could be bought to replace the cow's milk. The aspirin was truly a miracle drug that helped their arthritis and always a million thanks and a million kisses would end the letters.

I would fill in the letters with bedtime stories that my mother had told me about days when she would tend the geese who were bigger than her when she was a little girl. I would picture the storks that would build nests on the thatched roofs. I would imagine the village church spire in the distance where Mother would sing in the choir on Sundays and I could see the cherry trees and apple trees surrounding the farmhouse.

But today's letter didn't bring pretty pictures to mind. Instead I heard Mother speaking in whispers on the phone to her sister and stopping at times to wipe away tears. I knew enough not to interrupt or question why there were tears. After Mother hung up the phone, she put her hankie and the letter in her apron pocket and headed for the kitchen.

She dismissed me with, "Your Father will be home soon for dinner. Go do your homework."

Mother went off to check the soup pot on the stove. When Father came home, we all sat down to dinner in the kitchen. After the meal, Mother washed the dishes and announced in the same calm voice, "I have a letter from Lithuania."

We gathered in the living room. Mother took the letter out of her apron pocket and started to read about the weather and the usual lengthy thank-yous for the gifts and then the news. Her youngest sister had been diagnosed with breast cancer. Her sister wrote that she had been told that she needed surgery but that she was too frightened to have the surgery and could mother please send her some Lourdes water from the shrine in France.

She knew that if she had this miraculous water that she would be cured and wouldn't need the surgery. Mother finished the letter and folded it up and said, "What foolishness." Mother would send money for medicine and treatment. There was no way she could send this miracle. The Communists would not let you mail even a religious Christmas card and miraculous water was just nonsense.

Five months later, a letter arrived saying that her sister had died. She had refused surgery and there was no miracle. Mother was angry at the foolishness of her sister and the only holy water were my tears for an aunt that I would never meet.

I hate it when the phone rings. Perhaps it is my pessimistic nature, but I anticipate that the call in the least will be a nuisance business call, "Would you like to switch your phone carrier?" to the fearsome announcement of someone's death, "Your 98-year-old uncle died of unknown causes."

Today's phone call was from one of my best friends. We had met in college as we both struggled to learn the French language and became lunch mates and lifelong friends. Struggling to master nasal pronunciations and sharing drugstore lunches had created our bond. Today our conversation started with the usual catching up on news and the activities of our daughters, a few reminisces, a few laughs and then THE NEWS.

"I didn't know how or when to tell you, but I've been diagnosed with breast cancer."

A hug would have meant a lot more that the few words of support that I was able to murmur in response to this news. The conversation reverted to the practicalities of the impending treatment and her initial shock of the diagnosis. I ended the conversation with, "I love you, I'll pray for you."

After I hung up the phone, the shock hit me. Wasn't this a repeat of a conversation that I had had two years earlier with my friend of high school days? Here were two of my dearest friends with the same diagnosis. One friend had been Godmother for my first daughter and the other had been Confirmation sponsor for my youngest child. They had both been bridesmaids in my wedding party. One had been there to help me pack up my Mother's belongings and to close up the house when my Mother died, the other had sat and cried with me as I told her about my undergoing emergency surgery.

When my high school friend had been diagnosed with breast cancer two years earlier, my response had been disbelief. Breast cancer was just statistics that you hear on TV and it happens to people out there not to people who are healthy one day and end up facing a life-threatening disease the next. During the years of my friend's treatment, there were the phone calls where mostly I just listened. There were bad days and some that were not so bad. I sent get-well cards and little gifts to lift her spirits and I would save my tears for when I hung up the phone. We planned banquet meals on the phone for when she would be past chemo and past eating only Jell-O and cottage cheese and we debated about if she would look better as a blond or a red head with her new wig.

Again, when I hung up the phone, I would cry. The good news is that she is now cancer free and now, we start again with another friend and the same disease and the same journey, hopefully with the same good outcome.

When I hung up the phone on this day, there were no tears, just shock and disbelief. I called my husband down from his hideout, the computer room, and I matter-of-factly told him the story of my phone call. He listened to all of the details and then I saw him tear up. He had told me a long time ago that because he was a logical engineer by profession, he wouldn't know that he was supposed to have feeling if I hadn't told him. Seeing his tears, opened up my own numbed senses and released my pent up emotions. We both hugged and cried.

The tears dry but the heartache stays. I went to my desk and found a prayer card for healing. It said that the recipient of the card would be remembered at the Shrine of Our Lady of Lourdes in France, the shrine of the miraculous water. I addressed the envelope and sent the card to my friend with the hope of a miraculous healing. Love, support, prayers, medical treatments can go a long way but adding a little water can't hurt.

Tango Bar
By William Baldwin

Is it too much to ask—
A little tango bar,
A half-filled glass of Pernod,
A lamenting band,
A dark-haired, dark-eyed beauty,
A song of love, betrayal,
Remorse, longing, madness,
Sung with ghetto bluntness?
Wistful regret
For what was once but can no longer be?
A sliver of consolation
In this stinking, rotten world?

The Poisoner's Handbook
By Marjorie Johnson

The flag is up on our rural mailbox. It's come at last, a plain brown envelope from Underground Press, addressed to me, Betsy Mills. I slip *The Poisoner's Handbook* into my apron pocket and head back to the house: two rooms, tarpaper roof, red-clay yard. I hurry past my husband Wayne: blond, twice my weight, six years older. He has the old Chevy in pieces again, the hood leaning against a pine tree. He pounds on something with an oversized wrench, throws the carburetor across the driveway.

In the doorway I spot an aspirin bottle, pick it up. I pull out my box of treasures from under the bed and add two small seed cones, just right to make a porcupine for my critters-in-a- bottle collection: Wilbur W. Worm, Al E. Cat, Lady R. Bug. I build them using tweezers in empty glass aspirin bottles, all saved after Wayne empties them.

Wayne takes too much aspirin. They make your stomach bleed, I tell him, but he says no way, besides his shoulder hurts all night. He tells me I'm too young to know much. Not that he got that much out of high school, except a ruined shoulder from playing football. Any who, I'm plumb tuckered out, what with him not sleeping at night.

I hide my new book beneath my underwear in the dresser drawer. Wayne stomps in, shakes out some aspirin, his jeans covered with oil and red dirt.

"Mail's here," I say.

"Win any contests yet," he says, moseys back outside. "Sweepstakes," I say to the back of his head.

That night Wayne listens to the radio in the dark, water glass on the dresser beside the radio, aspirin bottles lined up. The radio does a fade-out, like most nights in the mountains. He fusses with the bottle cap, can't get it off. Having a tizzy, Wayne throws the aspirin bottle across the room, cusses, and slaps at the radio as usual, only this time he hits the water glass. Breaking glass. Radio crashing. I turn on the bare-bulb ceiling light. Blood spurts. I wrap a white dishtowel around his wrist. The bleeding doesn't stop.

The car isn't running. I pull on pants and a shirt and run to the neighbor's house, a quarter of a mile down the road.

"Hey, it's midnight, what's going on," the neighbor says. He gives me a ride back in his pick-up truck, oak wood in the truck-bed, window stuck open. I help Wayne and my best dishtowel pile in. I clean up the mess.

Come four o'clock I hear the truck rattle and bang on down, wood bouncing in its bed. Wayne says, "Thank you for the lift, much obliged," slams the door. Wayne kicks off his shoes and comes to bed. I play dead.

Wayne sleeps 'til lunchtime. When he finally goes to work on the road crew, I read my new book. I want to know about poisons like in those murder mystery stories, but this book from Underground Press tells how to poison people, how to inject poison into a piece of fruit like the witch in *Snow White*.

Something about nicotine catches my eye: one drop of pure nicotine in the ear canal kills a person. The murderer on tiptoe, holding out a medicine dropper . . . It might work with gophers.

Early next morning while I tend the garden, I light up the burn pile. I save Wayne's cigarette butts and roll the tobacco fibers for him to smoke later—makes my fingers stink. I'm thinking I'll make some nicotine like in the book. I put some fibers and a little water in an empty tomato juice can over the coals and let it simmer. I don't breathe the fumes. It makes nasty brown goo.

I catch a gopher out behind the carrots. I lift the trap and the ugly critter dangles down. I keep away from those yellow teeth, dab a little tobacco paste on his nose with a stick. Sure enough, in a few minutes he's dead. I dig a hole in the garden and cover the dead gopher. I don't know if he will turn to fertilizer or if he will poison my plants.

I need to dry out the nicotine concentrate and divide it into small doses. I try dipping aspirin tablets into the goo. When the brown coating dries, I push the capsules into an empty aspirin bottle—I use a stick, don't touch the stuff. I hide them under my underwear next to the book on poisons.

Next afternoon Wayne works on the car again. I go to my garden, admire the tomatoes, water the plants. I hear a big commotion, Wayne yelling. He smashes the car roof with a big rock and throws a greasy car-part across the driveway.

I pick the first red ripe tomato and start dinner. I make a salad with fresh greens and boil

p some spaghetti. I put his spaghetti in the middle of the yellow plastic plate. Wayne takes his time coming, like usual. I say, "Spaghetti's getting cold."

Wayne sits at the table, pushes the salad away. He puts some spaghetti in his mouth and spits it out. "You trying to poison me, woman?" he says, flings his dinner plate across the room. It smashes against the wall. The plate bounces and rolls. Paints a splotchy red trail, clatters to a stop. Spaghetti drools down, down, sliding slowly, piling up in a red sauce puddle.

"I make you something nice for dinner, and look what you do. It's not my fault it's cold." I cross my arms over my chest and frown.

"What was that stuff, anyway?" He sits there, knife in one hand, fork in the other. "An onion and tomato sauce. And cinnamon. You always say, put in spice." "That's crazy, woman. Nobody puts cinnamon in spaghetti sauce."

"Spaghetti's still there. You gonna clean it up?"

"You don't tell me what to do, woman," he says. He shoves me hard, makes a fist. "My name is Betsy," I say and shove him back. We yell and scream, bump one another

around, have a terrible fight. I duck and move farther away and start to cry. "I wish you were dead," I say.

He sits down on the bed, folds his arms across his chest and crosses one leg over, big frown on his face. He massages his shoulder, clenches and unclenches his jaw.

I clean up the mess. I wash down the walls and scrub the floors. Same old thing, come bedtime, he listens to the radio in the dark. "I need some aspirin, woman," he says.

I get the tobacco aspirin from my dresser drawer and put them next to him, within easy reach. Now we'll see, Roger Q. Rat, I think. I hook my leg over the edge of the mattress so I won't roll downhill to the center. Wayne starts to snore. I'm thinking like, you can't just kill somebody, even if you want to wring his neck. What if that bedspring breaks through again, wakes him up? First thing, he'll grab those pills. No, I'll hear him for sure, trade bottles then or in the morning.

I edge myself back over the uphill mattress and go to sleep.

Middle of the night, he sits up, pulls off all the covers. "Help me," he moans. "I just threw up."

I turn on the light. I see blood, a lot of blood. I wipe him off with a damp towel. "Car isn't running, and us with no phone. Just stay right here," I say. I run for help.

You again? Are you crazy?" the neighbor says, leaning out of the upstairs window in his underwear. I use his phone.

I run back home. "Ambulance a-coming," I say. Wayne doesn't answer. He doesn't move. I throw the aspirin bottle from his nightstand in with my underwear. Wouldn't want him to take one by mistake.

It takes a long time for help to come. Wayne just lies there, white against the blood-red sheets. I hear the siren, see the whirling red lights coming down the drive.

The ambulance driver rushes to the door. "Where is he, Ma'am?" "Right here," I say, "too small a house to lose him."

The helper rolls in a stretcher. They both wear white uniforms and white shoes. They try to make him breathe. Sure enough, he's dead. The sheriff's here before Wayne leaves in the ambulance, red clay dust boiling up, like a cloud of nicotine gas.

"What happened, Ma'am?" the sheriff asks. He has a pistol in a black holster. "I don't know, I just don't know."

The sheriff picks up an aspirin bottle from the floor. "Is this what he's been taking?" he asks. "You have to come in tomorrow." He drives out, his taillights aglow in the dust.

After the sheriff leaves, I change the bed. I throw the sheets and the bloody pillow on top of the burn pile. That aspirin bottle, did he swallow half a bottle all at once, there in the dark? I look for the nicotine-flavored ones, right there with my underwear. Only six tablets, I thought there were a dozen. *Oh-my-god. I must have killed him!*

I cannot sleep.

Come morning, I catch a ride into town with the neighbor. This time I'm the one in the pick-up, kind of cold with that window stuck down, lots of rattles. Rough ride, too, his springs are shot. He drops me by the sheriff's office, half a dozen posters on the wall, mostly wanted for murder.

Murder! I shudder and swallow spit. The sheriff comes in.

"You say he took lots of aspirin." The sheriff writes that down. "Wait for the coroner's report, don't go anywhere." Then, friendly-like, he says, "There's coffee and donuts in the waiting room."

I wait. The donuts are stale. Coffee doesn't help my guilty conscience. They'll find nicotine—he smoked by the carton.

Time passes slowly. Finally the sheriff's helper comes, says the coroner wants to see me. "How much aspirin did you say your husband took, Mrs. Mills?"

"Way too much. He took it by the bottle."

"Wonder it didn't kill him sooner, with that bleeding ulcer," the coroner says. He has a bushy mustache. "What do you want to do with his body?"

"His body? I have to do something with his body?"

"Well, are you having a funeral or something? What would he want done?"

"No sense having a funeral. No family to speak of."

"Okay. The county will cremate him and mail his remains to you. Just fill out these forms here." He asks if there is anything else he can do for me.

"Sure could use a ride home," I say.

Next morning early, I light the burn pile, put the book right on top of the bloody sheets. While I'm at it, I throw in the nicotine aspirin. Right next to the beets, that's where I'll plant his ashes. Make him eat his vegetables after all.

A Bit of the Unnatural
By Rudie Tretten

It had been a long time. Though we live close together, almost enmeshed, we had not encountered one another in months.

I was walking down our front ten stairs clutching the metal railing with my left hand and holding my red metal cane in the other when I glanced down and there he/she was sliding toward the wall. I watched for a moment then took the next step.

California was in the middle of one of its driest droughts in decades though this day was cool and overcast. Not wet, but the sun was sheltered behind some clouds. This gave rise to the thought that the daily warmth was keeping my neighbor indoors or, more accurately, ensconced somewhere within the rock wall bordering the stairs.

It was about a week later that I had a similar meeting with a smaller version of my longer stairmate from that cloudy day. Perhaps the entire family was throwing off the drought and getting out and about more often. My curiosity inspired me to reach into my jacket pocket and put out a piece of notepaper which I placed in the sliders path so that I could pick up the crawling one without touching my stairmate.

I carefully lifted the paper with my left hand, turned around and walked back up the stairs to the deck with its table and chairs. I sat down placing the paper and its very quiet short inhabitant on the table. Maybe we could have a conversation though I wasn't sure there was enough trust in either of us to promote much sharing.

"So," I said. "This situation seems strange to me. Something unnatural about it."

The voice responding was quite soft and my hearing aids were challenged but I was, I think, able to pick up most of the conversation. Though some of what follows may be an interpretation of what was intended to be said.

"Yes. Unnatural is a splendid way to describe what we are doing. In the past you have simply reacted to our presence. Usually your response has been hostile. You haven't shown any desire to communicate in a peaceful manner."

"Well, your perception of any hostility is accurate. As I watched your progenitors over the years I was appalled by your appearance. Your eating habits also triggered my hostility."

"Sorry about that. But it wasn't us who declared war. Your inability to accept peaceful behavior on the part of your neighbors was a sign of immaturity – rather child-like."

"But look at yourself. That God-awful color you wear. The way you slither across the ground. And what you have done to some of my rose blossoms. You have invited my antipathy!"

"Hold on there, big neighbor. We've been around for a long time. Most of you have come to accept us and our way of life but you, on your own, set out to destroy us. I know of three different approaches you took to this task. My being here in this conversation is proof you have failed."

"There were actually four ways I undertook to rid us of you. And I attempted to limit any suffering on your part. Two years ago I started capturing your relatives and placing them in a garbage can used for plants and cuttings from our gardens. There was food there for them."

"So what! Your intent was the same—poison us, starve us, ship us away. We deserve to be treated with respect, like now, you're listening to me."

"But—"

"Who was here first? Who is a natural resident of the area? Who will be here after you've gone away?"

"Okay, but are you going to do something about your appearance and stop eating what I plant?"

"No. I am what I am and I do what I do. Get used to it!"

"I can't do that. But maybe we could meet again and continue to talk things over."

"That's all right with me. But I want you to call me by my formal name, Ariolimax Columbianus. No more of the banana slug stuff."

My Spiritual Guide
By Ryann Murrin-Desouza

Arising,
Color of energy and growth.
Praise to earth,
The strength, grandeur, expansive, radiant center.
This sacred space,
May you enlighten me along my path.
And guide me with your spiritual radiance.
Allowing me to continue the growing center of my spirit,
To keep on growing.
Listen and receive it.
Slow down to receive more and more spiritual guidance,
And save me for future support and assistance.

Half Foods, Whole Moments
By Katie Burke

As I stepped out of my San Francisco apartment one recent morning, I decided to buy a cup of coffee at the new Dolores/Market Whole Foods, and to drink it in the beautiful parklet just outside its doors.

I sat on a neighboring bench to a man who was looking up at the Whole Foods sign and muttering, "Whole Foods ... Half Foods ..."

Just as I thought, Quarter Foods ... One Eighth-Foods.., the man turned toward me and engaged me in conversation.

David and I chatted for an hour, mostly about the history of theatre in San Francisco, where he has lived since 1983, in a rent-controlled, single room occupancy hotel in mid-Market. We discussed several plays that we'd each seen in San Francisco and New York.

David rarely has two nickels at once, but when he does, he rubs them together and transforms them into discounted theatre tickets that he wins every few years, as a reward for his patience to stand in line every weekend that he has money.

I told him about Custom Made Theatre, a small production company to which a friend and I have had season tickets for years. While CMT doesn't have a discounted ticket lottery, its prices are on par with the cheap seats that David tries so hard to score for Broadway productions.

David and I also traded opinions about our city's rapid development of late, and the sweeping displacement that has been happening in both glaring and insidious ways...particularly in mid-Market, where Twitter and other startups, and their high-earning employees, have become neighbors to David and other longtime mid-Market residents.

Without a trace of self-pity, David shared his worry that the changes could eventually leave him homeless, even though he lives in a historic building whose residents are protected from Ellis Act evictions. A petition that circulated in his building for signature, pleading with management to let the rent-controlled tenants stay, shook David's previous sense of security.

Also, David's landlords have tried twice to evict this self-described "clutterbug"—and though he prevailed in court both times, these experiences scared him into renting a public storage unit, for which he pays almost 200 dollars per month that he can't really spare. He is trying to conquer his hoarding tendencies, so he can rid himself of this expense.

David was good-natured about these burdens he was laying down. Despite his personal concerns, he applauded the city's growth, and voiced his understanding that everyone has a legitimate side to this story—that the widespread "tech v. homeless people" polarization serves no one.

This is not to suggest that David is passive about the issues that he and other low-income people face. A couple of days ago, David participated in a City Hall protest on behalf of the city's homeless people, because he knows he is dangerously close to joining their ranks at any moment.

After we'd talked for an hour, David was off to sit in the outdoor patio at Castro and Market. I had to go into the office, since our firm is moving this week, substantially shortening my time to get work done. As we parted, David asked, "What's the name of that theatre company you told me about again?"

"Custom Made," I answered.

"I'm going to check that out," David replied.

As I walked away from Whole/Half Foods, I immediately regretted that I hadn't suggested we see a play together. David and I had exchanged only first names, but he had told me some of his hangouts, as well as the name of the building where he lives.

Conveniently, I walk along Market to get from home to work, so David's hotel is right on my way. While walking toward his place, I decided to leave David the following note, along with my phone number and email address: "We met at Whole Foods this morning. Be my guest to a play at Custom Made Theatre."

With his joy for life, and the responsibility he takes for creating his own happiness, David inspired me to be grateful for my relatively secure spot in the best city in the world...because, despite his circumstances and occasional doubts, David feels thankful for the same thing.

Naming Rights
By Evie Groch

The open, yellow streaked lands rise
up above the horizon
in a seamless ascendance
to the newly baked sky.
One could travel for days
not knowing when one's
trip is close to an end.
Freedom and desolation
are in tension
fighting for the right to
name this ground.
We who view it from afar
define it as the opposite of
fences.

Barefootin'
By Terry Toomey

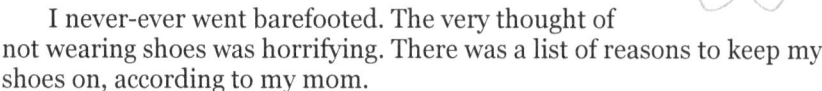

I am worried about my feet. I am sure that they are getting longer and longer every day. If my mother was still alive she would be horrified; she warned me time and time again that this would happen. I should have listened.

I never-ever went barefooted. The very thought of not wearing shoes was horrifying. There was a list of reasons to keep my shoes on, according to my mom.

You might step on a rusty nail and get lockjaw.

You'll get ringworms.

Glass will cut your feet.

Heaven only knows what else you might step on.

You will get hard soles and your feet will be crusty,

You will have BIG feet.

Your feet will grow and grow.

Men don't like woman with BIG feet.

The worst thing on this list was to have BIG feet. Small feet were more attractive. I think she might have been right on that account. I don't remember anyone bragging about having big feet. I knew a lot of girls and women who did brag about having small feet.

I followed her advice most of my life. I seldom took off my shoes. I wore sandals at the beach. I did not, and still do not, like the feel of sand on my feet. I did worry, and still do, that terrible things might be hidden in grass and sand that I might step on. Taking off my clothes at a doctor's office is not stressful if I can leave my shoes on. I suppose I was one of only a few patients who left their shoes on in the stirrups. At home I kept my shoes on until I got in the bathtub or went to bed.

The last few years I have been forgetting my mom's advice. First, I started taking off my shoes in the house after I had dinner. Then, I started to take them off when I came home for the day. It has been a slippery, downhill, barefoot walk since I went to the doctor and took them off. First, I would open the door and get the newspaper barefooted. Next, I ventured a bit further out the door to get something from my car. Next, I stepped on the lawn and on to the sidewalk.

I'm doomed! I know when I go to the shoe store I will not be able to find any shoes that will fit me. I am sure my feet have gotten bigger and so will my shoe size. It was hard enough to find the perfect shoes before I started to wander about bare footed. Stylish shoes, or any shoes for that matter, are just about nonexistent for short, wide, fat feet. I doubt if there will not be any footwear at all for a person who did not follow her mother's advice, took off her shoes and let her feet grow.

147

O Bind Not My Words in Paper Edges
A sestina
By Frank Saunders

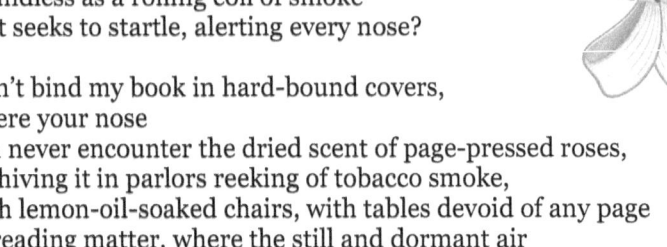

Where in the seed is the scent of roses?
Why do you want to cage my meaning in a page
of paper, straight-cut, with edges that bring
uniformity to thoughts wanting to be free as air,
boundless as a roiling coil of smoke
that seeks to startle, alerting every nose?

Don't bind my book in hard-bound covers,
where your nose
can never encounter the dried scent of page-pressed roses,
archiving it in parlors reeking of tobacco smoke,
with lemon-oil-soaked chairs, with tables devoid of any page
of reading matter, where the still and dormant air
has no living vibrancy to bring.

Shout these words with all your strength. Let your voice bring
a bracing call to the hearer, so he knows
that a new song, a new breeze stirs the air,
blowing out the dust of ages, bringing in the scent of roses
tinged with the acrid smell of blood, of hordes in full rampage
running closer, closer through the smoke

of turmoil. Can your voice pierce the pall of smoke
and fear that paralyzes us, we the speechless? Can you bring
a hint of hope that future writers can record a page
of history more peaceful, where every citizen knows
that, stronger than decay, a drop of oil of roses can
dispel the stench of cordite hanging in the air?

Even a simple spider, weaving a dew-jeweled web in the air as
dawn-warmed moisture rises from the ground like smoke, feels a
shiver as a bee, back from breakfasting on a bed of roses,
blunders into the sticky net, to bring
itself as breakfast, signaling to the spider's quivering nose
that food has arrived to support, in his life's book, another page.

So make haste to free the words imprisoned on this page.
Release their message to the shimmering air
for all to breathe, pointing a direction for each nose to
follow, pervading the universe like smoke.
Publish this score so that all the world may bring, in
singing, a worldwide harmony fragrant with roses.

Burn this page. Let its smoke rise
into the air, and bring
to every nose the scent of roses.

Remember Me Not
By Anastasia Breeze

I remember your first few days as a newborn.
I remember when your body was as big as my forearm.
I remember your finger paint always making its way
to the kitchen walls.
Bouncing and chasing after red rubber balls,
Reading the same book for storytime everyday.
Skipping, singing, laughing,
Life for you was endless play.
Your first day of kindergarten, and you didn't say a peep,
Driving me crazy when you couldn't fall asleep.
I remember how nervous you were to start middle school.
I remember buying your first pair of high heels,
Going to your first PG-13 movie, you felt oh-so cool.
I remember how impressive you played that season.
Along with those careless decisions made without reason.
I remember the constant dedication
through the years of your education.
Your first date,
And those frog legs you were dared to, and actually ate
I remember the streaming tears as you wore that cap and gown,
and later, learning to love that incredible husband you found.
How excited and blessed I was to see my first grandson,
Whispering to him lullabies when the day was done.
Going to his first soccer game.
Of course I remember...
Yes, I remember...
I remember...
No,
I don't
remember...
Who the photographs in my home are of.
The house where I am eating Christmas dinner.
That I am married.
This man who asks me if I am okay
Why is he saying "I love you"
Who is this young lady
What is "Mom"
Who is this little boy
hugging my leg
What does he want from me

My name.
My life.
I do not remember
a thing.

There it is,
a single memory,
my own name.
I have returned.

Storytime?
High heels?
Soccer game...?

I remember.
I remember not.
I remember...
not.
Sitting next to me, patting my back, watching me breathe,
You are with me.
But my distant tone, confused expression, not knowing who you
even are
I am not with you.

Memories engulf memories.
Jumbled thoughts galore.

I was there, yes I was
I should remember, yes I should.

Though I may not remember the past,
Remember me not of this present.

needle worker
(a tribute to Nelson Mandela)
By Maurine Killough

the stitch that took a lifetime
obliterated a bridge dividing worlds
the stitch that took a lifetime
began the healing for a continent whole the
father of a people
who rebuked intolerable injustice a
stitch at a time
is on the other side now matriculated
into Everything
seeing his life in a blink, the tortures barely a flick 27
years imprisonment hardly a dot
his radiant smile views his stitch on a patch in
a blessed quilt
that changed the pattern of everything

C. elegans
Renae Keep

Back in '03, the nematode C. elegans made the news
when several survived the Columbia Space Shuttle disaster.
After ecstasies of rain, the street glowed like a cactus flower
as it embraced their hermaphroditic forms.

Inside a hotel restaurant, surrounded by colleagues
whose headsets pump music like oxygen, dutifully
the cello prodigy talks to her breakfast broccolis,
tells them how good it is to be human, offers to eat them to prove it.

Likewise, the elegant Caenorhabditis, native to temperate soils, readily
embodies RNA strands ingested from transgenic bacteria.
This ability to take up RNA from ingested bacteria has been mapped
down to a single gene, which, when inserted as a transgene in other species

allows them to do the same. As though a secret handshake held tickets to
a philharmonic séance. No one knew it would knock out 20,000 genes
and establish a functional role for only 9% of the genome
which would then pose for a self-portrait as a corporate logo.

Light and electron microscopy reveal the reflective consciousness:
a thought as a spore contains one or two nuclei and a coiled polar tube.
Within the gut of C. elegans, it finds a host cell and insinuates itself.
Soon, the cell too speaks in spores. And so on, to the death of an individual.

Our catacombs rustle darkening memento morendi.
The present moment arrives on time, but we have already descended
having divined from dripping eaves that it might not come at all.
The line is longer by then, its evolution accelerating with each new body
added,

so the punctual present alone admires a pretty park's morphologies as a
general will consents to set the day aside, to let the stars slide, to
multiply into a myriad of independent, suspended volitions
like particles of Rubidium, spontaneously igniting into pink and purple

bloom and petiole. The sense that the most important things remain unsaid
happens in result of the incursion of one or several new languages.
Nosing, undulant, bloodless, Caenorhabditis strains to hear: what
would you want if you could want anything?

For scientists studying C. elegans, pricey robots procure results.
The ossuary folds like a labyrinth laughing at a secret it contains: the heirs of
inevitability got what everyone else avoided.
Apparently, even, they had it about them.

Whispered Confession
By Gail Jenner

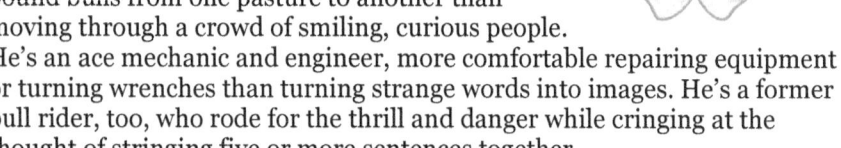

I'm the writer in the family: author, freelancer, and former English teacher.

That's the irony.

My husband is a rancher, a man more comfortable moving arrogant eighteen-hundred pound bulls from one pasture to another than moving through a crowd of smiling, curious people. He's an ace mechanic and engineer, more comfortable repairing equipment or turning wrenches than turning strange words into images. He's a former bull rider, too, who rode for the thrill and danger while cringing at the thought of stringing five or more sentences together.

People have often called us an odd couple: me—the lover and manipulator of words—married to a man who was, for many years, considered tongue-tied.

That said, I must confess: the most profound words ever written to me came at the height of despair by my farming/ranching, slow-talking husband, a recovering alcoholic.

This was not a love letter in the traditional sense. Indeed, during our courtship almost twenty years earlier, he had written only six letters while we were separated over a summer. Terse, filled with little more than a "Hi, how are you," he was simply not a man given to speaking or writing what was in his heart.

Through the tumultuous early years of our marriage, however, when I discovered we had an issue no one wanted to address, I wrote hundreds of letters to him—begging him to think, begging him to feel, weeping over the pain our children and family were enmeshed in as a result of his drinking. Instead of moving him, though, my endless chatter only clattered to the bottom of the black pit we'd fallen into.

Not knowing what else to do, I stopped talking, or—more precisely—found myself withholding the callous words that only added to the chaos around us. But, whether it was as a result of the silence or the silent prayers I prayed—or perhaps both— suddenly we began moving in a new direction.

It didn't happen overnight, but it became clear that things were changing.

My husband suddenly asked for help, and, facing his own fears, agreed to enter a recovery center.

One of the assignments given to him during the first week of recovery was to write. For a man who could hardly wrap his weather-beaten hand around a pencil, this was a monumental task. According to him, he spent hours looking at the blank pages of his journal. What was he supposed to write about? What was it he felt?

Most of all, he wondered, would his words convey the despair in his own heart or the regret that overwhelmed him? Could they really make a difference?

As the questions and conflicts with which he struggled finally spilled out onto the page, he began to find the words; he began to find his voice.

In the end he wrote about a dozen pages, which, by a writer's standard, were hardly the introduction to a small body of work. For him, the pages constituted a major opus.

When he handed his journal to me, as required by the counselor, during the final week of the program, he was almost shaking.

I remember sitting there in the bare, cold conference room of the recovery center. At this point, I was filled with more questions than answers as to our future or joint recovery. Hope was wrapped in fear.

As I glanced down at the notebook, chills ran up and down my back and I couldn't speak. He anxiously apologized for the sloppy writing and squirmed as I opened to the first page. Then he seemed to hold his breath, a question in his glance.

Could he trust me with his confession?

I studied the tight, labored scrawl and instantly recognized the price my husband had paid for this sober examination of the bitterness and confusion he'd carried for so long. The first page represented little more than scattered, random thoughts, but by the second and third page, his words were filled with an intensity and clarity I'd never experienced in our life before this.

I read, and reread, his heart-felt yearning, and my own heart broke open in response. Miraculously, my husband's words not only touched me, they transformed me.

And in that moment, I fell in love all over again.

My Love
By Brenda Hammond

Just give me all you have
I will not break your heart
I know that things seem bad
You don't know where to start
I know you're in your head
Where you feel alone
Tangled in words once said
But none of them your own

Just come lay down with me
Just close your eyes

All the secrets that you keep
All the lies in which you speak

You don't need to hide from
me
My love
Just give yourself a chance
Untie your guarded heart
Everyone must learn to dance
With the courage to fall apart

Just come lay down with me
All the secrets that keep
All the truth in which you
seek
You don't need to hide from
me
My love

When the Lights Went Out
By Stanley Gedzelman

No! This is not a memoir about a special night of passion, or a blackout, or a natural disaster.

It is about two days when the lights went out. For the first, I was about 17. The exact day I'll never remember. My brother, Jack and I went down the block from our home to play two-person baseball with a high-bounce rubber ball called a Spaldeen. But, before we began the game that day, Jack took the opportunity to prove the accuracy of his throwing arm with my encouragement. A squirrel was running along an electrical wire about 20 feet above the ground. Jack grabbed several rocks. The first rock he threw would have hit the squirrel, but the squirrel saw it coming and did a vertical loop around the wire and continued running. It was quite acrobatic. The next rock followed two seconds later. It hit the squirrel flush on and knocked it off the wire. The squirrel fell to the ground, bounced a few inches, and Jack hit it with a third stone. For us it was a remarkable display of accuracy.

For the squirrel, it was something else. It twitched on its side, struggled to lift its head, which then collapsed back on the sidewalk a second and final time. I looked into its eyes and saw the moment when the lights went out for that little squirrel. I felt devastated and I think Jack did too. With and without intending, we had terminated a life – Jack through direct action, and I through eager complicity. It is the only creature other than insects and jelly fish, or while driving that I have ever killed. That little murder gave me a deep, intense feeling for the sacredness and miracle of life. What we had taken so quickly - so easily -no one could restore with all the expertise in the world. There lay the squirrel, complete before our eyes minus one vital, irreplaceable ingredient – life.

Forty years passed. It was a Tuesday morning – just another morning that I stayed home in New Jersey to do my research. I enjoyed my work but mourned its insignificance and my anonymity. I was seated at the kitchen table, writing a computer model to simulate the colors of the sky. It was pretty, especially when the sun set and the colors of the horizon sky changed. It was pretty, yes, but what was its value?

Thus, the day started as a morning like so many others that would have faded from my explicit memory. It started that way but did not end that way. My work was interrupted when the phone rang. It was my daughter, Elise calling from San Francisco. "Daddy, did you hear the World Trade Centers have collapsed?" It was 9/11, the day when the lights went out for over 3000 people in the primes of their lives.

I immediately had two thoughts. First, I regretted I had not seen and photographed the event from reasonably close up. As a meteorologist it would have been extraordinary to see the downbursts of debris-laden air produced by the collapsing towers.

My second thought was that neither I nor anyone whose life was imbued with a love of nature could ever have executed such evil. And, since much of my career had been devoted to describing and explaining the majesty and beauty of nature, I may have given people a reason to live and love and not to kill and die. It justified my teaching, my research, and my life. Later I found that this thought resonated strongly with my colleagues.

Of course, my thought is not true. There is always the paradoxical image of the highly cultured Nazi exterminator. We are all constructed in a certain sense to be schizophrenics. We can be simultaneously creators, inventors, builders on the one hand and raving, murderous ideologues on the other with no awareness of any inconsistency. We are born with a desire to be free but apenchant to be programmed. We are doomed to struggle with horrible impulses we have all been designed to crave. We are fashioned to see reality clearly with bright eyes and then embrace self-deception with equal delight, so that far too often we see the results of our actions only when the lights have gone out, and still don't sense what we've done or why we are groping in the dark.

I am a member of the club. I mourned the squirrel but eat fish, chicken or meat almost every day, turning an oblivious eye from the wholesale slaughter. I've had monstrous resentments, towering jealousies, and murderous moments. I feel rage towards Muslim mass murderers the world over without feeling commensurate pity for the victims. I still covet revenge against any colleague who years ago sought to harm me. And I feel no guilt about any of these feelings.

But there is one more strange incident that perplexes me. I had one chance to kill with impunity. Two teenagers attempted to mug my brother in Rio. I yearned to kill. A teenage boy was holding my brother. His accomplice — thin girl—was tugging at my brother's video camera. I sprinted to the conflict ready to smash her chin up into her skull. It was almost the time when the lights went out for her. But in the decision of an instant I merely shoved her into her accomplice. What deep-seated taboo withheld my hand from murder?

Let me add intolerance to my human virtues. I cannot abide those who have found ways to overcome the taboo against murder, neither the leaders and officials who cavalierly advocate, institute and execute war nor the drones who crave orders that enable and ennoble their taking of life. I sneer at any form of coercion, even if it appears to be complicit. I am repulsed by the hoods, veils, and shrouds of the orthodox of any sect or religion as a banner that signifies to me a war cry. I think them not innocent; to me they all goosestep to the tune, "Today I wear this, tomorrow you will."

All week long, I didn't know how to conclude this essay. All I could think of was why me? Why have I, who have withheld my hand from murder and from so many other crimes I wished to commit, why have I been forced to watch in one silent stroke when the light went out in my right eye? So now, ironically, I can see a moat in my eye but cannot see even a beam in anyone else's. But ending this essay in a bath of self-pity, one more of our many glorious human qualities, is not appropriate.

What is appropriate, and what is the real point is that after the squirrel, I didn't murder. And if everyone could say that and never have to look back on a time when the lights went out because of their actions, we'd all be far better off.

The Content Remains
By Don Rogers

Used books..used by whom? hard
to know... does it matter? used for
what purpose?
hard to know but it's probably does matter.

Used books.. used up ?
Hardly...the content remains.
so merely used and now for sale again what
had been $25 is now only one dollar. Still
the price did not change the content.
It only acknowledged the new designation.

Used books.. sign in a local store.
Drawing in bargain hunters and treasure seekers.
Who are often one in the same
I belong to that dual classification.
I quietly rejoice at finding a treasure
At a bargain price.

Used books.. used by whom?
Hard to know and it probably doesn't matter.
What does matter is that...
The books were used and recycled
Sent out to be used again
To be found by treasure seekers and bargain hunters
Used books... used up?
Hardly... the content remains

When I Stumped the Doctor
By Evelyn Safiri

So there I was, approximately 10 hours after the amputation, sitting up in bed and talking and laughing with my darling husband, Tom, and my dear brother-in-law, Steve (actually, I refer to him as my brother-in-love), when in walked the surgeon, Dr. Rosenman. The ensuing conversation went as follows – and this is my story and I'm stickin' to it!

Dr. Rosenman (DR): Well, Evelyn, I expected you to be less conscious right now. The nurses are complaining that you are not releasing enough morphine.

Me: I am not in a great deal of pain, which surprises no one more than me, I assure you, and you know how I am regarding all drugs, especially narcotics: don't want 'em if I don't need 'em.

DR: You have a very high tolerance of pain, apparently. (I laugh - who'd have thunk it?) Ok, then, let's talk about your stump.

Me: STUMP?!!!

DR: Yes. That is the common term for referring to a residual limb. Why are you making such a face?

Me: A stump is the dead remnant of a once-magnificent tree (and I love and hold a great reverence for trees). It is covered in lichen and moss and toadstools and thousands of creepy-crawlies who are intent upon slaughtering and devouring and excreting one another as rapidly as possible, leaving trails of oozing, yellow-green slime in their wakes. I firmly believe in the mind-body-spirit connection and I am so not having that mental image for healing purposes.

DR: Hmmmm... well, okay then, what would you like to call it?

Me, after pondering the matter for a moment: Well, I do believe that I will call it what I have always called it: my left leg... (Dramatic pause)... because it is, after all, what is left of my leg!!!

(And then I giggle hysterically, using what one of my wicked sisters refers to as my trademarked cackle... harumph!)

DR: Tom, I guess that she still is at least partially sedated, right?

My Darling (proving once again why he's my Darling): No... she's always like this!

DR (after a few seconds, and finally laughing at/with us – a goal that I have had for weeks): I can see that I do not have to worry about you two. You are going to be fine.

AND WE ARE!!!

What Matters
By Nadine Moreno

"Nadine!"

I heard her screaming my name, half a block away. I could just see her, standing on her porch with her hand on her hip.

"Yeah?!" I responded.

"Put that recycling bin back in front of that house!"

My friends and I had been kicking a green recycling bin along as we walked home, and I wasn't even sure which house we had found it in front of. My friends looked at me, mischievous grins awaiting my response. I knew they expected me to say something smart mouthed, something to let this woman know that she couldn't tell me what to do. I considered it, I did. I considered flat out ignoring her, or just leaving the bin there before we continued to walk home.

Instead, I turned around and started to kick the bin back in the direction we had come from.

"Nadine!"

What now? I turned back, "Yeah?!"

"Pick it up!"

Really? I picked it up, walked to the first house that didn't have a green bin out front and set it down. I wasn't sure if that was the house we had found it at, but it seemed good enough. When I got back to my friends, they had looks of disbelief on their faces. I just shook my head and kept walking, head down.

As we passed her house she gave a clipped "Thank you" before she went back inside.

When we reached my house, across the street from the one she went into, my friends were quick to make fun of me. They didn't understand why I'd bother listening to her, why I'd care what she thought. They knew she was not my favorite person. No one from that house was.

Except for him. He was my absolute favorite person. He was my first love, and even though we were currently broken up, I knew that we'd get back together. I knew that one day, what she thought of me, might just matter. She was his mom.

Seventeen years later, and what she thinks of does matter. She's my mother-in-law.

I'd be lying if I said that the day on her porch was the last time she raised her voice at me, or told me what to do. Nor was it the last time I ever considered smart mouthing her or flat out ignoring her. She's done her fair share of putting me in my place, and I've done my fair share of letting her know how I feel.

We didn't get the easiest start in our relationship. She watched me grow up from her kitchen window. She saw my awkward middle school years, my rebellious teenage years, all while being madly in love with her youngest son.

She would find ways to keep us apart. He'd be grounded, or have chores to do, or errands to run with her. Eventually we decided we'd keep the relationship a secret. We must have dated for an entire year without her knowing.

Over the years, I've come to realize certain things about her.

She's an insomniac. When we lived across the street from her, she'd call as late as 2 a.m. if she saw the lights on. My husband and I would be up late watching movies, and the phone would ring. "I saw the light on." It would drive me crazy, but now she's the one I call when I can't sleep, because I know she'll be awake.

She's horrible at keeping secrets. Seriously, within five minutes of getting off the phone with her, telling her that she absolutely could not tell anyone that I was pregnant, she told at least three relatives. Yet, I continue to confide in her every time I need someone to talk to.

She's opinionated. When my kids were babies, she'd constantly let me know how I could do something better. Always beginning with the famous, "Well when I raised my kids..." And even after I snapped back with a "Well let me raise mine!" I continue to go to her seeking advice.

Last year, she was diagnosed with an aggressive form of breast cancer. And what she thought about me didn't matter anymore, because all I could think about was what she meant to me. Throughout the years of driving each other crazy or flat out getting on each other's nerves, this woman had come to be more than my mother-in-law.

She's my stand-in mom. After having lost my own mother to cancer, my mother-in-law has done her best to be a mom to me as well as to my husband. She doesn't treat me like an in-law; she treats me like a daughter.

She's my go-to when I'm anxious. During the years that I struggled with an anxiety disorder, she was the one I'd call to talk me down if my husband was busy at work or school. To this day, I can call her and say "Just talk," and she knows exactly what to do.

She's my friend. We don't only get together at family events, or when my husbands around. We get our nails done together, talk on the phone every day, and laugh all night when she sleeps over. We've survived living across the street from one another, with each other, and in different states. We've shared tears of anger and tears of happiness. We've been angry enough at one another to lash out with harsh words, but love each other enough to always remember that that's why we get so angry in the first place.

At my wedding, her speech let everyone know that she wouldn't have ever accepted anyone else as her daughter-in-law. But now, it's my turn to let her know, I couldn't have asked for a better mother-in-law.

What I Learned from the Guru's Dog
By Helen Hansma

The guru moved out of his home on a hillside in Montecito, California. The house was to be sold, and the caretaker resident, Meenakshi, needed to get rid of the guru's little old dog Rama. She brought Rama to a sangha potluck of the guru's followers in Santa Barbara. My daughter was six at the time, and she begged to have Rama. We agreed. Rama came to us with his collar and leash and a knife that Meenakshi had been using to get his dog food out of the can.

"This is great!" I thought. "I'll get lots of good exercise," walking Rama on the bluffs above the ocean on West Campus, near our home in Isla Vista, the student ghetto beside UC Santa Barbara.

Little did I know! Rama loved walks. He would run with enthusiasm ... to the end of the driveway. Then he would creep along, at a most frustrating pace, to Coal Oil Point on West Campus and back. Sometimes, in his last months, we even had to go our house to get a green dishpan on a hand cart for bringing him home.

"What's wrong with him?" people would ask.

"He's 17 years old," I'd reply.

"Oh, he's so cute," they'd say, looking at his sweet little furry brown face, relieved that the dog was just old.

Rama got aroused, those early months with us, by any dog he met, male or female. My daughter now has some idiom for this – 'red rocket', I believe. My daughter took him to her second grade class one day, and the teacher said he got aroused there, too. "Some kids noticed and got excited. Some kids didn't notice," she said. Rama had, in fact, been known as a ladies man on the Montecito hillsides where he had roamed in his former home.

Rama was still a roamer, and we'd get phone calls to the phone number on his dog tag, from the people who found him. This was especially a problem if we were on vacation and Rama was staying with our friends. We'd come home to calls on our answering machine. But it all must have worked out OK, because my memories end there. One day, in response to a phone call, I walked over to Devereaux, a school for autistic adults near Coal Oil Point, to retrieve Rama from where he was lying by the desk of some administrative assistant.

Another time, Rama was even a Special Delivery Dog. The doorbell rang, and the mail woman – i.e., the letter-carrier – was there at the door, holding Rama. She had found him wandering around Camino Majorca and Del Playa, just above the beach. Knowing where he lived, she brought him home.

I'm surprised we didn't discover how he was escaping and fix our fenced back yard to prevent the problem; but Rama was our first dog, and maybe we just weren't careful yet about keeping the doors closed.

Rama's eyesight was poor. His hearing was probably bad, too. I've heard that directional hearing is one of the first things to go as one ages. In any case, I developed a routine for getting Rama to come from the back yard into the house.

I'd call, "Rama Rama!" and he must not have responded, because then I'd start clapping. He'd turn around in circles, trying to locate the source of the clapping. Given his poor vision, he could keep turning for quite a while without noticing me, so then I'd start waving my hands in the air when he had turned to face me, and that usually worked for getting him into the house.

Rama had a tumor on his rear end under his tail. It oozed and left gooey spots on the vinyl flooring in our dining room. When Rama lay out in the sunny back yard, flies landed on his rear end. I started covering his rear end with a yellow bath towel when he was lying out in the yard, but soon there were maggots in the tumor in his rear end. As I pulled them out with fine-tipped tweezers, I felt terribly martyred. But I had a delightful insight:

"This is how the world is! Looking at the world in one way is delightful. Looking at the world in another way is horrible." In Rama's case, the view from one direction was of a sweet furry doggy face; the view from the other direction was an oozing tumor and maggots!"

Rama didn't worry about all this. He just lay in his corner on his blanket and licked his rear end when he wanted to. I realized how much grief is caused simply by the act of worrying, and how much grief Rama was spared by not worrying.

Rama had an annoying belief. If he couldn't get outdoors to relieve himself, he though it was better to use the brown shag carpet in the living room instead of the vinyl floor of the dining room. We built little barriers of wood blocks across the doorways to keep Rama in the dining room. We stepped back and forth over them quite easily, but they sufficed to keep Rama on one side. When the guru visited us, however, he waited at the barrier until we removed it before going through the doorway.

When Rama came to us, he was not used to eating in public – i.e., in our dining room. He had been used to eating alone in the utility room of his previous home, and this was something new for him to get used to. He also was not accustomed to being a lap dog, because his previous caregiver was not a dog person. But he learned to enjoy being held on my lap and petted, as I sat cross-legged on the dining room floor.

The guru had gotten Rama from a rescue shelter many years before. He had selected a dog, but then another dog was leaping up on the cyclone fence, barking intensely, and this dog seemed to be begging to be chosen. So that's the dog who became Rama.

Photos show many of our other experiences with Rama – sleeping on the dining room floor with my daughter Joy's arm around him; being dressed up in doll clothes; eating from his dog dish while the cockatiel is perched on it; sleeping while our cockatiel pecks at the fur between his toes; looking adorable while standing in tall rye grass on the bluffs above the ocean.

As Rama aged, the question became, do we need to have the vet put him down? The good vet, Bill Wallace, explained that Rama would get two shots – one to relax him or put him to sleep and one to kill him. Even the guru thought that Rama had finished living out his karmic life, though some of the guru's disciples would probably be horrified and disbelieving about this. We saw Rama lying on his blanket in the corner of the dining room, suffering, or not suffering, and we talked with our daughter and son, seven and eleven years old, about whether it was time to end Rama's suffering. I've discovered that death and dying are the pits – one never knows when death will occur, or when the time has come to take some sort of action! We decided that the act should occur on the upcoming Saturday, but when the day came, Rama appeared not to be suffering, so we postponed the act. Finally a Saturday came when the decision was made. I took him to the vet. Unfortunately the other vet was on duty, and Rama, lying in my lap, was killed with the single, killing, shot, baring his teeth, which was not a happy way to die.

I brought him home, and we planted – I mean, buried - him in his blanket under my daughter's bedroom window, and planted a jade plant on top of him. Then the kids' dad made us french fries and frozen peas and we ate lunch; we were good vegetarians at that time.

Forgetting
By Michele Jessen

I cannot remember what is lost
No matter the focus or the cost

Was it life or death to be?
Was it simply the past of me?

Our future is our present, here today
Our past was our future, yesterday

So confused, this chaos is not mine
So perplexed, my soul lost in rhyme

Love in snippets darn the holes
Weaving patches of my soul

Needle threaded, to stitch in time
A life in pictures passing, now sublime

What I know is true, that I don't belong
What I know my due, for which I long

That this identity is all wrong
Searching for serenity, now just a song

Visiting
By Ruth Stout

Mom was a widow for fifteen years. Then one day in 1975 at the age of sixty-five, she up and married the man next door. We, her children, were astonished. Our mother, getting married? We were perfectly happy having her to ourselves. We were all married, but assumed she would spend the rest of her life alone. We suffered a communal failure of the imagination. She didn't want to live alone any longer and she wasn't going to.

We knew a little about the man she married. His name was Bill, his first wife had committed suicide, he was fifteen years younger than my mother but looked older, and he was obsessively neat. After the wedding, we discovered traits that made liking him difficult. However, we loved our mother, so we needed to get along with Bill. We made it a habit to fly from the Bay Area to Portland, Oregon to visit them several times a year.

Visits to Mom and Bill were always precarious, similar to driving on a poorly maintained road along the side of a cliff. It was almost impossible to avoid the potholes and very possible to drive off the cliff. By necessity, we avoided a number of subjects. Politics, race, house cleaning methods, eating too much, eating too little, and long hair on men were among them.

Relatives were usually a safe topic. Mom would gleefully give us an update on the foibles and missteps of various aunts, uncles and cousins. One aunt was always pretending to be sick, another refused to bring a flower arrangement to the Garden Club, an uncle was bone lazy, an aunt served spoiled peaches for dessert, a cousin inappropriately knitted at important family gatherings. All I had to do was listen and be glad I wasn't the current target.

Another generally safe topic was travel. Mom and Bill traveled a lot and loved to talk about and show slides from their trips. It was a seemingly harmless, if boring, way to pass the time. Yet one session of slide watching very nearly drove us off the cliff. My sister, Carol, and her husband, Jack, were also staying with Mom and Bill. Jack was long haired, hippyish, and thin as a snake despite never going anywhere without a six pack of beer.

Carol and Jack were decidedly liberal. Mom and Bill were decidedly not. We settled in for a night of watching slides of Mom and Bill's latest cruise. I was about to nod off when Bill showed us pictures of the couple they were seated with in the ship's dining room. He was clearly distressed when he talked about them. "We had such a good time with them," he said. "They seemed like very nice people, then," he said, as though he'd discovered a communist under his bed, "We found out they were Jewish!" Bill was struggling, trying to reconcile such apparently mutually exclusive facts. The couple were nice, friendly and fun, and they were Jewish. How was that possible? My ever sarcastic brother-in-law didn't miss a beat, "Oh," he said with a straight face, "they must have been White Jews." White Jews, Bill brightened, completely missing the sarcasm. He hadn't been fooled after all, they were White Jews. White Jews must be ok. Mom knew that her hippyish son-in-law had shown Bill up for a fool, but what could she say?

Carol and Jack survived the tale of the Great White Jew, but stumbled into another misadventure on their next visit. They were practiced at biting their tongues when Mom expressed her admiration for Richard Nixon. They winced but tried to keep quiet when Bill maligned Jews, Catholics, Hispanics, uppity women and practically everyone else who wasn't him. When Mom suggested taking a trip to Bend, Oregon, they were not enthusiastic, but agreed. Bend is hot and dry and not their favorite spot, but Mom and Bill liked it, so to Bend they went.

When they got there, Carol discovered that Bill, in a truly excessive amount of thriftiness, had booked only one motel room with two beds. They were all going to sleep in the same room. Carol took Mom aside and hissed, "Mom, I never wear a nightgown or pajamas, how am I supposed to sleep in the same room as Bill?"

"You don't have anything to wear to bed?" Mom was slightly shocked. "No, nothing," my sister replied. "Maybe I have something." Mom said. She checked her luggage and came up with, she thought, the perfect thing. "Here," she said, thrusting the garment at Carol, "You can wear this." "Your swimsuit!", Carol cried, "I have to wear your swimsuit?" It was a vast rubbery garment devoid of any charm or comfort. Jack protested that she felt "scaly", but Carol wore it. Modesty was preserved if comfort was not.

In another visit Carol and Jack had to be hauled back up after going over the cliff. Carol and Jack stayed on the second floor of Mom and Bill's house which had a bedroom and bathroom. There was a small radio in the bathroom which they used to listen to music and the news. The visit seemed to go surprisingly well and they went home breathing a sigh of relief.

The next day my mother called me in a rage. "Do you know what your sister and her husband did!" She shouted. "No," I said, "what did they do?" "They changed the station on Bill's radio. The one in the upstairs bathroom." "They changed the station?" I asked, confused over why she was so angry. "Yes, I'm going to cut her out of the will." "What!" I exclaimed. "You're going to cut her out of the will?" "Yes!" "Mom," I said taking a deep breath to calm myself, "you can't cut Carol out of the will for changing the radio station." "I can't?" "No, you can't." "Well, it took Bill a long time to find his station again." His talk radio station was the 70s equivalent of Rush Limbaugh. "He did find it, though." I said. "Yes, he did." "Then Carol stays in the will."

There was really no chance that Mom was going to cut any of us out of the will. We might not be perfect children or married to perfect spouses, but we were her imperfect children and she would never quite leave us or let us go. She was an imperfect mother married to an imperfect spouse, but family is family and we were going to keep right on visiting.

To Hypnotize a Chicken
By Marjorie Johnson

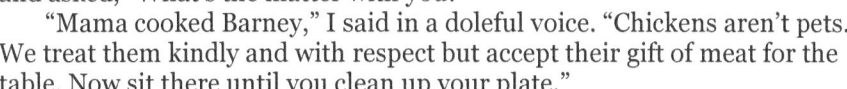

I stared at the fried chicken on my plate and twisted my fork through the mashed potatoes to move them away from the gravy. How could Daddy give my best subject to Mama to cook for Sunday dinner? I swallowed hard and announced, "I can't eat Barney."

My mother looked down and crushed her napkin in her lap. My younger sisters stopped eating and gazed at me in silent amazement. My father frowned and asked, "What's the matter with you?"

"Mama cooked Barney," I said in a doleful voice. "Chickens aren't pets. We treat them kindly and with respect but accept their gift of meat for the table. Now sit there until you clean up your plate."

That was the rule. I chewed two peas until they liquefied and thought back two years to when Daddy brought home the first baby chickens to add meat and eggs to his World War II victory garden. He built a chicken house in the backyard and invented an incubator by putting a light bulb under an inverted aluminum dishpan held two inches above the floor by blocks of wood.

The fluff-ball chicks ran in and out from their warm incubator to get food and water, peep-peep-peeping and poop-poop-pooping. Once Daddy nursed a droopy chick by bathing it and setting it in a cardboard shoebox in the warming oven of Mama's wood burning cook-stove to dry out. Mama didn't like having a chicken in the kitchen, but Daddy said it was all part of the war effort.

Daddy followed the advice he found in USDA publications on how to raise chickens and invested in White Leghorns, Cornish Hampshires, Rhode Island Reds, and Plymouth Rocks. The Plymouth Rocks were white with black and gray speckles like Mama's feather duster but with yellow feet and red comb and wattles. Daddy told me that the White Leghorn was the best egg layer, the Cornish Hampshire best for meat, but the Rhode Island Red was the best all around chicken. I thought so, too, from my studies in the chicken yard and because the Rhode Islands Reds were easier to catch.

I fed the flock every day. The chickens ate mash—a ground dry food that came in fifty-pound sacks—supplemented with dried corn, wheat kernels, sunflower seeds, and vegetable scraps from the garden. My father grew corn and table vegetables and sunflowers, giant sunflowers with nine-foot stalks and eighteen-inch heads, large enough that he took several blue ribbons at the county fair.

The chickens always ate the sunflower seeds first and left the mash for last. To find out why, I sampled all their feed. No wonder they weren't enthusiastic about the mash: the stuff tasted like dried alfalfa and stuck to the roof of my mouth. The corn was tough and tasteless, but the wheat developed a delicate flavor after extended chewing. However, the sunflower seeds were scrumptious and worth the time to pick them out of the dried heads that Daddy kept under his workbench in the garage.

In addition to a scientifically balanced diet, Daddy gave the hens crushed oyster shell to help harden their eggshells. I tried a few bites of it because I wanted to harden my teeth to avoid trips to the dentist. Instead, I cracked a tooth. Daddy said oyster shell wouldn't work for little girls because they don't have gizzards, and chickens grind up their food with rocks in their gizzards because they don't have teeth.

The chickens had their own house with clean straw on the floor, a closet rod for roosting at night, and nesting boxes with glass eggs in them to show the hens where to lay, but they didn't pay attention. Hens will lay eggs anywhere, singing cut-cut-cut-ca-docket outside under a bush. When one brown hen walked about cluck-cluck-clucking, feathers all fluffed out, pretending she had chicks, Daddy gave her half a dozen fertilized eggs from the feed-store. They hatched after twenty-one days, each wet naked chick pecking its way out of its shell and drying into a yellow ball of fluff.

I liked to hold a chicken just to feel its soft feathers. Afternoons after I finished my chores, I would sit quietly amongst the chickens to observe their behavior. I named them all, even though Daddy told me not to make pets out of them. Each chicken had a distinct personality and a place in the pecking order: some chickens always ate first, and the same one always had to wait until last. Chickens like to take dust baths out in their yard and scratch everything up, looking for bugs. Afterwards, a chicken cranes its neck, almost tying itself into a knot, to reach the oil sack above its tail with its beak and then to preen its feathers.

I found a book on animal behavior in the library and wondered what chickens could learn to do. At the movies, I had watched a hypnotist who induced relaxation with a soothing voice while his subject stared at a slowly swinging watch suspended from a gold chain. How could I make a chicken with a habit of bobbing his head around all the time pay attention? I picked one up and stroked it and told it a bedtime story until it relaxed in my lap. Next, moving slowly and gently, I lay the bird on its side on the ground to prevent head movement and to force it to focus with only one eye. I hypnotized the chicken by slowly rotating my hand over its eye, then releasing the bird and moving farther and farther away. The chicken would remain prone for several minutes before stumbling to its feet, always shaking its head a few times as if asking, "What happened?" I got the same results when I rested a chicken on its breast, beak to the ground, and drew a line in the dirt outward from the tip of its beak. Teen-aged male and female chickens—cockerels and pullets—behaved in the same way; I never tested an adult rooster. My best subject was the cockerel I called Barney, but I should have chosen a pullet.

Daddy slaughtered a chicken every Sunday, usually a male that had awakened the neighbors by learning to crow. Daddy started by cutting off the head with a hatchet and draining the blood. Then he poured boiling water over it and removed the feathers and held the naked bird over a burning newspaper torch to take off any hair. Except for the yellow feet, it wasn't a chicken anymore, only meat.

Finally at the kitchen sink, Daddy gave me anatomy lessons, a different one each week: muscles, tendons, and cartilage; windpipe and lungs; entrails and a gizzard that held rocks to grind food; the liver with a gall bladder that had to be removed without spilling any bitter bile. The hens had eggs inside, small eggs not yet within a shell, and the grooming sack on the tail contained one drop of oil.

Once we looked at a chicken's tongue with a magnifying glass to see its taste buds, and Daddy said I should study anatomy. "You learn this so fast you could be a doctor someday," he said.

Mama looked up from stirring applesauce on the stove and said, "Now don't you be filling her head with fool notions. A nurse, maybe, until she gets married."

I shrugged my shoulders. I didn't care because I didn't want to be a doctor. I was more interested in how to teach chickens than in what they had inside.

On Sundays after Daddy cut up a chicken, Mama would cook a special dinner. I usually peeled potatoes while Daddy cleaned up the mess. He dug holes in the yard for all the entrails and other leftover parts such as the yellow feet, and he mixed in poop from the chicken house to make his special fertilizer for the sunflowers. Daddy never wasted anything.

Everything was reused until it was hard to say which came first, the chicken or the giant sunflower.

I should have known that Barney's turn was coming. I sat with my dinner still on my plate and watched everyone else enjoy apple pie. After my sisters were excused and my father left the table, I had a five-minute window of opportunity when my mother went into the bathroom to clean her false teeth. I scooted out to the chicken yard and threw the gravy-coated potatoes over the fence. Then I put Barney's drumstick into a hole in the garden and hurried back to the table with my clean plate.

I felt sad about losing Barney but Daddy was right: the chickens did give us the gift of meat for the table. Maybe this was my bit for the war effort. I gave up my studies on chicken hypnosis, but I didn't eat Barney.

Self
By Nicole Justine Cavanaugh

I pour myself a
sudden rush –
thunked gracelessly,
in any place that will hold me
Looking for shelter,
I smash sanctuaries thrashing against
my homelessness
A moment steady and still
I peer into the window of home past
my flesh, beyond bones deep
in the blood:
The raw, red spirit crying
white, soft tears

This Old House
By Marcia Healy

We were just kids, fourth graders actually. He was one of the smart-alecky boys, always acting silly, talking loudly and constantly getting in trouble. I was one of those teacher's pets, goody-goody, prima-donna girls. Oil and water, hot and cold, good and bad--never the twain shall meet.

In the sixth grade, our world turned completely upside down. Returning from summer vacation, we were now giddy, laughing flirty femme fatales and slouchy, swaggering macho guys, with crashing, swirling raging hormones. That's when Steven and I became girlfriend and boyfriend, a couple, inseparable.

Then, as a fifteen year-old high school freshman, I did the unthinkable. I ditched him. As has been documented, teenage girls can be ruthlessly brutal. I mean, upper classmen, who drive their own cars could not be avoided or resisted. We drifted apart into a casual friendship throughout high school, each dating others.

A good-bye kiss on grad-night sent us each out into the world. It would be thirty years before we would see each other again. In between, we would each marry, raise families, and be alone again.

Then out of nowhere, I got a call from him. It was the day after our thirtieth high school reunion, which I had been unable to attend. He said he would like to drop by and see me. We talked and laughed all afternoon. Crazily, we repeated a catch up afternoon ten years later, after our fortieth reunion. The more we talked, reminisced and compared our youth; we were astonished at how similar our early years had been. Both of us were born in San Francisco. We had both moved down the Peninsula, from the city at about the same age. We laughed as we tentatively planned a San Francisco excursion to try to find our city homes.

Right after Christmas this year, Steven called. In early February, he is driving down from Northern California and we are spending the day in San Francisco house hunting. The fashion Gods had been kind. The pile of rejected clothes on my bed had finally resulted in the perfect, casual, yet alluring slacks and sweater.

The hair Gods had been kind. It was a good hair day with waves falling just right and the cowlick under control. Stylish, but not styled.

The weather Gods had been kind. The day was clear, bright and promised to be warm for the end of February, even for San Francisco. Steven had promised a perfect day when he called to plan our odyssey.

As we laughed our way toward San Francisco, we had already decided I would read the map, but leave the driving and street choices to him. We both acknowledged that since I had no sense of direction, I would keep my mouth shut and offer no suggestions. Steven proved to be a good driver and almost before I could get my emotions in check he announced, "Here is Whipple Street, right where the map shows it. You did good."

The map reminded me that the street was only three blocks long, between Mission and Alemany. Almost immediately, Steven stopped the car and waited. I looked to the left, gasped and voice shaking, declared, "Oh, my God. It is just as I remembered." The double set of steps up to the landing, one for each of the houses, sitting side by side. On the side of the wall, next to the right hand staircase, the numbers one seven five in shiny white were familiar.

As I stared at the memory of my childhood, I wondered what had happened to Doris and Alice, the two sisters who lived next door. Doris was my age and Alice was three years older. Doris and I spent most of our time tormenting Alice, sneaking into her room and riding her bike, all of which we had been forbidden to do. I remembered the tears we shed when my family moved.

Bless Steven's heart. He stayed parked in front of my old house long enough for me to remember the happy times, but slowly started to drift down the street as I became sad and teary eyed. He wanted me to remember only the good. "One down and two to go," he declared. Let's see if we can find my old houses."

We spent the next two hours driving across San Francisco, the outskirts of the Presidio area and all over the Marina. Even though the map showed the street in the Presidio area, we could get to every street around it, but it eluded us. We decided the recent reconfiguration of the area had lost the street to progress. We did find the street in the Marina, but Steven wasn't sure he recognized the house that had been his grandparents. So many of the houses had undergone remodeled front entrances, making it difficult to identify an original home. Steven wasn't too disappointed; we had a least found the street, which was somewhat familiar.

Deciding we had had enough of detective work and were starving we decided to get lunch. As homage to our San Francisco births, we headed to Fisherman's Wharf and Crab Louie salads.

Snow
By Ryann Murrin-Desouza

The newborn snow falls,
Gently from the sky.
Like a precious child,
Being born from its mother.
The snow covers the land,
Like a blanket covers a baby.
The life of the snow is,
Just like the child that will grow.
The snow is a great beauty to behold.
Just like having a child to hold.

O Priest of God:
By Frank Saunders

Do you not proclaim,
whenever you declare the essence of your faith,
      "He will come again in glory
              to judge the living and the dead"?
Stand, therefore, in your pulpit,
looking over the upturned faces of your congregation, and
pause, seeing deeply into the heart
of each person that God puts before you in your path.
Ask from the depths of your soul: "Are you Jesus?"

Stop your speech, and wait,
and listen for the susurrating response that comes from
here: "I am He,"
and from this side: "I am She,"
and from the back: "I am He,"
and from the person before you: "I am She."

When you approach, drawing near with an
open and willing heart,
I promise you:
you will find me:
you will find God.

Moon in My Tea
By Cheyenne Wiseman

The moon always sits in my cup of tea
Does it see my eyes, does it even care?
An opaque sphere of ice, cooling my drink
Did you know that tea is the liquid of my soul?
No, I don't think the moon listens,
Otherwise it would have sunken with my prayers.
It's more of a show in the sky, a queen
who does not hear the cries of her peasants,
Who enjoys being all alone with sparkling gems,
To forever gaze at her king.
My tea is half a raindrop to the sky,
There's no one to say it happened,
No one to call my name.

The Principal of the Matter
Evie Groch

As I left the office in the modern, suburban, school in Concord, one day in the late sixties, I didn't know how I had handled the interview and if it had gone well. I had never been asked these kinds of questions and had no idea if I addressed them well. Walking back to the car in my gray interview suit and black heels, I felt like a phony. What did I know about how to interview? No one had prepared me; however, I knew I could teach, especially Spanish, and would do a great job if given the chance. When the principal asked how soon I planned to start a family, my jaw dropped. Did he really want me to share my private plans with him? I wanted to say, "None of your business," but what came out of my mouth was, "Not right away." There was no visible reaction on his face. Next came another zinger, "What was your college GPA?" How odd, I thought. Does he want to know my GPA or if I can teach? Why doesn't he ask me questions about teaching? Ask me about my ability in Spanish. I was student teaching at the school, and he had been in to observe me many times. Why ask about my college GPA now?

He looked very professional sitting behind his desk wearing frameless glasses, hardly any papers showing. Way too neat for my taste. Everything in the office was immaculate, bordering on sterile. Even the potted plant looked artificial. Would I even like it here? Could I work for someone who was so concerned with answers to questions I deemed inappropriate and off limits? Yet, I loved working with the students and wanted the job; this would be my ideal position: a fairly new school with supportive parents and bright students in a high school setting where I felt much more comfortable than at middle school. However, I could not work for a school whose principal didn't believe in my capability. At this point, I had already built up a barrier in my mind against liking the principal.

I feared his values were so different from mine that we might just not mesh working together. Still hopeful, however, I offered him a final statement as I left the interview: "I know my subject well and will work very hard. I won't let anyone down."

As I drove home, I tried to gain perspective and rethink some of my answers. They were all a blur. The Caldecott Tunnel was not only a physical barrier between my work in Concord and where I lived in Berkeley at the time, but also a mental one. It was like crossing from one culture to another. As I headed for the tunnel, I could feel the cooler air welcoming me. People east of the tunnel were much more rural and conservative. Students could ride their horses to school and tie them up behind the bleachers. The smell of manure contrasted with the pot odor through the tunnel. Walnut groves lined the single lanes leading from the freeway to the school, and traffic lights were scarce. The Berkeleyites west of the tunnel were hip, academic, university types. The scent of marijuana mixed with incense accompanied us through the campus as we traveled to and from classes. Protests were common, and at times we couldn't get into our apartment without showing our ID or fighting tear gas. What would that principal, Dr. Wutzke, know about my city west of the tunnel? Had he ever run the gauntlet down Telegraph Avenue or eaten pizza at Blondie's?

He knew much more than I realized. He did offer me the job, and I now had a career. About 75% of the staff he had hired at Ygnacio Valley High School came from west of the tunnel. He appreciated the younger generation educated at UC Berkeley and welcomed its new ideas and teaching methods into the school. Who else would question authority, challenge the status quo, or bring the controversial Ms. Magazine into the library? He didn't fear change despite his never-changing appearance. Standing close to six feet tall, from Germanic roots, he was a respected and admired leader, even though many made fun of his hair transplants visibly showing on his scalp.

At times we found him a little awkward in social situations, but he had our backs as teachers and defended us to parents and the district. At one graduation ceremony, he instructed the students to "pick up your diplomas at my rear," while everyone chuckled. Students had planned to each hand him a marble as they shook his hand on stage. As he resorted to filling his pants and jacket pockets with overflowing marbles, faculty rushed to aid him with containers to house these pesky tokens of defiance. He took this in stride and didn't show anger or disappointment.

Every time we were observed in the classroom, we were anxious for class to end so we could run to our mailboxes and find that special little note from our principal, Ernie, (which I couldn't call him for years) thanking us and applauding what we were doing. I recall walking deliberately with huge strides, just below a running pace, to reach my mailbox after an observation he did of me. Yes, he left a note! I savored the view of the envelope in my mailbox with my name on it in his handwriting. I fingered it for a moment before tearing it open to read "I enjoyed your class today. The students were engaged, and you did a nice job leading the lesson." My day was made. It meant something special to us, his personal notes in his familiar handwriting. I saved them for years.

After teaching for about five years at the school, I became pregnant, and at first, was almost afraid to tell Ernie. My loose fitting tops would only hide my condition for a short time. I planned my meetings with him seated behind a table until the table had to be moved further and further away from me. When I finally told him, he seemed to already know. I shared with him that my plan was to come back to teaching as soon as I could. I even asked him to save me my job. He agreed.

When the teachers went on strike in 1975, Ernie felt for us and came around with donuts for us, glazed, chocolate covered, and crumb, as we marched in front of the school. He did want us back in the classrooms, but he understood the unfairness under which we were teaching - - being the lowest paid teachers in the county under a new superintendent whose goal it was to break the unions.

After the birth of our second daughter, I returned to work immediately, having exacted another promise from Ernie to save my job yet a second time. I picked right up where I had left off and stood solidly with my peers as we endured protest after protest from the student body for a variety of reasons ranging from anti Vietnam War sentiments to student rights. This response from students was the first in the history of the school, and it may have had something to do with the proximity of the UC Berkeley campus and its effect on our students as they became aware of the free speech movement and demanded more from teachers and administrators. As teachers, we weren't allowed to protest, but we supported the students in their anti-war stance. Throughout it all, Ernie stayed calm. He met with students, allowed them to have rallies, and most of all, listened to them with an empathetic ear, refraining from judging them. In hindsight, I can understand that to have done any less would have ignited a greater surge of protests.

I stayed at Ygnacio Vally High School for 23 years, outstaying Ernie. Before he retired, I stopped by to ask him if he thought I had made good on my promise to be loyal and faithful to the school in spite of my decision to become a parent and not caring so much about my college GPA. It was evident he didn't remember this, but neither did he deny it. We had a good laugh.

All these thoughts ran through my mind as I sat next to Phyllis in the Fireside room at Rossmoor for a memorial service for Dr. Ernest Wutzke. Many former faculty members and students were in attendance. They say we always remember our first, and he was mine. What I learned from him I used in my own administrative career, and it still serves as a basis for my supervision of new administrators. No other principal had as much influence on me and my career as he did, many times by his modeling alone.

Beyond Words
Thomas Ekkens

A look beyond words to something deeper
That lies hidden in clarity revealed
By the obvious — mourning doves concealed In
furrowed dust, stalk the morning reaper.
Irony of words on slopes no steeper
Than a poet, wandering far afield
Of dreams, can climb — red-tailed hawk, talons
steeled
In blurred descent, close on those that keep her.
Pictographs, hieroglyphs, beyond words,
Beyond the broad brush stroke of paint and form
Where poet meets silence — fires glow warm
Against canvas of thought, bats become birds.
Words are clouds on trade winds — above the storm,
Albatross span motionless; sleek, white herds.

The Middle Bedroom Closet
By Sally Shunsky-Hernandez

During WW II, our grandmother and father purchased the three bedroom brick house in Detroit. Grandma Shunsky lived in the upper flat while we lived on the first floor. Our parents slept in the front bedroom; my brother had the third bedroom near the kitchen while my sister and I shared the middle room. All the bedrooms were small, approximately nine by twelve feet. Fitting even a double size bed in those rooms was a squeeze. When my sister was born, she slept in a crib in our parents' room until they thought she was old enough to share a bed. I had the middle bedroom and closet to myself for several years.

My only problem – that closet was filled with ghosts, critters, and demons. They lived there and came out in the middle of night when all the lights were out. I called out often for my mother because I was afraid. Mother came in several times a night when the visitors were making noises in the closet. In their bedroom, she slept closer to the door and could hear me calling her. Dad was hard of hearing because of his job and slept facing away from the door. Mother never found anyone hiding in the closet and told me that I was dreaming. She would force a sip of water on me and urge me to go back to sleep. But, how could I sleep when all those characters were still in the closet? When I heard the voices, I would tighten my eyelids and pull the blanket up over my head.

My visitors came out of the closet in pairs and they didn't always arrive in the bedroom with the same partner. In all, there were five to six guests. Scariest of all was the old man with the dirty, gray, hair that was matted. He smelled like rotten tuna or cat food. There was a toothless child that didn't walk properly; her one leg was shorter than the other. There was an old lady who resembled the witch in my fairy tale books. She smelled of moth balls like Grandma Shunsk. There was a boy who had hair that glowed in the dark. He always had a blank expression on his face. There were also two indescribable globs that appeared on some evenings. One glob was greenish and the other glob was bluish green. It was a strange grouping of characters but they were all scary.

"Click, click", was the sound of the closet doorknob turning. Hearing that sound, I grabbed the satin edge of my blanket tighter and pulled it closely around my shoulders. Quickly, they crept into the bedroom and then I heard them open the bedroom door which made a creaking sound. Next, they walked out into the hallway and into the dining room where they walked around the table multiple times. Our parents' bedroom was located right beside the dining room yet they swore to me that they never heard anyone in the dining room. One night, my mother searched the first floor and went down into the basement to assure me that no one was in the house that didn't belong there. My father always said that it was the ghost of the previous owner who had died in the middle bedroom. I would ask, "If only one man died here, who are these other people?" Dad said that they were friends and family members of the dead man. Then my mother would be angry with my father for putting such ideas into my imagination.

The question of who the nighttime visitors were and why they came to visit me was never answered in my opinion. I don't remember when they made their last appearance, but I don't remember them coming again after my sister moved in.

Years later, my mother told me that she thought I heard the old house creaking with noises from the new gas furnaces that were installed to replace the coal heat in both flats.

I want to agree with my mother's last theory but I know what I saw. I never told her but one time, I jumped out of bed when I heard the clicking of the doorknob. I ran to the closet door, turned the knob and quickly pulled it open. Then I knew the truth.

Eternal Mystery
Bernadine Fornesi

Heat from the scorching ball of fire
Wills blood red roses to bloom
Blushing fruit hangs heavy on overburdened limbs

All too soon the gossamer clouds in unblemished skies of blue
Gather in dark grey palettes
Clearly harbingers from the North

The merciless winds start to howl
The velvet nights turn frigid
Stripped of blooms and leaves

Beauty no longer prevails
Thorns offer no resistance
As they wither with decay

The perfume soon exhales
As the roses in coma
Lie beneath suffocating blankets of snow

They wait till the system devised by nature
With laws of cosmic drama sends forth green
A mystery hard to solve as the Rosetta Stone

The circle softly humming now complete
No mockery as it survives
Only to repeat again and yet again

The Gift
Brenda Hammond

I was 25 the first time I noticed that something was wrong. Having been in perfect health for all of my life, it was easy to see that my body was not acting as it should. Twitching. Jerking. Pulsating. Hundreds of times a day, muscles contorting ever so slightly underneath my skin. It was visible to the naked eye. I was concerned, but I was in shape. I had a great job. I was pretty. There's no way anything was wrong with me.

It was summer when I started noticing these changes. We had a family history of Amyotrophic Lateral Sclerosis (ALS), though no one really knew if great granddad actually died of it. It had always scared me as a little girl, and I remember my father telling me that it ran in families, and how fearful he was of developing it. He told the story of witnessing great granddad's awful demise, suffocating and soiled, as he died a merciless death in a 1950s hospital. There was nothing anyone could do for him, dad said, and there's still nothing they can do for you today.

Growing up with the subtle anticipation that at any moment you or your family members could be stricken with a horrific and fatal disease contributed to my increasing worry with my health. I was almost expecting it. Nervously, I did a quick search on the internet for early symptoms of ALS. The top answer: body twitching.

I made an appointment with my general doctor. I explained the twitching and she ordered a full physical. My results were normal and she told me that the body twitching was nothing to be alarmed about. That it was likely just stress and I should relax. Unsatisfied, I went to Google, where I would spend every spare moment for the nextnine months researching my symptoms and asking strangers in chat rooms what they thought I should do. It turns out there are many people who believe something is wrong with them. Isolated and panicked, they find comradely and comfort through the shared frustration that such ambiguity brings. They find hope. They find connection, when traditional care has failed.

The final time I visited the generalist, I asked for an MRI. I had become her worst nightmare. She said insurance wouldn't cover it, as there was no medical reason to run one. She wrote me a Prozac prescription, instead. Then a Paxil prescription for the anxiety. I didn't need Paxil, I needed an answer. I decided to take my health and life into my own hands and scheduled an appointment with a neurologist, who did a full exam and wrote me a clean bill of health. I begged her for more tests. She agreed to do a lumbar puncture. The test came back inconclusive, and she reinforced that there was nothing wrong with me.

By this time it had been months and months of body twitching and internet surfing. I was convinced that I was dying. I knew that I had ALS. But worse than dying, I was losing my mind. The endless medical appointments, the guessing, the symptoms, and the loneliness were an obsession like I'd never known. I couldn't eat, couldn't sleep, cried all the time, and lost 15 pounds. Yes, you can worry yourself sick. I did.

I had little support from friends and family. They continually reminded me that several doctors had cleared me and that I should keep taking the meds. This alienation drove me deeper into my depression and mania about my own impending death. Night after night, I would come home and go into the spare bedroom in my house, sit on the futon and cry. Sobbing and praying, clutching my faded childhood bible in my hands, I begged God to spare my life. I asked tough questions. How could a God who is known to millions as being loving, tender, merciful and kind, allow this to happen to me. How cruel it is to give a life only to end it before it comes to fruition. I had dreams. I had plans. I was just getting started.

I made one final appointment with the neurologist. I told her I thought I had ALS. She pointed out that it was an extremely rare disease, especially for women and those under the age of 40. I didn't believe her. I had myself so convinced that I was dying, I'm surprised my will alone did not kill me. I was desperate. I told her please, please just run an MRI. She said, "Ok. I'll do an MRI. But I really doubt I'm gonna see anything." One week later she called. There was one 1 mm non-specific lesion residing in white matter aroundthe left ventricle. She referred me to Stanford Hospital. "What do you think this is?" I asked. "MS," she replied flatly. "You fit the criteria for it."

Within a month I was sitting in the MS clinic at Stanford Hospital. I met the neurologist, a good looking blonde woman who was about ten years my senior. She was stylish, and she liked my shoes. She ran her own tests and concluded that the body twitching was simply a condition called Benign Fasciculation Syndrome, (BFS), and that the lesion was not a big deal. Sometimes lesions develop, absent of disease, but it was not the cause of the BFS. She theorized that I had a virus affecting my peripheral nervous system which would go away on its own. Feeling some relief, I happily accepted her verdict as truth. And, I realized that by now, it had been at least nine months since my first appointment with the generalist. If I had ALS, I would be in declining health; I would be peeing all over myself. We agreed that an MRI in one year would confirm this theory.

The follow up MRI that winter was easy enough. I was confident that I was fine and that the visit to MS clinic was just a formality. It seemed like an eternity when the blonde neurologist, Dr. Gould, finally came in the exam room to give me the results of my latest MRI. "So, I have some not so good news. You have five new brain lesions; you have relapsing-remitting MS. I'm sorry." Tears immediately streamed silently down my checks. I was in shock. She reached out and touched my arm. She continued, "I'm sorry that I said it was a low-likelihood that you had it. Your symptoms had not advanced enough so we could confidently diagnose it."

This September will be my tenth anniversary living with this disease. I have too many lesions now to count. Bladder issues, weakness, body twitching and numbness are just a normal part of my day. One year I landed myself at Stanford Hospital to receive intravenous corticosteroid treatment for three days after a large, problematic lesion developed on my spine. Dr. Gould told me I was extremely lucky. That if the lesion had been just a little to the left or the right of where it was, I would not be walking. That lesion still exists today, though is considered inactive.

Another two have developed just below it. I will never know when one will develop that will disable me.

My journey to diagnosis was the most frustrating, demoralizing, and terrifying experience that I have ever known. No one listened to me. No one walked with me down that road of despair. The disappointment was crushing. I am certain that living with uncertainty is one of the hardest things in life. We live with an assumption that we have control over what happens to us. We are focused on the outcome of our lives; the goal, the plan. But it's never about the outcome; it's always about the journey. Having a plan helps us feel in control. But it's the journey that provides the opportunity for real growth and a true expansion of your spirit and soul. That's where the gift is. The gift is the opportunity. But most of us are so focused on an outcome, that we miss the gift. I was so desperate for an outcome that I made myself sick trying to fit symptoms into a disease that I didn't have. I was ready to accept dying as my fate just so I could feel better. I almost missed the opportunity.

I still deal with the uncertainty of this disease, but I've made peace. I've accepted the gift of my journey. Today I am integrated. I am weak and I am strong. I am humble and I am fierce. I accept life on life's terms. And I understand now that family and friends were just as inept, just as unprepared, and just as upset as I was. And I forgive them. We are all doing the best we can, wherever we are in the journey.

Boston, April 2013
By William Baldwin

Well—and blood-stained bodies groan along the street.
The Festive Day is wracked
By nails, ball bearings, smoke, and fire; Anger,
rage, obscure intent.
Joy is bloodied once again by malice,
Hate snickers taunts in the lovely April air.
The dead, the mangled, stunned and living
Ask: For what, dear gods, for what?
What ill consumes the springtime citizens,
Children, athletes of the fair land?
What malevolent force leers up against us? What
Higher Power calls us to reply?

The Flashlight Next to the Glove Box
By Kevin Arnold

When Ensign Art Anthony dropped out of the Navy flight program, he received orders to a ship in Virginia Beach, with a stop off first to Damage Control school in Philadelphia, to learn how to save a ship in an emergency. He drove a roundabout way from Pensacola to Philadelphia, stopping by Madison, Wisconsin, to see a girlfriend.

His orders required he be in Philadelphia by midnight on Saturday, so he set his alarm for eight AM in Madison, which would give him time for the fourteen-hour drive. The problem was, someone parked behind his car so he couldn't leave until 10:30. Even if he didn't stop, he had time to make up.

He would need to exceed the speed limit, and used a technique he'd used before. He'd drive lawfully until some serious speeder would pass him. Thirty miles into Indiana, he pulled in behind just such a speeder, and sped with him, half a mile behind. The technique worked. Halfway across the next state, he passed a jackbooted Ohio Trooper writing up the other driver. By the time Wade entered Pennsylvania, even with the time change, he'd made up enough time to report to Philadelphia by midnight.

Three months earlier, in an automotive store to buy conditioner for his car's dried-out dashboard, he had impulsively bought a flashlight with a magnet, which he attached next to the glove box.

Past Pittsburg, he had the road pretty much to himself. It was pitch dark at quarter to nine when he passed a few trucks—no cars around—before three tunnels. He was two and a half hours from Philadelphia, so he was going to arrive in time.

As he entered the last of the three tunnels, he obeyed the sign Please Turn Off Headlamps. The tunnel was a mile long, very well lit. As he'd done at previous tunnels, at the tube's exit he pulled out the light switch. The switch, instead of turning on the lights, came out in his hand. He braked to a complete stop in the pitch black outside the tunnel.

He fumbled for his flashlight. When he found it and shone it on the roadway, he found out he'd parked across the two freeway lanes. The trucks he'd passed would be coming, soon, with no way to avoid him. Working to ignore the glow of an oncoming truck in his mirror, Art maneuvered his car to the shoulder just before a fourteen wheeler came whizzing by.

Not long later a trucker, an ex-Marine, stopped and fiddled with the headlight switch and got Art's lights going again. He didn't think the trucker was any miracle—acts of kindness had been, in Art Anthony's experience, much more plentiful than evil doings—but the flashlight . . .

Art still wonders what led him to buy that flashlight and affix it to his dashboard. He'd not done so before or since, nor did anyone in his family ever have such a flashlight.

Loss
Darlene Schwartz

Too many words
Not enough words
No rhyme
No sense
This poem seems at a loss

The stanzas don't come out right
They don't say what I mean
They don't express what I feel
This poem seems at a loss

I ponder and I think
I rhyme and I try
I tear up and start over
This poem seems at a loss

The poem doesn't express the pain
It doesn't express the anger
It doesn't express anything
This poem seems at a loss

My soul is on fire with anger
Devastated by the rudeness and exclusion of others
How dare they judge
How darethey condemn
This poem seems at a loss

The poem doesn't capture the anger
It doesn't capture the hurt
It doesn't capture the exclusion
This poem seems at a loss

Or maybe. Just maybe. I am at a loss.

The End
By Kimberly Schultz

The phone screamed at me as I wiped the dust from the picture frame of a hand drawn lighthouse that hung on one of the cream colored smooth walls in my bathroom. I had a sinking feeling it was her.

"They admitted him," my mom's tiny voice said through the phone.

"Do you need me to come?" I whispered into the phone. Five minutes later and I was in the car with Celeste, then 18 months old, driving to the hospital. My mom took my father into the hospital because he had been sick for the past week. The last years of my dad's life were filled with many scares, but this one was different. This scare would define the person each one of us in the family became.

With Celeste in her stroller, I rushed into the emergency room and was met by my mom, whose sunken face held a hundred pounds of worry. The small, grey room spun around me. My mom took hold of Celeste's stroller handles and pointed me through the double doors. She sat down in the waiting room with a sleepy Celeste.

"I messed up, Kimmy," my dad said to me as worry filled his face. He looked up at the ceiling, his eyes watering as he lay helpless on the hospital gurney. His once tough exterior now broken down by fright and shame. "I am sorry I am always doing this to you guys," he uttered apologetic.

A hard knot grew in the back of my throat and tears burnt my eyes, demanding to fall. But I would not let them fall. At that moment I decided that I would be strong for my dad and never let him see me weaken. "It is not your fault, Dad," I said calmly and bravely as I took his hand into mine giving it a hard squeeze. "We do not blame you for anything. Just listen to the doctors and you will be home and healthy before you know it." Feeling the pressure of uncertainty slowly overtake me, I gave him a hug and quickly made my exit. Once my back was turned, I walked out of the emergency room through the two grey double doors and the tears fell.

The tears continued to fall as the days turned into weeks and weeks turned into a month. Every single day I would make the ten minute drive to the hospital to visit my dad. Some days I had no choice but to bring Celeste with me. She was so young and did not know what to make of "Ba-Pa" in the hospital. The elevator rides that took me up to his floor were torturous. I had to lie to myself that everything was going to be okay, although I knew it was not. I wiped any tears from my cheeks that escaped my wet eyes, held my head high, and put on a smile when I entered his room.

Although his condition worsened, the whole family hoped for the best. "He has a 30% chance of passing away if he goes into surgery," the hospital staff explained to us. I believed them. I put my trust into them while the whole time he was slowly passing away before my eyes.

While my dad slowly deteriorated, my older sister prepared for her wedding day in Tahoe. "I will make it to the wedding," my dad said when he entered the hospital. As the days and weeks passed, he no longer promised he'd be there because quite frankly, he knew he wouldn't be able to make it. The day before the wedding, he was admitted to the ICU. "This is better for him," my mom tried to convince me. "This way, he will get one nurse to himself and he will be better taken care of," she urged. For one brief moment I believed her. I believed her because I wanted to. I needed to. I was leaving for Tahoe the very next day for my sister's wedding and I needed her to tell me it was okay for me to go.

On the day before my husband, Celeste, and I departed for Tahoe, I visited my dad in the ICU. I stood at the locked doors in front of the Intensive Care Unit in the basement of the hospital. "I'm here to see my father," I called into the intercom. It felt as if my dad was locked away in prison. In some way he was. Despite his failing condition, I kept my composure before I walked into his cubicle. He sat helplessly upright in his bed, hooked up to many machines that beeped and buzzed. He was so weak and fragile. I sat beside him and made small talk, promising I'd visit him as soon as I got back from the wedding. As I turned to leave the cubicle, I looked him in the eyes and told him I loved him. He pulled his oxygen mask away from his mouth and whispered, "Come here and give me a hug." I wrapped my arms around him and gave him a kiss on the cheek not knowing that that was the last time I would ever see him alive.

I stood at the entrance to his cubicle and turned toward him. "I love you," he said softly.

At the Harris Casino and Resort in Tahoe, the phone rang at 6 a.m. on the morning of May 22. "His blood pressure is dropping," my mom told me over the phone. "You need to come home." Shock and desperation sprung my family into action and we left Tahoe in a heartbeat. After four torturous hours on the road, we pulled into the hospital parking lot and rushed through the long, winding corridors to the ICU. I pressed the intercom button and was let in without even telling the nurse who I was. When I walked into the room, all monitors that beeped and buzzed were silent. My dad lie motionless on the bed as if he were only sleeping. In that one frozen moment when the second hand on the clock stalled, my life as I once knew it shattered into a million pieces. Nothing could tame the emptiness my heart pumped throughout my entire body.

As our family left the hospital torn apart by utter sadness, the cool breeze blew across my tear-stricken face. I stopped walking and looked up at the sky. How could the sky still hold such a beautiful blue? How could the clouds waft through the sky as if the world is still revolving? I looked back at the white box that was the hospital where my dad no longer was. His body was there, but he was gone. It felt as if he had just vanished. No matter where I looked for him, I would never find him. I searched my older brother's face, red and stained with tears, for answers, as if he was going to tell me that dad was waiting for us at home. In my heart I was begging for him to tell me that everything was going to be okay. But he didn't. Because he knew everything was not going to be okay.

My entire family went to my parent's house to grieve. Shock and silence began to divide us the minute we stepped into the once happy house. I couldn't fathom why my dad was gone. The man who was my world was nothing but a fading memory. The house felt empty and grey without him. The kitchen chair where he sat many nights watching his favorite movies with my mom sat empty. The bed where he once slept was still molded with the outline of his body. His cuckoo clock that once ticked every second and a cuckoo bird chirped every hour hung in calm silence.

Death not only stole my dad from me, but it also severed the once strong bonds that tied our tight-knit family together.

My Dream Shoes
By Ida Lewenstein

World War II caused extreme hardship for many people around the world, the likes of which we, here in the U.S. never had to face. Nevertheless, our comfortable way of life here was beginning to change as shortages and rationing found their way into our life style.

I was only ten years old when we entered the war and I, personally, didn't feel deprived of anything until that fateful day my grocery store no longer stocked my favorite candy bar—the U-NO bar. Oh, yes, I had heard that sugar was in short supply, but, come on, taking away a kid's favorite candy bar was going a bit too far! But then I was only ten—what did I know.

As you may remember, each family was issued a ration book which limited each member to three pairs of shoes a year. But to a child who never experienced rationing before, that number didn't mean very much, but I was yet to be tested. And tested I was—rather painfully, I might add.

Wearing what was fashionable at the time was always important to young, impressionable girls, and I was no different in that respect. Well, it so happened that stylish clogs were all the rage at that time, and anyone who wanted to be 'in' had to have a pair. Not just the ordinary clog (wooden shoes) that Hans Brinker might have worn, but stylish shoes with leather uppers in various shades. And the ticket for me was a pair of rich chocolaty, brown suede uppers that I had eyed in a shoe store window. Oh, how I wanted those shoes! They were my Dream Shoes.

As you might expect, my mother wasn't too happy with my choice. She warned me that we were being rationed and that we had to make some wise decisions about what we buy. Those kind of shoes, she admonished, would be most uncomfortable over time, and if you insist on wearing them, you will have to live with your choice.

Nevertheless, rationing or no rationing, I was not going to be deterred from getting my Dream Shoes. And besides, I reasoned, my cousin was wearing them, so it seemed to me that they couldn't be all that bad. But little did I know what would be the fate of my cousin's shoes. As it turned out, her clopping up and down their staircase in those clogs so annoyed her father that he was driven to chop up those special shoes with an AXE! So much for my cousin's shoes!

In a short time, my mother relented, and I got my Dream Shoes, and just as she predicted, I found them to be most uncomfortable. And in no time, my feet became sore, red and blistered. How I wished that I had never bought them!

Soon I began to think the unthinkable.... I began to wish that my father would do to my clogs what my uncle had done to my cousin's. But that wasn't to be. There was a lesson to be learned here, and I was forced to learn it.......the HARD WAY!

Stone Hearts
Ellen Six

One night, I overheard my parents talking about moving to a new house. I was four years old and it didn't mean much to me until my mother started to pack all of our belongings into boxes.

"Mamyte, what are you doing?"

"We are moving to a new house, a bigger house. Go play. I'm busy."

Mother never felt that she needed to explain herself to a child so it was up to me and to my imagination to figure out exactly what moving meant. A new big house sounded nice but where and when were not part of the puzzle for me.

The day that the moving van arrived, I watched as men hoisted boxes with straps on their shoulders and carried loads down the flight of stairs to the truck. In two hours, our apartment was completely empty. While Mother negotiated outside with the movers, I ran from one end of the room to the other shouting, "We're moving, we're moving," not so much because I understood the words but because I was caught up in hearing my own echo in those empty rooms.

When I first saw my new home, it looked like a brick fortress. It was a three-story, six-flat apartment building, with three units on each side. We were moving into the second floor apartment. My parents would tell their friends that they had traded up from a two flat to a six flat and that this was making it in America.

It was much bigger than what they had owned before. This time I could run from the living room, through the dining room, to the kitchen but Mother quickly put a stop to that.

"There are tenants living downstairs. Elyte, be quiet."

My Mother took to her role as landlady like a Queen taking possession of her castle. Her apartment was her palace. This domain came with crown molding, a wall of mirrors above the fireplace and a glass, crystal looking chandelier in the dining room. Mother would hold court with each of the tenants as they came to pay their monthly rent. She listened to their stories of births and commiserated with their aches and pains and wished them good luck until the next month's rent meeting. She could turn on tears or laughter as needed and then turn off the emotions when she closed the door. She was fair with everyone but she would say that they have their own lives and she had hers and that's why we have doors on our apartments.

What brought my mother so much contentment brought me only sadness. I felt alone in the world, no playmates in this new neighborhood. I lost my appetite and had trouble sleeping. My mother took me to the doctor because a child who doesn't eat must be sick. The doctor's diagnosis was that I missed my old house and my little friends and that the remedy was to take me back to visit the old neighborhood, which was only two miles away. My mother's response was that this was all nonsense and if there was nothing physically wrong than I would just get over it and with time, I did.

184

A few years later there was a chance meeting with one of our old neighbors. I was in the grocery store shopping with my mother, when my best friend's mother approached us. I was delighted and as I eagerly looked for my friend I heard the conversation between the two mothers. The neighbor wanted to know why my mother had not attended the funeral for her daughter. After all, she had sent Mother a notice of the death. My mother didn't explain that she couldn't read English and so she just apologized for missing the event. I heard them talking about how my friend had died of polio. That was a scary word even to a young kid because adults were always talking about how polio could kill you and that you needed to stay away from public swimming pools in summer. I knew then that I would never see my first best friend ever again. I felt a real hurt in my chest. I remembered my friend's blond hair and blue eyes. She looked just like my favorite doll. One day at the old house when I couldn't come out to play with her, I had dropped my doll out the window to Margaret Mary but she missed it and as it hit the sidewalk, she said, "I think that you broke her heart." That day in the grocery store losing Margaret Mary broke my heart.

Up in the Air
Nichole Justine Cavanaugh

He was looking to be grounded.
She was looking for escape

They crashed into each other
on the way to looking
for what the other couldn't give.

Road Kill
Jane Christmas

One frosty morning, a friendly young man pulls up in his truck. "Here's your firewood," he says as he pulls a lever that tips up the truck bed causing half-a-cord of almond, walnut and oak logs to fall, slowly at first, and then sliding and tumbling onto the driveway with a loud rolling clatter. I look at the sprawling, unruly pile and wonder what possessed me to order so much wood at once.

Following right on the heels of that thought is the realization I have to move it quickly out of the way so as to not block people from leaving or coming home. I look at the young man expectantly and open my mouth to ask him, but he anticipates my question and shrugs as he takes my check. "Sorry," he says and drives off with a wave. I sigh loudly to myself and begin, picking up an armful of wood and trudging up two flights of stairs to the recess in the landing outside my apartment.

I wonder how many trips it will take and start counting, but give up because I start thinking about other things as I find myself in a rhythm, up the stairs with an armful of wood, down the stairs for the next load.

I do not consciously hear the car coming down the hill until it hits the deer. There is a loud crunch and I look up as a large doe is struggling to get to her feet after being hit. The woman driving the car looks shocked and throws one hand up over her open mouth. And she drives off. She does not stop.

Either one or two of the deer's back legs are broken. It cannot run off the road because its legs keep collapsing under it. It tries and tries to run, but its legs will not work. I run down to the road and some teenagers who came out when they heard the noise are also standing there. I can hear another car coming too fast down the hill and run onto the road to try to help the deer. The deer growls at me while it is still trying to get its legs working.

"Get off the road!" the teenagers call out to me. "Leave the deer alone!"

I stand back and watch as pieces of bone from the deer's leg fall onto the road. I cannot believe what I am seeing, but it is true. There are pieces of the deer's smashed bone lying on the road. The deer somehow manages to drag itself off the other side of the road into the bushes at the edge of the open space, pulling itself away from me and all of the danger of being near humans.

"Can you call the humane society?" one of the teenagers asks me and I run inside, find the number and call. The woman I speak to sounds young.

"We can't do anything if the deer has run away," she says firmly.

"Well, I can't imagine it got very far because at least one of its legs is broken. Pieces of bone fell out of its leg onto the road," I say with some disgust.

I am not disgusted with the deer or the broken bones, but the whole idea of the woman who hit the deer just driving off like that and leaving us, me, with the mess makes me furious and fills me with a sudden, intense and hopeless despair.

The young woman on the phone hears my desperation and reassures me, although I am sure I hear her say deer can "shed" a leg and they will be fine.

When she says it, I think "Like lizards dropping their tails?" and, frankly, I am incredulous. She goes on. "Unfortunately, there is no rehabilitation for deer, because they are so plentiful. Injured deer are euthanized." I tell her I will call back if I can find the deer and we hang up.

I go outside to see if I can see where the deer went. I cross the road and look into the thick bushes, but cannot see anything, so I come back to my apartment and resume carrying the rest of the wood up the stairs.

I feel uneasy.

The next morning, I get up and go outside to collect the newspaper. I look across the road to the place where the deer had dragged itself and suddenly I can see ears silhouetted in the morning light through the leaves. I walk carefully, gently, over and peer through the foliage to where the deer is sitting behind a pile of dead branches, watching me. She is still, very still, just looking.

I retreat and go inside. I call the humane society again and talk to someone who says she will call the officer on duty. The officer calls me within ten minutes and I explain to her what happened the day before. I am also worried about what she will do.

"Are you going to shoot it?" I ask her. After an almost imperceptible pause, she laughs.

"No," she says, "That would be barbaric. We euthanize the animals by injection. It's gentle and doesn't hurt." Within half-an-hour, she pulls up in a small truck.

I feel reassured by her presence and, after going down the stairs to meet her, I point to the bushes where the deer is lying. She walks over and, peering through the leaves as I had done earlier, sees the deer. She steps forward a little and the deer responds by trying to get up but cannot even use her legs to lift her body off the ground. The officer nods and says, "Oh yes, she's in a bad way, poor thing." She goes to her truck and retrieves a long pole with a syringe attached to the end. She leans through the bushes and pokes the syringe into the deer's shoulder.

"This will calm her and take away her pain. It's too bad she has been laying there all night...probably in excruciating pain. It would have been better to have euthanized her when the accident happened."

I feel awful and wish I had made more of an effort to find the deer sooner. The deer has laid her head down and closed her eyes with a loud sigh and her body has relaxed. The officer talks to me about this process, explaining what is happening. We both push through the bushes and can now stand next to the deer without frightening her. The officer gently lays her hand on the deer's head and strokes her. He takes another syringe and injects it into a vein in the deer's ear.

"This one will make her heart stop," she says. We stand there as the officer places her hand over the deer's ribs, feeling her heartbeats. After a few minutes as we both watch the deer's ribcage rhythmically, slowly slow down and stop moving, she tells me the deer has died and I can see it for myself. Neither of us says anything and I find myself crying. The officer looks at me and nods.

I ask her if she needs any help and she says no, she has a winch. It is easy for her to hook up the deer, drag the body into the truck and take it away. I thank her, cross the street, walk back up the stairs past the pile of wood, and cross the threshold, closing the door very quietly behind me.

Arms of the Angel
By Carolyn Donnell

On the arms of the Angel a
line from a song
The hum of the music rises to
my tongue whenever I see
gray-haired bent
ladies wobbly walkers
crossing ... at lights ... insufficient time
to catch the train
closed doors don't wait, schedules to keep.
Guy in the wheelchair.
Unwashed, feeble, maneuvering down
Main Street. To where?
veteran of wars sent
to kill returned home
to die untended.
Mothers with children no
home to keep.
Bankers' golden balloon. Others,
no place to sleep. Where are the
families, sons, daughters or
friends? Church and charity they
say but too often they really pray,
"Thank you God, I'm not like them."
Where is the angel for all of these? Are
angels that selective and few?
On the arms of the Angel, do
you have one?
Lucky you.

My Encounter With King Kong
By Pat Callaway

I have become quite accustomed to getting up at 5:30 a.m. most mornings over the past three weeks while traveling through the African countries of Tanzania, Burundi, and now Rwanda.

My internal clock always rings before the alarm does, and this morning is no exception. But unlike other mornings, I feel a peculiar emotion of excitement, apprehension, and adventure all rolled into one. Today we will take an incredible journey into the forests of the Virunga Mountains in search of the mountain gorilla.

The volcanic mountains peak into the clouds, bringing to life the images Dr. Dian Fossey portrayed in her book, "Gorillas in the Mist". How exciting! We are actually here, in the very same spot the famous scientist spent studying the gorillas we hope to encounter.

We walk a ways on the flat farmland, maneuvering through the rows of carefully planted sweet potatoes. Then we approach the forest; the entrance is a dark thicket of bamboo. Our hike will take us through dense foliage which often has to be hacked away with a machete. Protective gloves and long sleeved shirts and pants are worn to keep from being cut by the sharp edges of the stinging nettles.

The altitude starts at 7500' and the climb is strenuous. My walking stick helps me up the steep inclines and over the heavily matted vines that are like a thick carpet, but with deep holes that could easily twist an ankle. Sometimes the guides proceed ahead and we relish the opportunity to catch our breath.

We are told the gorillas have been spotted. It has taken two and a half hours, which suddenly seems condensed into minutes as our energy is renewed with the excitement of our encounter. We carefully proceed forward, but with a reserved enthusiasm.

A large silverback gorilla sits several feet away, content with our presence, but keeping an eye on us. His massive forehead overpowers the small dark eyes he views us with. Further along, we come upon the rest of the family. They forage at the base of a wide tree trunk.

An infant, a cuddly bundle of fur, looks more like a fluffy owl than a gorilla as it clutches to its mother's side. It looks at us in wonderment as a young child does when viewing the world for the first time. A youngster frolics around the bamboo, and persists on making a nuisance of himself. His intrusion into the eating area is not welcomed and his elders gingerly push him away. He rolls over from the gentle nudge and then, with a renewed itinerary, toddles our way to get a closer look.

We sit within ten feet of the group for about an hour, elated that we have this privileged opportunity to share the domain of these wonderful but endangered animals. There isn't time now to think about those first encounters where gorillas were shot out of fear or for museums, or to recall the stories about poachers who mutilated them just to sell a souvenir. There isn't time now to reflect upon the encroachments of their habitat by developing farmlands.

A small adult, full from the morning's meal, flops on her back and crosses her arms under her head. She yawns and reminds me of a content human resting after a hard day's work. Another curls into a fetal position in a ray of sunlight that filters through the forest canopy. He looks my way and then closes his eyes as if to say its okay that I am there.

The silverback approaches the tree now and when he stands up, the full impact of his immense size becomes evident. The silver hairs banding across his back contrast with the blackness of his husky body and magically affirm an earned position of wisdom and authority over the family.

My earlier apprehension is blanketed now by the serenity of the moment. We must not loose these incredible animals to extinction. I sit in awe.

Menopause
By Jeannine Gerkman

Soaking wet
Glistening with Tears
Seems I've hit the
Menopause years

Sleep eludes me
Memory too
My middle thickens
What can I do?

I once had beauty,
vivacity and skill
Now I'm but a puddle
Drowned against my will.

I A groan escapes me
And then a worried sigh
Dread enfolds me,
Yet I don't know why

'm a stranger in this body
Flailing in the dark.
My head throbs in misery.
The arrow's made its mark.

When did life get so intense?
And Simple things so Hard?
Why am I so Perplexed?
Will I ever be restored?

County Fair
By Karen C. Hartley

Hurry to the ticket booth!
Pay so you can stay all day
The clicking turnstile makes you smile
Then you're bombarded by a cacophony of sounds
And brightly painted horses on the
Dazzling carousel turning 'round and 'round
Noises – lights – colors
What to do first
Rides – midway – games
Thirst
Food – drink – music
Laughter – big kids – little tykes
Demos and blaring mics
Exhibits – art – quilts
Merchandise – what to buy
Jewelry – hats – items to try
From the latest fry pans and
Cooking things – to samples and sparkling bling
Barbeque – hotdogs – popcorn
Ice cream logs
Beer – wine – animal time
Rides to the sky – the Ferris wheel and
Roller coaster – whirling things
Flying swings – balloons popping – ring tossing
Children's laughter – what's left to do after all of this?
Exhausted – tired and before you know it
The lights go out one by one and suddenly, sadly
All too soon
No more fun!
Your day at the County Fair
Is done

Mr. Bo Jangles Danced
By Sherrie Gant

I knew better; I had had a lifetime of experience. I should have practiced and prepared at home first, in a familiar environment. But I didn't, so I had to deal with the issue under pressure while everyone watched and waited on me.

Everything went smoothly while I saddled my four-year-old sorrel gelding for the morning hunt. Bo stood quietly until I carried the long thin leather scabbard towards him. His big Arabian eyes grew wide and wary as I approached his offside with the strange and scary device in my hand.

"Whoa, Bo Bo, it's okay," I said when he puffed up his body with uncertainty. My soothing voice helped settle his anxiety and he allowed me to press the rifle scabbard against his neck and shoulder and buckle it to the saddle.

I raised the scabbard and slapped it gently against his shoulder. I wanted him to hear and feel the leather case; he flinched then settled again as I soothed him with my voice.

That wasn't so bad, I thought as I headed to the truck to retrieve my rifle. I really had no intensions of using it on the hunt but knew I should take it along just in case. Bo stood quietly as I approached.

I thought the worst of the training session was over until I lifted the black frightening rifle up over my shoulders to slide it into the leather sleeve now attached to Bo's side. His big brown eyes doubled in size as he jumped away to avoid me, nearly breaking free from the trailer where he was tied.

I quickly stepped back while Daddy untied Bo from the trailer and led him into the open; he held my edgy equine while I once again tried to put the rifle into the scabbard. With each attempt Bo danced a circle around Daddy, away from me and the metal club I held high in my hand.

Nearly fifteen minutes later the dance was over and the 30.30 was safely ensconced in the scabbard. I mounted my spooky steed and headed out of camp following Mom and my sister Karen on their horses.

At the base of a steep butte, Karen and I split up from Mom. Bo and Dancer, Karen's leopard appaloosa, were both fast walkers and could cover a lot of territory so we took the longest route. Dancer was a strong seasoned trail horse and the herd boss and young Bo gained courage in his presence. The ride was nice, but uneventful, without the sighting of a single deer. As Karen and I rounded the backside of the butte, we spotted Daddy in "Old Red," his classic Chevy pickup, and headed over to the parked truck. Mom and Taffy were already there, awaiting our arrival." "My allergies are starting to bother me," Karen told us, "and my eyes are itchy. I'm gonna head back to camp so I can take an allergy pill before my eyes swell shut." She turned Dancer and headed down the dirt road that ran along the edge of the butte – the shortest distance to camp. Mom and I remained mounted while Daddy chatted with his friend Roy.

Roy finally started up his truck and headed down the powdery dirt road, but we waited for the dust to settle before heading out.

As Roy drove past a thick patch of trees on the edge of the road, a three-point buck jumped from his bed under a tree and ran towards the butte.

"Buck!" I yelled and grabbed my rifle from its scabbard. I jumped from the saddle, but, unfortunately, when I snatched up the rifle and leapt from my horse, Bo skittered sideways. The commotion that followed and Bo's reaction spooked Taffy, causing her to run backwards and sideways as Mom tried to dismount, making it difficult to pull her rifle from its scabbard.

Instinctively, I threw my gun to my shoulder, took aim at the running buck and fired a single shot just as he disappeared over the ridge.

The sudden roar of Old Red's engine caught my attention , and I turned and watched as Daddy raced down the road after Taffy.

Bo, however, was nowhere in sight.

"I hope Daddy catches our horses!" I said.

"Me, too," replied Mom. Then she and I headed out on the trail after the buck. If he was shot, we needed to get to him as quickly as possible. We learned soon enough that Daddy was able to catch up to Taffy. She had slowed at the sound of his voice through the pickup window and he eased up to her. She then allowed him to step from the truck and catch her, even as she trembled with fear.

Mom and I were elated to see Taffy when we returned to the road.

Expecting to see my horse tied up somewhere nearby, I asked Dad, "Where's Bo?"

"Probably back in camp by now, as fast as he was running," he chuckled.

"Taffy couldn't keep up with him. The last I seen of Bo Jangles," he added, "he was headin' back around the butte."

I sighed. "All he had to do was follow Dancer down the road to camp. It's half the distance."

Dancer was already unsaddled and in the corral munching on hay when Bo reached camp, still at a dead run. Karen ran from the trailer and grabbed his loose rein as he slid to a stop at the corral gate.

"Whoa, Bo, where's Sherrie?" she asked him as she lead him over to the trailer.

She pulled the saddle from his sweat-soaked body and began walking him in large circles around camp to cool him off. Then she went to the trailer and called Dad on the two-way radio.

"Bo's back I camp," she said. "I assume Sherrie got off to shoot? I see her rifle is missing."

"You guessed right," Daddy replied, his smile to me indicating my horse was back at camp, safe and sound.

An hour later we drove into camp. I was relieved beyond measure to see Bo standing in the corral with no injuries, and I was happy I didn't have to walk back. This was a lesson I'd remember on learning new things in the safety of my own barnyard.

meditation
By Maurine Killough

this is the way life is
with its boxes and swirls
appearing as snares, suction cups and mazes
they are everywhere
you step into them everyday
get boxed in
circle around and around
then trip into a dead end
before you see clearly, after so many lifetimes
that the boxes are windows
the swirls are clouds to carry you away
the rubik's cubes are your own lethal thoughts
so i lie down to not think
i am awake but i do not participate
i recline quietly as
ancient labyrinths order my hair
secret mazes mark my body
sacred swirls coil my mind
cyclones siphon my drops
i shut my drain pipes
to all that is going on
like music in the background
and fall into myself
into my infinity
spiral like a snake where gaia meets the cosmos let
the energy flow
fly above where the patterns take helix shape
until i am free of the circling thoughts material
traps
and can wrap my being around the
divine pattern of all that there is

Pictures and Words
By Nadine Moreno

All day I've gone through the pictures I have of my mom. I've gone over the things I've written to and about her. I could write about her every day, the words seemingly endless. The pictures though…

She loved pictures. So much so that when I packed up her house, there were totes upon totes of pictures, negatives, photo albums, and frames. I go through them from time to time. There are pictures of her as an infant, a teenager, a reckless 20-something,
and as a mother.

The pictures though… they do end. They end abruptly, with almost no warning. The only suggestion that an ending may be coming is the one picture I took of her in the hospital. Her hair is clipped back, the porcelain angel I bought for her is visible, and she is wearing a nasal cannula. She is smiling still… We were still hopeful, oblivious to how short the time we had left together would be. It was the last picture I
ever took of her.

Sometimes I look at pictures of her, and when I see her smile, I can almost hear her laughter. Not in that last picture though. That last picture reminds me of how long it's been since
I've heard her laugh.

Today marks ten Christmas Eve's without her. She would have been fifty-eight today. But instead of celebrating, I'm realizing that it's been just short of ten years worth of holiday, birthday, and wedding pictures that she's not in. I have no pictures of her at my wedding, or with my children.

None of the pictures I have of her feel complete anymore. They feel too old, too used up. Perhaps I've exhausted the emotion they once held. They are all I have left, and sometimes they
just aren't enough.

I'm not sure what to do with that though, and so I write. I write because the words are seemingly endless, and there is always
more than enough.

Missal Crisis
By Sue Barizon

I sit with the subject of my "Most Memorable" gift beside me nestled in the folds of the comforter for inspiration. I close my eyes and tilt my head back against the headboard. I promised myself a few moments of meditation before taking pen to paper. Much to my chagrin, I ask for divine guidance. Damn! Now my meditation smacks of prayer. The gift has been a thorn in my side for over five decades. This memoir serves as its Last Rites.

When I was ten, I got a "missile" for Christmas – a pretty neat gift if I had been a boy and the missal had been a missile. But on Christmas morning in 1962, there was only one package under the tree with my name on it. The tag read "To Susan, from Santa" – odd, Santa calling me Susan. In those days I was "Suzie," "Suzie Q" or as Papa liked to mispronounce with his thick Italian accent, "Sussie Girl." My mother was the only one who called me Susan. Mom was like that, very exacting. No doubt she had scrutinized my birth certificate before signing it, methodically inspecting each line. Once her brain registered "Susan," it was as if chiseled in a stone no term of endearment could penetrate.

The lone package couldn't have appeared more unremarkable to my ten-year-old senses – a smallish, thick rectangle wrapped in thin paper with dancing Santas falsely promoting the merriment inside. It didn't even have the gumption to rattle when I shook it. Up until now, my Christmas world had been a sparkling fantasy of little elves merrily toiling away all year on glorious toys for us good little girls and boys. I counted myself one of the good little girls, confirmed by my rebellious teenage sister, Elena, who referred to me as "Miss Goodie Two Shoes."

I remember peeling back the paper, exposing a sinister looking sheath of black leather. What was this? It felt like a book. I held it up to the parade of twinkling lights bouncing off the aluminum tree Mom decorated with redundant silver ornaments. The tree rotated on a motorized stand in front of our living room window. How many rotations did it take before my brain fully grasped the book's title, Saint Joseph's Daily Missal? Santa brought me a bible for Christmas?

"It's not a bible. It's a Missal, see? M·I·S·S·A·L." My sister stood over me and tapped the letters out with the pointed finger of one hand while holding her new transistor radio up to her ear with the other. I was too stunned with disappointment to speak. Intuitively, Elena read the "What's the difference?" expression on my face.

"It's to follow along during mass. See, it's in English instead of Latin."

I sat staring at the morose little book – both of us were devoid of any Christmas cheer. Even the five skinny multi-colored ribbons dangling from the bottom of the spine looked as if trying to escape suffocation between the seemingly endless stack of tissue paper thin pages. Finally, I opened it to the cover page, Saint Joseph Daily Missal, the official prayers of the Catholic Church for the celebration of daily mass. What was Santa thinking? Did he confuse me with my 80-year-old Nonna Angelina or any one of the other shriveled up old ladies dressed in black attending mass at St. Peter and Paul's?

I got up and double checked under the tree. There were no more presents to be found, except the usual unopened panettone from Aunt Ana and a jar of cherries in brandy for Papa. Good little girl be damned! I demanded an explanation.

"Is this all I get for Christmas?" I held the missal up for all to see.

The inquiry was directed at no one in particular but loud enough for the whole family to hear. My sister still had her transistor radio glued to one ear, and my little brother was oblivious to anything but the fort he was building with his new set of Lincoln Logs. Papa turned to my mother with an inquiring expression. I remember my mother's response, "That's what she asked for!"

The shock reverberated through my body. I asked for a missal for Christmas? Why would I do such a thing? Going to 9:00 mass on Sunday was something I did just to get it over with, so Mom wouldn't nag me all morning, although she rarely went with us. Tuesday afternoons were my least favorite day of the week because the kids in the neighborhood who didn't attend parochial school had to go to catechism. I learned the true meaning of boredom in catechism, watching the clock on the wall over Sister Agnes Bernard's head, appearing attentive as I counted out the 60 seconds it took for the minute hand to jump from dot to dot.

Mom was the Santa connection in the Capella household. She noted who was being naughty or nice, and was not opposed to breaking out into song when she perceived an impending infraction.

"You better watch out, you better not cry…" Her crackly, out of tune voice was enough to make any kid stop dead in her tracks.

When she asked what you wanted Santa to bring you, you had one shot at it. Our Santa didn't go in for lists you got one present under the tree on Christmas morning and a stocking full of perfunctory underwear, anklet socks, pens, pencils, a candy cane and a net bag filled with gold foil wrapped chocolate coins. It wasn't that our Santa was on a budget or was particularly miserly, we just accepted it as our family's custom.

So how could Mom have gotten it so wrong? I don't exactly remember telling her I wanted a tea set or a hula hoop or a fake white rabbit muff with matching clutch purse like the one I saw in a Shirley Temple movie (all of which my cousin Carla got that Christmas). In fact, I don't remember her asking me period. I do remember coming home from catechism the day Sister Agnes touted the Pope's decision to have mass performed inEnglish, and telling Mom that sister suggested we add a missal to our wish list. Did Mom not see me roll my eyes at the suggestion? Was she too preoccupied with chiseling a mental note to herself to hear the mockery in my voice?

I sat fanning through the pages of the missal, searching for some redeeming feature of this disaster of a Christmas present, perhaps some folding money tucked in between a page or two. All I found were pictures of Jesus and his cohorts in various stages of pain and suffering - the Technicolor pictures graphically depicting saints and martyrs looking up to the heavens. Evidently, the ribbons were intended to mark favorite passages. I used the red one to mark the Stations of the Cross and the green one for the Mass of Several Virgin Martyrs (my sister was too busy to explain why three terrified young women in an arena were being stared down by a couple of healthy looking lions).

By the time Mom summoned us for Christmas dinner next door at my aunt and uncle's house, I had read about the plight of enough martyrs and Saints to take the edge off my self pity. Before leaving to face my cousin Carla and the cache of gifts she'd be flaunting, I found a page in the missal beckoning me to write my name and the date. In my best cursive handwriting, I wrote "Susan Capella" and dated it December 25, 1962. Admiring my penmanship, I noticed three numbers at the top of the page written in pencil - 6.95.

You'd think that Santa would at least have had the decency to erase the price tag!

I've vowed to banish this pimple of a present from my life once and for all, but its familiarity has become a charming nuisance. Besides, I'm afraid it might be a sin. Maybe, I just save it for the end when we can share our LAST Rites together.

I Love
By Thomas Ekkens

I love sushi
I love chocolate
I love roast beef on rye
I love cracked crab with butter

I love a walk on ocean's beach
I love a walk in forest's shadow
I love a walk on desert's floor
I love a walk on city's street

I love a time alone
I love a day of rest
I love a peaceful feeling
I love a quiet moment

I love a baseball game
I love a crack of bat
I love a roar of crowd
I love a slide at home

I love to cook
I love to eat
I love to find new foods
I love to share with friends

I love life
I love health
I love spirit
I love emotion

I love could go on forever
I love could end tomorrow
I love could include me
I love could include you

I love you

Mind Shots of Moorea
By Patricia Bradley

The roosters salute the day in a competition, one calls, another answers, another says "I'm here too." I, too, greet the day between 6 and 6:30 AM each morning. In Moorea, clouds rest on the ocean and the sky starts from the water up. These clouds look like whipped cream around a lime pie. Some mornings the pink begins behind me and wraps up and over the peaks. As the sun begins, it casts a shadow of the mountain behind onto the mountain in front, an astonishing peak on a peak. The tallest peak has clouds that roll up one side, hang around the top in a halo, then tumble on down the other side like an enormous waterfall. Any morning can bring a surprise. A lovely sailboat may have dropped anchor right in front of us. Once a beautiful couple emerged from one in the early morning and dipped their perfect bodies into the Bay in their natural state. It was a lovely thing to see. One morning two gray naval ships appeared across the entrance to Cook's Bay. The French we supposed. It turned out to be the Japanese. We watched that evening as they formed on deck, played a song, probably their national anthem, and retired the flag. It caused me to imagine what the experience would be like to arise and find hostile ships in my Bay. Some days the "Windstar", a beautiful white sailing cruise ship has arrived under full sails and that evening it will sparkle at us across the water, its masts lit and all lights on as music drifts across to our over the water deck. What will I see in the lagoon that surrounds us? A manta ray flies by silently in the water looking dark and mysterious. It looks like the Stealth airplane of the sea. Suddenly what had appeared to be a part of a rock, moves to a new location, changing colors as it does. It is an octopus. Each day we get a loaf of fresh French bread and I drop some crumbs into the water. Beautiful Angel Fish with their yellow and black stripes and graceful tails, schools of four inch silver fish, Picasso the multicolored and aggressive, long blue Needle Noses, come to check. None of them really like the bread but I enjoy the visit. Directly across from me these astonishing mountains spring up from the sea. One has a hole close to the top. I can see the sun shining through from the other side. The clouds change constantly around the tops of the peaks and in the quiet of the morning I can hear the ocean beating on the reef which surrounds this island saying, let me in, let me in, let me in. Parrott fish, so beautiful – I wonder if they realize it. Silently a canoe and its paddler move across my field of vision, one on the water, silently. We revisit those darlings of these waters, the spinner dolphins, the babies not more than three feet long. Suddenly one springs toward the sky and spins in a corkscrew on its way back down. Why? Perhaps for the sheer joy of it. The air is so soft on my skin and the people, both men and women, don't feel properly dressed until they have a flower behind their ear. Even the small children. There are many blossoms to choose from. There is much laughter here as those who live in paradise go about their lives, giggling and guffaws and tee hees behind a hand. We lunch next to a table of laughter and it goes on for an hour. Soon we laugh from the sound of it. Mahi mahi burgers are the menu. We saw it arrive in one large fish earlier in the morning. A large catamaran has made its way into the Bay and dropped anchor. Suddenly a man picks up a child of four or so by his arm and tosses him over the railing to squeals of laughter. He swims like a baby dolphin. The peak peaks at us from a wreath of angel hair. Soon the sunset creeps through the sky turning it fifty shades of pink and reflects on the still Bay making it pink also. As darkness falls, more stars than I have observed in the last four years appear together in this one night. A universe up there so broad and deep and sparkling it numbs my mind with the possibilities and the secrets it holds. The waves slap gently underneath the bungalow – over and over and over, lulling me to sleep.

Naptime
By Jeannine Gerkman

Let's snuggle together with some crackers and juice,
And turn the pages of my Dr. Seuss

We'll read about creatures big and small,
Watch their antics and have a ball.

I've been reading since I was four,
We'll read a little and then
Read some more.

About ships and spoons and
Cats and owls,
We'll slide with verbs and
Skip with vowels.

We'll play in water both wide and deep.
We'll slosh and splash
And then drift to sleep.

A Cloud
By Maria Barr

International Women's Day

One cold morning, I stepped into my jasmine scented garden
to enjoy a cup of sweet repast.
I surveyed the beauty before me then, glanced up
and saw a puff of gossamer, that myriad forms did make.
The swirls of white rapidly unfolding as a form came into view.

She, appeared before me, moving swiftly, floating by
her long hair flowing, left hand gripping tightly the edge.
Right hand held slightly back as if hiding precious cargo.
Female in white on a sapphire sea, is the imaginary portrait.

Behind her, a tiny figures clutches at her flowing robe.
Beyond their image a majestic immensity of cold blue.
Practically, alone her eyes fierce are focused ahead.
Determined, she searches the distance, chin held high.

A woman and her child, fleeing, drifting far into the blue,
Her grip tight, as she looks furtively at the child behind her.
Her eyes turn forward as she wills herself to move a head.
Faster, faster they move as the image grows dimmer.

Reflecting, I recognize her, she is woman, with her child.
She is you, she is me, she is our daughter, our sister.
She is female, alone against the blue. She needs help!
Too proud to beg, she fights the blue alone with her child.

Tears streaming down my face, I set my cup down to wave.
I want to save her before she is lost!
I search the blueness that forces me to blink.
Frantically, I look up but she is gone.

She was just a cloud. A faint blur. A mirage?
Yet in the few moments that she lived in my heart,
I saw woman, child, floating thru life, fighting, struggling.
What was the blue they were fleeing? Was it a man?

Lonely Wyoming Highway
By Sherrie Gant

Feeling the need for fresh air, I roll the side window down. The outside air is warmer then it is in the cab and I don't like it blowing my hair, so I immediately roll it back up. Alone in the cab, I scan the scenery—not much to look at, just short stunted bitterbrush and sage as far as the eye can see—the view hasn't changed for miles. The only visible life form is an occasional pronghorn antelope dotting the sparse desert canvas. Tired and not feeling well my mind drifts with the steady hypnotic hum of the diesel truck engine. There is no change of speed or shifting of gears needed on this stretch of deserted Wyoming highway. The road is straight and flat which I'm grateful for today. The horses in the trailer I'm pulling are standing quietly, probably napping taking advantage of this curve less road. After days of travel they have settled into the routine. As the afternoon sun begins to set it fills the cab of the semi-truck, lying heavy across my lap like a thick winter blanket. My eyelids feel weighted. I shake my head blinking back the weariness, fighting to stay alert. I turn the air conditioner on high, adjusting the vent to blow cool air directly into my face. Sixteen hour days over the past two weeks plus last night's event is beginning to take its toll.

My husband Dennis usually drives on our long commercial hauls transporting horses across the nation. On several occasions in the past when we were empty I had asked if I could drive, Dennis always answered "Not now, I'd rather be driving than just sitting in the passenger seat doing nothing." I didn't just sit "doing nothing", I am the navigator—I read the map, study the landscape and sleep. Yes, the harmonious buzz of the motor and warm air often makes me sleep—like a baby according to Dennis—with my head resting against the side glass and my mouth wide open, drool slowly creeping its way down my cheek. I cringe at the thought. He hadn't given me a chance to practice my driving skills until today when there was no other option. I was not excited.

Last night we didn't sleep well; Dennis had a stomach ache and fever and he was nauseas. He thought it was the stomach flu but after a quick trip to the bathroom he suspected food poisoning from dinner's Italian sausage lasagna. A few hours later I was deathly ill too. For hours we took turns emptying the contents of our stomachs. This morning, Dennis drove for as long as he could bear it, allowing me to rest, before pulling off the road. "You're gonna have to drive, I can't go any longer," he said. It was the worst time ever to get sick— we were loaded with eleven horses in the middle of nowhere and it was getting hot outside. We had to keep moving for the welfare of the animals.

After a five minute instruction course on how to shift the gears, Dennis climbed into the sleeper and I took over behind the wheel—we had to arrive in Salt Lake City before dark. An hour later I pulled over at a road side park to tend to the horses—feeding and watering without help from Dennis was brutal and time consuming. We always strive for 500 miles a day but today we are falling way short of that goal. The horses have to be delivered to several clients along the way to California then up into Oregon. I am so anxious to get back home to Central Oregon.

Southern Wyoming can be a quiet and lonely state to drive through when the wind isn't gusting 100 miles per hour, attempting to blow trucks off the road. The breeze whistling from the air conditioning vents remind me of that. The air flowing isn't as cold as it should be. It must be hot outside, I thought noticing the blurry wave hovering over the sand. I turned the radio off a while ago when I couldn't recognize the song for the static. This is a boring stretch of highway and I am growing more tired by the minute.

Gazing aimlessly down the highway, I notice the horizon begins to glow growing more intense the closer I get. The blinding radiance makes me squint—my path appears to be turning to gold right before my eyes. Puzzled and confused I ponder, am I delirious from this fever or am I staring at the gates of Heaven? The road's luminosity is that of a precious stone—it gleams the glory of God.

The truck groans under the heavy load as it pulls a slight grade towards the still blinding light. I place my hand on the gear shift knob then step on the clutch successfully dropping the transmission down into a lower gear without a hitch or a grind. Hmm, I thought, that was easy.

All morning I struggled when down shifting, grinding gears trying to convince an objectionable transmission to submit. Earlier today I needed a break and wanted Dennis to take over driving again and give me a chance to rest. I spotted a REST AREA sign and prepared to slow the 60 foot vehicle for exit. As I rounded the corner watching for another sign, several orange construction cones lined the roads narrow shoulder. Without any additional warning the entrance to the rest area immediately appeared at the end of the cones. I flipped on the exhaust break to slow the engine and quickly stepped on the clutch to shift down. I easily moved the stick placing the transmission into fifth. When I let up on the clutch the engine revved sending the tachometer into the red zone. Terrified of destroying the transmission, I immediately realized I had completely missed fifth and fourth gear and shifted straight into third. With lightning speed I stomped on the clutch shoving it to the floor and rode it hard coasting the truck smoothly into the rest area sparing the transmission and keeping the horses on all fours. It baffled Dennis how I managed such a task with ease.

My focus remains on the radiant light guiding my way through the desert—red and blue beams of light flash at the edge of the glow. The black tar road becomes dotted with silver and copper then quickly it's flooded in a pool of precious metal appearing liquid in the gleaming sunlight. I remember the Bible describes what Heaven will be like. One of the things it says is "the great street of the city was of pure gold" (Revelation 21:21). I have never seen anything like this before in my life. Is this real? Then I see him, standing guard over the treasure making his presence well known. His dark uniform boldly stands out on the light colored backdrop. His weapons glisten.

In disbelief I recognize the precious metal that paves my way—it's coins! Sparkling new nickels and dimes and quarters mixed with shiny copper pennies covering the pavement turning it into a street of gold and I'm driving on top of them! This is surreal.

I see a large shiny black metal box toppled on its side in the nearby brush with doors twisted and ripped wide open—its valuable contents of its belly spewed out across the land like last night's lasagna. As I creep past, I see the word SECURITY.

Soon I recognize the wreckage—an Armored Car. It appears to have left the road and violently crash into the rocks—possibly the result of the driver drifting off or the victim of Wyoming's brutal wind gusts. Maybe robbers blew the vehicle up with explosives to steal the precious cargo? I've been watching too many crime shows. My imagination wonders. Nothing stirs. The only sign of life is the State Trooper standing guard, armed with rifle in hand beside his patrol car—lights flashing, warning curious passersby to keep on moving.

Fully awake now and feeling revived and grateful I move on picking up speed and shifting gears without any grind. Reaching down I turn the radio on—a joyous noise of song rings out. I smile as I continue traveling toward home safely over this fascinating Wyoming Highway.

In the 'Hood
By Evie Groch

House hunting, my realtor asks
What are you looking for?
Which neighborhood is calling
you?
Which style do you adore?

My ideal, I share with him
comes from a list I made.
Although it's well thought-out,
it's picky I'm afraid.

Next door would live the journalist
forever checking facts.
Two doors down, an essayist,
enjoys his own wisecracks.

On the corner, a novelist who
spins full tales of fiction.
Six doors down, a poetess with
powers of depiction.

Backing up to my own house, an
editor of note
who polices words and voice,
errors make him gloat.

Four doors up, a columnist who
gets paid by the inch.
At times his themes elude him –
finds himself in a pinch.

A short story writer
is somewhere in-between, and
I, the memoirist,
would simply serve as queen.

This is where I'd to live
and welcome all who knock,
for then I shall not ever fear
having a writers' block.

If the Shoe Fits . . .
By Jo Carpignano

I've been intrigued by how often, when at a loss for descriptions of day-to-day events, we resort to adages. According to Webster, an adage is "a saying in metaphorical form that embodies a common observation."

Several years ago, the adage "Anything that can go wrong, will ..." applied to me, several times, and all on the same day.

After moving from Millbrae to San Mateo, several routine chores had accumulated which badly needed to be done. I had to have my car washed, fill a prescription for new glasses, close a safe deposit box at one bank and open another, and cash in some coupons at Safeway. Simple enough, I thought.

First on my list was the car wash. My Toyota mini-wagon had been used and abused shamefully for several months during my move from Millbrae to San Mateo. I had offered to drive a friend grocery shopping, and bird droppings came off on her hands from grasping the handle on my car door. I was humiliated, and ashamed forhaving waited so long to get it detailed.

At my new home in San Mateo, I asked dinner companions where a car wash might be found nearby. The recommendation was for Ducky's Car Wash on North San Mateo Drive.

"You can't miss it," my new friends assured me. I followed their directions, and saw the sign for Ducky's entrance - just as I passed it. Damn, I swore to myself, how do I get myself back there without making two U turns? I saw there were no cars behind me, so I decided it was safe to back up. Luckily, I made it before traffic arrived. All's well that ends well, I told myself. It was to be the last bit of good luck I would have that day.

Taking the elevator to the fifth floor of Kaiser Medical Offices in Daly City, I handed the receptionist my prescription for new glasses.

"Will you want new frames or just lens replacement?" she asked.

"Just the lens, the frames I have are fine," I assured her.

I was asked to wait, and when the optometrist appeared, he informed me that since I did not want new frames, he would need to keep the ones I wore while preparing and changing the lenses. Why had I not thought to bring my spare frames, before I left home? What is it they say about hindsight?

As I was leaving, I saw frames in the display cases and wondered if it might not be a good idea to get new frames after all. My other frames were ancient and might not withstand the stress of inserting new lenses. I wanted so much to get this done today, I thought.

After trying several frames, I selected one that I felt might be appropriate, and went back to the optometrist. I smiled, and explained, "I changed my mind, and I think I'd like to get my prescription in these frames. How much will they cost?"

The glasses had been marked at $85. I thought that was a fair price, but there might be a discount for seniors?

Hope springs eternal. The optometrist used his calculator and said, "That will come to $265."

"Excuse me?" I said astonished, "Those were marked $85."

"That's only for the frames. The laboratory fee and lenses are additional."

"There must be some mistake," I insisted, "Kaiser provides for glasses every two years."

Obviously in disagreement, the optometrist and I adjourned to the desk, where the receptionist consulted her computer. She informed me that since I was no longer on the Kaiser plan for optometry, I would indeed have to pay full price.

"You must have been notified by your employer that the optometry provider had been changed?" she questioned.

In the midst of packing for my move from Millbrae to San Mateo, I vaguely remembered receiving a notice from the Health Services System, but I had not registered the information, and forgot all about it. Out of sight, out of mind.

I picked up my prescription, expressed regrets for my forgetfulness, and left. I would need to make some calls about which provider had replaced Kaiser optometry. My glasses would have to wait. Oh well, if at first you don't succeed . . .

On the way to the bank in Millbrae, I scolded myself for being so careless with notices about health plan changes! I'm sure there's an adage for carelessness? Would "A stitch in time saves nine," apply here?

In Millbrae, I intended to empty my safe deposit box at Chase, and then, on my way home, place the contents into a new box at the San Mateo branch. I explained to the teller why I needed to close my safe deposit box here.

"Jamie will take care of you," she said, pointing to a young man seated at a desk. When I arrived there, Jamie was very busy sorting papers. I stood for several minutes, then coughed, just in case he had not seen me standing right in front of him. He sorted a few more papers, and then looked up.

"Yes?" he said shortly.

"I'd like to close my safe deposit box," I stated.

"Just get in line and talk to one of the tellers," he said curtly.

"I already did that, and she told me to come to you."

"Which teller was that," Jamie said accusingly.

"The young lady in the red blouse," I pointed.

Jamie left his desk, walked over to speak with the teller, and came back. "What is the box number," he asked grudgingly.

When I told him the number, he filled out a paper, had me sign it, and said dismissively, "That's it."

I hesitated, waiting for him to accompany me to the safe deposit box. He looked up eventually. "That's all, we're finished," he said abruptly.

By this time I was aware of the intense desire to call attention to the rude, inconsiderate behavior this young man was demonstrating. However, when not perfectly confident about achieving the desired outcome with a temper tantrum, I take a deep breath and become excessively polite.

"I'm sorry, I guess I didn't make myself clear. I also want to remove my documents from the box," I said in the sweetest tone I could muster. We must suffer fools in silence, I said to myself as impatience gnawed at me.

"Oh, you still have something in it?" he asked.

"I have eve-ry-thing in it," I responded slowly. "I also have a refund coming for closing early."

"No you don't. The amount paid for a safe deposit box is not refundable. Once you pay for it, it's done."

I was aware of the fury about to erupt, and took another deep breath. "Oh, but I do get a refund. I talked to the teller about that before I came to you, " I said, again using my sugary voice.

Off went Jamie to consult with the teller, and once again he retreated angrily, this time with teeth clenched. Fortunately, he did not return to his desk. Instead he stepped aside, and assigned the task to a young man with a nice smile who issued the refund, and accompanied me to my safe deposit box.

Thank God for small favors, I thought. I did not think I could have held back much longer. Should I have been alone with Jamie in the isolated area of safe deposit boxes, I doubt that he would have been safe from my outrage.

"Do you have a bag I can use or borrow?" I asked.

"Sorry ma'am, we don't provide bags," he said apologetically. So I relocked the box, and I walked away to return another day. After all that, I had failed to accomplish anything here as well. Another strikeout in my five item pitches for today, I thought.

I was parked near the Millbrae Safeway store, so decided to complete my fifth task there. Surely I could accomplish this objective easily.

The store was packed, but I had carefully prepared coupons for things I needed, so this time would be efficient. My refrigerator was almost empty, and shelves bare, so coupons for mayo, orange juice, bread and cereal were exactly what I needed. I am not usually seduced by coupon offers, but Nothing ventured . . . With a change of address, Safeway had offered these free items when registering the new address and phone number. I had diligently made the necessary phone calls, and a new card had been issued, all bases covered - or so I assumed. To assume, makes an ass out of u and me . . .

After collecting all the items for which I had coupons, with a few more basic needs, I lined up to check out. Smiling, I handed coupons, along with new Safeway card, to the cashier.

"Sorry, those coupons are only good at the San Mateo store. We can't accept them here," the clerk stated.

"What? Why only the San Mateo store?" I complained.

"The ad and new card were issued by the San Mateo Safeway, and we are not allowed to cash their coupons," she said firmly.

So there I was, loaded down with groceries, fully anticipating that almost half of them would be free. Chagrined, I paid the full amount, loaded the groceries into my car and headed home. Strike four . . .

Of the five chores I had assigned myself this day, I had accomplished only one successfully. Perhaps I should be thankful that I did have a sparkling clean car. Besides, Tomorrow is another day.

I Lived for a Year in the Sanborn House as a Marycliff Academy Student
By Dr. Audrey Lynch

On a recent visit to Boston my niece, Michelle Dickson, a member of the Winchester Historical Society invited me to take a tour of the old Sanborn mansion. She was so excited about the house that she said, in her best Gatsby voice, "How wonderful it must have been to live here. I would have loved it."

To her amazement I replied, "I actually spent a year living here during my junior year at Marycliff Academy." That started a whole chain of memories that began when I was thirteen years old. Now I am 80 so that meant looking back sixty-seven years in time.

How did it all start? I had won a four year full scholarship to Marycliff. My freshman and sophomore years had been full of wonderful experiences but my parents noticed a change in me the next summer when I turned 16 on Cape Cod where we spent our summers. Suddenly I bloomed physically and then socially.

I discovered boys and they started appearing at our cottage every day and when we arrived at the West Harwich Beach. Looking back I realize that my parents must have been surprised by all this constant activity into their usually peaceful summer. It reached somewhat of a peak on my sixteenth birthday when three different boys gave me pearls as a gift.

My mother's best friend found the situation hugely funny and referred to our vacation "as the summer of the great pearls". My parents started having a lot of private conversations together. I discovered the gist of these conversations when they announced just before Labor Day, "We've decided to let you live at Marycliff this year because we think that all that commuting between Cambridge and Winchester is too tiring for you." "Tired" was a euphemism for bad behavior which my parents often used.

They didn't make it sound like a punishment so I looked forward to my year at the Sanborn Estate as an exciting adventure. The nuns always had a few live-in students every year. Some of them were from South America ostensibly to improve their English. In my class there was one—Merille Burlie—a beautiful dark-haired girl. Privately I wondered if she, too, had been "tired."

If my parents' goal was to isolate me from the male sex, they had picked the right place. The only male in sight was dear, old Father Garrahan, a retired priest of advanced years who occupied a loft with the science teacher's class specimens over the garage, the former carriage house. He often said Mass for us.

There was one additional discordant male presence. It was a large print of "The Laughing Cavalier" on one of the stairway walls. He was a handsome and leering gentleman, one of the first subjects to smile in the portraits of the Flemish School of painting. In the Cavalier's case it was more of a smirk than a smile. It was a daily reminder that there was a big world out there that probably differed from Marycliff Academy and the Sanborn estate.

Our rooms on the top floor of the Sanborn Estate were small and sparse in my memory. Two items of its old grandeur, however, remained seared into my memory forever. One was the wide, sweeping front hall staircase where I used to imagine myself descending to attend elegant balls in the future. The other was the beautiful stained glass window. I had only seen such windows in churches until I moved there.

Of course the rolling green lawns – white in winter – were perfect for sledding. They reminded me of one unforgettable evening we had with Reverend Mother Cloonan. As the head of our school she ruled with an iron hand both the nuns and students. She was efficient and formidable and everyone admired her but no one dared to approach her. Imagine our surprise one night when she suggested that we make fudge. It was a night filled with laughter and the delicious smell of warm fudge. It also taught us that maybe, just maybe, Reverend Mother Cloonan just might be human after all.

Without any boys in sight, we spent a lot of time thinking and talking about them. That brings up the matter of sex education which is a staple of modern, public education. The closest we came to that was a yearly lecture on menstruation given by our science teacher, Mére Haché. It was an embarrassing event and rather overdue.

Instead, we existed in an underground of myths and misinformation. Any sort of make-up, even the palest of pink lipsticks, was totally forbidden. The underlying message was that the use of make-up to attract boys must be some kind of sin. The minute we left the school grounds the first thing we did was to put on make-up. We didn't have mirrors so I mastered the art of putting on lipstick without one while running for the bus down High Street. It's a rare talent that I still retain much to the amazement of my current women friends.

Patent leather shoes were used as another example of the occasion of sin. Supposedly a boy could stand close to you, look down at your shoes and see the reflection of your panties. This has never been verified to my knowledge but women of my generation avoided these shoes – just in case.

Our social life, if you could call it that, consisted of two yearly dances with St. John's Prep School. It was run by Brothers and one of its charms I suppose was that it was located in Danvers, a good safe distance from Winchester. The boys were eager but always gentlemanly. We girls, attributed the latter fact to the story that we heard that the Brothers put saltpeter in the boys' food just before the dance to calm them down.

In addition to the saltpeter, there was another deterrent to fraternization. The dances were sharply patrolled by the Brothers who kept an eye on all potential danger spots. Towards the end of the evening as the dancers grew closer, they would be startled by a rap on the boy's shoulder and an admonition to "leave room for the Holy Ghost."

If the sex education was rather non-existent the rest of the curriculum was way above average. The nuns, the Sisters of Religious Education, a small congregation whose Mother House was in France, were totally devoted to us. They watched over us, taught us, and were totally involved in our overall welfare. I've worked in the field of education all my life and have never witnessed this type of devotion anywhere else.

Two experiences stand out in my own memory. Mére Haché, our science teacher, invited me to participate in a science fair at the school, city, and state levels. She drove us and helped us and always turned out winners. In my senior year she apprenticed me to a biologist at Harvard University to oversee my project. As a result I was exposed to that wide academic arena when I applied for college.

In French Level 4 there was just me and Mére Janin. We worked on my French and she required a senior thesis of me and gently guided me to the subject of Blaise Pascal and his Pensées. Can you imagine the rich, provocative discussions we had? I was very well prepared for the Ivy League by these intelligent, dedicated women.

Since the order came from France there were some other emphases in the curriculum. They worked on our French and we were expected to use it (i.e. "Bonjour, Ma Mére") when we ran into them outside or in the corridors. I learned to love the language so much that I took it in college, too.

The nuns also tried to turn us into little ladies. They demanded courtesy at all times. I've heard that in their southern academy, in Ashville, North Carolina, the girls even had to learn to play a good hand of bridge before graduation.

I had a little trouble with some of the "lady" requirements. The nuns spoke of the virtue of a well-modulated voice but I had a loud voice and was of the opinion that "the louder the better." In addition, I liked to run, rather than walk anywhere. As a boarder the nuns suggested gently that I should emulate the fine example of two sisters who lived in the house with me. They spoke softly and walked with dignity. In fact they seemed to glide rather than walk. Of course I hated them.

In my sophomore year the school moved from Arlington to Winchester. The nuns oversaw the building of a brick high school as well as the purchase of the Sanborn house. I saw the new school building as a challenge and it prompted my first big prank. I brought a flashlight to school and told my classmates that we needed to explore our new school. I led them down to the basement and we went in to explore the underpinnings of our new school. Perhaps the custodians complained. The nuns met us on the way out.

They were angry and looked like they would like to punish us. Of course there was no specific rule which we had broken so we weren't ever punished. Looking back I think they might have even been amused by our boldness.

There were some activities outside of classes. We had a newspaper and a yearbook. These were my favorite activities. There was sodality and sports. I even played basketball although I was terrible. The vice-president of the class, on the other hand, was the star of the team. Everything was open to all of us and we were encouraged to participate.

For the parents, there was the annual Dessert and Fashion Show. It was a fund-raiser and kept the mothers busy all year. Sometimes the fathers were called upon to provide special skills like fixing things or helping with the finances.

Some of the girls came from wealthy families. For example two little blonde sisters arrived every day in a limousine driven by a liveried chauffeur. It was a show-stopping daily occurrence for most of us.

Despite the disparity in wealth, there was no overt snobbery. One of the great equalizers was the mandatory requirement for uniforms. This eliminated all clothes competition. The uniforms consisted of blue jumpers, white blouses with Peter Pan collars, and navy blue blazers. Looking back now atour class picture I think we looked very neat and nice. As teenagers we cordially hated these uniforms. As an adult I have never purchased anything with the color of navy blue.

Another classmate told me she has never purchased a blazer in her adult life. The year after we left, the uniform changed to a plaid skirt.

As graduates, we did very well in our college placements. By now we were a class of 12, just half the size of our freshman class. Two of us went to Harvard and the rest went to other colleges and we mostly graduated with one exception and another one of our class who became a nun.

Our senior year ended in a flurry of excitement. There was the prom which was preceded by an invitation to dinner at the Winchester Country Club. The invitation came from our classmate Betty McCormick ("Chicken") whose father sold Willys' Jeeps. This classmate was a cute little redhead full of life and very social and, unfortunately one of our first classmates to die.

Dates had been a problem for most of the girls so some male teachers at Cambridge High and Latin School had been commandeered to "find dates" for the girls for the prom which they did. The gym was decorated like a fairyland and we were one of the few girls' schools who danced to live music by a popular local band leader who was related to one of the girls.

Then came graduation day which we thought meant the beginning of real life. I remember particularly the dazzling colors that day although not one word of Cardinal Cushing's speech. Our nuns had come to Boston at his request and so he was their protector. He was always the commencement speaker.

The weather was gorgeous – all blue skies and rolling green lawns. Cardinal Richard J. Cushing, our commencement speaker, was clad in the brilliant red berretta and vestments of his office. We were dressed in floor length white lace gowns, scoop necks, with a blue underskirt. The dresses were designed by Bianchi, famous for her wedding gown designs, because she was a relative of one of the girls. In our arms we each carried a dozen red roses. Looking at our picture, I now know that we didn't suspect on that beautiful day that never again would we look so young, so pretty, and so innocent as we did with the lovely Sanborn House behind us as a backdrop.

Gone
By Valerie Stoller

HONORABLE
MENTION

I exit an elevator into the lobby of the Memory Care Unit and stop at the entrance. My mother has just moved up here from her assisted living apartment, and I've flown in from California to visit. A small wooden set of letters painted with blue and yellow flowers squats on a mahogany sideboard. The letters spell out "RESPECT." A reminder for visitors.

My stomach clenches. Respect? What's on the other side of the door? Maybe a confused, agitated resident cursing me. Or a flock of frail bodies strapped to chairs, drool dribbling down their chins. Will my mother be one of them?

I push open the door. It's only locked from the inside. An empty hallway greets me. Oh, thank god. I let out my breath and move down the hall towards the new room assigned to my mother.

Mom has been in this assisted living residence for eight years, uprooted from her New Jersey four-bedroom home to a one-bedroom apartment here in St. Louis Park, Minnesota. Near my sister and her family, but light years away from her previous life. And still far from me.

Most of her old friends are dead now, as she likes to remind me. So is my father. He died in 2002, and a year later we helped her sell their home and move here. But she often forgets this, when she's lonely or remembers something she wants to tell my dad. When I remind her that he's gone, I feel like he's just died again.

My mom has Parkinson's, a disease that has shrunk her world in countless ways. A relentless river of losses. Her short-term memory is just one of these, drifting, tumbling downstream. Her body has betrayed her, too. Her legs refuse to walk, her arms no longer remember how to pull her through the ocean. All gone.

Mom's apartment is at the end of the hall. Most of the doors I've passed are open. I glimpse old men and women, alone in their recliners facing TV screens, asleep despite the deafening volume. So exposed. Here loneliness trumps privacy.

Mom's door is open too. She looks up at me from the couch. She's dressed in a gray lamb's wool cardigan, maroon paisley shirt and pants I bought her last year. Silver earrings, bright lipstick smudged at the corners. Never without lipstick. Her hazel eyes, magnified by large reading glasses, lock on my face. I know she is trying to place me, pull open that drawer of memories. Yes. My daughter. I know you.

"Hi, Mom." I lean down and kiss her cheek. Skin soft as a baby's.

"Oh, it's Valerie." She scrunches her eyes, peering up at me. Mom holds the New York Times Magazine with both hands, a familiar pose, though now she has trouble getting through most of the articles. She used to linger over the double acrostic, no help needed, triumphant when she'd announce the source of the puzzle's quotation. Now the crossword puzzle squares are empty. Still, this ritual, holding tight to those pages, seems to comfort her.

"I thought you were Elle Bishop." One of her friends who is dead. "I forgot you're a platinum blonde now."

"Yeah, it's me." I smile and squeeze her hand. Small as a child's. Bony, cool flesh. "Not blonde. Just silver- haired."

A male nurse's aide knocks on the apartment door, then enters. Tall, thin body, dressed in a purple polo shirt and khaki pants. Staff attire, but he, Kefir, could just as well be headed out for a game of golf.

"Hello, ladies." His voice is warm, accented. . His ebony smooth skin and chiseled features mark him as not native to the Midwest. More Masai than Minnesotan. "I come to give you your medicines, Miss Beryl."

Mom smiles at him. He unlocks the small toolbox containing the meds my mother takes. Does she recognize this man who takes care of her? Or does each day bring a new collection of strangers who lean, dress and feed her?

His careful fingers arrange a small mountain of pills in a paper cup. I watch as he places the first large pill in a spoonful of applesauce. It's the only way to get the medications down.

"Here you go." He feeds Mom each pill, waiting until she swallows before offering the next. Like spoon-feeding a baby.

His kindness is so touching. Gratitude washes over me. Is his respect for elders natural or learned? I envy his patience. Maybe he can teach me.

Parkinson's makes swallowing difficult. A perfect metaphor for the disease itself. How can I learn to accept Mom's progressive deterioration? Will this be me someday? Is the disease encoded in my genes? What will I do if I can no longer swim, or follow a conversation or dress myself?

"Now, ladies." Kefir flashes his smile. "Please come down to the community room. We have a guest musician."

Great. Mom has always been a music lover, jazz, classical, show tunes. I push her down the hall in her wheelchair, past fishing rods and nets dangling on the walls—all, they tell me, to make it feel like home. Maybe so, but not like Mom's home. Most New York Jews don't fish.

Guitar chords echo into the hall. Mom and I find a place in the back of the community room. An attractive petite woman in her forties, hair dyed an unnatural reddish brown, perches on a barstool. She cradles an acoustic guitar in her lap, her sparkly fake nails strumming the strings.

The lyrics, amplified and familiar, envelop the small gathering. I back up a few steps.

She's mid-way through Johnny Cash's "Ring of Fire."

Several residents tap their feet and clap in time to the thudding bass notes. Loving it. Probably the highlight of their day. At least while they hold on to the memory.

Oh god. Country music. Mom's always hated it. For rednecks only. I peek at her, bracing myself for her indignation. Why have you brought me here, subjected me to this pathetic excuse for music? Instead, she smiles and, yes, taps her foot. Even claps. I'm stunned.

Maybe she's just faking it. The new girl in class, wanting to fit in. I lean down in between songs.

"Mom," I whisper. "Do you want to go back to your apartment?"

"I like this." Mom shakes her head. Smiles up at me from her wheelchair. "No, let's stay."

I can't believe it. How did this happen? Where is that vital, opinionated intellectual snob of a woman who raised me? I want to grab her by the shoulders, tell her that her old self would be appalled by this new one. Who is she? Where is my mother?

She's slipping away, and I'm helpless. My ninety-three-year-old frail mother, unable to track conversations or swallow her food, is disappearing before my eyes. There is less of her each time I visit.

Meanwhile my new mom is very happy to see me. Even if she's not sure who I am. And I'm happy to see her, too. She's much easier to be around now. Still, I miss my mother, the one who drove me crazy, who I tried so hard to please, who I loved so much. My heart aches. Now I understand why they remind visitors about respect. I have a lot to learn.

Things I Learned from my Dog
By Jeannine Gerkman

- Stretch thoroughly upon awakening
- Drink plenty of water
- Exercise but don't forget to smell the flowers along the way
- There are times you're going to have to humble yourself, but it's okay as long as there is a reward at the end
- No matter how late your friend is, greet him with joy and enthusiasm
- Guard your boundaries
- Adapt your approach based on the other person's style
- Forgive freely
- No matter how serious things get, take time to play
- There is no such thing as too much affection
- Be mindful of your colleagues and don't let anyone get left behind

Evelyn's Fantasy
By Judith A. Guarnera

The frail woman with white, cotton-candy spun hair framing her weathered face, looked up with rheumy eyes as I opened the door to her room in the assisted living facility which she had called home for two years. Aged eyes squinted, as her memory tried to place the visitor in her doorway.

"It's Judy," I said. I repeated my name in a louder voice, as I moved closer, squatting down so that I was right in front of her. Whether she finally heard or dimly saw something that sparked a memory, her grin suffused the wrinkles in her face.

Evelyn's age calendar will flip over in April, when she reaches the 103rd anniversary of her birth. Ten years ago she began the litany, I'm ready to die," and continued it until the encroaching dementia robbed her of the memory of that desire. Her mind and her memory have failed her, but her body, though fragile, refused to cooperate.

My house sat catty-corner to Evelyn's at the crossroads to two quiet small- town streets. Although we waved at each other, several years went by after I moved into the neighborhood, before we actually met. We were both perusing a lovely garden during our town's annual garden tour, when we recognized each other. I offered my condolences over the recent loss of her husband. I don't remember how she responded, but her spunk touched me and we became friends.

Once a week, I would take her to breakfast, then to shop at Farmer's Market and other local stores. I knew our friendship had progressed, when she asked me to take a key to her house in case of an emergency. Even though Evelyn had a life alert necklace, whenever she fell, she called me first. Together we faced the onslaught of paramedics and firemen who gallantly came to her rescue when the button on her necklace was finally pushed.

When our weekly trips became too much of a chore for her, I would bring her fresh raspberries and home-made triple berry jam from Farmer's Market. Food forays also included the doughnuts she loved along with a McDonald's burger and vanilla shake.

Evelyn, a bright woman, attributed her droll sense of humor and stubbornness to her Norwegian heritage. Long before her hearing had deteriorated to the extent that hearing aids offered little help, she religiously practiced selective hearing, making it impossible to win an argument with her.

Macular Degeneration played another of life's nasty tricks on Evelyn. She loved to read, but the disease robbed her of that pleasure. Imagine having a smudge on your glasses right in the center and having to read around that smudge. Evelyn could see the shape of a face, but the details—features—were missing. She would peer at the occasional piece of mail she received (her important mail was forwarded to her son) or at the daily newspaper, but her eyes tired quickly. For a while she could watch her beloved golf matches on TV. Now she no longer reads anything.

Evelyn used a walker to ambulate. After several falls, her caregivers restricted her walking unless someone was with her. Finding that someone became her mission. Now, the walker sits idly by her chair, for she's forgotten what it's for.

Most visits I sat down, prepared to follow whatever direction our conversation would take us.

"I'm glad you came. Are you Mary?" Evelyn would ask.

"No, Evelyn, it's Judy. I brought you some of those cinnamon grahams you like."

"What?"

I held the container in front of her, but she couldn't see what it was. Before I could change the subject, Evelyn would beat me to her favorite topic.

Okay, Judy, now's the time to use your creative writing skills and lie through your teeth, I would tell myself.

"I thought you were that other person, the one who won a big prize," she said, as she cocked her head trying to remember. "It wasn't the Nobel Prize, but something like that."

"That would be me, Evelyn. And you're right, it wasn't the Nobel. It was for my book."

'Oh what tangled webs we weave, when first we practice to deceive.'

A Musing
By Beth Mostovoy

the world
gleams in your smile
smiles in your eyes I am
not that world and my
revelations
are not in the revolutions by
which you live
I am a moon
a hint in the darkness which
shadows me from you that you
can't see thru
the flow of my tide is endless deep
within the currents of myself you see
my face
its many phases
you see the face I choose gleaming and
shining above you out of your reach
but not too high for your hopes let my
light shine softly on you

216

Curiosity
By Margaret Vose

The guns were hidden way back in the small dark closet in my Dad's den behind the heavy red-checkered wool hunting jacket, water-proof pants, and a lighter jacket worn shoveling snowy sidewalks. A red hunting cap with ear flaps rested on the shelf next to half a box of shotgun shells.

The shotgun was used to hunt birds and for "skeet shooting", where circular clay plates were slung out into the air for target practice. It looked heavy with its twin barrels of gleaming blue-black steel and smoothly polished wooden stock. In contrast, the other gun was lighter, graceful, almost feminine; a single barrel rifle used for deer hunting week-ends in the north woods.

I was firmly warned never to touch the guns in my father's closet but often the forbidden is irresistible to a curious child. One day when I was alone, I opened the closet door, reached my arm through the clothing until I felt the cold barrels of the larger weapon standing upright in the corner. Carefully, and with some effort, I pulled it from its hiding place with both small hands and drew it out into the room, laying it on the floor before me. I felt excited and at the same time frightened to be alone with this forbidden object. Of course, it wasn't the first time I had seen this gun, but it had always been in my father's hands. My fingers slid up and down the metal barrels as I looked closely at how the parts fit together, but I lacked the courage to put my small finger in the trigger to see how it moved. I examined the design my father had carved in the hardwood of the stock.

When I finished I had no further interest in that gun. I didn't want to load it or shoot it or even see it again. I quickly replaced it in the corner of the dark closet, behind the hunting clothes and shut the door.

My Dad and Grandfather Leland always hunted pheasant and quail in the autumn on the farm in Michigan. They might even come with a rabbit or squirrel, enacting a ritual when early settlers provided game for the family table. They would bring the still-warm feathered or furry creatures home in their large coat pockets for my grandmother to dress and roast in the oven with butter, herbs and potatoes.

I watched the men clean and oil their guns after the hunt and carefully hang them high on the wall of the garage attached to the farm house. There was once a need for guns in America, but that was a long time ago, before the horror at the Sandy Hook Elementary School.

Cheesy Memories
By Terry Toomey

Sometimes I wander along Highway 29 with no particular destination in mind. The drive is pretty and there are interesting places to stop and browse. Both the Oxbow Market and Dean and Deluca have upscale foods and wines. And oh my, the cheese shops in these stores carry expensive cheeses; some are imported and some come from small cheese makers.

When I say expensive, some of them would require a bank loan for me to purchase. When I was looking at these cheeses I knew I never had them as a child. But they reminded me of the meatless Friday night dinners my mother cooked for us. The fish, and frozen fish sticks were baked in the oven they were always a big hit and so was cream tuna on toast. The fish sticks were my brothers' favorite Friday night meal; mine was creamed tuna. However, we did have cheese dishes for dinner and sometimes we had them at lunch.

The biggest Friday night treat was Cheese Strata a tasty combination of bread and cheese with Campbell's Cream of Mushroom poured over it. The casserole was placed in the oven and then baked until it was bubbly. I liked it more than macaroni and cheese. I guess that's why I can't remember how my mom cooked the Mac. I suspect it came from a package. Sometimes it might have had some type of Campbell's Soup over the noodles and maybe with some tuna.

My favorite birthday meal was spaghetti with a tomato and meat sauce my mom made. Sometimes it came out of a Chef Boyardee can. I didn't care, I liked spaghetti both ways and I covered it with cheese that we sprinkled from a cardboard container. Homemade cheese cake was my brothers' birthday choice and my mom made a good one. Spaghetti is still one of my favorite meals, although I usually have don't have cheese on it from a paper cheese shaker, not because I don't think it is cheese, but more because I like spaghetti without it better.

When I got a little older my mom and I would go to the mall and have lunch at Woolworth's. I would order a grilled cheese sandwich with a dill pickle spear and a Coke. This was a real treat. They sure tasted good then. I'm not so sure they're as good now unless they have added some tasty cheese. We often went out to dinner on Friday nights as a family, but these Saturday lunches were just for the two of us.

Cheese figured into weekends in other ways, too. There was a cheese factory on Main Street in Pleasanton. My family would drive to this pretty town, taste some cheese and I guess we bought some. Then, we might have dinner at the historic Pleasanton Hotel.

When I first lived on my own I would drive to a cheese factory in Sonoma and buy a small amount of cheese. And when I spent Saturdays at my mom's house, she would put cheese and tomato sauce on an English muffin and place it under the broiler until it melted and was bubbly.

All of these cheese treats are wonderful memories; I wonder if the artisan cheeses will ever match them.

monet's garden
By Maurine Killough

like holding her cloth napkin could
make a difference
monet's splash of color on this cotton square bleeds
memories into my heart...

the nasturtiums in her postage stamp garden
pot roast on sundays, looking up at her sheepishly
after dripping stains on her table cloth, again

like holding this piece of fabric,
held so many times at her table
could melt me away from here bring me back

to the comfort of life when it was new to
the safety of a grandmother's garden
playing scrabble with her on tuesdays
watching fog swim past her plate glass window

no mortgage or threat of foreclosure
no clients or projects aching their demands in my head
no marriage to reconcile or find
no health issues or the kinds of hurts that surely come with years

just free falling at that maiden age
drudgery hadn't set in yet.

like holding this piece of her could
bring me back to her
make this tedium of bills and chores and worries melt away
make life a monet garden
like holding this napkin of feather-tipped colors could
bring me back to life.

Anxiety in the Grass
By Stanley Gedzelman

Anxiety was his problem, or more accurately, his constant companion. It seemed never to leave his side. Others might be bipolar and broadcast their depression or mania to the world. His anxiety was an almost secret companion. Most others could not see any hint of it. But it was there and if he got close enough they felt it. It was like a cat's purr absent its endearing quality.

When had it started? Fittingly, at the time of puberty. A simultaneous change of schools and classes without a friend did not help. Suddenly, every test became a cause of great anxiety. The nervous feeling heightened from the moment the test was announced to the moment it was given if he knew the material or the moment it was over if he didn't. He knew when he did well or poorly—there was no illusion in him that way. If he did well he felt greatly relieved. If he did poorly it was as if every failing and shortcoming he knew about himself had been confirmed.

Nervousness beyond agony occurred when the teacher announced that everyone in the class had to give an oral presentation. You would think that he would prepare meticulously and rehearse his little two-minute speech. You would think wrong. Instead, he just allowed the anxiety to crescendo throughout the week. His presentation was a fiasco.

He joined the track team. Before every meet he felt sick. Sometimes he threw up. The nervousness ended at the starting gun, but if he ran in two events it began anew as soon has he had recovered his breath. He noted that physical exhaustion trumped anxiety. It helped him keep in shape his entire life.

Asking girls out was another source of anxiety. This one was interminable because the fear, indeed the certainty of rejection kept him from asking but the anxiety remained because he kept mentally preparing to ask out the girls.

The car broke down the first day of a cross-country trip. The car was towed and repaired. For days afterward he was sure the car would break down again at the first moment he relaxed his guard. Suddenly he had a revelation. He realized his vigilance had no relation to or impact on the condition of the car. All the anxiety in his life was purposeless and fruitless. It didn't prepare him for anything and was furthermore was counterproductive. But he could not internalize that precious insight.

He diagnosed anxiety as a result of a feeling of lack of control. An aide to President Woodrow Wilson once said that Wilson was so controlling he appeared to feel as if the grass would not grow if he did not oversee it.

School years passed. He got a job at a bank, eventually did get married, and even had children. Two decades into the job all seemed secure and the anxiety abated. Then the epoch of downsizing began. Joe, who had the cubicle on the left, was fired. Fred quit when he was demoted and transferred to Anchorage. One by one, they went. Then his job was threatened directly. The anxiety returned. Nights were almost sleepless. This went on for five years. He worried greatly about his heart.

One night after a heavy dinner he felt as if he had swallowed a boiling potato. He recognized he was having a heart attack. His wife called 911. They saved his life. Quadruple bypass.

The heart attack only increased his anxiety. Every moment he was certain another attack would creep up on him if he relaxed his guard. It became impossible to sleep. Eternal vigilance was required. He became somewhat like Woodrow Wilson.

It was as if the grass could not grow without his constant attention. He could not dare rely on his old revelation that anxiety was at best counterproductive.

More years went by. Still alive, the anxiety became more episodic. There were times he could forget it for hours at a stretch! No joke – that was a major accomplishment.

Throughout his lifetime of anxiety he wondered where it had come from. But he never got an answer. He just seemed to be the just about the only anxious person in the universe. Surely, from time to time he saw other anxious people practicing their art. They all gave undue importance to some trivial item or issue of the moment. They gave the impression that everything had earth shattering importance. It appeared so ridiculous to see it in others. His anxiety by contrast was real. That brought to his mind the old saying that Comedy is when you break your neck; Tragedy is when I stub my toe. But he could never internalize the knowledge of his self-absorption.

Where did it come from? Where did it come from? It couldn't be purely genetic. It couldn't!

Then one day in the park with his granddaughter he witnessed an unpleasant scene. A mother shook her three-year-old son violently for some unseen and unheard infraction and then growled to him, "Just wait until I get you home!"

That was it! That had been his childhood. One memory welled up – then another and another in quick succession. His early childhood had been filled with various ingenious or even pedestrian punishments. But all so often the punishment was preceded by a long waiting period of, "Wait until...."

"Wait until I get you home!" "Wait until your father gets home!" He had suffered the sadism of suspense.

Why did the anxiety wait until puberty to appear? Before that it was there but was submerged below the surface. Then it metamorphosed as his body metamorphosed. All things had been taken care of in his child world. But from adolescence he was on his own. And what was the lesson of it all? – "Wait until the inevitable failure or disaster!"

The revelation was the birth of freedom. The anxiety would take time to dispel–how much he couldn't tell. For this though, he could wait! Suddenly he had acquired some newfound patience. Finally, he could let the grass grow on its own.

Mama Sails Home
By Bhawna Panwar

She spent most of her life repairing boats and securing anchors
around shipping docks
Watching and enduring what came towards her and giving them
new home.
Now seventy years passed by her, her bronze twig-like fingers of
her hands roll two hefty barrels of wheels.
Pushing all of her presence ahead,
Her surroundings resemble a gray and turbulent ocean surface,
Swinging and swaying by the pull of a winter's sea storm.
She rides each hump and bump of a carpet as the brutal and
violent tide that surges and tries to tumble her over.
She struggles and sways just to hold on to the steel wheels as to
hold on to the walls of her shaky and crumbly world.
She is relentless to carry her own load across the sea of her room
once more.
Whispering words of comfort that are carried by her phone's dial
tone,
Slowly fading voices of sympathy disconnect and end.
This winter's snowstorm withers and welters her broken skin and
bones.
Hollowing and scraping against the roof top of her wrecked
world.
Each day she watches, her skin shrivels up and dries out like her
sinking courage with each breath;
As if to disappear with a heavy whip of the ocean breeze.
Despite this unfounded journey she discovers herself struggling
against cruel Nature's attack against her.
She tries to navigate and tries to survive.
No matter how hard it is for her to taste the bitter taste of this
helplessness
She has to drink the metallic fluid of her pride that weakens and
sheds her willpower with each passing day,
She has to gain the strength to sail ahead towards the sun and
restore her independence. Once again.

69 Lengths
By Mary Ruth Coffey

This morning, I was pregnant with twins –
Grief and Regret. They sat in my belly, side by
side, Grief on my left and Regret on my right,
Grief facing forward, Regret looking back. My
bloated belly bulged larger on the left and I knew
it was because her eyes were swollen with tears
and the strain to see a future without Regret.

I've always loved to see pregnant women in
bikinis. I think they're beautiful and I know, in
my heart, you would agree. So I let my growing babies be free and hang over,
especially on the left, of my light blue teal string bikini bottom, melon-
colored abstract birds entwined in each other's black beaks and legs. I looked
in the mirror of this foreign bathroom at my profile and rubbed my belly and
wondered if this is how you would photograph me if you could, if I had let
you when you asked me back in September. How would you have painted this
belly then, when our twins had just been conceived, and how would you
capture it now, six months pregnant with the offspring of our stubbornness?

The tiny string of my bikini top resting in the center of my chest only
partially covered the bright red sore that I had seen the dermatologist about
last week. She said it was just a scratch, but I knew it was a hole in my heart,
and that my heart was trying to seep through it and squeeze out of my chest
to transplant itself into yours and save your life. But the hole was too small
and already starting to heal, imprisoning my heart to try to save my own.

It was my last morning at the Ritz--Carleton in Sarasota, my last morning
to swim in the luxuriously heated pool overlooking Sarasota Bay, the great
divide between this monstrous hotel and the Cypress Bed and Breakfast,
where you always were, in the kitchen of my memories, drinking coffee,
laughing with the guests, baking scones and cooking the perfect extra cheesy
omelet with avocado and tomato, because you knew I was a savory, not sweet,
girl.

Downstairs, I could smell the chlorine and closed my eyes in my strong
wish that no one else would be in the pool this morning. I could only swim
with Grief and Regret alone, all alone this morning that was becoming the
next scene in the one-woman show I was writing, producing, directing and
starring in: "Sarasota – In Memoriam".

The air was cold and I could see the steam lifting off the warm water and
floating above it like I imagined your spirit did when your heart finally went
to sleep. Although the sun had shone brightly the last four days, today the
Sarasota sky wept, and shades of lavender and silver filled the breeze and
settled on the thick fog above the pool. This is where you and I meet, I
thought, beneath the sun, in a place where souls float in blue-grays and
purples.

I stepped into that fog and saw my ankles disappear into the three-foot
end of the pool. The scars on the inside of my lower left leg from the bug bites
I took as a souvenir from Sarasota in September submerged in your spirit and
I thought about how you must have felt those four days in the hospital as

your body slowly left you right before your eyes. I know you didn't want to die. I know.

The next step into the pool covered my bruised knees and skirted the top of my thighs, the base of my bikini whose birds floated like pelicans on waves. And finally, declining stair to stand on the bottom of this three-foot end of the pool, my belly, my twins, Grief and Regret, brought to my life by your death, rested just beneath the surface of the water.

Normally, I swim around 30 lengths of a pool, 15 laps. Sometimes, 40 lengths, 20 laps. Often I lose count, but mostly I have an intention. As I breast stroked my first length this morning, I had no intention, only an idea of a painting whose brushstrokes were moist with the mixture of my tears and this pool water.

Throughout my second length, a backstroke, I wondered if tears could be dried by water? Third length, breaststroke, I thought this merging of liquids was akin to what the curator at the Tampa Museum of Art said yesterday about the artist Luke DuBois, and other contemporary artists, that they are post-genre. On my fourth length, I realized that this was what my writing is— post-genre, and on my fifth, I thought about you reading my piece where I reworked the Miss Universe bathing suit contest and how you said just this, that it didn't fit into any one genre–it was all of them—post-genre.

And so it went, breast strokes on the odd numbers, backstrokes on the even. Breast stroking length 13, I thought about Nina, dead now nearly nine years, July 13, 2005, age 42, my best friend, and how I swam 13 laps for years after her death in the pool of my downtown Chicago apartment, 13 precisely, to remember her, to pray desperately, to wish, fruitlessly, that she would come back. As I swam then, I was pregnant with my second child, Pain, shingles wrapping the nerves of my belly like the holes you think you can see on the moon from your front porch as a child, when bellies of future unwanted children are far, far away from your wildest imagination.

By length 16, I was mesmerized and meditative, until a shock of cold water swam across my belly as the pool attendant placed a hose into the pool. And then I remembered my fourth child, swept away from me violently, suddenly, on January 16, aborted by the hands of the community that allowed me to carry and nurture this baby back to health, spin doctors who led me to believe she would then be mine to keep. They ripped her from my belly and left me openly wounded, telling her I was dead. When I carried her, I named her Beauty, but now I understand they call her Anger.

Backstroking length 23, I became warm again, and my belly began to rumble with words, hundreds of them, spinning and dancing and swarming in and out of each other, kissing sometimes as they caressed vowels and strokes and ink and sentences without punctuation. My first child was in me now, again, a child of language, of rhythm, of kindness, my brother's child, my brother who was engulfed in flame and smoke when only 23 years old, when I was the young mother, just 14, of his only child, Poetry.

I breast stroked and backstroked, caressing my spine and massaging my twins. When I got to backstroke 50, I began to sob. The tears flowed down the sides of my cheeks into the pool as I extended one arm and then another above my head, reaching far beyond me, trying to reach you, but just momentarily embracing a palm full of water that dissipated as soon as I touched it. It was like our love, I thought. It had just begun and it was brief and like the afternoon storms of Sarasota—sunshine, thunder, rain, lightening, rainbows, wind, moving quickly in spirals and ending abruptly with the aftermath of puddles. And now there were the babies, Grief and Regret, swimming in my belly as I tried to grab for you, hopelessly, in a pool that did not distinguish my tears from the pool water, from the hose, from the Sarasota Bay, from thunderstorms, water that knew nothing of us when we were nothing of us together when we were a solid, an embrace that could have, should have, conceived a different baby–Art.

At 50 lengths, my intention became clear. Regret was kicking inside the right side of my belly, and Grief remained still save for small tremors and the kind of tiny gasps you get in the back of your throat when incessant crying finally becomes just a whimper that no one wants to hear anymore.

My intention was clear. I was swimming 69 lengths, one for each year of your life. I was swimming 69 lengths because our twins were six months old and, although I wished they would leave me now, I knew they would stay there, the babies, Grief and Regret, for nine months and be born full-term. And I prayed, that as I raise them with their siblings, Pain, Beauty and Poetry, that you would come back into my spirit and father my one last child—Art. But then again, maybe you already have.

Freedom
By Nicole Justine Cavanaugh

Where inside myself do I linger?

I felt myself hovering near the truth, sometimes wanting
to claim it

Remembering a good meal, the
salt on my tongue,
the wine fresh and red. You.

And then, white bars closing in on
me,
salt dripping down my face,
flushed red.

I disappeared.
Once slipped from your grasp, I
leave the white fence behind

a trail of freedom in my wake.

Finicky – Finicky
By Ida Lewenstein

No mother like me should witness the scene I'm about to describe, especially a mother who is an avid recycler, a picker-upper and a supporter of environmental causes.

It was the day of my son's noontime dental appointment. I picked him up at his high school, drove him to the dentist and waited to drive him back to school. When he came out, he told me that he was hungry and asked if I would buy him a submarine sandwich.

"OK," I said. "But to get back in time you will have to eat it in the car."

BIG MISTAKE! I should have known better. This kid of mine was such a finicky eater – there was always something he didn't like, and this time was no different. The meat and cheese he liked, but all those "other things," you know like onions, peppers, pickles stacked in between, had to go. And go they went.

All I could do was watch in utter disbelief as he rolled down the window, picked through the layers, and one by one, threw out all those 'other things' into the street.

To tell the truth, I didn't know what to do at that point. Should I have stopped the car, ordered him to get out and pick up all those 'other things'? No, I don't think so, that would have been too dangerous. Should I have stopped the car and make him walk back to school?

NO, I couldn't do that, it would have made him too late for class. I did think of wringing his neck, but that too would have made him late to class. All I could do at that point in time was glare at him. However, I swear that if ever I agree to buy him another submarine sandwich, it will be on the condition that he eat it in a SUBMARINE, not in MY CAR!

Amsterdam at Dusk
By Lisa Meltzer Penn

Amsterdam at dusk
Luxurious glitter
The slip of the railing beneath my palms
Garble, melt
Disobliging gulls renege
this moment, this narrow boulevard in a thimble
This caress of brilliance.

Max
By Linda Brown

After all the multitudes of birds, fish, lizards, cats, and dogs that had been part of our household had become fond memories, and all the children had left home, I began a new relationship with a man named Frank.

I was staying briefly in Southern California with my mother while I helped my daughter, who was home from Belize to prepare for a symposium she was going to attend in Australia. She had been having severe back pain and I had arranged for her to visit a chiropractor. She was feeling better, but at the last minute before boarding her flight, she decided she could not take a 20 plus hour plane ride to Australia with such on-going pain.

At loose ends, Lisa turned her attention to me. She decided that I had always had a dog in the household and it was time for me to get a new dog. I refused, as I had promised Frank, that when he was ready, we would pick one out together. Frank was not in Southern California; however, my daughter insisted that we at least go look.

We went to the Irvine Animal Shelter. We walked through the entire shelter but did not find a dog that we liked. I was relieved as I knew Frank would be unhappy if I came home with a dog. But unbelievably as we were walking out to the car a man was unloading an odd looking dog from of the back of his jeep.

Lisa said, "Hey, what are you going to do with that dog?"

He turned around after hooking the dog to a leash and said, "I'm turning him in to the animal shelter."

"Why? What's wrong with him?" Lisa persisted.

"Nothing," he said. "I am on the road a lot and my wife is pregnant with our second child and she can't handle him. He has a lot of energy."

"Do you mind if I take a look at him?" Lisa questioned, "What kind of dog is it?" "No, go ahead. He's a cross between a Rhodesian Ridgeback and Bull Mastiff."

The poor dog's name was Keanu, but I refused to have a dog by that name living in Richmond. So I renamed him Max.

Lisa took the leash and held it close to his head. Then she ran her hand over his body and head and mouth. The dog seemed pleased to be getting the attention.

We ended up talking with the man and handling the dog for over an hour.

"Mom, I think you should take this dog. He's a good dog."

"Um, Lisa, I think that dog is too big and too rambunctious for me to handle"

"No, mom, this is a great opportunity. You will love this dog."

The man had the dog's file which he gave us. I reluctantly agreed to take "Max" on the spot. We exchanged phone numbers in case we had any future questions. The owner did not give us the dog crate, and in retrospect I should have been suspicious about that.

As Lisa had few days before her return flight back to Belize she exercised the dog and spent time playing with him. Max had one bad trait; if he got loose he would run away. He was definitely a runner. But when we chased him down with the car, he would stop and get into the car without hesitation.

Lisa left and the dog was obviously worried and missed her presence, but he did know my car and seemed resigned to be with me.

I bought him a new dog crate and a pillow, which he immediately shredded. I figured he was nervous about all the new things in his life.

We had a horrible trip home, we got delayed on the highway and poor Max developed a bad case of diarrhea. By the time I found a place to pull off to get more water and paper towels, the dog was shaking like a leaf. He appeared terrified of me, but I kept assuring him that all was well and that it was not his fault. He finally calmed down and we continued our journey home.

When we arrived, Max bounded into the house, Frank, initially stunned when he first saw Max went a little berserk at his size and exuberance.

The dog was about 60 pounds, and looked a little like a boxer on steroids, but his ears and tail were not clipped. Poor Max immediately reacted to Frank by eliminating again, which caused another round of swearing by Frank as Max loosed his pile on the living room carpet.

We discovered in the next few days that Max was afraid of newspapers, hoses, and men's hats. We concluded that he had been beaten in his previous home. His paper work only indicated that he had been a two-time rescue dog. The previous shelter handler had noted that he was an "exuberant bimbo".

None of this information was reassuring to Frank.

After about two weeks, Max's former owner called up to say that they were back from vacation and missed the dog. He said he would like to come to take him back. Huh! So that's why he kept the crate.

Max also didn't like leashes. But we persisted. We took him to Carmel and fearing that he might run away in his excitement and he might not come back when we called him, Frank decided to keep him on leash at the beach. Max did take off running at the dog beach. Frank, who weighs in well over 200 pounds, had absolutely no control over Max. Max literally flipped Frank over on the beach trying to get away in his excitement to visit other dogs. The other dog owners didn't hesitate to tell Frank he wasn't handling his dog well. This frustrated Frank all the more.

However, Frank did not give up. He took him to dog obedience class. The trainer insisted that Frank squirt Max with bitter apple essence in an attempt to discipline the dog. Neither Frank nor Max liked that suggestion. Following the second class session the dog trainer offered us our money back if we would just never come back.

It remained obvious that Max wanted to please us. With perseverance on both Frank and Max's part, Max continued to improve. One morning something clicked with Max and he figured out Frank wanted the dreaded newspaper. After bounding out the front door Max pounced on the paper and kind of flipped it up so he could get his mouth around it. He carried it very gently and happily presented it to Frank in the kitchen.

During that first year Max and his new family grew to love each other. Max trusted us. Then a friend begged us to take on a small kitten that she had found at the dog park, Point Isabel.

I said, "I don't think we can, we don't know how Max will react. He is clumsy and kind of crazy."

"Please, please," she begged. "I already have four cats and cannot have another one. I will get thrown out of my apartment."

"Well," I temporized, "you can bring her and we'll see how Max does."

So she brought the little black two month old kitten over and all of the humans stood around the scene to see how Max would react.

He looked at her and he looked up at us and I think if he could have spoken, he would have said, "For me? Gosh, thanks!"

He very gently leaned over and gave her a big full body welcoming lick. The kitten didn't cry or run away and even in all his excitement of getting a new friend, Max was careful not to step on her. She became Isabel or Izzy for short.

Over the years Max grew into our family which kept expanding to include three cats and two granddaughters. Max took them all in stride happily adding them to the family pack. He had unending patience with the kittens and the grandchildren. He taught every one of us lessons in tolerance and acceptance.

Lisa was right. Max was a good dog. But he was more than a good dog; he was a great dog and lovingly accepted all who came into his world.

Dreams
By Nicole Justine Cavanaugh

Poles stuck in water
Thighs of wood, holding the
long deck out to sea
I walk this plank in my dreams
bare toes
scratching possible splinters the
gauze of my gown peeling
flapping against
soft thighs holding
me up,
my spirit melting into the sea
The sea slamming against the poles

Life of Many Passions
By Thomas Ekkens

Life of wisdom, voluminous and deep,
Giving and sharing, daring one and all.
Look to the unknown for answers to keep.

A passion for knowledge, what it could reap
In the days and years that pass eternal.
Life of wisdom, voluminous and deep.

A passion for cooking, baking, would heap
Bounties of food on the family table.
Look to the unknown for answers to keep.

A passion for crafts, hands that never sleep,
Creating shape and form that are central.
Life of wisdom, voluminous and deep.

A passion for art, the heart takes a leap Into
unknown space, the reverential,
Look to the unknown for answers to keep.

A passion for poetry, words that sweep
The universe for clues, a pivotal
Life of wisdom, voluminous and deep.

A passion for love, a heart that will weep At
the joy love is, to always enthrall.
Look to the unknown for answers to keep.

The mountain is hardy, rugged and steep,
A worthy passion for those who struggle.
Life of wisdom, voluminous and deep,
Look to the unknown for answers to keep.

Warning Signs
By Valerie Stoller

I knew we were in trouble when the small brown spider inside our tent scurried up to the top pole, followed by all the other insects who'd been lounging outside the nylon tarp. Some kind of bug radar had alerted them. Something not meant for human ears.

My boyfriend John and I had just gotten back from a strenuous hike down to the third waterfall. Havasu Canyon, Arizona. Seven miles below the canyon rim, unbelievably lovely. Limestone pools where swimming felt like a spiritual rebirth. A sacred home for Native American Supai, who begrudgingly allowed hikers access, and only permitted their photos be taken if paid first. Not really welcomed, we ignored the undercurrents and embraced the magical setting.

A light rain sprinkled against the tent. No worries. John lit up a joint. We'd just relax in our little cocoon and enjoy the afternoon reading and napping. After all, we were alone in paradise. There were hardly any other campers nearby.

We'd found a perfect spot to pitch our tent. A small patch of land, almost an island, with a gentle stream on either side. A heavy wooden picnic table stood under the large tree that provided shade from the scorching midday sun. Perfect.

The rain shifted to a loud insistent tap-tap-tap against the tarp. I looked out the tent flap and saw the streams had picked up their rhythm too. Our island campsite was just a little bit smaller.

John told me not to worry. Just a summer rain, typical in the southwest. It'd be over by dinner time, and we'd cook up our ramen noodles and finish off our last Hersey bar for dessert. Of course he was high and food seemed more important than a little rain.

I climbed out of the tent and pulled on my jacket and boots. Rain splattered my hood and prickled my face. This was no sweet summer rain. The swollen streams on either side had picked up speed and grabbed branches, shoes and canteens upstream, carrying them past me in a crazy blur. Our island oasis was being devoured.

"John." I yelled over the noise. "Come out here." I began packing up our gear from the picnic table. Stuffing everything into my backpack. We had to get ourselves over to the other side of the stream. Quickly. The water kept rising. A foam sleeping pad floated past, coated with mud. Then a flip flop.

John emerged from the tent and slid his bare feet into hiking boots. "Holy shit." At least he didn't try to talk me out of worrying. We both knew that our two week camping trip would be ruined if we lost our gear. There was no time to waste.

He helped me dismantle the tent and we strapped the poles and tarp onto his backpack. My mind raced through our options. We could climb on top of the picnic table and wait out the storm there. The water had crept up to the campsite. If we crossed the stream now, we'd be pushing through a knee high tumble of debris and soak our leather hiking boots. How high could it possibly get? Submerge the picnic table? Jesus. I hoped not.

John wasn't about to wait and find out.

"C'mon. We have to cross over." He pulled on his loaded backpack, weaving under the weight. He stepped into the stream and sunk to his waist. I watched a slow-motion horror reel; the rushing water swept him off his feet, carrying him downstream towards the waterfall we'd visited that morning. Oh my God.

Out of nowhere-- really, I was not stoned and could not make this up—a man appeared on the other shore and yelled at John to hold on to his pack. Our Canyon Angel trudged through the rushing torrent, grabbed John by the backpack and pulled him over to dry land. I was left alone perched on top of the picnic table. The water was lapping at my boots.

"C'mon." Canyon Angel yelled to me. "And hold on to your pack." Okay. Either I did what he told me, or I stayed on the table and prayed for a miracle. Doing something seemed like a better option. God might not be listening.

Step down, I urged myself. I was crying and shaking and ready to puke. The guy kept yelling at me to come on, so I wobbled into the stream, feeling my backpack pull me down. Then my feet slipped out from under me. Maybe wearing that pack wasn't such a great idea. Too late. I was going to die. Helpless, at the mercy of the raging water. My mind flashed to the next day's newspaper headline. Woman drowned in waterfall by freak storm in Arizona. My parents would be so sad. John would feel so guilty. And I would be so dead.

Somehow, amazingly, Canyon Angel got across and pulled me over just as he had with John. I lay on the ground, sobbing, shocked that I'd survived. He shrugged off my weepy thanks, then told us to climb back up the canyon walls to sleep that night.

Anyone with any sense, he told us, knew not to camp at the base of an Arizona canyon. Not during flash flood season. Apparently the picnic table had been shoved downstream during a previous deluge. We were the dumb California hippies who didn't have a clue. Who couldn't read the signs Mother Nature had posted.

Heavenly Halos and Their Angelic Arcs
By Stanley Gedzelman

Then up and spake an old Sailòr,
     Had sailed to the Spanish Main,
"I pray thee, put into yonder port,
     For I fear a hurricane.

"Last night, the moon had a golden ring,
     And to-night no moon we see!"
The skipper, he blew a whiff from his pipe,
     And a scornful laugh laughed he.

The Wreck of the Hesperus
Henry Wadsworth Longfellow

In December of 1839 a series of violent gales, two with hurricane force winds, wreaked havoc on the coast, the ships, and the lives of New England. The storm on the 15th provided the inspiration for Longfellow's poem. The body of a woman lashed to the wreckage washed up on shore. Longfellow transmuted that body to the Captain's delicate daughter.

It was, however a relatively minor incident that gave the poem its name. The schooner, Hesperus, presumably safe in Boston Harbor during that storm, broke her chains and smashed into the dock and a nearby building, causing modest damage.

You might think I would use this opening salvo to tell you about the power of storms - their ferocious winds, monstrous ocean waves, and burying snows or drowning floods. Indeed, that might be the story for another time. Here though I draw your attention to one of the poem's more subtle, delicate features - the storm's silent sentinel, the golden ring around the moon.

The poem's golden ring is a 22° ice crystal halo. Its appearance has been known for millennia as a precursor of large cyclonic storms - blizzards and hurricanes. But the 22° halo is only one of the huge family of ice crystal halos. You can see such halos or bits of them around the sun or moon on many days each year, even in California. Most are subtle creatures, camouflaged almost as well as hidden animals in a hildren's puzzle, so that only a trained eye will root them out. A precious few, however are breathtaking visages that traverse the sky with arcs of color purity and brightness that exceed the most glorious rainbows.

I will describe some of the major players in the halo family but a picture is worth innumerable words and a sighting is worth innumerable pictures. The annotated gray tone photo (hopefully included here) shows a magnificent halo display captured by Claudia Hinz on the ski slopes at Fichtelbergin, Germany, along the border of the Czech Republic. The 22° halo is the small ring around the sun. That small ring is actually quite large. When the sun is 22° above the horizon, the bottom of the ring rests on the horizon and the top reaches halfway to the zenith.

The upper tangent arc touches the top of the 22° halo and resembles a pair of wings. It is capped by the Parry arc, which merges with the wingtips. A sun pillar extends vertically from the sun while the parhelic circle passes horizontally through the sun and has two bright spots, the sun dogs, just outside the 22° halo. Other arcs appear more than twice as far from the sun. The infralateral, supralateral and circumzenithal arcs appear just outside the 46° halo, which however is seldom seen.

Whereas rainbows are produced when sunlight strikes raindrops, halos are produced when sunlight strikes ice crystals. What knowledge do we need to understand halos? First, we must know how ice crystals form, what they look like, and their orientation as they fall. Second, we must know what happens to light when it strikes a crystal. Third, we must know geometry, a subject all high school graduates once studied.

Let's now trace halos from the moment of their conception. The sun shines down on the sea, warming it and agitating the molecules, which break free and escape into the atmosphere. In more pedestrian terms, water has evaporated.

The escaped molecules move ceaselessly at about the speed of sound, but in random directions. When a nascent storm beckons the wind herds the vapor-laden air inward. The wind raises waves and shreds whitecaps, freeing and herding more vapor molecules stormward.

As the air enters the domain of the gigantic swirling cyclonic storm it is lofted as if on a great escalator. Air pressure decreases on the way up, and the depressurization chills the air as much as when it hisses out of a pressurized tire. As the air cools the molecules' agitated motion slows.

Water molecules are shaped like tiny H_2O boomerangs, with the oxygen atom at the center and the hydrogen atoms bonded at an angle of 104.5° on each side. This asymmetry polarizes the water molecules and attracts them to their comrades so that they cluster together once they cool and slow down enough. Thus, vapor molecules condense into tiny spherical droplets. The larger droplets begin to fall, striking and coalescing with other droplets below. They quickly grow to raindrops and head toward the ground. Should sunlight strike these drops, a rainbow will result.

Rain is only the first phase of the storm's precipitation. As the escalator continues ascending temperature continues to fall and eventually the triangular vapor molecules lock arms as tiny hexagonal ice crystals. Almost all ice crystals are built on a hexagonal or six sided plan, but there are such incredible variations, it is no wonder no two crystals are exactly alike. First are the different growth habits. Crystals can be shaped like new, unsharpened wooden pencils. If we shortened the pencil a bit by cutting off a thin slice at one end, that slice would resemble a plate. If we sharpened the pencil, not in a smooth, round way, but tapered each of the six sides the pencil would resemble crystals with pyramidal endings.

These are the simple crystals. Most crystals are more complex. Many form in clusters or are partly hollow. Many are coated with droplets that have stuck and frozen to them and look as if they had been engulfed by parasites. Then there are the classically branched snow crystals.

Scientists have mapped out the temperature and humidity conditions that lead to the various crystal habits. Crystals can only grow when the air is

234

slightly supersaturated with vapor for ice, in other words, when relative humidity is slightly above 100%. Branching snow crystals form when supersaturation is high and temperature is near -15°C. As humidity in the cloud pulses, each branch of the crystal experiences growth pulses, hence the infinite variations. When the air is only slightly supersaturated solid pencils and plates grow - slowly, patiently, and regularly, respectively above and below about -10°C. Even though the conditions for crystal habits are well known, we are just beginning to understand how the crystals get their shapes. That too is the story for another day.

No sooner have the crystals formed than countless sunbeams strike them. Some of the sunbeams are reflected, as by a mirror. Fresnel's law tells what percent are reflected. The beams that are not reflected pass into the crystal and are bent or refracted following Snell's Law. Each color or wavelength of sunlight is refracted by a slightly different angle, so the sunbeams are dispersed or split into tiny colored spots or spectra similar to those you see when sunlight passes through the glass crystals of a chandelier or a diamond. These sunbeams proceed to the back or bottom of the crystal where they can either exit it or bounce inside it. Ultimately, almost all sunbeams escape the crystal and head in a variety of directions. Classically branched snow crystals are exceedingly beautiful, but have so many facets that the light emerges from them in a host of incoherent directions –too many to produce halos. The simple pencil and plate crystals offer sunbeams the fewest departure paths and thereby produce the best halos.

We use geometry to trace the path of a sunbeam that has struck a crystal, but we must know the angle that the beam struck the crystal, and, if it is refracted, its path inside the crystal. To do this we must know the crystal's orientation as it falls and the sun's height in the sky.

Each pencil or plate crystal has 8 faces –6 rectangular sides and two hexagonal ends. Sunbeams that enter a side and exit two sides away are refracted by a minimum of 22° and either form the 22° halo or one of the arcs or spots near it. Sunbeams that pass through a side and an end are refracted by a minimum of 46° and either form the 46° halo or one of the arcs near it. To determine which faces are involved we must know how ice crystals fall.

Crystals can fall randomly or with preferred orientation. Oriented crystals produce the brightest halos because, somewhat like a magnifying glass, they focus the deflected sunbeams on a small part of the sky. Crystals tend to fall in an oriented manner with their longest dimensions almost horizontal. You can demonstrate this easily. Cut a piece of paper about 2" long and ½" wide. Hold it over your head and drop it. It will soon begin to spin with its longest side almost horizontal. Because of that, when light strikes one of the sides of a long pencil crystal and exits two sides away, the light will be bent either almost up or down to form the tangent arcs or the Parry arc.

Plate crystals fall with the six sides all vertical. When sunlight enters a side and exits two sides away it will be bent left or right and produce the sundogs. Sunbeams reflected from one of the vertical sides form the parhelic circle. All of the halo arcs that pass right through the sun are formed by light that is reflected by the crystals.

Crystals that do not have any long side will tumble in all directions as they fall. Sunbeams passing through two sides will still be bent by at least

22°, but now in all directions to form the 22° halo. This is also the case for crystal clusters.

The sun's height in the sky dictates which light paths through a crystal are possible. This in turn dictates not only which halo arcs are possible, but also their shape. Every summer somewhere in the United States some newspaper will report a local sighting of an incredibly bright "rainbow" without any rain. This is actually a circumhorizontal halo arc that forms when sunbeams enter a vertical side of a plate crystal and exit the hexagonal bottom. The circumhorizontal arc can only occur near the summer solstice near noon because sunbeams can only take this path when the sun is higher than 58° above the horizon. Its complement, the circumzenithal arc cannot form when the sun is higher than 32° above the horizon.

The halo's brightness and color purity also depend on the cloud thickness and height. To form a halo, a sunbeam can strike at most a single crystal. Any beam that strikes a second crystal will almost invariably be deflected into some incoherent direction. A good rule is when the cloud is too thick for the sun to cast shadows it is too thick to see a halo. When the cloud is high in the atmosphere the crystals producing a halo cover a volume much larger than a city of skyscrapers. The probability that most of the crystals in such a large volume have only a few simple forms is quite small, and so is the chance of seeing spectacular halo displays. But when crystals form just above ground level in mostly clear skies, as they do in the polar regions or on ski slopes, halos can be extraordinary.

Most of us cannot easily arrange a junket to Antarctica. But we can go out on the ski slopes even if we don't ski and with luck can see the most glorious halos with no worry we will be wrecked like the daughter of the Captain of the Hesperus

.

Granny Says Life Started Between Mica Sheets
By Helen Hansma

I have a passion for mica. This passion led me, in my 62nd year and almost a grandmother, to develop a hypothesis for the origins of life.

"Develop a hypothesis" is what I've been doing in the last many months, but the original inspiration came when I had not a scientific thought in my head. I was bent over the dissecting microscope in my apartment in Virginia, near the National Science Foundation, splitting mica into thin sheets to arrange around some crystals grown from a Smithsonian crystal-growing kit. As I looked at the bits of green algae and brown crud at the edges of the mica sheets, I thought, "This would be a good place for life to originate!"

My hypothesis is that life originated between thin sheets of mica rocks, which provided many separate spaces for the earliest prebiotic molecules to form, sometimes in isolation from each other and sometimes in association with each other, as they oozed around within and between sheets. The energy needed for life to evolve from non-living molecules might have come simply from the sun and the waves.

The mica hypothesis says that life developed as a 'sandwich filling' in mica 'sandwiches' or, as: 'life between the sheets.' This contrasts with the 'pizza', clay, and vesicle hypotheses, in which life originated on the surfaces of earth's mineral crust, in clay particles, or in lipid vesicles. There are also 'RNA World' and 'Metabolism First' hypotheses. My hypothesis says that RNA and proteins and metabolic chemistries could all have evolved between the mica sheets and then combined and emerged, coated with lipid membranes, as primitive cells.

My passion for mica came from my research in biological Atomic Force Microscopy, for almost 20 years now, starting soon after the Atomic Force Microscope (AFM) was invented in 1986. The AFM feels a surface by raster-scanning a tiny tip back and forth across the surface, with a sensitivity so fine that it can feel even bare DNA molecules on a flat surface. The flat surface we use is mica, a layered mineral with atomically flat sheets that can be peeled off with adhesive tape to expose a clean surface.

Maybe you are now asking, "How can you see bare DNA molecules on the mica when you said there was algae and crud on it?" The mica we use for AFM samples is high grade mica, free of bubbles and other defects. The mica that inspired my hypothesis for the origins of life came from an abandoned mica mine in a Connecticut state park, where my brother Jim had taken some his family for a hike the previous summer, after his stepdaughter's wedding. It had lots of bubbles and defects.

Theories and Hypotheses

Why do I call my idea a 'Hypothesis'? People use words in many ways, but one of the strengths of science is that it tries to use words in precisely defined ways. Theories are much stronger than Hypotheses. A Hypothesis is a starting point in the scientific method, while a Theory is the result of much research and testing. Once there were also scientific Laws, but now we know that even Newton's Laws are not totally correct. Therefore, newer scientists such as Charles Darwin call their well-tested ideas 'Theories' instead of 'Laws'. My idea is only a Hypothesis, ready for testing, by me and hopefully by many others in the scientific community.

How Discoveries are Made

Dan Koshland, a famous biochemist, wrote that there are three ways discoveries are made: Charge, Challenge, or Chance. He calls this the 'Cha-Cha-Cha Theory of Scientific Discovery'. Louis Pasteur said that Chance favors the prepared mind. I think mine was a 'Chance' discovery, by a mind prepared by decades of diverse education and research in biochemistry, chemistry, cell biology, biophysics, nanoscience and materials science. Koshland, and Einstein before him, said that the process of discovery seems to be the same in science and in other areas. Therefore we are all making discoveries in the same ways, whatever our areas of knowledge.

Discoveries range from small to earth-shaking. I wonder which kind the mica hypothesis will be: a big one that gets into textbooks some day or a small one that falls into oblivion. I'll get some clues about this when I attend the Origin-of-Life Gordon Research Conference next week and share my hypothesis with people who have worked in the field for years or decades.

Love Diss
By William Baldwin

Your words echo in my head—
Love, obsession, longing.
You wanted me so terribly,
Couldn't wait to have me;
Then, disillusioned, dropped me;
Dropped me with scorn, abuse, derision;
Abandoned and forgot me;
Shut me out of your future;
Slammed the door to your life;
Accused me of shallowness and callousness—
You who never really tried to know me;
You who,
When I didn't fulfill your fantasies,
Dismissed me utterly out of hand.

The Family Moroni
By Bernadette Fornesi

When first he came to the United States, Pete Moroni and his cousin worked in the coal mines of Pennsylvania. He became very lonesome for the girl he left behind in Italy. When Pete saved enough money from his wages, he returned to Italy and married his sweetheart.

Pete knew their future for a better life would be in the United States. In La Spezia they boarded the steamship Atholl McBean in the northern part of Italy, and arrived at Ellis Island. They were cleared quickly and boarded a train for Colorado where Pete was told living conditions were better than in Pennsylvania.

The coal company hired Pete, and each day he descended into the coal mines and found picks and shovels waiting on the sides of the tracks where coal was being hauled to be dumped down a shoot. It was hard work and Pete was grateful when a whistle blew and the miners could rest long enough to eat their lunch from tin pails they had carried into the mine.

The next few years Pete and Rose Moroni's family grew to include three boys and two girls. The last child born was a sturdy lad, and his Godfather had the honor of naming him. He named him Orado. He took the last part of the state of Colorado, orado, and the boy was so named. Rose didn't like the name at all but she had nothing to do with it.

Orado was now four years old, and weather permitting his days were spent marching around the front yard with a long stick that he pretended was a sword. He guarded his domain fiercely. No stray animal dared to come into the yard. He yelled and beat the ground with his sword until they beat a hasty retreat. Dressed in faded patched clothing he stepped briskly in scuffed black laced up shoes. One lace was missing and the shoes were two sizes too large for him. The toes turned up, and sometimes he tripped himself, and went sprawling in the dirt. On his shoulders he tied a piece of red flannel found in his mother's sewing basket. Now he looked like a miniature Roman centurion ready for battle.

Rose Moroni looked from her kitchen window, and watched the boy. So that's where my piece of red flannel went, she mused. It's all right you play soldier, but you never going to be a soldier, she vows.

All the neighborhood children liked to come into Orado's yard to play soldiers. He was the leader, and had a petulant look when his lower jaw jutted forward. Everybody in the small mining town knew who he was. When he walked down the roadway with his sisters to the company store they all called a greeting to him. "Hey little Mussolini, how you doing today?"

He always responded by waving his wooden sword at them and saluting. This was received with smiles and clapping of hands.

One night a loud clattering on the tin roof woke Orado. He was frightened and moved closer to his older brother in the crowded bed that slept three. He heard the kitchen door open and saw his mother in her long flannel nightgown grab a broom and walk fearlessly into the darkness.

Orado heard her say, "I fix you good, if you throw more rocks on my roof." He went back to sleep now knowing what the noise on the roof was.

Those Irish kids on the other side of the company store tormented them frequently.

The gathering place for the miners and families was the company store. All the necessities for living were sold here; groceries, clothing, implements, and medicines. In the basement a large hall boasted two lanes for bowling. Every two weeks a silent movie was shown projected on a sheet strung up on the stage of the hall. Silent film stars Tom Mix, Gloria Swanson, Rudolph Valentino, and Charlie Chaplin were met with enthusiastic applause. The seats were not always filled. The Moroni family never attended because the admission price was ten cents. Ten cents would buy a small bag of sugar from the company store.

Pete Moroni was contended with his life in the mining town. The different nationalities of miners, Irish, German, Mexicans and Italians all got along quite well with each other and formed friendships through the years. Pete liked to go to his underground cellar and count the bottles of wine stored, and know he had enough to last till the seasonal grape truck would come into town. Pete Moroni lived the old Italian proverb, "A meal without wine is like a day without sunshine."

Summer and fall days of glorious colors in the shrubs and trees of Colorado gave way to the frigid temperatures of winter. Winter clothing was removed from the trunks stored under the beds in the Moroni household. The cast iron stove in the kitchen was fed constantly and the family spent most of their time in the warm room.

Christmas came at last to the children in the mining town. On Christmas Eve the Moroni children bundled into whatever warm clothing they could find, and started walking to the Catholic Church for midnight mass. Along the way they were joined by Mexican families. At the entrance of the small church each person was given a lit candle for the service. The highlight of the evening for the Moroni children was the red net stocking given to them as they left the church. Orado's eyes lit with pleasure and he opened it immediately. He found an orange, a few nuts, and hard candies. He sucked on one of the candies all the way home, and forgot how cold his feet were.

Christmas morning the stockings placed on the oven door in the Moroni kitchen had additional treats in them, hard candies, and lo and behold, the unthinkable; a shiny silver dime at the bottom of the toe to be used at the company store to see a movie. Mama Rose had made raviolis for dinner and Orado thought it the best Christmas ever.

The years breathing the coal dust in the mines was causing Pete health problems. He coughed frequently and was short of breath. Rose knew she had to get him away from the mines. She saved money from the lunches she made each day for the miners and washing their clothes. Rose sold moonshine liquor to the miners from a man in the hills who distilled it. She charged by the shot glass, 15 cents. Of course enterprising Rose diluted the alcohol and made a good profit on a gallon bought from the moonshiner.

At the company store, Rose heard talk about a state called California. She heard the climate was good, temperatures were mild and no snow on the coast. Pete could find a job along with the oldest son to bring home enough money to live on. She counted her money and decided they had enough for tickets on the train to take them far away from the coal mines of Colorado.

After tickets were purchased, Rose sewed the rest of her money into the lining of her black coat, packed a lunch and they boarded the train for South San Francisco where Rose's sister had immigrated. Arriving in the town Orado saw what he thought was white smoke covering everything and told his mother there must be a big fire burning. People standing nearby laughed and told the Moroni's it was fog rolling in from the ocean.

FOG…a new word for them in what was to be their new home.

Red, White and Green
By Sue Barizon

I was almost seven the day Papa taught me that I wasn't annoying. This was contrary to Mom's opinion.

"Susan, you ask too many questions."

She said that every time I asked a question. This time, she sounded different, not as irritated as usual. I was surprised when Papa looked up from his newspaper in time to admonish her.

"How is she going to learn if she doesn't ask questions?"

"OK Primo," Mom challenged, "you answer this one." Mom motioned to me. I readily obliged.

"How can Mrs. Fratelli's daughter be having a baby when she isn't even married?"

I figured I owed it to Papa to stick around for the ensuing argument which had gained momentum when they switched to Italian. I planned to leave after the part where Mom banishes Papa from the house.

"Why don't you go back to your Pisani in Parma?"

It was worth the price of admission just to hear Mom roll her "rs." No one delivered a line with more Fellini-like passion than my mother.

So, I spent the rest of my childhood sitting around the dinner table asking Papa "too many questions." Papa came from Borgotaro, a country town in northern Italy celebrated for cattle grazing, porcini mushrooms and parmesan cheese. He lived with his mother, sister and maternal grandparents in the home that served the family for generations. According to the map, Borgotaro was in the province of Parma, the region known as Emilia Romagna. Most residents referred to themselves as either Parmesano or Emiliano.

"Why do you always tell people you're Genovese?" I asked him.

Papa shrugged his shoulders. "It's easier."

Later I learned that to Papa saying he was from Genoa was the same as my saying I was from the San Francisco Bay Area.

The day I asked how he came to America, he gave me the same shrug. He poured a glass of wine from the fiasco de vin (wine bottle) kept on the "lazy Susan" in the center of the table. I set another glass in front of him and he tilted the bottle again, splashing just enough wine to cover the bottom. Then he filled the rest with water and pushed it over to me. He took out his pipe and felt around in his breast pocket for a match. He stroked the match lighting the tobacco as he leaned back into his captain's chair.

"I wasn't even two when my father, Giovanni, and my Uncle Tony left Borgotaro," he started. "Uncle Tony was the first to get a job working as a busboy at the Palace Hotel (in San Francisco), then they hired my father on as a janitor. They shared a room in a boarding house. Uncle Tony wasn't married, at the time. My father saved all he could to bring us over. It took five years.

There were letters from America. Once in awhile there'd be a telegram – a big extravagance in those days. I'd bring it to school to show off. A couple of my friends had fathers working in America. I remember my grandparents teasing my mother about being married to my father, "Profumo senza arrosto" (the aroma without the roast). My mother said he came back to Borgotaro for a visit, but I don't remember. I was too young. The way I remember it, I was seven years old when I met my father."

"Seven?" I echoed in disbelief - I was almost seven, myself! The shock triggered me to take on an accusatory tone. "You mean to tell me you were seven years old before you even met your own father for the first time?"

Papa simply nodded as a fog of melancholy crept over his face. His square jaw locked in staunch defense against the lump forming in his throat. He sat wide-eyed, unable to blink as if the fog had short-circuited his eyelids. His dark brown pupils glistened as they fixed on the candor of my innocence.

"My father had come all the way from America to take us back with him," he continued. "Everybody was crazy. My grandmother had been crying for days and my grandfather had a face on him, "que faccia!" (What a face!). When I saw my father coming up the walk, I ran out the back door and across the field to hide. I was crying when he came looking for me. He called to me, but I wouldn't come. I saw him crouch down behind a rock and heard him shout 'BANGO, BANGO,' trying to imitate an American cowboy with his thick Italian accent. He was acting like a big kid, ambushing me with the cap gun he brought from Hollywood, California. It had the Cisco Kid's face burned into the handle. My father liked to tease. He made me laugh, but I didn't want anything to do with him."

"But, why Papa, he was your father?" I questioned.

He sucked on his pipe taking a couple of long thoughtful puffs. "He was a stranger to me," Papa admitted. "Giacomo Vignali was a father to me."

The revelation worked like a tonic. It dissolved the sadness from Papa's face, replacing it with a subtle glow. I'd seen it on him before - the involuntary release of pride whenever he heard the first few stanzas of Stars and Stripes. Papa wore his loyalty on his sleeve.

"My grandfather was Giacomo Vignali, the town go-between." He went on.

"If a guy had a herd of cows and wanted to trade them for another guy's plot of land, they'd call on my grandfather to make the deal. I followed him around like a puppy. My job was to carry his fiasco di vin because in those days all bargains were sealed with a glass of wine. I respected my grandfather," he declared. "He could pat me on the head and kick me in the "culo" at the same time." He'd light his pipe again, blow out the match and flick it into the ashtray.

"My poor father stayed three months trying to talk me into coming to America. I cried and threw fits until my parents gave up. My mother finally promised to bring us by herself."

242

I listened as Papa told how his parents endured a long distance relationship for the next nine years, how his father visited again staying for several months at a time. Once, his mother reciprocated by making the voyage on her own intending to bring both her children. Papa wanted no part of it. His home was in Borgotaro with his grandparents. His mother and sister sailed without him.

"After a couple of months, relatives called my mother to come home. My grandfather was sick. As sick as he was, he'd go into town after dinner and stay out most of the night." Papa knocked on his head with his knuckles. "He was 'testa durra' (hard headed), my grandfather. My mother and grandmother would be sick with worry. They'd send me and my sister out to look for him. One night, I found him propped up against the side of a building."

"What happened to him, Papa?" I asked.

"He couldn't pee," Papa said. "His bladder exploded."

How quickly the sadness crept over Papa's face. I remembered the soulful expression many years later when he learned of his own diagnosis with prostate cancer.

"So why did your mother wait so long to bring you over?"

Papa shrugged his shoulders. "...because now I didn't want to leave my grandmother alone."

"But you'd let your father live an ocean away from your mother all those years?" I was incredulous. "What a spoiled brat you must have been!"

Papa returned a sheepish smile. "I was the only boy in a house full of women."

Papa's mourning period finally came to an abrupt end when his mother discovered a poster of Benito Mussolini hanging on his bedroom wall. With the threat of World War II and the certainty of Papa being drafted, and probably killed, his parents exchanged a flurry of telegrams. In no time, Papa, his sister and his mother stood on the steerage deck of the ship taking them to their new home in San Francisco.

"I was 16 when I came to this country," he said. "That was back in 1936." His voice wavered. "I didn't want to come."

"But Papa, how did they finally convince you to leave Borgotaro?" I asked. "My poor mother lied. She tried to convince me that my father had a big surprise waiting in America, but it was a secret. I threw a fit. I kept throwing fits until I wore her down. Finally, she confessed that my father bought a brand new house. When she saw how disappointed I was, she made a last ditch effort, '...and your father said to tell you that we'll be living next door to a nice family of cowboys and Indians!' "

Papa gave an apologetic shrug.

"Really, Papa," I scolded, "how annoying."

Hold your Head up High
By Madeline McEwen

"You're right," I said to my husband, probably for the first time in living history, "But this is hotter than Hades." We were driving away from San Francisco Airport on our first day in California. The skies were an unfamiliar, dazzling shade of blue with no hint of a cloud in any direction. August, the height of summer in 1997, without so much as a whisper about Global Warming, and I thought I'd been thrown into a furnace.

The hire car had air-conditioning, a rare and luxurious treat, but it took most of the journey for the sun-baked leather seats to cool down. During the fifty minute drive I gazed at the banking hills either side the vast, four and sometimes five-line, snaking, freeway and watched a haze of eddying heat waves rise from the straw colored terrain without so much as a green stalk for miles. I thought of the lush hills of home and felt a lump in my throat. How were we ever going to survive in this parched prairie?

"Is it too late to change my mind?" I asked my husband.

"No," he said, gripping the steering wheel. "We can always transfer to Boston. That was the other option, but I'm sure you'll like California more."

Glad he was sure, I was certain I'd made a terrible mistake. Every freckle on my pale face threatened to explode as we arrived at the hotel for our first jet-lagged night in the United States.

Drenched in sweat, we unloaded the luggage. We laughed at the bed the size of a launch pad and a fridge large enough to climb into. Who knew we'd moved to the land of giants? The tall tales were true; things were so much bigger and better in the States: thick plush carpets, automatic everything, super-sized, and seizmically retrofitted. I hoped it would be a very long time until I had any experience with earthquakes.

Dazed, overwhelmed and bewildered, we went outside to wander around in our new neighborhood to find our bearings and possibly a few locals. We hoped they'd be as friendly.

By this time, it was close to eleven at night and considerably cooler. The wide streets, more than six lanes if you counted the emergency vehicle lanes, were deserted. Where were all the people?

It was Saturday night, the high social focus of the week. Where were the revelers, the party-goers, and the nightlife?

After complaining about the dry environment since our arrival, I was amazed to see the dark green banks of manicured lawn around the strip mall. So lush, so green, so irresistible. Unable to avoid temptation, I slipped off my shoes and wriggled my toes in the long cool grass. I don't think I'd ever seen such a perfect weed-free lawn in my life.

"Why is it so spongy?" I asked.

My husband watched from the sidewalk as I jumped up and down to demonstrate its trampoline-like qualities.

"Maybe it's Astroturf," he said, "You know, artificial grass."

"No, I'm sure it's real. It feels real. It even smells real. This must be an incredibly important area to have such decadent and indulgent green strip around it. Do you think it's an embassy or something?"

"No, it's just a regular mall. They're everywhere."

"Like this? Everywhere? Really? This truly is the land of kings."
"It's a republic."

A door swung open across the street and a blast of music blared into the silence. Just then, I heard a strange gurgling noise and the ground seemed to rumble. Please, not an earthquake. Not now. Not already. Tectonic plates shifted beneath my feet, grinding and moaning. Why had we ever come to live in this disaster area? Such madness.

Suddenly short black pipes erupted from between the greenery below my feet. Fountains of water sprayed in every direction, squirting and spluttering, in a fabulous display of modern engineering. Drenched to the skin by the automatic sprinkler system, we returned to our hotel artificially weathered and thoroughly baptized by American plumbing.

Isn't
By Jeannine Gerkman

To tell you what she isn't is my goal humble,
I'll try my best and hope not to stumble.

She is not thin nor grown nor suave. She is
not green or back or mauve.

She is not evil, she is not blind
She is not flat, she is not kind

She is not idle, she is not still
She is not feverish, she is not ill.

She is not simple, she does not cook;
She does not listen, she does not look.

She is not generous, she does not observe;
She is not thoughtful in deed or word.

She is not my brother, she is not my friend;
I cannot breathe and now must end.

Lovely Oliver St. John Gogarty
By Meghan Tucker

"Soul, I hear you calling..."
We practically screamed the song
The balmy air of smoke and Guinness
Hugged us. Singing and dancing,
We couldn't look away
Smiles glowed in the dim lit pub

My hands wouldn't stop
Grabbing his skinny waist
The scent of old wood,
Some three hundred years ago, seeping.
Oranges, greens, and whites,
Draped. Complimented his tight shirt.

Dozens of voices
Yet we were alone,
The night stole us.
Intoxicated, our rights, wrongs – inexistent.
Clinging to his energy,
My blistered feet hit the cobbled road

Dizziness hit me, a smirk gleamed
Drunk, or excited,
Spontaneity instigated my moves
Innocent with experienced looks
Our fingers groped the hotel door
We stumbled inside.

The want pushing and clawing within me
Like his hands upon my black skirt
Our flesh meets, lips twisted
Eyes fall above my horizon

From Munchenberg to the City of Angels
By Evie Groch

At the age of three in early 1949, I was living in the tiny village of Munchenberg, Germany. I often played in a snow-laden street, dressed in a heavy coat with an eared cap and mittens. As snowflakes tumbled down from the sky, I remember asking my mother, "Vehr shit arup die feideren from dem kishon iber unz?" (Who is shaking the feather pillows above us?) "Dos iz shnei (This is snow)," she would answer patiently, as if that explained it all; however, she thought this was such a clever question, she never stopped retelling this story.

We had few belongings or toys, but I recall a doll I named Lisa. She had a cherubic face and cloth body with plastic arms and legs. I dressed her in a rag-tag style because there was no fashionable attire for her. She rode in a woven straw baby buggy with a fixed half cover. The push handle resembled the symbol for pi (π), and I made a point of placing one forefinger of each of my hands on each bar and letting my mittens, which were threaded through the sleeves of my coat via a string, hang down from the π.

Two of my uncles and their families shared the tenement apartment with us. Uncle Zvi would lure me into the warm tiny kitchen for my bath he knew I didn't like, by opening the oven door and speaking to a mysterious little creature inside of it. "Vos tiest du dort? Kim arois." (What are you doing in there? Come out.) Curious, I would tiptoe in. Once in the kitchen, I was trapped, and my mother placed me in the basin of heated water.

I was later to learn that these living accommodations were probably a form of a Displaced Persons Camp (DP Camp) for people who had to flee their country of origin toward the end of World War II. The full story would not unfold itself to me until many years later, but I understand we were stationed there awaiting permission to leave for America.

Soon we were in steerage, aboard a freighter, the US General Hauser, making its way from Bremen to New Orleans in a voyage that lasted 16 days. Today, whenever I smell the sweet and tangy fragrance of oranges, I am immediately taken back to the infirmary on that ship where I was kept while being treated for measles. I had no appetite, and my father would sneak oranges in to me for nourishment. They were honeyed, juicy, and pulpy and something I could easily swallow with little chewing. They were my diet. The lovely color of the oranges brightened up the totally white, sterile room in which I spent many days.

Once out of the infirmary, I had to endure what everyone else did. That entailed sleeping on a mattress on a urine-stained floor, amid strangers who gave off smells of sweat mixed with old clothes. I had no sense of how long sixteen days were, but as we were approaching the port of New Orleans, I was as excited as everyone else. We all stood out on the deck, watching the multi-colored houses pass by as we waved to no one in particular. I had been told we were going to stay with my Uncle Morris, my father's brother, in Los Angeles. Not knowing the difference between New Orleans and Los Angeles, I repeatedly annoyed my parents by asking, "Iz dos di hois fun fetah Moishe?"

as each house on the shore came into view. "Nein, mein kind, nochnit" (No, my child, not yet) they took turns answering patiently at first, but soon they stopped answering at all.

A train took us to Los Angeles after we docked and debarked from the ship at New Orleans. We got off at the Union Street Station near Olvera Street in East Los Angeles, where refugees entered the state. Many aromas surrounded me, all of them strange. There were foods I had never seen or imagined. Piñatas were hanging from stalls, and people were speaking in a language I couldn't understand. Someone picked us up in his car and took us to West Los Angeles, where the more veteran refugees resided. We entered a home so large, I couldn't believe it wasn't crowded with people. This was to be our home, for next couple of weeks or months – I can't recall which. The street was called Drexel, and I had not seen a more beautiful one. It was tree-lined, with each house having its own lawn and bed of flowers. There were lampposts that turned on at night and structures filled with food just a few blocks away.

Uncle Morris could speak to me in Yiddish, my mother tongue, but I couldn't communicate with his wife, Andre, or their three daughters, Lucy, Carol, and Maxine, my cousins. The first English words I learned were from Maxine, the youngest daughter and closest to me in age. The words were "Shut up." I repeated them over and over with pride, until I heard Uncle Morris telling my father that I shouldn't be using language like that. My father replied with a musing, "Mmm, I wonder where she could have learned that."

A month or so later, with hardly any English vocabulary to rely on, we found ourselves in an apartment of our own, in a drab downtown section of East Los Angeles. A colorless paint was peeling from a wall in the living room, inviting my little bored fingers to help it along. The well-worn furniture that came with the tiny apartment blended in so seamlessly with the color of the peeling paint that I could not easily discern where one ended and the other began. This was my first experience with linoleum on the kitchen floor, and I couldn't understand what it was. My spilled drinks could easily be wiped up from it, and the blue and white pattern it had that resembled tiles was challengingly repetitive. The miniscule dining area was in the kitchen, and no one needed to lure me into the kitchen for a bath because we had a separate toilet (what my father called a water closet). Whenever the landlord would enter the premises, I was supposed to run and stand in front of the peeled paint and hide it with my body. As soon as his heavy footsteps were heard on the stairs, my parents would cry "Er kimt, er kimt" (He's coming, he's coming,") and I would run to the sore spot. We had a dented and discolored icebox that had enough room in it for some cubes of butter and bottles of milk which were delivered to our door. What service! My father started disappearing during the days. He was off looking for work in a strange city with no language skills and no work skills either. He had been a merchandiser of grains in Warsaw, and when he fled from Poland to Kazakhstan, he lost the family business and had no means to support himself, much less a family he found himself heading soon thereafter. I will never understand how he so quickly learned to sew and construct women's coats and jackets and eventually co-own a shop that manufactured these items. I have believed for a long time that there was no smarter, more industrious, or more loving man than my father. Many others agreed with me.

A series of moves took place that found us in various rentals, from a two-bedroom apartment in a dark green fourplex on Third St. with its landlady, big Mrs. Woofsey, to a small detached house behind the owner's house on New Jersey St. Mrs. Elster was the kind and welcoming landlady who allowed me to dig tunnels and trenches around the perimeter of our house and always spoke to me in a gentle voice. By that time, I was enrolled in a private academy on a scholarship from the Joint Distribution Center for immigrants, learning English, Hebrew, and the basic elementary school subjects. Even there it was cliquish and very strict.

During my time at the academy, my parents were learning English, and I was helping them, having now served s their translator for a few years. After five years of residency, they applied for citizenship. I remember quizzing them on the study questions they needed to master to pass the test. It helped me learn about the government as well. They were proud to become US citizens, along with me, in a public ceremony in a huge stadium. We all raised our rights hands and repeated some loyalty oath I truly didn't understand, but the importance of the occasion wasn't lost on me. I was now a legal member of this country.

Ice Cold Beer
By Meghan Tucker

Pulsing pressure, oozing euphoric transcendence
Glazed eyes, pinched by a smile
Warmth-encompassed chest
Memories flood, fogged and deciphered
Shoes hitting the white sheen tiled floor
Crispness chapping my knuckles

Clinking necks, introduction cheers
He smiles, shy, walks away
Grabs another, towers, converses 'til close
Digitally connected, pancakes at three

Right hand grasps the sharp handle
Cutting cardboard, indented palms
Wallet and keys entangled
Rushed decision, maybe this time,
A blue moon? No, always my bud
Heavy, weighted arms, pulled shoulders

Exchanged book, for his Slayer tee
Women. Awkward persons but
Comfortable pair, a reintroduction
Anda continual kiss goodbye

Rapid walking, sheened floor, glisten
Florescent lit ceiling, undesirable complexion
Vision focuses ahead, nothing seen
Reaching an unpleasant encounter
Hi, how are you tonight? Fine, you?
ID please. Scrounge for crumpled bills.

Hard cream counter, at my waist
Soft lips, warming bare shoulders
Delivered pizza steams, a quivering body
A Sunday evening, Californication

Hands clawed, lugging canned memories
Flip-flops slap the pavement, gravel pokes
Key-ready, open my silver-stickered door
Toss wallet, phone. Secure my purchase
Ignition turned, engine warms, lights illuminate
Drive away to my next four-line stanza

Hello, beautiful. Hello, kiddo.
Give me a hug. Big arms wrapped
Warmth within us, curled gentleness
Soothed souls, easy love

The Cat with No Meow
By Kimberly Schultz

Dinky tried to meow. She really did. But what came out of her mouth was more of a squeak. Her mother always told her to practice her meow, but Dinky always became discouraged and felt like giving up when her meow didn't rattle the mirrors like her brother and sister's meow. Her brothers, Max and Punkus, and her sisters, Belle and Jinx, all made fun of her whispery meow.

"Hey, Dinky," Max would laugh, "I can't hear you. You have to squeak louder!" he would say rolling around on the ground, holding his belly laughing.

When it came time for meals, Max, Punkus, Belle, and Jinx pushed her aside, eating most, if not all, the food before Dinky could even get a pebble. "Squeak," is all that escaped Dinky's mouth, her tummy loudly growling for her.

During playtime, Max, Punkus, Belle, and Jinx enjoyed chasing birds. They'd creep up behind the unsuspecting birds and roar a boisterous meow, causing the birds to flutter away in fear. Although many times she tried to join them, the birds laughed at her and chanted, "Dinky, Dinky, with no meow, chasing us is not allowed!" They would all laugh, leaving Dinky so sad that all she could mutter was a quiet "squeak."

One day, Dinky sat alone on a tree branch in the big Oak tree in their front yard. She was supposed to be practicing her meow, but instead she watched her brothers and sisters scare the birds with their loud meows. How I wish I could join them, Dinky thought. All of a sudden, from nowhere, came Bullie, the meanest bulldog on the block. He came up behind Max and Punkus and let out a loud RRRUUUFFF! Max and Punkus ran around in circles, terrified. Bullie then ran up behind Belle and Jinx and let out another loud RRRUUUFFFF, scaring them as well. Bullie then nipped at the bird's tails, terrorizing them.

Without a second thought, Dinky leapt from the tree branch and headed straight toward Bullie. Dinky took a deep breath and blew out the loudest squeak she could conjure up. However, what left her mouth was so much more than a squeak–it was a meow! Terrified, Bullie howled all the way down the street without looking back at the cat that came up behind him with the thunderous meow.

Max, Punkus, Belle, and Jinx (and even the birds) gathered around Dinky and praised her for her courage. "Let's hear that meow, again!" Max said.

Dinky could not believe she was capable of such a loud meow. She opened her mouth to try out her new meow, but what came out was the same squeak she was born with. "Squeak," she said. So she tried again. "Squeak." Dinky's head fell down in shame as she headed back to her lonely tree branch.

"Wait!" her brothers and sisters called out to her. "From now on, you can play with us. We are sorry we treated you so bad!"

"But I lost my meow," Dinky said sadly.

"That doesn't matter anymore. You are a brave cat whose squeak is louder than any meow we have ever heard!"

Red Dragon
Ryann Murrin-Desouza

You entered the dream of another.
You told them things of my Ancestry.
Telling them that I need to open up and let my receptors receive.
That I'll be important to the "New America".
What does that mean?
My lineage is strong and devoted to lead.
A new people?
What does all of this mean?
Who am I suppose to be...
The Leader, Creator, Bearer of my people.
DNA, you say.
What are you trying to tell me?
A new race!
Am I supposed to be the bearer of this new human heritage?
I want to believe you,
But it's hard when I can't see you or hear you.
Open my receptors, How?
Red Dragon if you are there.
I need to know you're here.

i dream
By Maurine Killough

they come down from their gated thrones ask
for a typed page
or notarization

their eyes roll around my lopsided office
cracked steps
rusted roots
musty windows and happy spiders

i don't have time, time for details
like spinning ewebs, crystal windows
or sinking sunsets

my plants are thirsty
but i place my stamp on their beloved page or
spin a resume
charge half price
then return to the flickering screen the
inbox and data entry

i recall my choice of business major to
dispel the family joke of being a
Basket Weaver

i type their jobs calendar
their dates
sticky web with its html is beyond me but i try i
try
and i am all tangled up

yet inside
a world away from all of that i
dream
i still dream

Small Fry
By Madeline McEwen
CHAPTER ONE

On the top floor of the townhouse, Binky Stroud yanked the cuffs of her black, leatherette boots and cinched the garters beneath the purple net tutu. The color matched her hair drawn out into rigid icicles from her scalp. She drew a peachy pencil cupid's bow over the natural curve of her thin lips. Stepping back, she checked her reflection in the full length mirror. Her critical eye noticed the satin sheen of the bustier didn't match the illustration hanging above her bed. She grabbed two pairs of rolled up socks and stuffed them inside, shrugging her shoulders until the soft mounds resembled the real thing. Her thighs were too bony, bow-legged and pale-skinned. The silver nail varnish on her stubby fingers was already smeared. Too late to fix now. No one would notice except Terah Ladin—nothing got past him—detail orientated to the point of obsession, even had his ears modified at a fancy clinic in San Francisco—more like mutilated. Was he going tonight?

There was a gentle knock on the door. "Nearly ready," Binky said. Mom cracked open the door, a folded newspaper tucked under her arm. Her eyes widened.

"What do you think?" Binky said.

Her mother came in further wearing a weak smile of encouragement, her voice breathy with restrained disbelief.

"You've done a great job on the costume, and your hair is...spectacular."

Binky waited for the 'but.'

"But you're not going to walk down the street like that, are you? Couldn't you wear a coat?"

"The Queen of Avatars isn't afraid of rain."

Mom squinted at the poster through her smudged glasses and said, "What about a cloak?"

"I've got to be authentic. Everyone has to wear the exact costume, no deviations. I must stay in character, otherwise I won't stand a chance in the competition. It says in the rules."

She nudged the leaflet towards her and surreptitiously closed the laptop.

Mom ran an eye down the lengthy Roxville's Annual Cosplay Convention Rules.

The small town hosted the event where fans gathered together from as far east as Sacramento, and as far south as San Luis Obisbo, a vast radius, drawing fans decked out in the most outlandish costumes.

"Don't worry, Mom." She had already spent all day at the convention, but now it was time for the evening competition. Mom wore a dubious expression. Binky noticed the well-thumbed newspaper with the headline story about a spate of missing runaways. "All my friends are going. Make sure Dad waits on the corner to pick me up, not a minute before two. Later, if possible. I don't want anyone seeing him. You do understand, don't you, Mom?"

"Sure, but I'm not sure it's safe for you to walk there on your own. Dad wouldn't like it."

Mom said it was Dad who was afraid, but Binky knew they were both afraid of their own shadows, afraid of her growing up and becoming independent. Sad. They'd have nothing once she left home. Two lonely old empty-nesters. Luckily Dad didn't finish his shift until ten. She decided to be gentle. Kissing Mom on the cheek, Binky gave her a squeeze, the kind that made her giggle and broke the tension.

"Is Terah going?" Mom said, hands clasped.

"Why do you ask?"

"He's an unusual young man," Mom said. "And so much older than the rest of your friends."

"He's okay, intense but harmless."

Binky ran down the stairs, three at a time, calling after her, "Love you, Mom, later."

Across town, Angela Guardian sat on the toilet at ten o'clock bedtime in her glorious Californian home. She examined the empty laundry hamper. Beneath it, her husband's discarded clothes were strewn across the floor with deliberate abandon.

She reached for the toilet paper and touched the bare cardboard roll with several scraps of torn tissue. She ignored his toothbrush balanced on the windowsill with its lava flow of encrusted toothpaste—revolting.

This is what she had witnessed daily for her entire married life. She had a premonition of the following morning when she'd find his empty glass in the center of the gleaming dining table, welded into place with a milk slick of viscosity. She knew with dogged certainty that a thin stream of water would flow from the kitchen faucet in case his wretched cat became thirsty during the night.

These crimes of sloth and neglect greeted Angela with habitual regularity. And if that wasn't enough to turn a woman's heart to concrete, now there were the nebulous doubts about his fidelity. Was her sacrifice worth it? Years of casual torment and indifference only to be discarded in favor of some nubile replacement, probably one of his patients, one he'd perfected with surgical precision.

No doubt Peter didn't think she noticed, but a diligent wife always knew, awaiting betrayal as sure as stubble shavings in the sink or a brand new condom in the wallet. Small changes n his regimented routine, furtiveness with the mail, unexpected appointments. The thought of his premature retirement and lack of occupation, milling about the house restless and purposeless, fired her into action. She might be too late to stop him filing for divorce, but she was more than early enough to defeat the competition, but fair means or far more deviancy than pathetic Peter could ever imagine.

Doctor Peter Guardian, the husband, sat downstairs, oblivious and mired in his own middle-aged crisis at the time of his wife's decision to eliminate the opposition. Angela, his wife, was an erratic and eccentric transplant from the UK so he frequently misunderstood her, even after all these years.

Slumped at his desk, dressed in a plaid fleece robe, he sipped a glass of milk. He deliberated over his choices: make a fuss and risk admonition—if not lose his license—or stay silent and quash the psychological consequences. He couldn't risk losing his medical insurance along with his job, not with Angela's state of health—mental health.

Gorgeous, his beloved cat, pressed himself against Peter's naked legs, chafing the hairy skin with adoration. Sighing, Peter reached down to tickle him under the chin. Pity nobody checked the cat's sex before the name stuck. That's what happened if you attracted strays. He heard the toilet flush upstairs, acutely aware of its position directly above his balding head. The pipes gurgled and rushed.

"Okay," he said, "It's time." He shut the laptop and shuffled to the kitchen sink in his broken backed slippers. Gorgeous leaped onto the counter and rubbed Peter's arm in a frenzy of anticipation. Turning on the faucet, Peter allowed the finest stream of water to fall, and listened to the satisfied purr as Gorgeous lapped fastidiously, his eyes shut tight in ecstasy.

Peter's phone vibrated in his pocket. A last minute call from Crystal Kanvas, his eager would-be intern. He was too soft-hearted, he knew that now. Never do favors for friends. Crystal was certainly word-perfect when arrived at the office without an appointment. Her resume was too good to be true, convincing enough to fool him. Her photograph flashed on the screen but hardly did her justice. Such a pretty girl. He'd seen too many pretty girls lately, although he blotted them from his mind. Their bodies were perfect, why alter imagined imperfections? He tried to decipher Crystal's text message. Most of the vowels were missing. Was it 'Meet me at the hotel?' She didn't specify a time. He'd never get away without Angela noticing. What was he thinking? Why didn't Crystal understand it was impossible? Was his explanation unclear? What would people think? Crystal was a minor. He startled as Angela yelled from on high, "Move your arse you muppet. Are you never coming to bed?"

Less of a question, more of a command. Finding Angela already in bed with the covers pulled up to her nose, her back towards him, Peter sighed. The canister of her nightly medication was empty. Slipping between the cool sheets he sensed the distance between them in the king-sized bed, far greater than the barrier of the body pillow, more like the Great Wall of China. In some ways, Angela's silence was a blessing, avoiding another lashing from her acerbic tongue.

How long did it take him to fall asleep? He didn't know, but when he awoke at one in the morning, he was alone.

Sharon Stroud, Binky's Mom, had watched her daughter flutter down the street like a bedraggled moth in the half light. Strips of ragged fabric trailed from her shoulders like party streamers. Sharon was pleased when Binky started showing an interest in Japanese Manga characters, but never guessed it would become an all-consuming passion. New interests, new people, new friends. Sharon hoped Terah Ladin was only an acquaintance. What if he became a friend, or worse, a best friend? Could he ever become a boyfriend? Not that, please.

Dressing up in costumes seemed like an innocent pastime, but when she read a volume stuffed between the mattress and the wall of Binky's bed, Sharon found another side to the Anime stories verging on a cult. The cartoon-like figures were a peculiar blend of androgynous youthful faces and sexually voluptuous bodies. They made Sharon uneasy, but not half as uneasy as seeing her own daughter transformed into a flesh and blood facsimile of The Avatar Queen. Teenage hormones had changed her from the demure and docile child they adopted ten years ago. The green face-paint gave Binky a surreal expression, making her hardly recognizable.

Sharon never expected her to grow up so quickly. Binky's treasured collection of stuffed animals were relegated to the back of a dusty closet and smothered by complex costumes squashed together in vacuum packed bags. The smell of musky cedar hinted at a whole new persona, alien, with a hint of unfamiliar sophistication.

Checking Binky's web history, Sharon found a whole slew of sites on something called body dysmorphia, and private clinics which performed the most bizarre procedures, before and after hotographs, all at extortionate prices. Sharon's private fears of body piercings and tattoos seemed banal by comparison. These modifications made her wince: hideous implants in unlikely places, scars arranged with incredible precision, and small stubby horns inserted at the hairline.

Sharon clicked over to Binky's Facebook page where she had already uploaded photographs of the day's events before this night-time transformation and party. Terah leered back at her from the screen. Why was this freakish boy in Binky's life?

Sharon hoped his vampire teeth were fake, but where his long hair parted, Sharon flinched at his pair of elfin ears the delicate tips pointing up, pale, almost translucent, but definitely real.

Buttons Down
By Evie Groch

They lie in muted charm alone
in bunches
or strung on threads
reds and golds, greens and browns
four-holed and two
rimmed and plain
hard plastic and well-worn leather
sturdy satin and tarnished metal
corded cloth or warped wood fallen
in battle, lost in duty
cut off in spite, ripped out in rage
found between cushions
or on closet floors
they're collected and
fed false hope
of being employed anew.
How they once served
on royal sleeves and blouses sheer will
remain a secret as they rest
in funereal cardboard boxes and discolored jars, a
handful reduced to discs on a poor
child's board game of checkers.

Mr. Wattle's Mission
By Sue Cobian

Mr. Wattle felt very nervous. A messenger from the King had arrived moments before with a letter ordering him to appear at the palace that afternoon. Why? He worried.

After taking a few deep breaths to calm down, Mr. Wattle worked out what he would do. First, he would eat lunch. He could not think straight when he was hungry, and he needed to be thinking straight. After that, he would clean up any mess he had made. He liked having things in order, just like they did in the army. Next, he would decide what to wear for this important occasion.

He ate and cleaned up his mess quickly. Deciding what to wear didn't take long either. Mr. Wattle would wear his best suit, which was green and beautifully trimmed with pink ruffles. The large yellow hat with its fine, long, white, feather was fabulous. The new blue flip-flops trimmed with sequins were the perfect finishing touch. He loved the way the sequins sparkled with every step he took. He got dressed. It was time to go. He set off at a fast pace.

Soon, Mr. Wattle found himself before the palace gates. They were made of large, heavy pieces of wood and iron. The gates were set into high walls that surrounded the entire palace. Soldiers dressed in bright orange uniforms, blue boots, green belts with silver buckles and sailor hats, guarded the entrance.

The in-charge guard asked Mr. Wattle his name and business. "My name is Mr. Wattle and I have been ordered to see the King." The guard carefully checked the list of permitted visitors. "ENTER," he commanded.

Once inside, Mr. Wattle found himself in a garden at least 100 times bigger than his house. It was so big that he was sure nobody would be able to count all the flowers, plants, and trees. There were so many different kinds. He couldn't believe that some of them even existed.

Mr. Wattle especially liked the bright orange, blue and green flowers shaped like birds' heads and the blue ones that looked like bells. He kept his distance from plants with sharp needles that could give him a good poke if he went too near, and could probably throw their needles at him if he did something to make them angry. Shocked, Mr. Wattle watched a pretty looking plant capture and eat a fly. In the distance he saw tall trees with something looking like basketballs hanging from them. Were they for playing games?

After a few minutes, Mr. Wattle reminded himself that he was there to see the King, not to look at plants. The guard had not told him how to get to the palace and there was no one to ask. He would have to figure this out for himself. Which path should he take? There were so many, going every which way. No signposts except for one, which said STAY ON THE PATHS.

As he liked to do when he was feeling unsure of what to do, Mr. Wattle stood very still. Just as he expected, a very clever plan showed up in his brain. From where he was he would take every right turn. If that didn't work, he would start again, taking every left turn. And if that didn't work, he would start again, taking one right turn, and then one left turn. He started off. On his third try, he reached the palace door. One of the king's men welcomed him with a friendly smile and led Mr. Wattle into the presence of the King.

The King sat majestically on his golden throne and from there he looked at his subject, but he did not speak. Mr. Wattle bowed and said "Good afternoon, your Gracious Majesty."

As he stood there in the silence, Mr. Wattle noticed that he and the King were dressed almost alike. The only big difference was that his majesty had a great crown shaped like a lampshade on his head. As for the King, he always noticed what people wore and approved of Mr.Wattle's choice of clothes, so similar to his own. He knew immediately, since Mr. Wattle had also so cleverly found his way to the palace, that Mr. Wattle could be entrusted with important matters. Mr. Wattle was the one for the job.

When the King finally spoke he said in his very big, loud, round voice, "Mr. Wattle, I have chosen you for a very important task. I have been told, to my great surprise, that an ugly child exists. I want you to bring that child here. My wise ministers say that this child lives in some part of my kingdom, but they have no idea where. Your mission is to find and bring that child back to me. I have never seen an ugly child."

Mr. Wattle was so amazed that he had been chosen to do this that his kneecaps started jiggling up and down. His hands shook a little. He didn't know what to think, but he did know what to do. Whenever he felt jittery like this, he counted backwards from ten to one. He did not like to count backwards to zero. It just didn't feel right. Mr. Wattle knew from experience that if something didn't feel right, it was probably better not to do it.

After the King wished Mr. Wattle a successful journey, a palace guard took him back to the big entrance gates. He started for home. Today he would not be stopping to look at interesting things along the way: worms who somehow ended up on the sidewalk, birds flying,or clouds. He had a mission to plan.

When he got home, Mr. Wattle sat down and started to think. He had seen many children in his life. Tall. Short. Big feet. Small feet. Different colors. Long hair. Short hair. Big ears. Little ears. He wished he had a thinking cap to help him figure out what to do, but he didn't. He finally decided that he would only know who the ugly child was when he saw him or her.

No time to waste. What was he going to pack for his trip? Not too much, not too little; only comfortable flip-flops and suits. Who wanted feet that hurt and suits so tight that your stomach felt squished after you ate?

The most difficult decision had to do with his hats. After much thought, he decided he would take only one. He did like to wear a different hat every day, but there was no room in his bag for all of them. It would be hard to choose which hat, so he would put them in a circle and spin around in the middle until he felt the urge to stop. The hat in front of him would be the one. With that settled, it was time to get a map of the kingdom and plan his journey.

A map, but not just any map. After all, this was a great expedition ordered by the King himself. I will go to the mapmaker's shop and ask for the best map of the kingdom, he decided. Off he went, determined to come back with the map that very day.

What luck. The mapmaker had the perfect map for him . It looked like a game board. Every town came with its name and was painted its own bright color. A road shown in black connected them. Bridges were marked. Since there were bridges, there would be no wading through swamps full of snakes, or crossing rivers and getting wet, or worse. This was going to be easier than Mr. Wattle had expected. He felt happy and adventurous.

In the morning, Mr. Wattle put his bag of belongings, three bottles of water, and some apples and bananas into the shiny red metal wagon he would be using. It would be easier to pull a wagon than to carry the bag. Also, if he got tired, he could take the bag and food out of the wagon and use it as a place to sit. The towns were not far from each other, so a place to sleep and a place to have breakfast and dinner were not a problem.

It was a pleasant morning, not too hot or too cold, and not too windy. The sun was shining. As Mr. Wattle walked down the street, people wished him well. The news about his mission had spread quickly. Everyone was excited. They wanted to know what an ugly child looked like. Who had ever heard of such a thing?

After three hours, Mr. Wattle arrived at the first town. It was called HOORAY. Mr. Wattle asked a friendly looking man with white hair where he could find the mayor. People with white or gray hair usually know a lot, he thought. The man, who said his name was Jeffo, knew where the office was. They went off, with Mr. Wattle still pulling his shiny red metal wagon.

When they reached the mayor's office, the mayor welcomed Mr. Wattle to the town. As ordered, the first thing Mr. Wattle did was present the mayor with the letter of introduction which the King had given him. The letter explained that Mr. Wattle was on an important mission. All mayors were to give him a good place to eat and to sleep. The mayors were even told that they must do anything that Mr. Wattle wanted them to do. The mayor immediately rang the "everyone this is important" bell. Within minutes, everyone had gathered in the town square. The mayor told them that Mr. W attle was on a special mission for King His Highness. Everyone started yelling "Hooray". In this town, it was the polite thing to do. After two minutes, the mayor told everyone to go do something else. They had been polite enough, he decided.

The mayor walked with Mr. Wattle to the best hotel, the only one, in town. The hotel's owner, Boffo, grinned and shouted "Hooray" when they entered. "Please come with me and choose the room you like best,'" he said.

Boffo showed the three rooms to Mr. Wattle. They were all very nice. One looked like a cabin on a ship. One looked like the inside of an Arabian tent. One looked like the inside of a cave. Mr. Wattle yelled "Hooray" and took the ship's cabin. He liked the porthole windows and pictures of the ocean. Best of all, you turned a ship's wheel fixed to the door, not a doorknob, to enter and leave the room.

Once he had chosen his room, Mr. Wattle and Boffo went to the dining room. Mr. Wattle sat at a sea captain's table and ate fish. After thanking Boffo for dinner, he yelled "Hooray" and went to his room. It was time to sleep. Mr. Wattle slipped into the ship-shape bed. While he slept, he dreamed of sailing near and far.

The next morning Mr. Wattle went to the school. All of the children were there, playing and having fun. Now it was time for him to pay attention to details so that he could spot the ugly child. Some of the children were taller, some shorter. There were thin and not so thin. Hair came in yellow, red, black and brown. It could also be curly, straight, wavy or frizzy. Skins went from dark to light. Noses, eyes, eyebrows, ears, lips, mouths and chins all matched up in different ways on faces. Nothing unusual here, he thought. I'll leave tomorrow and try again in the next town on the map, RUN. If I need to, I'll search in FUN, GITTY UP and ABC too! I will complete this mission.

Vats
By Evie Groch

Beauty at a price –
vibrant oranges, earthy browns,
emerald greens, royals blues encased
in dyeing vats
on the roof of a North African factory.
Rugs to be woven
with color-infused threads to
sell to Americans
after the tour.

The stench of the vats
overpowers like stagnant sewage --
over-ripe eggs turned green
unassisted by dyes.
A mint leaf to hold
under our nose so
we may breathe as
we observe.

I cannot linger
or I will faint and go over
the rail to fall into a blood-red vat.
I climb down quickly and am escorted to
the salesroom
where I am offered tea and sugar until
they are convinced
I will not buy.

Mara & the Hedgehog
Rita Beach

The sound coming from the other room caused Mara to awake from her nap. The cry was not loud but mournful and frightening. It was a call for help, a plea for someone to come. What could she do? I'm so little, but I am almost three now. I must see what's happening. "Help, help," it seemed to be crying.

I must hurry, she decided. Everyone must be asleep, or they surely would have done something by now. Just then, she heard Henry, the hedgehog, cry out extra loud. There was a thrashing sound as if he was being slammed against the floor, and each time, he cried out for help.

That last desperate cry was all it took to give Mara the super-strength she needed to climb off the side of her bed. Her feet dangled as she tried to feel for the side rail. Her little fingers grabbed onto the bedspead. Granna had taught her that. Her little brother had outgrown his crib and moved into Mara's baby bed. Her landing wasn't as smooth as when one of her family was there to help her down from the new twin bed. She sat down hard.

Mara was unsteady on her feet when she stood up, but she quickly made her way into the living room. There stood Bandit with Henry in her mouth. At first Bandit dropped the hedgehog to rush over to greet Mara. Bandit loved to play with Mara. The young puppy was surprised when Mara walked on by her and picked up Henry.

Mara pulled Henry close to her. She hugged him so tightly he let out a squeak, but she was sure it was a sound of joy. Henry's squeaker box was located right where his heart was, and it had its own sweet sound, different from the others. Mara examined his two-tone tan fur, wet from Bandit's repeated attacks. His little snout with the button-like black nose seemed to be okay. His tiny mouse-size ears were still standing up straight. Henry was very round in the middle with stubby little legs, almost too short to be of use. Mara looked into Henry's sweet eyes and then at his tiny little mouth, hardly big enough to make those horrible cries. She was relieved to see everything was intact.

Bandit was jumping up on Mara. She lifted Henry as high in the air as she possibly could to keep the stuffed animal from ending up in Bandit's jaws. She had not been able to save poor Fred, the fox, but she was determined that Henry would not suffer the same fate.

Bandit had been relentless in his quest to remove the squeaker from the fox, along with all the stuffing. She triumphantly threw the squeaker up in the air after she tore it out. Now, Fred silent in the basket among all the other stuffed toys could, no longer utter a single sound, just like the others.

Mara resisted Bandit's efforts to grab Henry from her little hands. Bandit was quicker, stronger, could run faster, but that did not stop Mara. Bandit circled Mara and Henry and in an instant locked her teeth into the hedgehog's short leg. Bandit pulled as Mara tugged, trying hard to make Bandit release her tight grip. Henry let out a loud squeaky cry, and Mara felt an extra burst of strength. She dug her heels into the carpet more determined than ever. Suddenly, Bandit let go, and Mara fell backwards, sliding across the floor. Bandit lunged for Henry. Mara rolled over on her belly with the hedgehog under her.

Bandit thought all of this was great fun. She had never seen her little friend so active. Mara loves to wrestle with me for this stuffed toy. They rolled, tumbled, stood up, fell down, but Mara held on to Henry.

They battled until the end, but Mara won ownership of Henry, the hedgehog. Bandit wagged her tail, then walked over and licked the side of Mara's face. After that decisive battle, Henry and Mara were inseparable. He was always right next to her whenever Mara rode in the car seat. At bedtime, she wrapped him in her arms, where he stayed all night.

A few days later as her father was coming in the back door, Mara heard a new squeaking sound, unfamiliar, and different from the rest. In his arms he was holding the cutest baby panda bear she had ever seen. "Bandit," her father called, "come here girl. I have a new toy for you!"

Oh, no, Mara thought, not another one to save!

Hillside Lot W/ Valley View
By Robert J. (Jamie) Miller

What does a little four year-old dream? Yellow
bulldozers and big green trucks, Walks with Daddy
through fields on his farm? Scary dark sounds,
monsters under his bed, Daddy will keep him from
harm.

What does a big ten-year-old dream? Bullies who
mock him, threaten him hurt. Sunlight on fields
of daddy's farm.
The scary dark forest not far away.
Heroes like Batman will save him from harm.

What does a sturdy sixteen-year-old dream? A girl
(the one girl!) a dream, a plan.
They know this land. It'll be their farm. But
formless fears stir in distant lands. It's his time
to keep her from harm.

What does a brave twenty-year-old know? That
not all lands are a welcoming green, That
colored ribbons fade in the sun, And those
letters "USMC" are finally all.
And his homeland, this valley, their fields...

Who will remember? The girl? Those folks who
said "We'll never forget", then ask "Iraq? What
was that about?" Or the farm? Daddy's farm, where
they walked the fields, When daddy kept him from
harm.

Dragon's Baby Teeth
Carolyn Donnell

"Come on Sarah. We need to get home." Evan called to his little sister who had stopped to play in the park after school.

Sarah didn't answer.

"Sarah! Come on. What are you doing?"

"Shh." Sarah put her finger on her lips. She whispered and pointed into the bushes. "Do you hear something?"

Evan walked over to her. "I hear a sniffing sound. Is it a dog?"

"Or a hissing cat?" Sarah pulled back a branch.

"Be careful." Evan helped her pull more branches back.

"Oh!" Sarah pointed into the shadows at a green scaly animal a little smaller than herself. A long tail wrapped all the way around to animal's head. "What is it?"

"A giant lizard?" Evan took a step back. "Look out."

"No." A soft sound came from the bush.

"Who said that?" Sarah looked around.

"I didn't say anything," said Evan.

"I'm not a lizard." The voice spoke again.

Evan and Sarah stared at each other and then bent down to get a closer look.

"What are you then?" Evan asked.

"A dragon," the animal mumbled.

Evan snorted. "There's no such thing as a dragon. Besides, you don't even have ..."

The dragon wriggled and two small wings popped out of his back.

"... wings." Evan said quietly.

The baby dragon let out a breath that sounded like a soft sob.

"What's the matter?" Sarah reached for his paw. "Are you crying?"

"I am not crying."

"Yes you are. I heard ..."

"Shhh." Evan put his finger over his lips.

A deeper voice sounded somewhere behind the Evan and Sarah.

"It came from over there, I tell you."

"Quick." Evan grabbed Sarah's arm. "That's Davey's voice."

"Ow," Sarah yelped. "Who's Davey?"

"You know, the boy who likes to fight. Hide."

Evan drug Sarah into the bushes next to the little dragon.

"Everyone be very quiet," Evan ordered.

"Over here." The deep voice said. "Try those bushes. I'll teach him to cry."

The cold laugh made Sarah shiver. One of the boys with Davey swung a stick into the bushes. It barely missed Sarah's arm. She had to hold her breath. Three boys shook the bushes further down and then they all moved on to the forest.

"They must have gone into the woods. Their lucky day." The three laughed and pushed each other around as they left the playground.

Evan and Sarah hid with the dragon for what seemed like hours.

"I think they're gone." Evan looked out to the playground.

"Careful," Sarah relied. "It might be a trap."

Evan stepped away from the shrubs. "It looks okay from here, but wait a minute to be sure." He walked toward the woods, then turned and came back. "Come on out, the coast is clear."

"What about him?" Sarah looked into the bushes at the small dragon who shook his head no as Sarah waved to him.

Evan scratched his head. "We can't carry him. He's too big. We can't walk with him either. People will notice."

Sarah stomped one foot. "We have to do something."

"Okay. I have an idea." Evan pointed to Sarah. "Give me your sweater."

"My sweater? Why?"

"To put around the dragon. It has a hood."

"No. Not my new sweater. Use your old jacket. It has a hood too."

"Your sweater's longer. It'll cover more. Besides, I thought you wanted to help."

"Yes, but …"

"Don't bother about me." A whiny voice came from the shrubs.

"See, Sarah? He needs us. You're the one that said we had to do something."

"I know." Sarah ran her hand down her new red sweater coat and felt the flowers sewn on the pocket. She looked back and saw a tear in the dragon's eye. "Okay, but be careful." She took off the sweater and handed it to Evan.

Evan motioned to Drrrag, "Come on out."

Drrrag shook his head. "No."

"Come on. You can't stay here. Where do you live?"

"Doesn't matter. I can't go home."

"What do you mean, you can't go home?" A noise came from the woods. "Those guys might come back. Come on. Now."

The dragon unwound his long tail as he scrambled out of the bush.

Evan looked at the dragon. "I'm Evan and this is my sister Sarah. What's your name?"

"Drrrag."

"Drag?"

"Not Drag. It's Drrrag."

Evan tried to roll his r's. "Drr-rrag."

Drrrag laughed. "I guess that's close enough for now."

"Can you walk on your hind legs?" Evan held up Sarah's sweater.

"For a while." Drrrag stood up on his short back legs, swaying a little to one side.

"Put this on." Evan helped Drrrag. "Pull your wings in as far as you can."

Drrrag took a deep breath.

"Careful." Sarah pulled the hood over the dragon's small head and big eyes.

"There," said Evan. "All done."

"Not quite." Sarah pointed to Drrrag's tail. It stuck out about a foot behind him. She reached down and picked up the end of the tail.

"Watch it!" Drrrag spun around.

"Sorry," Sarah said, "but this tail has to go."

"What do you mean—has to go?" Drrrag cried out.

"She doesn't mean cut it off or anything. Just hide it."

Evan joined his little sister. "Here." He brought the end of the tail up to Drrrag's hand.

"You'll have to hold this." Sarah and Evan laughed.

"What are you laughing at?" Drrrag snorted.

"I didn't mean to laugh." Sarah bit her lip. "It just looks very - er... lumpy, that's all."

Evan stepped in front of Drrrag. "It'll be all right until we get to the house. Let's go now, before anyone comes back."

The sound of voices came from the woods. "There they are!"

The dragon tried to crawl back in the bushes.

"No," Sarah cried. "Not with my sweater."

Evan reached out and grabbed Drrrag. "This way. Everybody. Follow me."

Sarah pushed the dragon. "You'd better do what he says."

Davey and his bullies came out of the woods pointing and shouting.

"Get them!"

"It's Evan and his sister."

"Who's that funny looking kid in the red sweater?"

"Just catch them!"

Evan let the way through the woods. "Hurry up, dragon," he shouted.

Drrrag stumbled and then fell over on all fours. His tail flipped out the back of the sweater.

"Look," Davey shouted. "What's that? A dog?"

"Looks like a lizard," another boy panted as they all ran after the trio.

"A lizard! That's crazy. Hurry up. When we catch them we'll find out. Come on."

Sarah looked back and saw the bullies getting closer. She screamed.

"Quick. This way." Evan suddenly turned to the right. "Follow me exactly."

Sarah followed. Drrrag turned so sharply that his tail slapped the side of his face. "Ow," he cried.

Sounds came from behind them.

"Aieee."

"Ohhh. No."

"Help!"

Sarah paused to look back. Evan had turned them just short of a very steep hill.

The bullies didn't know the hill was there and went down, one sliding on his bottom, another rolling over, all scattering rocks and twigs as they rolled to the bottom.

"Now!" Evan motioned to the other two and pointed to a trail of rocks. "Follow me." They passed through the woods and came out on the other side behind a house next to the playground. Evan stopped for a minute and turned his head from side to side. "I don't hear anything. I think we lost them. Let's go home."

"How far is your house anyway?" Drrrag mumbled as he tripped on the hem of the sweater.

"Hey! Be careful." Sarah stepped closer to him.

"We're almost there." Evan pointed to a tall house on the side of the hill." Drrrag sighed.

"Don't worry, there's a little playhouse in the back."

Evan pulled Drrrag through the side gate and into the back yard. "You'll be safe here." He pushed Drrrag toward the door of the playhouse.

"Give me back my sweater first." Sarah reached up and tugged on the hood.

"You and your old sweater," Evan complained.

Sarah glared at Evan. "It's not old and it better be OK too or you're in trouble." Sarah helped Drrrag out of the sweater.

"Evan!" A voice called from the house.

"Who's that?" Drrrag started to shake.

Evan jumped in front of him. "That's my mom. Quick, into the playhouse."

Drrrag pushed the doorknob. "I can't. The door is stuck."

"Oh no." Evan stared as Drrrag shook harder, starting at his head and working down to his toes. Sarah's eyes got very big. "What are you doing?"

The edges of Drrrag's body began to blur. His whole body looked like fog. Evan heard a popping sound and then Drrrag disappeared.

The Kiss
By Lisa Meltzer Penn

The hallucinations of the pungent tongue
Fragment into whispers
Did you see? Did you taste? Did you smell?
The tongue has smell sensors
The nose can taste
And the kiss underneath beckons and breathes,
Issues from lips parted by day, pressed tight by dark.

The Last Seed
By Jo Carpignano

This tree remembers well how
things once were, when
saplings grew
and rippling waters flowed
between the rocks.

Then hills and valleys
shouted vibrant green.

Now, that green earth is dry, its
nurturing expired.
Depleted soil rejects all
hope for growth.

Evaporated rivers left deeply
furrowed scars.
Eroded mountain tops have crumbled into
mounds of dust.

This last small pine persists from
that far distant past.
Its roots sank deep then
final aquifer expired.
Its limbs now stark and bare.

From one shriveled branch a
shrunken cone slides down,
regretfully embraced by dry
exhausted earth.

A single seed slides out from
shelter far inside.
It lies exposed,
and has nowhere to go.

Bag Girl
By Robert J. (Jamie) Miller

"Allie! Earth to Allie, come in, please!"

"Hm? Oh, sorry, Megan." I glanced up at the lady in the grocery checkout line, to find her trying to stifle laughter. "I'm sorry, I was just thinking about this veggie. Instead of bagging things. Like I'm supposed to. Sorry." I tried to concentrate on fitting the lady's groceries into bags in the proper order, and finally looked up in triumph. "There! May I carry this to your car for you?"

"No, that's fine. This doesn't look very heavy. I hated to disturb you. I've never seen anyone so fascinated by a head of cauliflower. I half expected you to speak to it, like Hamlet talking to Yorik's skull."

"I'm really sorry! I first thought it was just a green cauliflower, but I found out that it's called a 'Romanesco', and I hadn't seen anything quite like it before. Just look at those patterns in the—"

"Allie, you're babbling," Megan said gently. "Give her the bag of groceries and let her go."

"Well," the lady said, "Perhaps I could use a hand out to the car, after all. And, Megan, don't give her a hard time. I think she's delightful."

I followed her to her car and loaded her groceries into her trunk.

"You seem to enjoy this job," the lady said.

"Oh, I do. It's fun watching people. I'll be studying psychology in college, and this job is so enjoyable. I watch people. Kids, especially. Have you ever noticed the differences? Five-year-old boys are already practicing karate moves. Girls that age are dancing. They always dance."

"I've never noticed. Thanks for helping me. I've enjoyed you."

"Well, not all little kids, it seems. She's not very happy." I pointed out a little girl who was hesitantly following a man to his car. "She doesn't look like she belongs with him. She's—what do you think? Chinese? And he's—."

"Bye, Allie, that's your name, right?"

"Yes ma'am." She started her car and I stepped back to watch traffic. As she pulled away, I glanced toward where the man and girl had been. The girl was nowhere in sight, and the man had started his car with the radio blasting at full volume. This was weird, I thought. Old guys don't play music that loudly. Something was wrong. What if it was an abduction? No, that's crazy, I thought. But what if... I sprinted between parked cars toward the exit lane, and looked around. What if the loud music was to cover the girl's cries? I spotted a couple of carts nested together and grabbed them, then pushed them into the path of the man's moving car. He crunched into the carts and stopped, then backed up.

"OmiGaad! What'd I just do?" I said out loud. I raced up to him.

"I'm terribly sorry!" But even as I apologized, I scanned the inside of his car. No little girl. My hands were shaking and my pulse pounding in my ears. "I'm really, really sorry!"

"You're in trouble, young lady! I'm going to sue. This is going to cost you big." He swung out of the lane and burned rubber leaving the lot.

I noticed his license. "BDB266" I said aloud.

A guy outside the coffee shop called. "You are in trouble, girl. I think you pushed those carts."

The two carts lay in a mangled heap in the lane. I dragged them aside. "BDB266" I repeated as I walked shakily back toward the market. "Oh, God, I'm dead. What'll I do? That probably wasn't an abduction at all. Just an old guy with a loud radio." I wanted to just run somewhere, anywhere, and never come back, never go home, never face my mom. Good-bye work-experience, good-bye college. I forced myself to walk into the store and up to Megan's check stand. "BDB266, Megan. Help me remember. And call Marty. I'm in trouble."

"He's busy."

"Please! I've trashed a couple of carts. BDB266."

"Forget carts. He's busy."

"I'll go look for him."

"He has worse problems. They're looking for a missing child."

"Missing? A little girl, about 5? Maybe Chinese?"

Megan's jaw dropped, and she stared at me. "Yes. Why?"

"I know what happened. BDB266."

"What are you saying? And what are those numbers?"

"The car license. Help me remember it."

The police must have arrived in just minutes, but it seemed forever. I told my story, then told it again and tried to answer their questions. They left but I stayed. I wanted to be there to hear any news. My mom arrived and yelled at me, but didn't make me leave. One of the officers came back to tell us the little girl had been dumped at a party store in the mall a mile away, where the kidnapper thought she wouldn't complain. She had been in the guy's car trunk. She was safe and her mom was there. The guy had just disappeared, but the police know his license number, and they are looking. Marty said forget about the carts. They weren't important. So I guess my work-experience program is safe, and my college applications won't have to show a conviction for Assault with a Deadly Shopping Cart or something. So it all turned out good.

But still, I keep wondering about things. What would have happened if I hadn't been paying attention to people? And if I hadn't been crazy enough to push those carts at him? I'm sure somebody else would have paid attention and done something.

Right?

I keep wondering.

A California Summer with Marie
By Jo Carpignano

In 1970, my Aunt Antonia, invited her Italian sister, Marie, to come to visit us in California. Being a teacher and on summer vacation myself, I volunteered to drive the two of them wherever they wanted to go on the West Coast.

Marie, a well-educated, retired accountant living in Lucca, Italy, had never been anywhere in America. This being her first travel by plane, she was apprehensive about flying the considerable distance from Italy to San Francisco; but finally convinced herself that our invitation was too good to be refused. Therefore, setting aside her concerns, Marie accepted our plan to visit the sights in California, which she had read so much about.

Her arrival was met with enthusiasm among friends and relatives living in and around San Francisco. There were numerous lunches, dinners, picnics and outings, to welcome and entertain the charming Marie from Italy. After a couple of weeks of celebratory engagements, Marie grew restless and asked, "Cuando si parte?" (When do we leave?).

We promptly packed our luggage, climbed into my 1960 Ford Mercury, and set off on our journey to visit as many attractions throughout the state as possible in eight weeks. While stopping for a short visit with my parents in Soquel, we took a day trip to the Big Basin Redwood Forest where we had a picnic lunch among the tallest living things in the world. Then, heading south along Highway 1 to Carmel, Monterey and Big Sur, Marie was enchanted by the California coastline. "Che meraviglia!" (What magnificence!) she exclaimed with sincere appreciation for those extraordinary vistas along the California Coast.

Continuing south, with the aim of reaching San Diego, where my brother Robert was studying engineering, we stopped at San Simeon State Park and a tour of Hearst Castle. Again, Marie expressed admiration for the exceptional beauty of the rolling hills and elaborate architecture of Hearst Castle. With a little time to spare the next day, we stopped at Redwood Shores to see Marine World U.S.A. where we enjoyed the antics of marine mammals then continued south to Los Angeles.

During the following week, we stayed with cousins in Hollywood, and enjoyed the delights of dinners at the Trocadero and Brown Derby. I talked everyone into a day at Santa Monica State Beach where I enjoyed a luxurious swim in the warmer currents of the Pacific Ocean. Next stop was in San Diego where we spent a few days with my brother. Here we enjoyed Balboa Park and the San Diego Zoo. In Italy there are few opportunities to view exotic animals from all parts of the world, and Marie was duly impressed by the extent and variety of animal species there.

Leaving my brother to complete his exams at Northrop Engineering , Antonia, Marie and I crossed into Mexico for a day. Marie was concerned about leaving the United States without her passport, and was much relieved upon reentry. "Grazie a Dio" (Thank God) Marie whispered in the back seat as we drove back through customs.

Las Vegas was next on our itinerary and the highway through Death Valley was truly impressive in its desolation during the shimmering heat of July. The lights and sounds of hyperactive Las Vegas proved a bit too much for the shy Marie, and after a visit to Hoover Dam and its electricity generating turbines, we returned to California.

In Yosemite National Park, Marie was astonished by those largest living things on earth, the giant Sequoias. Also impressive was Half Dome and Glacier Point near the Ahwahnee Hotel where we had lunch. We looked at some of the cabin rentals, but Marie shook her head, and we moved on to a comfortable motel outside the park.

Thirteen miles east of Yosemite was Mono Lake, another spectacular State Park. This is 65 square miles of water over one million years old. It is fed by mountain streams and natural springs but has no outlet The interaction of minerals from mountain streams and fresh spring water has created a landscape of "Tufa towers" in the lake. The watery landscape has an "other world" appearance. When Marie turned to me for an explanation, I had to admit ignorance, and consulted a park ranger.

In Lassen Park, the lava beds and bubbling mud pools were most intriguing to Marie. She asked if it was air causing the bubbles. She was skeptical when I told her that it was volcanic heat that made the mud boil. But when she touched the boundary of the pool, she conceded, "E vero! Molto caldo!" (It's true! Very Hot!).

Walking through the lava tubes was another experience that astonished her. Few of the many California Parks were neglected in the eight weeks that Marie spent with us. We visited nearly every corner of the state.

Although I did all the driving, I enjoyed every moment of travel with my two appreciative companions. Antonia and Marie contributed generously to my learning as well as to my enjoyment. In addition to developing my skills as tour guide, I had the privilege of hearing exquisitely spoken Italian during their long conversations.

When she returned to Italy, I'm not sure what Marie considered her most memorable experience in California. It may have been watching the bubbling mud pools, then walking through a lava tube to Lassen Park, or walking around a Giant Sequoia, Even more impressive may have been hearing the roar of water pouring over Hoover Dam, then visiting its huge hydroelectric turbines. Since McDonald's had not yet invaded Lucca, Marie might have laughed with her friends while explaining trying to eat her first hamburger with a fork and knife. Perhaps her most memorable event, was at Macy's in San Francisco when, with great apprehension, she experienced her first escalator ride. Marie expressed pleasure with all of these experiences, but she was most enthusiastic about her eight week tour of California State Parks.

Each experience was also memorable to me for different reasons. However, what I remember most vividly was what Marie said on Twin Peaks one crystal clear night, as we stood overlooking San Francisco Bay. I will never forget her wide-eyed wonder as she whispered in her impeccable Italian, "In Italy we have beautiful coastlines and majestic mountains, great cities and grand coastlines, but never have I seen such beauty as this breathtaking city and bay, bathed in glorious illumination."

A Day With Granddaughters
By Lisa Johnson

All day it's playing.
It's parks and swings and jungle gyms. All day
it's running:
it's chasing balls and bubbles in the sun.
It's lunching on nuggets with tiny toys in boxes:
it's called McDonald's Happy Meals.
It's in and out of car straps and buckles.
It's exhilarating, it's exhausting.
It's making memories with my two
young granddaughters.

At day's ending:
it's into the car again to chauffeur
them home,
down El Camino, through Millbrae, San Bruno, into
foggy South City.

On the way it's sibling ruckus in the backseat.
It's I, tough Nana, issuing stern warnings.
It's tears and sniffles and pleading:
It's Katie begging: "Nana, I need to kiss you," as I
try to ignore this tired drama for safety's sake,
but it escalates.

I pull the car over to the curb. I get
out to console, to kiss, then It's back
on the road again. But it's still
pleading and sniffling.
Then it's I, pleading: "Please, Katie, I've
already kissed you."

"Nana," the older, wiser Natalie
informs, interprets:
"Nana, Katie isn't saying I need to kiss you."
"What is she saying then?"
"She's saying I need a tissue."

It's all so aggravating and amusing: it's
another day of
bonding with my granddaughters.

Gun Smoke
By Linda Brown

Frank had been a licensed private investigator in California for over twenty years now he was thinking of taking Wendy in as a partner on many levels. Frank and Wendy were still in the first blush of a new relationship. It was in the days when they still got dressed up and went out for Sunday brunch and long meandering drives.

Over breakfast, Frank explained the particulars of his latest case. A contractor was suing Frank's client for $2.5 million in damages for personal injury. Frank told Wendy that he gave his cases names; this one was called "Gun Smoke". He expounded that the contractor/ plaintiff was a hunter and long-time gun enthusiast. The contractor had been loading his own ammunition, mainly shotgun shells for years. One day the contractor came across an old bolt-action rifle that he just had to have. He bought it and decided to load his own ammunition to use at the local firing range. He had always used an old manual gun owners referred to as a "bible" to research what type of shell, shot, wadding, and powder that was appropriate for his specific shotguns. This was a totally different type of process to load ammunition for this new rifle than he had used before.

Instead of going himself to research the new process, he had sent his wife to the local sporting goods store with a list to purchase items he thought he needed as outlined according to his "bible." When the contractor's wife produced her husband's ammunition order for his new rifle, the gun store clerk told her the requested products were not available in their inventory because they were out of production. He suggested that her husband should either call or come in for a full explanation. However, the contractor also had requested powder and pellets for his regular shot gun shells.

When the wife returned home, she neglected to tell her husband that the specific gunpowder he needed for his new rifle was no longer in production. According to the contractor/plaintiff he did not recheck the order, but used what was in the bag to load the casings for his new rifle ammunition.

The contractor went to the firing range with the new ammunition and new rifle. When he fired the gun, instead of the bullet firing, the breach exploded in his hand and the rifle disintegrated, blasting the bolt through the wooden table that the rifle was resting on.

At this point, Wendy involuntarily raised her hand to her mouth and shook her head in disbelief. But Frank continued. The contractor was rushed to emergency room by ambulance; and, he was treated for numerous injuries to his hands, arms, and face.

Of course he sued the sporting goods store. His lawsuit claimed that, in addition to his hand and arm injuries, he had sustained permanent brain damage and was no longer able to work as a contractor. He wanted millions of dollars for his injuries.

Wendy couldn't understand how it became a lawsuit, but Frank patiently explained that anyone can sue anyone else. All they need is a lawyer trying to sell the plaintiff's complaints to a jury.

Frank was hired by the sporting goods store's insurance to do an investigation. Frank told Wendy the investigation took a turn during the process of doing a background check on the contractor. Frank explained that he discovered that the contractor had suffered a brain injury resulting from a traffic accident for which he subsequently had filed a lawsuit. In the subpoenaed medical records of the contractor, Frank also noted that the contractor had already attended what is called a "brain school" for his automobile accident injuries. Frank discovered that a brain school basically dealt with people who needed therapy to relearn coordination and thought processes that had been lost due to their specific neurological injury.

"Can't you just tell everyone the contractor already did this once?" Wendy asked naively.

"It's not that simple, Wendy."

Wendy began to realize that this was not just a romantic date, but a working breakfast. Frank went on to say that he wanted to show Wendy how to set up for surveillance. It just so happened that Frank had chosen a brunch spot very near to the subject/ contractor/ plaintiff in "Gun Smoke". Since Wendy thought it would be fun to be included in Frank's case, other than just helping with the computer searches, she agreed to accompany Frank to the contractor's neighborhood. As they drove over to the address where the subject lived, Frank began talking in his teaching voice. He explained that when one is doing surveillance that the most important thing is to be prepared.

Frank continued, "The first thing one needs to do on surveillance is notify the local LEOs (Law Enforcement Officers) so that the local force is aware of what you are doing lurking around in a neighborhood."

To demonstrate, Frank pulled to the curve and called the Sheriff's office.

After the phone call Frank continued his litany, "You need your camera equipment, a notebook, some food and water, and you need to case the area so that you will know all the entrances and exits."

As it turned out, Frank was not really prepared for surveillance; he thought he was just going to show the ropes to Wendy.

Since it was a Sunday, many people who were outside observed Frank and Wendy driving back and forth in this small residential neighborhood. Frank drove a fairly inconspicuous white Blazer. Frank said, "We have a good cover, we could conceivably be just looking for an address."

He told Wendy that he was not concerned about burning himself in the neighborhood. Or, as Frank further explained, "I don't think that a man and woman riding slowly through a neighborhood as though we were really looking for an address would send any red flags up."

After determining more than one entrance and exit to the area they drove past the house again. Frank and Wendy immediately noticed a man in a Boy Scout's uniform carrying a large 42-quart cooler out to the car parked in the driveway.

"Oh, my gawd, Wendy, it's him!"

As they slowed down to observe, the contractor actually loaded two more coolers; then a couple of preteen boys in Boy Scout uniforms ran out and climbed into the car.

They could not believe that they had stumbled onto the contractor and observed him doing things he supposedly was not able to do. He had claimed in his lawsuit that he had lost the ability to lift or hold anything. Frank raced the car around the corner and executed a U-turn so that he would be in position to follow in whatever direction the plaintiff chose to drive. The plaintiff pulled out of his driveway and they began to discreetly follow.

"What are you doing?" Wendy asked.

Frank turned his head and stared at Wendy. He was amazed that he would have to explain it to her. "Well, when you find your subject doing something suspicious, you have follow the action."

"But I thought you were just talking in the abstract," Wendy said quietly.

"Well, yeah, I was giving you an example, but if the situation presents itself you hafta go with it! Don't you understand? This guy has been contending that he can't even lift a hammer since the accident, and there he was lifting and carrying huge, heavy coolers! He's obviously up to something; otherwise why would he be in the Scout uniform? Let's see where he goes."

Wendy just nodded.

They followed him to a local park. It quickly became obvious that the occasion was a Boy Scout Jamboree and picnic. It turned out the plaintiff not only carried the large coolers from the car; he also transported a large snow cone making machine quite a distance, and also tied heavy ropes around trees so that the Boy Scouts could have contests shimmying across them.

What an opportunity for Frank to collect evidence against him. Frank had developed an incredible amount of disdain against people who fraudulently sue insurance companies. Frank told Wendy that there was actually a trade term: litigious litigants. Basically these were people who sued for just about any reason, just to get someone else to pay their way. Frank saw himself as the White Knight Investigator, righting all these wrongs.

Unfortunately, Frank had expected to spend a lazy romantic Sunday with Wendy and had not done the minimal prep for an on-the-job surveillance. He did not have all his sophisticated camera equipment with him. He did have an older model Sony digital camera, which he always carried in his car, but it did not have the nice large telephoto lens that he had back at the office.

So the dilemma was how to get photographs of the plaintiff with the limited capabilities of the camera without being obvious or without people thinking he might be some kind of pervert hanging around taking pictures at a Boy Scout's picnic.

Frank told Wendy that this was a perfect opportunity for her. She had a new role as a decoy. She got to stand by every object and tree where the plaintiff was working. While she posed, Frank pretended to take a picture of her, but he actually was shooting over her shoulder so he could capture the plaintiff and his activities. Fortunately, this strategy was palpably believable. After all, they were in a park on a beautiful sunny Sunday; Wendy even had makeup on and was wearing a skirt.

When Frank had finished photographing the plaintiff's activities, he and Wendy settled down to sit at a picnic table in order to continue to watch the contractor. Frank and Wendy appeared to be having an intimate conversation as they whispered back and forth.

Apparently they must have looked forlorn at the table with out any food or drink. Seeing this situation, a young Latina woman came over from a loud, boisterous birthday party. She carried plates with tortillas and beans, placing them on the table for them. She said she saw that we had no food and that they had plenty. She shyly added that she would bring them some sodas too, and asked them their preference.

For the next couple of hours, Frank and Wendy watched in amazement the plaintiff's activities, including when he demonstrated his ability to grasp the rope with his hands and ankles so he could show to the Boy Scouts how to shimmy on the rope from one tree to another. The trees were about 15 feet apart and the rope was about four feet off the ground. He even was observed throwing several snowballs, taken from the shaved ice machine. He threw overhand using his so-called bad hand and arm during a snowball fight with several Boy Scouts.

Thus Wendy's first experience "in the field" was ended .

She did go with Frank to the sporting goods store to interview the manager and the clerk who had served the plaintiff's wife. The clerk insisted that he told the wife that the store did not carry what her husband had requested and that the clerk needed more current information. He had suggested that the husband should call the store or come in so they could determine what he actually needed. The contractor never came in and he never called the store.

At trial, Frank testified as to what he had observed during that Sunday and used the images to corroborate his testimony. With this evidence the jury could conclude that there was sufficient questions as to plaintiff's real injuries and cause doubts of the validity of his claims.

The contractor's attorney was furious and attempted to discredit Frank's evidence by suggesting that Frank and Wendy were not really present at the Jamboree and someone else had taken the photos and provided them to him. Frank stood his ground under the intense cross examination. He offered to present the Sony digital camera that he had used that day.

The jury did not need any more proof corroborating Frank's testimony.

The jury verdict, although in favor of the contractor, reduced the dollar award using a jury instruction of "contributory negligence". The final award was $35,000, just about enough to cover the contractor's medical bills.

The insurance company considered it a "win" on their behalf. Wendy was disappointed that none of the photos had her in them to commemorate her first surveillance, but she was proud that Frank's investigation had been successful for his client and had contributed to a small award.

Frank and Wendy considered it a successful conclusion to bring truthful facts to the jury that made a difference in the outcome of the trial.

Frank observed, "Some days luck and perseverance are all that it takes."

Wendy looked forward to more cases with Frank.

Death on Route 66
By Carolyn Donnell

Further Examination Unnecessary

Deputy Dennis Roscoe groaned as he leaned against the door of the ranch house. He scanned the room one last time. A lavender and teal Tiffany lamp by the stone fireplace cast intricate shadows on the ceiling above the sofa where Mrs. Clayton's body lay. She looked like she had just lain down for a nap—a permanent one. He had felt for a pulse just to be sure. No need to check the other body slumped in the leather chair behind the mahogany desk. The bloody hole in Jeremy Clayton's head made further examination unnecessary.

Dennis rubbed his hand over his thinning hair. Was it a double suicide? A murder? He shook his head. He wasn't used to suicides or murders. His job usually consisted of breaking up a bar fight back in Vega or responding to Old Lady Potts and her reports of disappearing burglars or other imagined crimes. But tonight she had been right—tonight and fifteen years ago.

Something clicked into place in Dennis's brain. He punched a number on his cell phone. "Put me through to Detective Monroe." He backed out of the room onto the porch. "Jake? Dennis here. I know this is not your beat, but I knew you'd want to know. Clayton's house. Mrs. Potts called it in. Dead. Double—." Dennis hesitated. "Yeah, Jake. I'm still here. Same as last time. Except this time both of them are dead. Yes. Jeremy too, not just his missus. Only two times Potts has ever been right in her life. Get here quick."

Dennis snapped the phone shut and returned to his squad car to wait.

Jake To His Friends

Detective Jacob Monroe, Jake to his friends, drove west from Amarillo down Route 66. The mostly flat yellow land flowed out as far as he could see in every direction. Few trees grew in the Texas Panhandle. Elm, hackberry, cottonwood, and oak did manage to grow in the river bottom. Amarillo had a few tree-lined neighborhoods, and down in Palo Duro Canyon you could pretend you lived on a hillside, but in the area between Amarillo and Adrian, trees were a rarity.

His destination, the Claytons' residence, was an exception. Jake pulled into the drive and headed for the grove of oaks that spread from the side of the house to the back. He saw Dennis signal to him to park next to his car in the only shade for many miles.

Dennis stopped at the front door. "You can see the rest for yourself. This is a little out of my league. If you don't mind, I think I'll head on over to Maggie's. You have help arriving now." He indicated the Oldham County car driving up to the house.

Jake nodded. "Go on. We'll take it from here."

He stepped into the living room and saw why Dennis wanted to leave in such a hurry. Crime scenes were always a little surrealistic, but this one was particularly so. Mrs. Clayton lay peacefully on the couch, looking like she had just fallen asleep, but Jeremy Clayton's body leaned sideways in his desk chair with a hole through his head. The blood and tissue splattered on the wall made the scene even more bizarre. A large handgun lay on the floor near his left hand.

Jake walked over to the sofa and stared at the body. Amanda Clayton. She was the second Mrs. Clayton. Jake's aunt had been the first. Or had she been? Jake had been investigating Clayton even before his aunt's untimely demise fifteen years ago, but he had never found much information. Jeremy Clayton had managed to remain an enigma even in this small town where everyone knew everything about everybody else. One thing for sure, though, there wouldn't be any more Mrs. Claytons.

A Brandy or Three

Dennis pulled into the parking lot at the diner. The café had evolved from a greasy spoon one-room eatery with a dirt floor in 1928 to the present 1950s style diner/malt shop with stucco-covered posts that gave it the flavor of an outpost station. A patio in the back for outdoor dining, a souvenir shop and grocery store completed the new look.

The town of Adrian claimed to be midpoint (1139 miles each way) on the old Route 66 from Chicago to Los Angeles. It was home to twelve businesses and a population of a little more than 150. Maggie's place was the oldest continuously operated cafe on this part of Route 66 and the most popular stop between Amarillo, Texas and Tucumcari, New Mexico. Even though the current Interstate 40 now bypassed Adrian, people still stopped by regularly from as far away as Amarillo to mingle with the locals and enjoy a piece of homemade pie. The Café had changed owners and names several times over the years, but the food and the service remained the same —home-style cooking served with a smile. And if you were Dennis Roscoe, sometimes more than that.

He extracted his rotund figure from behind the wheel and went into the cafe. Pushing aside the last of the red balloons from a Valentine's Day party, he sank into the brown vinyl seat in the back booth, his usual table.

"Put a shot of brandy in it." He pointed to the coffee mug that Maggie had waiting for him. Sitting next to the mug was a slice of her famous chocolate cream pie. The trademark pie was dark and rich but not too sweet and was usually accompanied by stories about Route 66 and the Texas Panhandle. Normally Dennis's favorite, tonight he paid it no notice. After what he had just seen, he needed a boost of the alcoholic variety.

Maggie O'Brian lifted an eyebrow as she retrieved the bottle she kept under the counter for cold winter nights. But tonight was a balmy, for February, 58 degrees. And technically Deputy Roscoe was still on duty until midnight, but she didn't question him. She tipped the bottle over his cup for a count of two.

Dennis gulped down the coffee. "More."

Maggie waved two fingers at the waitress, retrieved a full pot of coffee and another cup and placed her ample derriere in the seat across from Dennis.

"Damn," Dennis muttered as he poured a third portion of brandy into the cup. This time no coffee joined it. He started again. "Damnedest thing. Never saw anything like it."

"Hmmm." Maggie indicated her attention with the single sound.

Dennis continued. "I was still on duty. I had to take the call. Had to. God."

Maggie finally spoke. "I thought you had the north end of town tonight. I didn't hear about any problems there."

"No. No problems there. A call came in about a possible robbery over by the 7-11. I started over, but then the dispatcher said it was under control. I was back here in Adrian when the other call came in. I was the closest one. Damn luck!"

He stared at the empty coffee cup.

"Dennis?" Maggie interrupted the silence. "Dennis? Who called?"

"Mrs. Potts."

"Nosey old Potts?"

"That's right. Old nosey parker Potts. Sees burglars under every bush, Potts." He slapped his forehead. "I thought, why me? What kind of goblin is old crackpot Potts going to have me chasing tonight?"

Maggie rolled her eyes in sympathy.

The waitress appeared at the table with two large platters: waffles and sausage with butter and blackberry syrup for Maggie and grilled ham and egg sandwiches on a heaping bed of hash browns for Dennis.

Dennis smiled. "You always get it right, old girl."

"Figured you'd be needing it about now."

He stared at the eggs. "Damnedest thing," he repeated. "I took one look and called it in. It's gonna be a long night. For Jake."

"Jake? Why?"

Dennis leaned back and stared at a poster hanging on the wall.

Adrian, Texas 1900.

Founded when Rock Island Railroad set up a station in Oldham County. Calvin G. Aten, a former Texas Ranger, was the first to build a dugout for his family west of the site.

Landmarks:

    *Adrian Mercantile and the Adrian Community Center (Formerly Giles Hotel)

    *Bent Door Trading Post

    *Antique Ranch-Mechanic's shop converted into an antique store and eatery.

    *Mid-Point Water Tower

    *Adrian Lions Antique Museum - Antique farm and ranch equipment

    *Maggie's Home-style Cafe

He looked at Maggie and narrowed his eyes. "Hard to believe we're just twenty-five miles from New Mexico."

"Closer than Amarillo, but a world away." Maggie smiled as she remembered trips she and Dennis had taken to New Mexico back in their wilder days.

"Yeah, even on a motorcycle, you hardly have time to get wet in a rainstorm before you're there." He laughed. "Maybe we should try it again sometime."

"Oh no you don't, Mr. Dennis the Menace. We're both a lot less nimble and lean than in those days." She glanced at his pie-fed tummy. "Probably couldn't find a cycle that would hold both of us now."

Dennis nodded toward the door "How about the car then?"

"Your patrol car?"

"That's the only car here, isn't it?"

"You mean now? Are you crazy?"

"Maybe so. But tonight has been bad." He slapped his hand on the table. "Let's just go.

We can come back tomorrow or whenever."

"I can't just up and go like that."

"Sure you can, Mags. It's your place."

She blushed at the old pet name. "God, I'd have to pack a bag ..."

"No bags. Let's go. I'll tell you all about this mess on the way."

Maggie gave him one last doubting look and then set her jaw. She walked back to the bar, removed her apron and whispered something to the waitress.

Mildred's eyes widened. "When will you be back?"

"Whenever." Maggie shrugged as she grabbed her purse and followed Dennis out the door. She smiled, remembering the look of shock on Mildred's face.

Dennis pointed the car toward I-40, the road that would take them to the Glenrio exit at the New Mexico border. This would be a better pick-me-up than a brandy, or three.

Hints of Gardenia

"Detective Monroe?" Two men from the Oldham County Coroner's office stood in the doorway. Jake waved them inside. Normally someone from the coroner's office would show up, take a few photos and file them with the city or county, whichever had jurisdiction, and investigate from that office. But after scanning the scene again, Jake made a call of his own. He wanted his Amarillo crime lab in on this one.

The house belonged to Jake's aunt, but Clayton had stayed on as surviving spouse after her death. Jake wondered if he would inherit it all now. He had always thought there was something fishy about his aunt's death but hadn't found even a whiff of anything else beyond the official report of an accidental fall and the resultant heart failure. Trying to investigate on his own was what had launched him into forensics in the first place. This time he wanted to be an integral part of the investigation. It was personal.

He had the others cordon off the house, front and back. The coroner's assistant agreed to keep watch until Jake could retrieve some belongings from Amarillo. He intended to stay here as long as it took. And he didn't want any nosy parker, Potts or anyone else, disturbing anything.

The next morning the team from Amarillo arrived. A member of the medical examiner's office joined the county representative. Men from the county office spread out to comb the house and grounds.

"This isn't our typical crime here," Jake explained to the medical examiner.

"There is no such thing as a typical crime," the examiner replied as he walked around the room. He stopped by the back wall and scraped a gloved finger across the wall.

"Brains," he said.

"I beg your pardon?" Jake raised an eyebrow.

"Often get bits of brain blown out from a wound like this." He pointed to the Colt .45 semi-automatic lying on the desk. "Depends on the type of round used."

A lady on the team took photos of the bodies and the items on and around the desk. After she finished, the assistant labeled everything and placed it in a large bag, to be transported to the lab. He went on to lift some hairs off the victim's shirt with tweezers.

An empty bottle lay on the floor next to the desk chair. The assistant bent over and sniffed. "Whew. Lots of Scotch." He used his tweezers to pick up a nearby handkerchief. He sniffed again. "And something else. Faint odor. Gardenias?"

He dropped the cloth and bottle into a plastic bag and placed it with the others. The team continued to document the scene in detail and collect physical evidence.

Jake retreated to the solarium at the back of the house. His aunt's first husband had built it for her. Clayton hated anything to do with plants and had avoided this area. It was her refuge. The horse barn and pen at the edge of the five-acre property was Clayton's realm. Jake had always wondered about a man who was so good with horses and yet so terrible with people.

He headed over to an oversized wicker chair in the far corner. Settling into the deep cushions, he let his thoughts return to the subject of Mrs. Potts. Fifteen years ago, when Jake was finishing his bachelor's degree at A&M, Verna Potts, then only 70, had called in a disturbance.

Police had found his aunt dead that night. He had received a call about the death at school but was not able to make it back home until after finals.

Clayton had told the ambulance crew that she fell off a ladder and suffered a massive heart attack. The paramedics pronounced her dead on arrival. The coroner ruled it accidental death. Jake never believed it.

He thought about his aunt. She always called him Jacob.

"Aw, Aunt Alice," he complained. "Call me Jake. Jacob is so not with it."

"With it?" she always asked. "With what exactly, would that be, that I can't call my own nephew by his proper name? And such a good name. My grandfather's name was Jacob and his mother's uncle before him. It's a good name, for good men."

Aunt Alice had been fussy, a perfectionist, so neat and clean she could hardly stand company in her house, but her heart was sweet and she had loved him. She had provided him with enough love and encouragement to make up for the lack of it in the rest of his life. Not that there was any real abuse at home—no hitting or drunkenness, some of the other things a few of his friends had to go through. But there was little love, less warm affection, or even much interest in him from his parents. If it hadn't been for his aunt, he would not be who he was today.

He had always blamed Clayton for his aunt's decline in health. Trying to find some sliver of evidence that would tie Clayton directly to her death had sent him down the path he now trod. Perhaps now he would discover some of the missing pieces.

"Mr. Monroe?" The assistant interrupted.

"Yes?" Jake looked up.

"We found a box with some papers and a few photos."

"In his safe?"

"This was in his desk." He held out a dusty metal box. "But there are more boxes in a safe or maybe you could call it a vault—behind a sliding bookcase, just like in the movies. Looks like some of the items go way back. We've finished listing the contents in this one. The coroner thought you would be interested."

He placed the box on the table next to Jake.

Jake pulled an old notebook from the top of the pile and opened it to page one. He began to read.

"I plotted vengeance against my father from the age of eight, but I never got a chance to act on it."

The Yoke of Dawn
By Nicole Justine Cavanaugh

The yoke of dawn stumbles over the hills.

I see her through the soft cages around my eyes
Gasping to inhale her brightness of being sudden shudders

The darkness, a slow, pulling embrace.
A pressure to come home to rest just a bit longer

And in these blurry moments, the
reel of my mind spins to you –
Memories shot at me Russian-Roulette style to
tip me at the cracking open of day:

into a slow, sweet slip and sigh

Or – jarred carelessly over the edge,
my brightness crashing on the floor,
my tender cocoon broken
Oozing –

Catch and Release
A partial novel chapter
By Madeline McEwen

CHAPTER ONE

Mythri Gupta, a tall, athletic student, unrolled the last campaign flyer—"Stop the Honor Killings"—one of a hundred. The photo of the latest victim, a girl with almond eyes and western clothes, was plastered all over San Jose Campus at Inkwells Community College, a warning to raise awareness. Their hotline number was emblazoned across the bottom. Had they won over public opinion? Tolerance only went so far, and outrage galvanized the community.

Mythri's hands chaffed. The light was failing, and the stored up heat oozed and rose out of the blacktop in the Californian night. The rest of the campaigners had drifted away.

Why was she the only one left? Didn't they care? Or had the initial enthusiasm waned. Who wanted to spend a Saturday evening posting flyers when there were dates and parties waiting?

Holding the flyer against the post, Mythri tacked it in place, nicking herself on a jagged wooden splinter. Standing back to admire her work, she saw a smear of her own blood across the paper flyer, casually scarring victim's brow. Mythri sucked her finger, satisfied it was worth the sacrifice. If four hours of flyer posting saved only one life, then not a minute was wasted.

The headline was bold, defiant, and assertive. If that didn't get the message across, then nothing would.

Not far away, Amita Chase, petite and petrified, pulled her dog close and hurried home along the narrow street. It was dark. She was late. Cowboy, her black lab gave her strength, like a talisman to ward off evil. Why had she wasted those last few minutes chatting in the changing room? She should have left straight away to beat Dad's curfew. Was someone following her?

She glanced behind her at a shadowy figure. Was it Lalit, the guy who leered at her in the cafeteria every day? She knew there was something wrong with him. Nobody liked him. Coincidence? He, if it was a he, also had a dog. Was she imagining it? Hadn't she just learned about facing your tormentors, standing up for yourself, being your own advocate? Was the point of assertiveness training if at the first glimpse of danger, she turned tail and ran? His steps sounded louder and his dog's claws rhythmically scraped the blacktop. She must confront him.

"Call off your dog." Her voice had conviction, more than she imagined. The mutt—neither Rottweiler nor boxer—snapped and snarled at the end of a long retractable leash. The owner holding the leash, not Lalit, but a taller guy, sidled over, Caucasian and casual, comfortable in his blue jeans and startlingly white T-shirt. His chest seemed to gleam in the moonlight, bloated with entitlement. "He just wants to play," he said, smiling, showing his teeth, more like a sneer.

"That's not play." She struggled forward hauling one hundred and six pounds of quaking Labrador. "Can you call him off?"

"T-bone just wants to be friends," he said. "Me too. I heard you're a friendly girl, a real easy friendly girl."

Amita winced, nothing was a secret on campus. She knew his type, big dog, flashy car, mega ego.

"I said, can you call him off? Who's the alpha male here? You or your dog?" She made for the house, increasing the pace, hoping to widen the gap.

"Bitch."

"Leave me alone." Nearly home, almost there.

"Fucking bitch."

"Do the world a favor," she shrieked over her shoulder, "—get yourself neutered." Turning, she crashed straight into her father, Abhay, his face a brittle sheet of slate, eyes narrow, lips tight. Cowboy whimpered, and Dad stroked the dog's velvet ears with rare gentleness. "Some guard dog you are!

"The man and his mutt had caught up, but his steps faltered seeing her father.

"I'll deal with this," Abhay said to Amita. "Please, take Cowboy inside."

It wasn't a request. Amita obeyed, but hovered behind the door to listen. Her father placated the man in his 'reasonable and rational voice,' the one he saved for anyone outside the immediate family. He played the humble immigrant, his broken English disguising his professional status. "Be quick," Gran said, fluttering her hands free from the light fabric of her sari. "Get to bed before he's done."

Amita made for the stairs taking three at a time with Cowboy galloping behind. They both panted with exhaustion and relief, but Amita shut Cowboy out in the hall, this once, and locked the door.

The next morning, Amita listened to her father padding around next door in his bedroom and then downstairs in the kitchen preparing his breakfast. She waited another twenty minutes until she was sure he'd gone. It was Wednesday. A late start for her, but not for him. Abhay's shift began at six.

Luckily, Inkwells College was walking distance. Dad worked there as a janitor, where Amita was enrolled as a student. She knew he took that job deliberately. Who needed a chaperone with a paternal protector prowling round every corner? But it was hopeless. He hadn't saved Mom, couldn't control everyday random events, like Mom's death beneath the wheels of a semi truck—driver asleep. Dad's efforts were futile.

Mom was asleep forever, or that's what people said. They tried to be kind saying—"She's not really gone, she's watching over you, always." That didn't help, despite their good intentions. They made it worse, creepy. Could Mom see her now, naked in front of the mirror checking for fat? No. Mom wasn't there. Amita was completely alone locked in her own body, caged in her own mind, and never free from the desperate gloom. This wasn't a home. Couldn't be without Mom, like an empty shell when the oyster's shucked.

Mom had kept dad in check, but without her influence, modern and western, they drifted. Dad's obsessions took hold.

His paranoia about dangers around every corner. Threats to the three of them: her, Dad, and Gran. Amita heard Gran singing old songs, familiar and comforting. At least Gran was protected. That was a better way to think of dementia, like a force-field for the mind. Everything stayed the same for

Gran, the present wiped out, stuck in the past. Most of the time. The odd blink of lucidity struck.

"Where's Salome, your Mom? Is she coming home? Has Salome left?"

Tears of rage followed until Amita calmed Gran down. This was her role, now Mom was dead, Gran's guard and advocate.

Mom and Dad had quarreled about Gran. "She's the mother-in- law-from-hell," Mom shouted. Amita listened and hid, but Dad hit back, venomous with rage and frustration. "A firebrand just like you," he said.

Without Mom by his side, Amita and Dad had learned to cope on their own. Dad didn't abandon Gran, or stick her in a residential home, or ship her back to the old country. Many would have, but not Dad. He craved order, peace and predictability, and Gran was none of those. She was more like Mom: warm, wild, and eccentric.

Maybe that was what killed her? Who else would run to the grocery store so late at night, on a whim, in a flurry of excitement to buy candles? Candles at nearly midnight? What was in Mom's head? Why the urgency? Amita still couldn't make sense of it. They had everything they wanted ahead of them in their adopted country and new home: freedom, safety and opportunities until that moment.

Dad's explanation made no sense when he told Amita later how Mom had clutched the candle when they put her on the gurney, and rushed her to the hospital, but it wasn't any use—the virgin candle was never lit, and yet snuffed out.

Break Away
By Jeannine Gerkman

Don't let 'em rent space in your head,
Kill your spirit or
Feed your dread.
No more "uh oh", here we go
Wildly spinning vertigo.
Your mind's elastic,
You can break free,
They're just plastic,
You hold the key
To break away in brilliant sunshine
Find yourself in dappled shade
You are beautiful
And so's your mind.
Golden filigree set with jade.

Table for Two
By Kimberly Schultz

The sound of Candace's nervous finger taps hitting the table top were drowned out by the sounds of the bustling café. "Why did I pick a café?" Candace thought as she blew the wispy smoke billowing from her hot cocoa. Candace inhaled the warm aroma of freshly brewed coffee into her lungs. The smell relaxed her. Although she didn't drink the stuff, she loved the smell. It calmed her in a not-so-calm situation.

Candace looked at her watch for the tenth time in five minutes. "She is late," Candace thought. "I am on my second cup of hot cocoa and she is late." Candace sat with nervousness building in her stomach as she listened to the sounds of grinding coffee, steaming milk, and porcelain mugs clinking together. She felt her stomach pinch with the excitement of today's breakthrough. The stifled smile she struggled to contain finally broke free. Though, the more she smiled, the more nervous she became. Taking deep breaths, Candace tried to control her feelings that were shifting from hopeful to doubtful every few seconds.

"Can I take this mug?" a barista asked, standing in front of Candace's table, startling her out of her thoughts. Candace didn't know how long the nervous barista must have been standing in front of her. Her smile tightened and she awkwardly shifted her weight from one foot to the other. The other two baristas behind the enormous espresso machine ducked from view, avoiding Candace's glance when she looked their way. They must have sent this girl over to her table. Her green apron was filthy with brown and chalky white stains and she stood in front of Candace with a dingy white rag hanging from one hand, her other hand reaching for the empty mug sitting on the table.

"Yes, please," Candace said, giving the barista a tight-lipped grin. The barista picked up the white mug and slowly walked away.

Baristas didn't just come to your table and act as your personal server. Candace knew she was overstaying her welcome, but she just couldn't conjure enough strength to pull herself up from the wobbly chair she was sitting in and walk out the door. Her legs were cramping up and her feet occasionally filled with pins and needles, but she just couldn't leave. Her sister was late. Not just ten minutes. Not a half hour. She was two hours late. The hours disappeared as the hands moved faster around the clock. Any remaining nervousness left in the pit of her stomach was replaced by a hard and heavy feeling of rejection. The thought of not reconciling their relationship brought tears to Candace's eyes. She held on to any little hope she had left and desperately watched the door hoping to see her sister rush into the café and frantically look around, searching for her. She would spot Candace at the table in the back and work her way around the long line of ornery people waiting for their caffeine fix. She would stand in front of Candace's table out of breath and say, "I'm sorry I'm late, but..."

"But would her sister apologize?" Candace thought. Would she utter those words that Candace waited to hear her say for over ten years? The day they stopped talking was engraved in Candace's memories like it happened just yesterday. Candace remembered how her sister could not look her in the eyes during their mother's funeral. She became even more distant as the lawyer recited the will. Hanging onto every word the monotone lawyer said, Candace realized that her sister and her husband changed their mother's will, giving her only a small percentage of their mother's assets. Feelings of betrayal thrust her into a horrible anger she couldn't gain control of. "Unless you give me half of what I am entitled to, I don't want anything more to do with you!" Candace yelled at her sister. Her sister felt entitled to the majority of their mom's assets leaving Candace no choice but to stop talking to her.

Days of not talking turned into months. Then those months turned into years. Gathering the entire family together for birthday parties; sharing moments of laughter around a large Thanksgiving Day table; ripping through Christmas wrapped presents were all moments lost. Candace lost precious moments watching her nephew grow up. He graduated from high school, bought his first car, and was off to college.

"Excuse me," a short, stocky woman with curly brown hair said, interrupting Candace's thoughts. For a brief moment, Candace thought this woman standing in front of her table could be her sister.

Candace wasn't sure if she would be able to recognize her since she hadn't seen her in years. Her sister's hair was curly like this woman's hair. But it was not as frizzy and short as this woman's hair was. And this woman was short. Her sister was not short.

"Yes?" Candace asked searching this woman's round face for a clue that might lead to her sister. "Are you using this chair?" she asked. Her hand was wrapped around the empty chair and she was slowly pulling the chair toward her as if to claim it for herself.

"Yes!" Candace shouted, a little too loud. Her voice echoed throughout the café and heads turned her way. When there was nothing to see, everyone went back to impatiently fiddling with their phones waiting for their coffees. Startled, the woman whipped her hand back from the chair.

"Yes, I am expecting company," Candace said, shooting up from her seat and reaching for the chair. There was a sense of urgency in her voice that even she didn't recognize. The woman pulled her hand back and took a step away from the chair. She scurried away, stopping to ask a couple at the table by the front door if they were using their extra chair.

Candace sat back down at her table embarrassed by her reaction. She hung her head and fiddled with her mug. She took a small sip of her hot cocoa, which was no longer hot. The cold liquid sliding down her throat almost made her gag. The chime of the bell above the café door caused Candace to look up suddenly. A man walked in and stood in line for coffee. Candace took a deep breath, pushing away the tears that were pulsating behind her eyeballs.

"She will come," Candace whispered. "She will come."

But the thought of her sister not showing up was becoming more apparent the longer she sat alone at the table for two. Looking at her watch, she realized that her sister was now three hours late.

The orange glow from the setting sun shone against the back wall of the café. A hurried barista made her way around the café hoisting chairs onto tables. She stopped at the front door and flipped the open sign to closed. Candace stood up, her body aching from sitting so long. Her legs were numb and her back stiff. She collected her purse and jacket and wandered past the baristas avoiding eye contact.

Her tears blurred her eyes, but she refused to let them fall.

"Have a good night," the barista sweeping the crumbs from under a table called out.

"Thank you," Candace said, her voice quivering as it left her mouth. She hung her head, the tears falling uncontrollably now. She pushed open the café door and the chill in the air hit her tear-stricken face. She stood in the middle of the sidewalk, her whole body violently thrusting with every sob.

Strangers made their way around her in a blur.

"Are you okay?" a young man asked, stopping in front of her. His hair was as brown as milk chocolate, his face as pale as cream. His strong jaw line replaced his once chubby round cheeks. The sweetness in his voice made the pain evaporate. Ten years helped the young boy she used to know grow into a man she had yet to meet.

"My nephew," Candace whispered. She looked up and down the long narrow street that was now deserted. "Where is..." Candace began her voice trailing off with the solemn look on her nephew's face. "I am the one that emailed you from my mom's account. My mom passed away last year," he said.

Crayons
By Darlene Schwartz

Red, yellow, blue, green
Crayons in a box
As a youth you color the pictures
Using all the colors of the
rainbow
Imagination is for the making
The crayons fall to the floor
It does not really matter
You quickly pick them up
Red, yellow, blue, green
Crayons in a box
You color the pictures with your
child
Using all the colors of the
rainbow
Imagination is for sharing
The crayons fall to the floor
It does not really matter
Your child is quick to pick them
up

Red, yellow, blue, green
Crayons in a box
You are alone
Your child has grown
You open the box of crayons
You stare at them
You cannot remember the names
of the colors
You are confused
The crayons fall to the floor
You are unable to bend down to
pick them up
You stare down at them as they
stare back at you
Crayons trying to remind you
Of all the colors of the rainbow.

Raindrop Flies to Heaven
By Michele Jessen

I met an angel, caught upon her garment's fold
To the heavens above, lifted awareness yet untold

As I flew along clinging to her hem
Where reality enlightens each being's gem

Where rainbows laugh conversing in tones unknown below
Where pixies watch over worldly visions that grow

From sleeping dreamers, open to what lies beyond
Treetops stretch to bend clouds with every frond

Rising on tiptoe, she lifted me to her cheek
To caress her lashes and hear her speak

In the flutter of her wings and the speak of her eyes
In the breathe of her skin, rhythmic heavy sighs

Made known was I, to be a mere droplet, less
Unable to walk and to talk as humans progress

As if significance, were all that mattered
As if my new awareness, could be scattered
Dispersed cosmic beauty lost, awareness shattered
Knowledge cannot be undone, flattened, splattered

Reminded of my place within this great mass
Of earth, land and water, to return so crass
Blinded to my race, replaced anew...alas

Bent to conceal me warm under feathered wings
As a fledgling seraphim, rejection to sing

Made to return among my kind
Down I fell unwrapped to find

My humble dew bent on the frond's fold
Slipping shinny nodding, upon leaves so cold

My sparkles melted, rainbows reflected
My glimmers gone and faded, never connected

Blending blurring, crowded pooled puddles
I joined masses, as they huddle and muddle

One to another, as many one Forced to
Fathom communal numb

Enlightenment Disengages Unassuming,
left behind sages

Yet I do not belong I'll rise solitary and proud
Chancing to touch an angel on the next cloud

Fore (4) Warnings
By Evelyn Safiri

(1) I am descended of Celtic Warrior Queens
　　　　And I am always triumphant and merciless in battle.
　　　　　　Whatever you do,
　　　　　　　　Don't slay with me -
　　　　　　　　　　I don't turn off that easily!

(2) And I have been known to hooooowwwwl at the moon,
　　　　While we spoon at the water's edge until the sun comes up.
　　　　　　Whatever you do,
　　　　　　　　Don't bay with me -
　　　　　　　　　　I don't turn off that easily!

(3) And I have a direct pipeline to God
　　　　And we commune sweetly and deeply for hours on end.
　　　　　　Whatever you do,
　　　　　　　　Don't pray with me -
　　　　　　　　　　I don't turn off that easily!

(4) And I will love you far beyond a mere human lifespan
　　　　And I can **still** ignite an all-consuming fire in your tired eyes.
　　　　　　But (For tonight, at least),
　　　　　　　　It is best,
　　　　　　　　　　My Darling,
　　　　　　　　　　　　That you rest.
　　　　And
　　　　　　Whatever you do,
　　　　　　　　Don't play with me,
　　　　　　　　　　Don't lay with me,
　　　　In fact,
　　　　　　Don't even think about having your way with me -
　　　　　　Because
　　　　　　　　　　You know...
　　　　　　　　　　　　(I do not turn off that easily!)

Knock on the Door of the House Where You Lived
By Kevin Arnold

CWC Most Promising Writer

Wade didn't like to think about why he'd waited decades to return to Barrington. His mother abused prescription drugs and alcohol and his father had a hard time keeping a job; high school had not been an experience he was anxious to revisit.

Leaving from the airport in San Francisco, Wade scribbled down the start of a list, or even a poem: Step One: Wait Twenty-seven Years.

The expensive suburb made him feel especially poor since his first love, Barbara, from a wealthy family, had unexpectedly left him. Wade used frequent-flyer miles to upgrade. Step Two: Go First Class.

How lush and green the land was as the airplane descended into O'Hare airport. His eyes filled with tears and he felt a little woozy. When he deplaned, he was pleased a shiny blue sedan waited for him, trunk raised for his luggage, another frequent-flier benefit. At least I'm not returning home in a potato truck.

He drove to the prospect's location, Hinsdale, a suburb twenty minutes south from the airport, where he met with a group of local investors who wanted to refurbish nine theaters. Wade's job was to sell them sound systems. He impressed them not only by his product, but by using pictures of their own theaters in his presentation. When they responded positively, Wade called his boss to negotiate a discounted price they could present to their board of directors. Pleased, Wade drove on to Barrington, thirty-five miles north.

The terrain seemed inexplicably familiar. He'd heard of a new concept in physics that says people are connected to their place on earth through patterns in the earth's molecular structure. He felt remarkably at home under towering white clouds, the kind he seldom saw in California.

Rather than heading to the northern part of Barrington, where he'd finished elementary school, Wade first drove into the center of town. Its rural feel was moving toward upscale suburban. He felt he was in two worlds—real people were walking about, looking like the people he'd seen in California that very same morning, but they were walking on streets that belonged in his childhood. He suddenly knew Step Three: Hit All the Old Haunts.

He passed the barbershop, its red-and-blue pole still swirling as it had when he was young. On haircut days, he would run the six or seven blocks from high school into town to get a jump on the other boys. It was Wade's earliest brush with tempis fugit; five minutes could save him an hour.

He drove past the high school, which, because it supported miles and miles of surrounding farm country, was surprisingly large. The school's clay-colored brick core was three stories, with wings of classrooms that protruded into the northern Illinois plains. He spotted the English classroom where

Mrs. Hautch introduced him to poetry. Wade had disappointed her. After her encouragement on his writing, Wade had worked hard to get into college, and earned an 'A-' the first semester of his senior year. But he'd slacked off after the college applications were in. She'd looked so pained when she handed the first quiz back with a 'D' on top—et tu, Wade?

Wade hung a U-turn and headed back to town. He searched for the drive-in, The Spot. It was the place Wade thought of when he watched American Graffiti, which he'd seen three times. That would be a good feeling to recapture.

Long before Spielberg's movie, Wade had cruised The Spot slowly in his dad's Pontiac Catalina, bought right before he'd lost his last job. Tonight Wade drove to The Spot in minutes, but when he found the place, the drive-in was gone, replaced with a Ten-Minute-Lube. He sighed, saying goodbye to long summer evenings and chocolate malts.

As the sun set among the massive clouds, he left town and drove north toward his home, turning in to North Barrington Elementary School. From there he traced the path he used to walk to his house with his friends. Ancient conversations came back to him: What about the Giants swarming out of the dugout to throw punches at Don Drysdale? Adults don't beat each other up, do they? Why did God put sex the same place where you go to the bathroom?

Unlike those slow walks, today's drive from school to his old house took just minutes. When he saw his childhood home, now with two modest cars in the driveway, he almost turned around. But this was why he came, right? What he should do is knock on the front door. Any chance they'd let me in?

Step Four: Knock on the Door of the House Where You Lived. When he worked up his nerve and rapped on the door, a woman's voice answered from a distant part of the house. "Who is it?"

He took a step back, not to seem too aggressive. "My name is Wade Middleton. I used to live here."

She opened the door wider, revealing her short gray hair and bright, kind eyes. Wade thought the style they called her hair was a "pixie." She introduced herself as Martha. "How long ago?" she asked, still tentative.

"I left in the early eighties. You've sure kept it up."

She opened the door wider. "Oh, we came in ninety-four. Come in."

A man with rolled-up sleeves stared out from the darkness inside the house. "I'm Tom," he said. "You say you're from California?"

Wade entered a foyer next to the living room. Looking at the intricate wood ceiling and stone fireplace, he said, "I don't remember it being so elegant."

Tom put down some wire-cutters he had in his hand and moved reluctantly forward. "I spent three months sanding down the ceiling. It had been painted over. Everything needed work. The toughest was the crawl space—the slightest rain would fill it up."

Wade remembered problems his dad couldn't fix. "So, Tom, what do you do?"

"I'm the vice principal at a high school on the North side, where Martha teaches English. It's a long commute, but we love the rural feel out here. How about you?"

"Oh, I work for a company that wires movie houses for sound; that's my day job anyway. I also write some poems."

"Really? Martha, where's that old book I found?"

"It's around here someplace—I just saw it last week. I'll make some coffee.

Tom, why don't you take him upstairs."

Wade followed Tom up a short stairway to a small room set among the sloping roofs. "This was my older sister's room." It had a tiny balcony overlooking the front yard. "I think she might have snuck out once or twice."

Tom laughed. "We raised a daughter in here, too. Maybe she did as well."

He and Tom walked into Wade's old room, built over the two-car garage. He could almost touch the plasterboard ceiling. "As I was growing up here, an aspiring basketball player, I used to jump to the ceiling, no more than oh, ten or twenty thousand times."

Tom laughed.

Wade had loved basketball in eighth grade, when he practiced shots for hours and made the team. He found his moment of glory when he'd fashioned an improbable hook shot to win a game. But he never grew past five foot nine, and when he got to high school the townies, from a bigger school with real coaching, ran circles around him.

He stopped in the hallway up on the next level when he saw his parents' room, where his mother often lay when he came home. Each day was slightly different. Sometimes she would be lucid but argumentative. The worst days she would lie barely conscious, sometimes half-dressed, her speech slurred. Another step came to him. Step Five: Inside Your Old House, Hold Yourself Together.

The thing about an alcoholic that you never get over is that you're always less important to them than their habit. These memories would keep anyone away, probably forever. Wade knew he'd stopped talking, but couldn't be social again. He started down the stairs with Tom behind him.

In the kitchen, Martha had filled three coffee mugs. "This house had had five or six owners in just a few years, and two divorces. The neighbors called it 'the troubled house.' Tom and I bought it after a young man's fatal car wreck."

Martha handed Tom a slim book, an old paperback with cardboard covers.

After he glanced at it for a second, Tom handed it to Wade. "I found it between joists in the crawl space off your old bedroom."

Wade fingered it. "101 Favorite Poems. I vaguely remember it, I'm pretty sure. It's a wonderful find."

Martha topped off the mugs. "Read and see if it brings back any memories."

Wade thought he might have remembered his father reading "Jes for Christmas" aloud to him and his sister. Could it have been from this book? Then he spotted his carefully-inscribed initials, WM, one the upside-down of the other, on the flyleaf. It was his. He kept reading.

Martha asked, "Are these the kind of poems you write?"

"Well I don't rhyme mine much. Sometimes. But these are great. Here, listen to the way Kipling starts 'If':

If you can keep your head when all about you

Are losing theirs and blaming it on you,
      If you can trust yourself when all men doubt you,
            But make allowance for their doubting too;"

Martha smiled warmly. "It should be yours."

Wade shook his head. "No, I couldn't take it from you. But here's the part everybody remembers, the last stanza:
If you can fill the unforgiving minute
      With sixty seconds' worth of distance run,
Yours is the Earth and everything that's in it,
      And—which is more—you'll be a Man, my son!"

Wade remembered wishing he had a father who would talk to him like that. We ask so much of our parents. Be here now. He looked at his hosts.

"Maybe I should work on rhyming mine more—there's a power there."

"It's yours now." Martha looked at Tom, who nodded in agreement.

Wade started to refuse it, but the next step came to him: Step Six: Accept Life's Gifts. "Well thank you, I'd love it."

Wade drove west toward the horsey-estates side of town, Barrington Hills. He passed the Country Club where he'd worn his first tux to escort Barbara to a cotillion. It wasn't until he took a right on Otis Road that he realized he was headed for Barbara's house. Step Seven: Ferret out the Pain.

That summer they'd spent so much time together, Barbara had sewn two sheets together. She would pretend to retire and slip out her first-floor window and join him in the barn, which, fortunately, wasn't visible from the house. Wade remembered the night when he gathered dry straw and Barbara stuffed it into the sheets, handful after handful, until they'd packed their love nest. He had never been happier than when he drank in her nakedness or, better still, held her, made love to her. He loved her confidence; that she opened herself to him without fear. In her warmth, Wade's concerns about his family and his future faded. They were in love—what else could it be—and that made everything right.

He never understood why she had broken up with him. They were going to school a thousand miles apart when the phone calls became less frequent, and her letters, which had been filled with details of her days and specific longings for him, stopped. Her father, a big-league banker, didn't like Wade. He referred to him as Barbara's "beau." Perhaps her father had convinced her to stop seeing him, maybe even with a reward. Wade would never know for sure, but that spring he did give her a new yellow convertible.

But that could just be paranoia. His letters to Barbara were, comparatively, sketchy. Maybe he hadn't let her know how special he thought she was. Maybe that was a lesson he needed to learn.

Barbara had become a raw memory, the girl who walked away. The sight of her father's name on the mailbox made Wade feel almost as hopeless as he had in his mother's room.

Lost in the memory of the many times he'd met Barbara at the barn, he walked toward the dark structure.

Lights went on everywhere, and a bell clanged. Dogs started howling. He must have tripped a security alarm. He sprinted back to his car in his leather-soled shoes, slipping—once scraping his hand so it bled—before he drove off. When he was well down the road, a glance in his rear-view mirror showed a police cruiser at her barn, red and blue lights pulsing.

On the night flight back to San Francisco, Wade was again up in the first class cabin. He befriended the man next to him. Unlike Wade, his tie wasn't loosened. Wade watched him remove his wingtips and change into slippers he carried in his briefcase. Wade admired how relaxed he seemed. He's a lot more organized than I am, a real traveler.

After some prodding, the man divulged that he was a University provost, which sounded vaguely powerful and learned. He introduced himself as Peter, with a long last name Wade couldn't quite distinguish.

When Wade pulled out the book Martha and Tom had given him, 101 Favorite Poems, the provost interrupted him. "That book looks familiar. May I see it?"

Wade handed it to him.

"I had a book like this back in high school," he said, handling the volume like a curator. "Mine wasn't this tattered, but close. It's a classic— Wordsworth, Shelly, Lord Byron—look, first copyrighted 1873. Moving toward 150 years. Imagine." He handed it back. "So, what do you do with your life?"

Shyly at first, since the man seemed so accomplished, Wade described his life in Palo Alto. "And lately I have a new lady in my life. Sometimes I feel I've found the right one, but . . . right now we're apart," Wade concluded.

"Palo Alto's a nice town. It's where I met my wife."

Wade envisioned Peter with a happy marriage. "So, do you have kids?"

Peter looked away. "My wife's no longer with us. She got cancer very young. No children."

"Oh my." He touched Peter's shoulder. "How did you get through?"

Peter shrugged. "I threw myself into my work."

Wade raised his eyebrows. "That seems to be what we guys do." He took a deep breath. He felt like when he stood outside his old house—he had an urge to take a chance. "I hate to impose," he blurted out, "but I'd like a little help here. I have seven steps for a poem or article on going home. I need one more."

"Steps?" Peter asked. "I don't know what you mean."

"Pretend you had to choose one pithy thing to say to people who are returning home after a long time. What would it be?"

"Distill life into one statement?" Peter laughed wryly and shook his head.

"All right, what have you got already?"

Wade talked him through the steps. He smiled when Wade told him Wait 27 years, Go First Class, Hit All the Old Haunts, and Knock on the Door of the House Where You Lived, but looked concerned when he mentioned Inside Your Old House, Hold Yourself Together. He smiled again at Accept Life's Gifts, and said, "Good advice there, people have the hardest time accepting gifts, but they resent it when they don't get them!" He laughed.

When Wade mentioned Ferret out the Pain, Peter looked at him like a country doctor doing a diagnosis. Wade didn't want analysis, he wanted a last step. "Whatever you say the last one is, that's it."

The provost said, "I'll think about it," and returned to the poetry book.

296

A half hour later, as the pilot announced the plane was on final approach, his seatmate looked at Wade.

Wade quickly said, "So do you have one for me?'

"I might. The one I concentrate on is about holding yourself together. This guy's confidence ebbs and flows. The trip home brings out his insecurities."

Wade didn't want to push deeper. "I guess. So . . .what's the last step?"

"This isn't going to end up in some newspaper as what the provost says, right?"

Wade laughed. "No, I'll steal it as my own, I promise."

"We need to buck this guy up. Kipling's poem encourages trust. Trust yourself when all men doubt you. Things have always gone better for me when I do that. How about just Trust Yourself?"

Wade hesitated. The step didn't sound as final as he'd hoped, and too easy somehow. But . . . this was a gift, and one of the steps was Accept Life's Gifts. If he took it, the list would be complete. Done.

In the terminal, just beyond the security exit, a buffed-out Hispanic driver in a Navy sport coat and tie waited for the provost. Wade thought he saw the bulge of a gun near the driver's shoulder as he shook Peter's hand. "So it's Step Eight: Trust Yourself?"

The provost nodded and said, "I fly quite a bit, and this might be the strangest thing that's ever happened to me on a plane. Still, I'd like to read what you finally come up with." With that, he handed Wade a business card, clapped him lightly on the shoulder, turned, and walked off with his driver.

Fruit of the Poisonous Tree
By Madeline McEwen

Laura, a Christian, lied as frequently as necessary, but only when she could do so with good conscience. Big lies came later. She started in a small way, like the time her mother offered temptation in the winter of 1972 when Laura was eight.

"You can stay home on your own while I run to the store," Mom said. "Would you like the responsibility of being a big girl?"

Laura, coddled and ambitious, nodded gravely and let her dark eyes go big. Mom liked that, it smacked of sincerity. Mom did the same thing when Dad spoke to her. She called it "demure" and "ladylike." A nice way to act, the way dad expected women to behave. Like many former addicts, he was a man of deep convictions and high principles, a lay preacher with upstanding values, now he'd left the black-jack tables behind him.

Mom brushed her hair at the dresser in her bedroom. Laura watched Mom's reflection in the tryptic mirrors revealing every flaw. "Striking," that's how they described Mom. Not pretty or beautiful. Dad said she was handsome, which was odd. Weren't men described as handsome? A fine layer of dust dredged the glass surface, but aura saw the thumbprint on the portrait of herself as a little girl with some unknown boy. A cousin? A friend? Whoever he was, Dad hated him--a gambler, a wastrel, and a lady's man. Mom defended him, "You'll never understand, Teddy." Was that his real name? No, Teddy was short for Edward.

"I won't be long," Mom had said. "Read the good book while I'm gone. You know your father's standards. Will you do that?"

Laura nodded again. This movement betrayed her, but she hadn't spoken a lie, unlike Mom who wasn't going to the store, not on a Saturday afternoon when Laura had her weekly piano lesson. Everyone in Laura's class wanted to watch the next episode of the serial, and Laura wanted to be one of them. None of her friends had piano lessons. None of them were either "demure," or "ladylike."

As soon as Laura had woken up that morning, the thought of watching the show, or rather, sitting at the piano stool while everyone else was watching the show, made Laura madder than scalded milk. Why should Mom get to meet with her secret friend, while Laura practiced boring scales? It wasn't fair. Besides, Laura knew about Edward Gunner. No big secret there, except from Dad.

Laura didn't say she had a sore throat nor pretend. Instead, she played with her pancakes and allowed a small cough to escape, more of a throat clearing. Her hang-dog expression caught her father's attention.

"That child's off-color, Evelyn," he said, snapping the top of the newspaper. "Shouldn't she be in bed? I can't afford to catch anything, ot when I'm meeting with the bank on Tuesday."

He reached across the breakfast table and put a cool palm on her forehead. Laura knew she was cheating, but she didn't care.

"Check her temperature too." His opinion confirmed the diagnosis, decisive, ambitious, and driven. "I'll be back late, don't hold dinner."

Kissing Laura on the cheek, smoothing her dark hair, he left without another word.

Evelyn, Laura's Mom, crashed around the kitchen, tight-lipped. How did it feel to have your plans ruined? Laura knew, and waited. She longed to curl up on the sofa and watch the show together, like they used to do, before Dad recognized the evils of sloth.

Who'd want to see Edward, when you could stay home with your only daughter instead? Edward reminded her of molasses, oily black hair, and shiny skinned. He spoke breathily, through reddish plump lips. They'd be soft to touch, like a girl's. Mom wanted to touch them. Laura could tell by the way Mom looked at him, all big-eyed on the night when they had hosted a cocktail party for potential investors.

"Delicious," Edward had said, formally dressed in a tux two sizes too small. He pierced a meatball with a toothpick. "My favorite. Your mother's so talented," he said, but spoke to the huddle of men around him, his eyes following Evelyn flitting from group to group.

The guests had divided themselves by sex, small collections of women, pairs and threesomes, and lumps of men, suited and dense like the heart of a forest blocking out the light.

Laura glanced at the rounded black patent toes of her own shoes and then her mom's high heels, every bit as high as the other ladies'. None of them had admired Laura's shoes, or even acknowledged her, invisible at elbow height.

Tension prickled through the air, all on account of the cash. They called it 'finance,' but they meant money, for Dad's business expansion.

Laura didn't understand everything, but she knew enough. Edward, the maybe millionaire, knew about money. You could tell by his big house, flashy car, and all the diamonds on his wife, though she looked more like a grandma. Those diamonds weren't paste—Dad said.

Dad had started going to the golf club for lunch at the weekends, even though he didn't play and didn't own any clubs. He hated golf. He liked bowling and loved playing with Laura. They always had the best time together. They hadn't gone for weeks, not since all the trouble of the money. Money had changed. Now it was important and tight, whereas before it never really mattered.

Mom had snatched back the empty tray of meatballs to refill with tiny succulent wieners. That was Laura's job: "take this one instead, circulate, be polite, offer them to everyone, not just the women, be brave, men don't bite." Laura wore her black velvet dress, the one with the ribbon, like Mom's but with a different neckline. A sweet-heart shape for Mom so you could see the necklace, eye-catching, but "made of paste." Mom fingering the chain with coral pink nails. The warm pearl wedged itself between her breasts. It looked stupid stuck there. Dad said it looked cheap. He never liked costume jewelry.

The messages from that night were too subtle to understand, but Laura caught the gist, enough to adjust her behavior. Although she didn't miss another piano lesson after that, Laura noticed more. Her harried mother once the finances were secured. How much harder Dad worked, rarely home. The infrequency of family time, family holidays, family in general. Dad got thin. Mom got fat. Divorce was just around the corner, and a coronary a few blocks further down, but by that time Laura was in college.

Laura met Evelyn in the hospital. Dad looked like a helpless spider trapped in a web of tubes, wires, and monitors. Any strangement vanished. Laura pulled up a chair, took her father's hand, and submitted to Mom's cocoon of disapproval. Laura's list of failings grew longer every visit.

"This is all your fault," Laura said, because the best defense was attack. "You pushed him too hard."

"Your father drove himself. I had no hand in that."

"He did it for you, and then you dumped him."

"I didn't 'dump,' your father. How you twist things. You're so like him."

"Better than turning out like you, a callous, cold-hearted bitch."

"We're more alike than you think."

"I'm nothing like you," Laura said leaning back, arms folded across her newly sculptured chest.

"You're a congenital liar, a fixer, a deceiver, just like me, although at least I acted with a good conscience."

"Who do you think you're kidding? You broke his heart with that affair. That's when everything changed."

"What affair?"

"Don't play the innocent with me. I noticed stuff. I understood more than you thought."

"You never understood anything, always fighting figments."

"I know. I know why I was stuck at home practicing scales every Saturday."

"So you could learn to play the piano. You wanted to be a concert pianist. I didn't discourage your ambitions."

"You led me on with my dreams, so that you could pursue yours, with Edward."

"Who? Edward? Not Edward Gunner? What an earth gave you that idea?"

"I saw him looking at you. He gave you that pendant? The one with the pearl. The one dad hated?"

"No. Someone else gave me that."

"Who?"

"Let's not talk about that now. Let's focus on your father."

"Don't change the subject. None of this would have happened if you could only have been satisfied with Dad."

"You're wrong, Laura. Dad wanted this. He wanted his empire more than anything else. He'd sacrifice anything to achieve his goals."

"And he did, no thanks to you."

"That's where you're wrong, where I went wrong perhaps."

"Finally, a confession."

"You mentioned the pendant, the pearl."

"Here it comes, I knew it. A gift from Edward Gunner."

"My brother gave it to me."

"Your brother? I have an uncle? How come I didn't know this before?"

"Because your father disapproves of people making their way in life through gambling."

"My uncle's a gambler?"

"Yes, and a very successful one too. Teddy gave me the pearl pendant."

"Teddy?" Laura remembered the photograph on the dressing table. "Your brother's called Edward?"

"That's right."

"It isn't paste?"

"No. Not only that, he gave it to me as an insurance policy. Something for me to fall back on if anything ever went wrong."

"Well you're okay on your own then with that little nest egg. I should have known you wouldn't fly the coup without a parachute."

"Oh Laura. Where did I go wrong with you? Why do you hate me so after all these years? I thought we gave you a happy childhood."

"Happy? How could I be happy when every second I was waiting for you to leave and run off with Edward. Why didn't you tell me that photograph was of you and your brother. I always thought it was a picture of me and some random kid?"

"I don't know. Your father disapproved. He didn't want you to know about him. You have to believe me. I would never run off with anyone, least of all Edward."

"Then why divorce?"

"Because your father couldn't live with himself when he found out."

"Found out what?"

"None of his investors took the plunge. He couldn't persuade anyone to put money into his business. They had no faith in him."

"But he's been so successful. He's achieved everything he wanted. The business keeps growing."

"I know, but to him the whole enterprise is a failure."

"How? Why? What would make him think that?"

"Because it's built on immoral earnings."

"What are you talking about? Prostitution? You're not making any sense."

"I gave your father the seed money. I told him it was from Edward Gunner, but really it was mine."

"You don't have two beans to rub together. It's not as if you've ever worked for a living."

"I resent that. I devoted my life to you and your father."

"A part-time hobby in between your love affairs. Did they give you money?"

"No. You're not listening. I sold the pearl pendant for seed money for your father."

"Was it worth that much?"

"Enough to get him started, enough to get a foothold on the stock exchange eventually, enough to fulfill his great dream."

"I don't get it. You're saying that now he knows where the money came from, he wants to quit. What difference does it make? Surely wives can help their husbands. Isn't that what marriage is supposed to be all about?"

"I thought so, but Dad's standards are far too strong, impossibly high."

"What?"

"If you trace the money back, it came directly from my brother, Teddy."

"Who cares?"

"Dad does. The money's tainted. Teddy's earnings were from gambling. As far as your Dad's concerned, that means every penny he's made is soiled by sin."

Dawned into Darkness
By Leigh Simpson

He was uninterested in cats, but he liked the old lady because she spent her modest social security income on this stray. Ted recognized goodness in people, and responded to it.

Now, he noticed a large abscess on the back of Blackie's neck. He was struggling to stand, so Ted threw his jacket around him, and raced to the emergency clinic.

The veterinarian questioned, "Is this your cat?"

"No. I've been feeding him, but he's a stray."

After pointing to the notched ear and numerous scars, the veterinarian replied, "His condition appears quite poor. He's old and semi-feral. I think he should be euthanized."

"No! No way! Do what you can, Doc. I'm taking him home."

"But he'll need to be kept inside until the shunt is removed, and the abscess drains, and even then he might not recover—"

Ted had become irritated with the veterinarian, so he abruptly interrupted him, and in a no-nonsense voice said, "If it dies, it dies! I'll do, whatever!"

He had only promised the old lady that he would feed Blackie, but he knew what she woud have wanted, if she were alive, so he had decided to give this sickly tough guy another chance.

Several days later the test results revealed that Blackie had the feline immunodeficiency virus (FIV), and Ted was informed that fighting could spread the disease.

He had seen Blackie fight several times with larger cats, and secretly respected him because he was an unyielding fighter.

He had never planned on making Blackie an indoor cat, but he did.

It took Ted seven long months and Herculean patience to train this former outdoor cat into using his many litter boxes. Ted was scratched and bitten more than a few times, but before the year's end, they were sharing the same pillow.

Nearly two years later, when Blackie could no longer stand, and had to be euthanized, Ted called a veterinarian to his home. As the needle was removed from Blackie's leg, Ted slumped to their bedroom floor with Blackie in his arms. His tears were painfully long, and he wept openly, without apologies or shame.

South African Tears
By Evie Groch

His missing leg spoke to us of daring escapades. He never offered an explanation, and we dared not ask. We took his tanned face and leathery complexion as additional signs of experience. He was a man of few words, yet the Afrikaans accent that carried them exuded confidence, reassurance, and calm, all the qualities a safari guide would need to communicate with his visitors on a trek through Kruger Park. He called himself Ben.

To say we were eager to begin wouldn't capture our high expectations and anxiousness. This People to People trip to South Africa promised us educators a deep look into its teaching and learning institutions after Apartheid, but also offered as a post-trip a colorful visit to the National Game Reserve in Kruger. And we were finally here. Our alarm clocks had awakened us at 5:30 a.m. After a hasty continental breakfast at our hotel, we hurried out to the specialized jeeps outfitted for safari, with their tiered seats, and camouflaged awning. We had on our recommended brimmed hats tied around our neck so they could flap in the breeze and not get carried off either by the wind or a native inhabitant. Our cameras were primed, our f-stops checked, and our shutter fingers ready. We were in the perfect frame of mind to capture wild life in Kruger as we bounced onto the roadway, our eyes peeled for anything that stirred.

About one-quarter of a mile into the route, Ben pulled off to the side of the road and spoke to us only in whispers. What could it be? A lone, huge, male elephant was crossing the road to examine what looked to us like a large skull and a small heap of discarded tire shreds. "Just watch – don't talk," advised Ben. Through whispers he informed us the male had discovered the remains of another elephant who had died and was nearing them to mourn, to pay his last respects. We were only yards from him and were able to observe how gently his trunk caressed every shred and how he was humbled by the experience. As we watched, a larger, bull-like alpha male appeared and headed over to investigate what the smaller elephant had discovered. He approached brusquely and tried to push the smaller elephant out of the way. We sensed the tension in the air as our hairs were standing straight up. The smaller of the two refused to cede ground, and the two of them faced each other, tusked locked, rocking to and fro.

"The larger alpha feels he has the right to mourn first," Ben explained. "The smaller one has to ingratiate himself to the larger one and receive permission to continue mourning." That is indeed what he did. He backed his tusks out of the hold, and bringing his trunk around to one side of the alpha's face, caressed it softly, in a loving and pleading manner. He then did the same thing on his other cheek, slowly, deliberately, while tears were flowing from his eyes, leaving darkened streaks on his face. Apparently, the larger elephant was moved enough by this gesture that he acquiesced and stepped aside to allow the smaller one to return to the remains and continue to mourn. This was a sign of compassion and empathy we had never imagined elephants were capable of.

Since the alpha elephant had now turned his attention away from the mourning male, he looked around and spotted us, only yards away and started to approach. We shifted uneasily in our seats and were warned by Ben to sit still and not move or talk. He reiterated that the elephant was not a danger or a threat to us as long as we followed his instructions.

I happened to be on the outside seat nearest the approaching male and instinctively pulled my arms into the vehicle. We were so tightly packed into the jeep that my elbow still protruded a bit. As the male ambled over to check us out, I realized he was larger than our jeep. He extended his trunk as I started to close my eyes out of fear, remembering not to move anything else. As I held my breath, illogical thoughts raced through my mind, like: if I were killed, who was going to make sure the safari hat I had borrowed from Barbara would get back to her? What part of me would the elephant destroy first? When would it be okay to get out and run? Damn, this was a fairly new camera I had purchased for the trip!

"Keep still, very still," Ben kept advising. "You're going to be okay."

When I opened my eyelid closest to the outside of the jeep, I found the elephant's trunk fewer than three inches from my protruding elbow, which was frozen into place. "Oh, God," I thought, visualizing South African national headlines reading "Alpha Male Elephant Drags Tourist from Jeep and Leaves Her for Dead."

We continued in this frozen frame for what seemed like hours, but later learned were only minutes. When the elephant had had enough of his smelling and checking, he started to slowly back off, and we audibly shared a communal exhale. For a while we all sat there, not speaking, still trying to digest and make sense of the adventure. Our guide told us we would never forget this experience, and he was right. He asked us to reassure future visitors to Kruger that elephants were not dangerous and not an enemy. Elephants have severe critics since they strip trees of bark and new growth and rub up against them to scratch. Many trees have been destroyed and groves leveled, especially since these herds have no predators. Nevertheless, our guide's love and affinity for them was evident. His feeling permeated us as well. I learned in this wilderness what true compassion, respect, and memory are – from two elephants whose encounter is always with me.

candy machine
By Maurine Killough

did i push the wrong button
pull the wrong knob
impulsively choose the colorful
wrapper with its tidy
birthday gift wrapped edges?
this hard candy
i have to swallow
instead of choosing the milk
chocolate one
with the chewy nougat and depth...
so much more depth
or the rich fried corn chips
so crunchy and salty
making me salivate
wondering how that choice would
have been
instead of this hard candy
the monotony of the same taste
taking so long to dissolve
and you can choke on it
trapping your airways until they
turn you upside down
and you hack it out then back in
your mouth it goes
is it too late
to spit this one out
watch it crack and bounce on
the pavement
leave my mouth empty
lost and flavorless
hoping to find all the delicious
but scary choices still open to
me?
or maybe i would find the
expiration date had passed
only to leave me
dry and strangling on my own
disillusioned breath
perhaps i should relish this
heady sweetness
aching my teeth, gritting my jaw
with its one-dimensional but
jolly and colorful flavor
celebrate this choice above all
others
desperately loving what belongs
only to me
this flavor
which button, does it matter?
but in how you savor
whatever the machine serves up

Ruben's Tales from the Amazon
By Dr. Audry Lynch

When Ruben turned 13, his parents decided that he should leave their village. They did not mean to be unkind. They had high hopes for Ruben and wanted the best for him. The village school was small, so they decided to send him to a high school in the city of Iquitos.

Compared to his village, the city of Iquitos was immense. It was a large port city at the junction of three countries — Brazil, Peru, and Ecuador. He loved seeing the Amazon River but it wasn't the same as at home. He couldn't dive in and swim any time that he wanted. The harbor was usually filled with boats.

He also minded wearing so many clothes. They made him sweat even though sometimes there was air-conditioning in some of the buildings. The shoes were the worst of all. He longed for the days when he ran along the Amazon riverbank with his feet sinking into the mud.

During the summers he returned to his village to visit his parents, his old friends and particularly, Don Jose. He swam in the Amazon, walked in the jungle, and begged Don Jose to tell him his favorite stories again. At the end of each summer when he had to go back to Iquitos, he felt sad again.

Ruben's parents were ambitious and they wanted him to have more opportunities than existed in their little village. They, too, cried each summer when he left but they consoled themselves that they were doing the best for their child. Ruben knew they loved him and he appreciated their sacrifice. But it couldn't stop the sadness.

The years passed and Ruben finished high school. Four years later he graduated from college. Then he married and had two children of his own. Through all this he never forgot Don Jose's stories. Each night he went to sleep wishing he could hear the jungle symphony again.

"As a tortoise grows older, it can't get around very well. It becomes harder and harder for them to move. Eventually they become immobile and can't move at all. That's what happened to Juana. Then plants and leaves grow over its body so it can deceive its victims. They approach it without fear. Then the tortoise turns and snaps its victims into its mouth while it looks as if the whole world is shaking.

"On the day in question, you and I were strolling in the jungle. It was very hot and you were thirsty and crying for a drink. I decided to go further into the jungle to find the plant that holds water in its leaves. I told you to sit down on what I thought was a mound of vegetation. Then I left to look for the water.

"In a few minutes I heard you screaming. I ran back just in time to pull you away from Juana's snapping mouth. What we thought was a pile of vegetation and a seat for you turned out to be Juana, a gigantic tortoise and the mother of all the jungle tortoises.

"I guess you looked like a good dinner," laughed Don Jose, and Ruben laughed too.

Then Ruben hugged Don Jose suddenly. "That's why I love you," Ruben said. "You've always been there to teach and protect me."

"Just don't sit on Juana again," warned Don Jose as the two friends started off for their daily walk in the jungle.

Ruben lived in a little village along the mighty Amazon River. The river was big and brown and reminded Ruben of the fierce anaconda, the most feared of all the snakes in the jungle. It was powerful and unpredictable. It could be calm as a lake or produce waves and dangerous eddies during storms.

The river brought good and evil. He knew people who had drowned in it. But it also brought the big ships with the tourists who bought the masks from the village housewives. They also gave the children candy and gum and pencils for the village school.

Each morning when he woke up, Ruben's day involved some time with the big river. Sometimes his mother asked him to bring pails of water from it for her cooking. Sometimes his father took him with his brothers to catch fish from it for their dinners. Sometimes he led tourists from the boats up the muddy slope to his village. Every night before bedtime he took his daily bath in it.

The Amazon River governed his daily chores but it was the Shaman, Don Jose, who also controlled much of Ruben's life. Don Jose was the Shaman of the village, its oldest and wisest man. People even from other nearby villages came to him all day and night to ask questions to inquire about good and bad spells, and to purchase little bags of his herbs.

Don Jose fascinated Ruben. As long as he could remember, he had visited the Shaman every day of his life. He watched his visitors come and go and listened to every word that he could overhear from their conversations. Finally, Don Jose asked him to come along on his trips into the jungle pharmacy as Don Jose called it. They collected herbs and plants together while the Shaman explained their many uses to Ruben. Sometimes Ruben thought Don Jose could cure anything.

Shaman means Teacher, and Don Jose was the best one Ruben had ever met. At first Don Jose told Ruben about all the plants and animals in the Amazon Jungle. As they walked on the green slippery carpet of the jungle, Don Jose pointed out dangerous plants and the hiding places of poisonous snakes. At dusk, the songs of the birds and insects became louder and Don Jose explained to Ruben each sound in the Jungle Symphony.

Like most children, Ruben loved stories. The best times that he could remember with his Father were when, after a hard day of wild boar hunting, his father would relax by telling stories around the fire while his Mother cooked the meat. Ruben knew that Don Jose told some very special stories about the animals and creatures of the Amazon. Finally, he had the courage to ask Don Jose to tell them to him.

"Yes, Ruben," Don Jose replied, "I will tell them to you. But, remember they are special and secret to our village. Only share them with boys and girls who will appreciate them." Ruben decided that he was one of those special people so here are amazing Amazon stories that he heard directly from Don Jose.

Tale # 1 — La Sachamana (Earth Boa)

"One of the most dangerous animals in the jungle, Ruben," said Don Jose, "is this one, the earth boa. When it is young it moves quickly and quietly through the jungle just like any other snake. But when it is fully-grown it is absolutely enormous.

"Then it stops moving and looks around for a clump of thick vegetation. That certainly isn't hard to find in the Amazon jungle. When it finally finds it, the boa settles down and parks there for life. No one notices it because it has such good camouflage. You're looking at one now, right over there, Ruben."

Ruben gave a little scream but still he could not see the evil boa. He and Don Jose stood quietly for many minutes hoping it would move. Finally, there was a little rustle in the leaves and Ruben could see the outline of the huge snake.

"Not only does it hide itself well," said Don Jose, "But some people think that the boa has some magical magnetism that attracts its prey. That might explain what happened to Juan."

"Tell me, please," begged Ruben.

"Well, it was a very sad story," said Don Jose. "Juan was a local boy who decided one day to go for a walk by himself in the jungle, always a dangerous decision. The sun came through the greenery that day in such a beautiful way that he walked longer and farther than he had intended.

"He became tired so he decided that he should sit down and rest for awhile. As you have seen, it's hard to tell whether you're sitting on an innocent clump of vegetation or an earth boa. In this case Juan made a bad mistake and sat on the earth boa.

"Perhaps it was fatigue or maybe the magic magnetism. Anyway, Juan fell asleep on the back of the earth boa. Soon after his family went into the jungle to look for him but it was too late. hey arrived just in time to see the last of Juan's feet being devoured by the powerful earth boa. After that, no village child was ever allowed to walk in the jungle alone again."

"That's too sad," Ruben told the Shaman. "Don't you have any happy tales?"

Don Jose laughed and said, "Well, maybe I should tell you the story of Roberto and Maria."

"Oh, good," clapped Ruben. "I can hardly wait."

Matwa and Pandu Help Their New Friends
By Anne Jayne

On the African plain, in a small farmhouse surrounded by sweet thorn trees, lived an old farmer. Each day he milked his goat, Afar, and fed hay to his cow, Kole.

One day the old farmer said to Afar and Kole, "I am too old to cut hay and tend this farm. I am going to live with my daughter in the city. You may live in this house. Instead of hay, you must eat grass that grows between here and the river. Good-bye." The old farmer tied his belongings into a bandana, and set off down the road.

"Well, Afar," said Kole the cow, "I'm ready for lunch." The cow and the goat left their farmyard and walked to the tall waving grass. They had eaten only a mouthful before Afar called out in alarm.

"Kole, there are two eyes staring at us through the grass!" They turned to run away, but a kind voice said to them,

"Don't be afraid. We have promised not to hurt animals in this grassland." A lion and a cheetah walked toward them.

"I am Pandu, the lion."

"And I am Matwa, the cheetah. Who are you?"

"Two farm animals, Kole, a cow and Afar, a goat. Our master has gone away, and we now must eat grass for our dinner."

"There is room for all," said Pandu.

From a clump of Acacia trees by the river bank, Twiga, the giraffe stepped with her long legs. She was hard to see because she had spots like shadows made by leaves in the sunlight.

"Welcome!" she said.

Lita, the zebra walked toward them. He was hard to see because his stripes were like the shadows made by sun shining through the grass.

"Welcome!" he said.

Tumbiri, the monkey, swung down from a branch. "I see a brown cow with a hump, and a white goat with curved horns," he said. You need shadows on your backs to hide from the hunters coming from the village."

"That is true," said Matwa.

"I could make stripes for you with mud from the river bank," said Lita the zebra.

"Mud would wash off in the rain," said Pandu.

"I could spread leaves on your backs," said Twiga, the giraffe.

"They would blow off in the wind" said Pandu.

"Lets look in your farm house for shadows," said Matwa.

Together the animals walked to the little farmhouse in the sweet thorn thicket. They looked at what the farmer had left behind.

"Here is the farmer's old blanket with zig-zag lines," said Tumburi, the monkey.

Using his clever hands, he took a piece of rope hanging on the wall, and tied the blanket on the back of Kole the cow. "Now you have lots of shadows!"

"Here is something for you, goat," said Matwa. In his teeth, he picked up the farmer's old straw hat. Tumbiri placed it on Afar's head. Afar's horns stuck through the hat and held it in place.

"Here is something else for you, Goat," said Pandu. With his paws, he held up the farmer's old flowered shirt. Afar stuck his front legs through the sleeves. Tumbiri pulled the shirt over his back.

"Now you have shadows, too," said Pandu.

The animals walked back to the tall grass to eat.

"Please visit us in our farmhouse," said Afar and Kole to the other animals. "We will!" said Matwa and Pandu and Twiga and Lita and Tumbiri.

"It is good to have new friends!" said Pandu.

Heat, Not Warmth
By Evie Groch

Sun-seared sidewalks pray
for shelter
under sheets of rust-colored dust.
Sandal-clad feet
bronzed by a Moroccan furnace make
their stamp
on unpaved paths.
A sip of water is
a sin,
a glance too long – a dare.
We're not clad
as modest women,
and so deserve the stares and
taunts.
Men mouth welcome,
but their eyes say otherwise.
They practice patience
as they sit and wait for sundown.
Ramadan in Casablanca.

Come Home Come Home
By Bernadine Fornesi

Out on the front porch
Granny shouts
Is'e a waitin' you worrisome thing
Come Home Come Home

Neighbors yell out front
You betta come home
Ungrateful one
Your Granny wails when the street lights come on

Stop shamin your Granny
Hawkin your wares at the corner of the block
Studs in your eyelids tongue and nose
Blood red lipstick a siren to the restless Johns

Your Daddy's in the prison
Your Mamma sniffs powder through a straw
Nobody to stop you when you took to the streets
With a wiggle in your walk

Shake your bootie and bicker for a price
To the shadows in the cruising cars
Looking for sports
Under the cover of night

Nosey neighbors have ringside seats
They call you trash and spit in the wind
You ruffle my feathers unworthy one
But I still loves you—come home

I all alone troublesome hussy
The grits cookin on the stove
Come home dull witted one
Before you gets dumped headfirst in the bay

You still my chile worthless one
Even though you be a "Ho"
I gonna love you till I up and die
Only Sweet Jesus knows why

Angel on high set her feet upon the path
She be safe when I see her at the gate
Sweet Jesus whisper in her ear
Real love waits for you...Go Home...Go Home

Index by Category

MEMOIR

POETRY

ADVENTURES IN SCIENCE

Index by Author

Acknowledgements

We only have a couple of weeks to format, set and print the over 200 literary entries to the San Mateo County Fair and create *Carry the Light*. Frankly, it's reminiscent of the Keystone Cops. We do our best to print at least one entry of each entrant in every category. In the case of short poetry, we can fit it in here and there, so some people have many of their poems printed. Although we don't change what people have written, we do need to check for missing text, text that has mysteriously run together and a host of other technical issues. Thank you to Ann Foster, Michele Jessen, Marjorie Bicknell Johnson, Lisa Meltzer Penn and Kim Schultz for volunteering to read through *Carry the Light* and spot problems. Thanks to Joanne Shwed of Backspace Ink for creating our cover. And as always, a great big thanks to Bardi Rosman Kooodrin, Literary Director of the San Mateo County Fair, for her patience and leadership.

Tory Hartmann
Sand Hill Review Press

www.ingramcontent.com/pod-product-compliance
Lightning Source LLC
Chambersburg PA
CBHW022135170626
46807CB00005B/1955

* 9 7 8 1 9 3 7 8 1 8 2 5 8 *